SUMMER'S REASON

SUMMER'S REASON

———— a novel by ————

Cherokee Paul McDonald

DONALD I. FINE, INC.

NEW YORK

Copyright © 1994 by Cherokee Paul McDonald

All rights reserved, including the right of reproduction in whole or in part in any form. Published in the United States of America by Donald I. Fine, Inc. and in Canada by General Publishing Company Limited.

Library of Congress Catalog Card Number: 94-071110
ISBN: 1-55611-409-5

Manufactured in the United States of America

10 9 8 7 6 5 4 3 2 1

Designed by Irving Perkins Associates, Inc.

This novel is a work of fiction. Names, characters, places and incidents are either the product of the author's imagination or are used fictitiously. Any resemblance to actual events, locales, organizations or persons, living or dead, is entirely coincidental and beyond the intent of either the author or publisher.

For my uncle,
Stephen Cwalinski,
and his Pauline.

Like most of my works of fiction, this story is taken from real life characters and experiences, from cases I handled as a police officer or private investigator, or those I have studied. The criminal activities described in the story are based on U.S. Government reports and summaries given to me by a current agent stationed in the Far East. The criminal activities portrayed are happening in real life, today.

—CPM

PROLOGUE

She has an old photograph, taken by her mother when she was unaware, that shows a little girl on a long white beach. The little girl is bending slightly, her face turned, her long white-blonde hair blown back by the wind. The girl wears a faded one-piece bathing suit and carries a small bucket. As she bends, she reaches for the sand, toward another treasure. They can't be seen in the old photograph, but the treasures are in the bottom of the bucket. Periwinkles, tops, trivias, doves, tritons, spindles, whelks, tulips, nassas, a magical assortment of shapes and colors and textures, each of them sought out, found, cleaned, recorded and coveted. There is one more, a very special one, but the photo doesn't show it, and it wasn't in the bucket that day anyway.

It was the last summer of her childhood. A summer spent on Sanibel Island, on the west coast of Florida, in a small motel near miles of sandy beach. The motel had a pool, but with the peaceful clear waters of the Gulf so close, and all that wondrous stretch of warm hardpacked sand reaching off in both directions, she had no time for the motel. She spent the summer in a bathing suit, two months exploring and dreaming, and collecting diverse and perfect shells she found along the edge of the water.

There was another reason she didn't stay around the motel, the man with her mother that summer. The way her mother talked, the man would soon be her new father, but she hated that thought. She knew almost nothing of her real father, and her mother never spoke of him, so she had created him in her mind . . . and this new man could not compare. The man was too loud and rough, and was often mean to her mother. When he tried to act nice or caring, it seemed put-on to her. He drank every day, and when he did he fought with her mother about stupid things. The man had friends on the island, had worked there at one time, and knew his way around. It seemed to the girl there were always parties going on, grown-up parties.

So she would wake with the first rays of the sun coming in the jalousie window across her small bed near the front door to the motel room. She would pull on her bathing suit, slip into the bathroom for a minute, then walk through the loud snoring coming from the bedroom. Then out the front door, over the pool deck, and across the two-lane road to the beach. People would smile and quietly say "good morning" as they walked past her in their Sanibel stoop . . . unconsciously bent at the waist, watching the clean sand in front of them, searching for the shells.

She was comfortable on the beach alone, smelling the early morning, hearing the wind through the feathers of the big pelicans as they glided overhead, occasionally having the thrill of seeing dolphins play just a few yards offshore. For the first hour or so the sand would feel cool between her toes, but as the day grew old the sand grew warm, almost hot. She loved to lie on it then, and embrace the comforting vastness of it. The sparkling granules of sand would be washed off her skin with a quick swim in the clear water at the edge of the beach, and she was off again, exploring, searching.

She was *not* comfortable that year with her body. Ten years old was pretty old, she thought then, and her mother told her she should think about getting a different bathing suit, maybe a two-piece. She'd want to show off for the boys, her mother told her, she'd want to look pretty for them. Actually, *she* thought boys were kind of stupid and strange to be around, and she knew her body was hopeless anyway. She was convinced that stuffing it into a two-piece wouldn't make it any better. Besides, that whole boy and girl thing still eluded her, and she didn't understand the fuss people made. She felt awkward and gawky and skinny and plain. Sure, she had pretty blonde hair, but that was about it, and who cared if boys liked her or not?

All she wanted to do that summer was stay out of that motel room, walk the beach, and hunt for the thousands of beautiful shells waiting out on the sand. But on the day she found the special one, the summer changed. She almost missed it at first, and because she almost missed it, she nearly stepped on it. Just in time it caught her eye, she gave a little hop, reached down, and there it was. She held it up to the sun, then turned and carefully washed it in the lapping waves. When she held it up again, she saw it was perfect, and she felt a thrill.

She hurried back to the motel, a mile or more down the beach, proud and excited and impatient to show her mother her treasure, to share its rare beauty with her. The late afternoon was clear, still and hot, and when she got back to the room, all she found was a note. Her mother and the man who might be her new father had gone to a party on the other side of the island. She should have dinner at the pool bar, then watch television in the room. She should not worry, the note said, a friend of her father-to-be would check in on her later.

ONE

Like a fleshed-out image of the running child's silhouette on a "Slow, Children Playing" sign, the little boy came racing headlong across the green expanse of lawn, focusing on a bouncing soccer ball, charging over the grass and onto the street. Too late he saw the movement to his left and jammed hard on his sneakers to stop his forward momentum.

The approaching Fort Lauderdale Police motorcycle patrol officer took in the bouncing ball, the running boy and the other kids in the yard in one glance, then timed it so the ball rolled against the front tire, and pulled on the brakes. The boy stood at the edge of the road, staring wide-eyed. The big motorcycle idled strongly with a hollow, bubbling sound, and there was a sharp, silvery thud as a cleat on the heel of the officer's boot hit against the hard pavement. The kickstand was swung out, the Harley-Davidson leaned into it, and the officer shut down the engine and got off. Sun-browned arms reached out and grabbed the ball, which had bounced away from the front tire of the bike to the center of the road.

Motorcycle Patrol Officer Jessie Summer spun the soccer ball in her hands, concerned and appraising eyes on the boy. She was straight and strong, over five-nine in those Colt leather riding boots, fit and tight at one hundred and twenty pounds. The riding britches with the dark stripe down each leg fit her like a second skin, and the crisp white uniform shirt sheathed her straight back, squared shoulders, tight flat stomach and full, shapely breasts.

Her blonde hair was cut short, not quite severe under the white helmet; aviator-type sunglasses shaded big eyes made darker green by the lens and sat on a nose just the right size for her open face. Below the nose were full lips, the lower now being bitten slightly by even white teeth, finely shaped into a wide and pleasant mouth. Jessie Summer smiled as she tossed the soccer ball back to the small boy, aiming it so it bounced once on the street before hitting his waiting hands. "Be careful," she said in a gentle voice, and the boy nodded, smiled back, and turned to race across the lawn to his watching friends.

Summer swung her right leg over the seat on the Harley-Davidson, lifted it off the kickstand, fired it up, and kicked it into gear. Before she released the clutch and began to roll forward, she looked to her right at the kids playing in the yard once more, smiling as she thought of what the brass would say if they saw her now, off on some side street behind a small shopping center in the south end of town instead of cruising one of the main roadways in the area. Well, it was her last day assigned to motors, her last Sunday to ride the streets of Fort Lauderdale as a motorcop, and she wanted to enjoy it for what it was.

She let her eyes sweep the area in front of her as she eased the big bike forward, then back to her left and across the street to the rear of the shopping plaza. All the rear access doors were closed and padlocked. All but one. At the bottom of the open door, just visible to her, was part of a leg and a loafer-covered foot. She let the Harley roll along the edge of the street for a few yards after she shut the engine down, put it on its kickstand, and swung off. She pulled off her helmet, hung it on the handlebar, and hurried across the street toward the open door.

As she got closer, she could see the stenciled letters above the doorway: "Sunport Jewelers," and she instinctively went into a crouch as she saw the leg disappear, pulled into the dark interior of the store.

Summer ran straight to the back wall of the plaza now, reached it two doors from the open one, pulled out her .9mm semi-automatic pistol with her right hand, and took a couple of deep breaths. The radio receiver on her left shoulder crackled. She bent her head to hear the dispatcher giving a description of a missing person and turned the volume down to a whisper. Biting her lip, she moved toward the door, the weapon held in front of her at an angle near her right leg—she was only two feet from the door now—and paused. She heard voices, not loud, but tense, almost hoarse.

"Close the door! Leave that stuff, man . . . close the door!"

"Hey, take it easy . . . this *puta* won't need this stuff now anyway."

It had to be a robbery, she thought, and they had already incapacitated the victim. Two voices, both male. If she moved into the doorway to confront them, she would be in the sunlight, they in the shadows of the store. She would have to chance calling on the radio for backups, but as she bent her head to the radio again, she heard another unit going on about some abandoned car.

"He's probably dead already, but . . ."

"Fool! That's not why . . ."

". . . I'd better give him one behind the ear to make sure."

It was decided for her, but suddenly she was assaulted by familiar images. Like old film still sharply focused, she saw rushing toward her those memories that seared her with shock, revulsion, humiliation and embarrassment. "Not now!" she thought. "I'm grown now, you can't do that to me now, leave me." She felt the flutter of fear from deep within her, an old, familiar, insidious fear that eroded her confidence, her ability to act. Around the doorjamb, inches from her right shoulder, death waited. But it wasn't the fear of a deadly confrontation that weakened her. She had faced death before and had tasted and controlled the fear that came with it. No, the fear that made her shudder now, even as she crouched slightly and prepared to swing into the doorway, came from her childhood and had never left her.

She had heard them, the two men, and immediately and instinctively knew what act they were seconds away from committing. And she knew *she* had to act, now. She would turn from the sun into the shadows, her weapon in front of her. She would be framed in the open doorway with the men in darkness, but they didn't know she was there, they wouldn't expect her. It would be close, and would only work for her with reflexive speed and sure hands. But the fear . . .

No. She had to *do it,* and as time stretched through microseconds, she *dared* the old fears to get in the way, and she spun around the corner with feline speed and balance, her weapon coming up, her eyes wide and searching the gloom for the target, her finger poised tightly against the trigger that would speak for her life.

Gun hand leading, she turned the edge in one fluid motion, all of her senses pointed at the interior of the store. At one glance she saw the crumpled body of an old man on the floor. Bent over the head of the old man was another—big, young, with dark, sweaty skin and shiny black hair. The young man's eyes glowed brightly in the gloom as they stared in wonder, then anger, at her. He held a small silver gun in one hand, pointed at the head of the man on the floor. She sensed more than saw the figure of another man behind the young one.

"Freeze! Police! *Drop the gun!*" she shouted, her normally rich voice strained and sharp. Even as she gave the commands, the young man with the gun tensed and his mouth went into a grin made of fear and surprise and something else. His hand with the gun came up fast. She saw his arm move, saw the barrel of the gun coming up in an arc, and she squeezed the trigger of her weapon rapidly, twice. The twin explosions rocked her back slightly, punching her eardrums and impacting her senses. She smelled the burning powder and felt the immediate heat against her hands even as she watched the young man's body jerk violently as he was lifted back and up, grunting as he fell spread-eagled onto the floor. As he fell she saw, rather than heard, the small silver gun fire three times. She saw the bright bursts of flame from the muzzle, and for one terrifying second she thought she could feel the hot slugs tear into her body. But no, they were gone, and her skin tingled with that realization.

As the young man went down, she steadied her weapon and looked for the figure behind him, but the figure was gone, moving with impossible speed over a glass counter off to the side. The figure was out of sight, then visible again near the front of the store.

She stood now and stepped forward near the edge of the wall. She glanced at the two on the floor, then back at the fleeing one and shouted, "Freeze! Stay right there!" But the fleeing figure bent down behind the counter again. She crouched quickly too, afraid he would come up shooting.

He didn't come up. Instead, there was a loud crash of broken glass, scrunching noises, and then silence. She counted to three, stepped over the two bodies on the floor, and kneeled over the young man's gun hand. He still held the small silver gun. She stepped on his wrist with her boot and slowly, cautiously, looked over the counter toward the front of the store. A large section of the front plate-glass window had been smashed out with a small potted palm, and she knew the scrunching noises she had heard were the sounds of the other figure escaping. Just to be sure, she kicked the gun out of the young man's hand, watched it slide under the counter, stood, and moved quickly to the front of the store. She hugged the near wall as she stood in the broken glass and carefully peered around the edge. She saw no one, and she knew that a running man had had time to make it to the far end of the plaza and be gone.

She moved back to where the two lay on the floor. The old one was very still, dead. As she kneeled near the young one, she watched and listened as he took two long, wet, shuddering breaths, convulsed, and died . . . his chest soaked a bright crimson. Jessie stood slowly, walked past the bodies, and stepped out into the sunshine. She took a long slow breath, holstered her weapon, and unclipped the radio from her shoulder.

"Tango Fifteen, ten thirty-three, emergency," she said.

"Go ahead, Tango unit."

"Tango Fifteen. I'm at Sunport Plaza on State Road Eighty-four. I've broken up a robbery in progress, I think. The victim is signal seven, and one suspect is signal seven by me. Advise other units it was a shooting situation. One suspect still at large."

"Ten-four, Fifteen. Description of second suspect?"

She paused, trying to picture the shadowy figure, "Uh, possibly a Latin male, medium height and build, dark clothes, sharp features and long black hair. No other."

"Copy that, Tango Fifteen," a different voice said now. Jessie recognized it as that of Kelly Verdine, the senior dispatcher. The concern could be felt over the radio as Verdine asked, "Are you injured?"

Jessie looked down at herself, aware for the first time how strongly her heart was beating. A picture of the silver gun's flame flashed across her eyes, and she saw the blood on the dead man's chest. She ran her left hand over her own chest and looked down the street and across the yards to where the group of children played in the grass with the soccer ball. Their game went on, and one yard beyond them a man rode a lawnmower in a precise pattern across his lawn. They had heard nothing, and were apparently unaware of what had just happened. The neighborhood was calm and peaceful, and Jessie almost smiled as she spoke into the radio, "No. No . . . we're all right."

Then she leaned against the dusty wall of the building in the warm sunshine and waited for the arrival of the cavalry. She took long deep breaths, which caught at the end, but she stopped them before they became sobs.

South end patrol units were the first to make it to the scene. One unit parked in front of the jeweler's, and another came roaring down the back alley of the plaza, lights and siren blaring. Both units were operated by veteran male patrol officers, content with their Sunday dayshift assignments, pleased to be enjoying a quiet morning until the first and only female motor cop called in with this mess. They crunched through the broken glass, they stood over the bodies gawking, they looked over the goods in the open display cases, they eyed the small silver gun speculatively, and they basically did all of the things first units do when "securing the scene" of a heavy crime.

The south end patrol sergeant arrived at the same time the first detective unit pulled up. The sergeant was young, with a carefully nurtured and trimmed mustache, a polished command bearing, an eye for detail and a desire for an upwardly mobile career. He took one quick look inside the store, then approached Jessie Summer and asked the immediately pressing administrative questions.

"Even though you're sure the older one is dead, you've called for the Emergency Medical Teams anyway, right? Let them make that determination. Good. The one you shot and killed, he was armed? And he fired at you?"

Jessie pointed to where the silver gun had come to rest. She nodded and waited.

"How many times did you fire your weapon?"

"Twice, Sarge."

"Let me see it, please."

Jessie pulled her automatic pistol out of the holster, popped the magazine, tucked it into her belt, and locked the slide of the weapon back, catching the live round that came out of the chamber into the palm of her hand. She handed the safe weapon to the sergeant, then slid the live round into the top of the magazine and handed that to him also. From where they stood they could see the two spent shell casings from her shots lying on the floor near the back door. The sergeant grunted, walked a few feet away, and began giving instructions to the dispatcher.

After the sergeant walked away, Jessie was approached by the first detective on the scene. Detective Melody Mitchell had already made a fast inspection of the interior of the store, checked out the bodies, reconstructed the shooting in her own mind, and contacted the Detective Division dispatcher to get more units to the scene. She knew the area would have to be canvassed soon to see if anyone had seen the second suspect fleeing. Mitchell stood next to Summer, looked into her eyes, and said quietly, "You did good, lady. Hear me? You did good. Now . . . are you okay? I know you weren't hurt, but are you feeling settled and all that?"

Jessie smiled at Mitchell and nodded. She was not surprised by the genuine concern she heard in Mitchell's voice. Mitchell had come out of the academy and onto the job one class ahead of Summer, and even though their six years on FLPD had taken different directions, they had stayed friends. Jessie saw Mitchell was sharp as always, even on a quiet Sunday morning at the scene of a double homicide. Mitchell was a black woman with uniformly brown skin and a head full of loosely curled black hair worn in a short style. On this morning she wore pleated slacks, a pastel cotton shirt and flat shoes. She wore a thin gold chain at her neck, a fine gold watch with a black leather strap, a couple of rings with different stones

...no wedding band...and carried a small notepad bound in leather. She had the overall look of a woman acutely aware of her appearance. She had a round, very pleasant face with big brown eyes and a quick smile that showed strong white teeth. Melody Mitchell was an intense cop and a generally well-liked and respected member of the department, even though she had experienced some career ups and downs along the way.

"I'm all right, Melody, thanks for asking," said Jessie. "And what are you doing here? This is a Sunday, for one thing, and everybody knows you're being formally promoted to sergeant tomorrow. I thought you were leaving the detectives and going back down to patrol?" Mitchell still surveyed the scene, but nodded and said, "I can ask you the same question, lady. Thought *you* were movin' on up to the division...gonna be a de*tect*ive, not to *replace* me exactly, but maybe to keep the balance between penises and brains up there...and here you are out riding that stupid hog motorcycle around town. So, yeah, I'm out of the division...came in today to clear my desk and finish up a couple of odds and ends. I've got a few days vacation before I actually take over a squad in patrol. I heard you on the radio and figured I'd better get my saucy butt over here."

Just then another unmarked car arrived, and Summer and Mitchell watched as Captain Bert Ford climbed out, adjusted his tie, and hurried over to them, already talking. "Mitchell," he said with a tight grin, "I don't have to call you *Sergeant* until tomorrow, right? So...what have we got here?" Jessie went through it for him, ending with, "As far as I can tell at this time, sir, I stumbled into a robbery-homicide in progress. I felt I had to take action before my backups arrived, and I did."

The captain, aware that Mitchell had quietly moved back inside the store, nodded and said, "Fine. The whole thing will be reviewed anyway, just as in any shooting situation. You'll have to go right into the Detective Division to give a statement as soon as you clear here, then we'll take the investigation the rest of the way." He looked perplexed for a moment, then went on, "You've just been assigned as a new detective...I knew you were on the list of possibles, then I heard you were coming up for general duty...and yet you're still out here joyriding? And what's a traffic unit like you doing *here* anyway, and a motorman, uh . . . motor officer, at that? And why'd you say you stopped in the first place? Oh yeah, that kid with the ball. Fine, fine . . .'' Then he turned away.

Jessie hesitated a moment, dazzled by the captain's complete lack of understanding, then walked into the hubbub of the investigation, which was now in full swing. She saw that the lab people were there taking photos, and the medical examiner and two paramedics were poking around the bodies. The two victims were pronounced officially dead by the ME as he bent over them, and for one tilting moment Jessie half expected to see the Munchkin coroner appear from the crowd with a scroll certifying this fact with a poem. She rubbed her face with one hand, saw Melody Mitchell speaking with Captain Ford, and joined them.

"I just have the feeling it's not that simple, Captain Ford," said Mitchell. "There's something about this set-up that doesn't play . . ." "Looks damned clear-cut to me, Mitchell," replied the captain. "They wait for the owner to unlock the door here and rush him before he gets a chance to re-lock it. He's already deactivated the alarm, of course. They beat him up, maybe force him to unlock his safe, which he does. Maybe he resists and they beat him a little too much, inflicting fatal injuries. Probably by the time Summer saw his leg sticking out the door, he was already dead. And this young guy here, his pockets are stuffed with watches and rings he took from the displays. Summer comes along after playing ball with the neighborhood kiddies, and while she's smoking this one, the other asshole smashes out the front window and hauls ass. A citizen witness saw a suspect matching the *brief* description given by Summer. Says the suspect got into a dark-colored new car, probably a rental, and drove off eastbound at a high rate of speed." He paused, and as he looked at Mitchell he thought, college-educated Negro female detective *sergeant*, huh? But he ended with, "I don't know why some of you dicks think you always have some complicated case on your hands instead of accepting a simple one at face value. My suggestion to you would be not to try to turn this into something it isn't. The patrol sergeant has Summer's weapon . . . you take custody of it as evidence." Then he turned and walked off to speak with the medical examiner.

Mitchell watched him go, then said to Summer quietly, "*Face value*? In *this* business?" Jessie shook her head and smiled. Mitchell motioned to her with one finger and Jessie followed her into the small office located off the hallway between the back door and the main display counter. It had been ransacked, the safe stood open, all the trays and compartments scattered on the floor, papers and stones and small tools all mixed together. And something else.

Jessie bent to look closer at the several slick and colorful pornographic photographs lying amid the jewelry. Then she looked up at Mitchell, a question on her face.

"Special stuff, these dirty pics, Jessie," said Mitchell with a hushed intensity. "Special, and hard to get. All children, all of it. *Young* kids and hard-core stuff. Stuff you'd really have to look for and be willing to pay for."

Jessie nodded, looking closer at some of the photos. She felt sick to her stomach for the first time that morning. Mitchell went on, "It has to come from some kind of special mailing list thing. No way he'd be able to walk into one of the local adult bookstores and buy crap like that." She stepped out of the office a moment to speak with the patrol sergeant, and when she came back she moved some of the jewelry on the floor around with the toe of one foot. "We'll do the inventory and see if there's something here, a label or address. Let me throw some questions at you for fun."

Jessie nodded.

"Why is our owner here so early on a Sunday morning? Could the bad guys really sneak up on him in this alley without him seeing them coming? Did he *know* these guys and meet them here? Why isn't the one you killed wearing gloves, and why is that stuff in his pockets such a haphazard bag? Hell, there's the good stuff on the floor there. And what's our little businessman doing with this rare and sickening collection of child porn? Hmmm?" She pinched her nose, gave a huff, and said angrily, "Face value, my chocolate brown ass."

Jessie saw the pain and anger in Melody Mitchell's eyes, and with a jolt remembered what she had heard about the female detective in the last year or so. She was considered controversial, aggressive, almost "militant" about any racial conflict within the hallways of the FLPD. This did nothing to lessen her popularity with the opposite sex, apparently, because it was well known that "the guys" were often jockeying for a shot at her *off* duty, which added to her reputation as a party animal. The other thing Jessie remembered was Mitchell's abrupt transfer out of the Juvenile Unit before being assigned to Homicide. She had done a good job in Juvenile, so good she found herself handling all the child abuse, molestation and murder cases that came along. Word was that they got to her, those cases, and both she and the PD narrowly missed some big legal problems when she had attacked a child molester in one of the interrogation rooms. The suspect had been laughing as he described how his last child victim had begged him to stop, and before Mitchell could be dragged from the room, the suspect had sustained injuries that hospitalized him for weeks. He later pled guilty and threatened to sue, but never did. Mitchell was "laterally assigned" to Homicide, and the word in the hallways was that she only got to keep her gold badge because she was a black female, and the brass were afraid to bust her.

Melody Mitchell handed Jessie Summer's pistol to her then, along with the magazine full of live rounds. She rubbed her face, tried to grin, and said, "We'll get this sorted out, won't we? You'd better not ride back into the station with your holster empty, Jessie. With your luck, who knows *what* you'll run into. I'll take it into evidence there."

Jessie snugged the magazine in, chambered a round, made the weapon safe, and holstered it. She nodded and said with a grin, "Thanks, *Sarge*."

Jessie Summer cleared the scene, rode the big Harley-Davidson to the station on Broward Boulevard, and collected her gear. Before she turned to walk out of the motor shed, she gazed down at the Harley leaning on its stand, the engine ticking as it cooled, and she laid one hand on the smooth leather saddle. "It was good for me, was it good for you too?" Then she went in the back door of the building and up to the second floor to the Detective Division. Word of her shooting had already circulated, but she was still surprised to be greeted by the chief, who spoke with her briefly, then went into a meeting with Captain Ford and the public information officer.

They knew it was only a matter of time before the news media were out in force.

Jessie felt the eyes on her when she went into the Division area looking for Mitchell's desk. The detectives, thinned out as they were because of the weekend, eyed her speculatively. She was surprised when one of them pointed at her and then at one of the desk phones. She picked it up and said, "Summer."

"You all right, darlin'?" asked the dispatcher, Kelly Verdine. "Got your act together for the hassle that's coming?"

"I'm . . . I'm okay. Thanks for asking about me."

"Hey, babe . . . you're one of *us*. You did the right thing and you're alive to talk about it. Remember that." Verdine hung up, and after a moment, Jessie did too.

She was relieved when Melody arrived, and she spent the next several hours with her, giving a statement and doing a report. It was late afternoon when they wrapped it up and Mitchell told her to go home and try to relax. Before she left, she was approached by Captain Ford, who told her he had been around a long time, understood the stresses involved in a shooting, and told her to call him later, even at home, if she "needed a shoulder." Melody Mitchell stood by listening, a small smile on her face.

Jessie had driven to work in her old Camaro ragtop. It had recently rebuilt guts, but the body and interior were a little rough. She loved the car though, and considered it a classic. She couldn't remember, as she climbed into it, why she had not taken her usual mode of transportation, and she felt mildly dazed as she started it up and drove home. As she drove, she could feel the exhaustion creeping in. She felt jumpy, and her mouth was dry. She lived in a small house she had purchased a year earlier in the Rio Vista section of Fort Lauderdale, in the southeast, between Federal Highway and the Intracoastal Waterway. She could hear the phone ringing as she unlocked the front door, and she got to it on the seventh ring.

"Oh my God," said her mother's strained voice across the line. "It's all over the news . . . are you all right, honey?"

"Yes, Mom, I'm fine, really."

"It's terrible, terrible. My friends have been calling me. The news said there were two men shooting at you. You're not hurt?"

"No, Mom."

"And you killed the one and one got away and they think you interrupted a robbery of that poor jeweler? It's terrible, that's what. Oh, honey, you just can't know how upset I am about all of this..."

"Mom..."

"You *know* I think this is crazy, what you do. And look at this, these horrible men *shooting* at you and you went all the way through college and you have your teaching degree and, instead, you ride around on that awful motorcycle in those boots and carry that gun and now you wind up *killing* someone and it's just crazy. I have such a headache now and my friends keep calling me and they showed that old picture of you when you were a rookie and your hair was longer and I really think it's time you gave this job some thought."

"Mom. Listen... are you listening? I'm fine, really. I'm very tired, and I need some time to myself. I'm sorry you're upset. Why don't you take some aspirin and a hot bath, and then a nap? I'll call you later and talk more when I'm rested."

"Are you sure, honey? Isn't there something I can do now?"

"Just love me, Mom."

"Oh, honey, you know I do. It's just that I'm so worried about you."

"I know, Mom. I want you to relax now, and I'll call later."

"Promise?"

"I promise, Mom. Bye-bye."

"Bye, honey."

Jessie hung up the phone, shook her head, and let out a long sigh. Then she leaned over and unplugged the phone from the wall.

A few minutes later, after caring for her small menagerie, she stripped off her uniform and ran a hot bath. She lay back in the hot water and thought about the day and the job. She had drawn her weapon in the past, prepared to use it if the situation demanded it. Before today it had never happened. I've never before had to *kill*, she thought. So it was easy... blow the life right out of him. She remembered the red blood in his mouth and bubbling on his chest.

She remembered his last breath. The cooling of the water around her in the bath brought with it the certainty that the easy part of the killing had been squeezing the trigger.

She got out of the tub, dried off, put on an old robe, and visited with her gang of house pets: one bird, one small dog and half a cat. She watched some of the news, switched it off, cooked up a dinner of steamed chicken and broccoli, took two bites and wrapped it up and put it away. She made a cup of tea and sat on the edge of her bed in the dark, sipping and thinking.

She felt drained but knew there was no way she could go to sleep, knew there was no way she could even stay home. She pulled on a pair of nylon/lycra cycling shorts, a jogger's halter top and her aerobic shoes with heavy socks. She put her hand-held police radio and the pistol they had given her to carry while hers was held as evidence into her small backpack and slung it on. She pulled on a pair of thin half-gloves, put on her Bell V-1 helmet, and wheeled her bike out of a back room and out onto the sidewalk in front of her house. She had been riding bikes as exercise for years and had for a long time zipped around the city on a radical ten-speed thin-tired rig. But she learned to like the fat-tired "beach cruiser" style bikes for urban riding.

She swung one leg over the bike now, rested one foot on the high pedal, and shrugged her backpack into a comfortable position. She looked over the bike and smiled. It was a Raleigh "Tactic" mountain bike. It was a metallic green, had an eighteen-inch men's frame, and weighed twenty-nine pounds. It was a twenty-one speed, with XCM derailleurs. She knew it as fact that there were few mountains to cross in South Florida, but she liked to give her legs a good workout going through the different gears. The bike had a chrome moly oversized frame and fork, Dia Compe "Short Stop" brakes and resin pedals. It was a serious bike, well-built, expensive and made in the U.S.A. She loved it and most of the time used it as her primary means of everyday transportation around the city.

The night was hot and clear, and she rode the bike through the quiet streets pedaling hard, her senses aware of everything around her, including the sparse vehicular traffic, while her mind worked in fits and starts until leveling off in relaxation. She rode through downtown, over the Third Avenue Bridge and the length of Las

Olas Boulevard, eastbound toward the beach. She got to click through some of the gears as she pumped over the Las Olas Bridge and cruised onto A1A and then south. She cruised slowly through the Bahia Mar Marina, looking at the yachts, and stopped for a few minutes on the beach near the Yankee Clipper Hotel to look at the stars. She turned off Seabreeze Boulevard to steadily pedal through the curving and bridge-connected streets of the wealthy Harbor Beach area, feeling the night air grow slightly cooler coming off the manicured lawns and canals. Then she was back out onto the causeway, over the Seventeenth Street Bridge westbound, Port Everglades off her left shoulder, and onto Cordova Road, which took her again into an area with fine homes, winding streets and lots of small bridges over curving canals. She slowed then, relaxed, resting on the handlebars as the bike rolled along. Then she turned for home, only a few blocks away.

She carried her bike back inside her house a little after two in the morning. She locked up, stripped off her clothes, took a long hot shower, and went to bed.

TWO

Detective Melody Mitchell sat in the anticipatory Monday morning quiet of the Detective Division offices holding a thick file containing the reports, photos, statements and other information on yesterday's jewelery store killings. It was still an open case because one of the suspects had escaped, and there was far more to be learned in the investigation.

Jessie was coming up to the Division today to begin a tour at being a detective-type cop. It was an assignment rather than a promotion, Mitchell knew, but most cops saw getting that gold detective's badge as a step up, a step into "real" police work. She also knew Jessie Summer had made the grade through the selection process. Her letter requesting the assignment had been on file for a year, and several other cops, all senior on the job to Summer, had been selected during that time. But now Summer had a shot at it because of the quality of her work on the street, not because she was a female cop.

Mitchell looked at the closed file lying in front of her. Jessie *should* be assigned to the general duty pool, she thought, but with this homicide thing on her shoulders right now, the brass might do something different. She looked around the area, searching for another detective who was usually there early too . . . a senior homicide guy. She knew his partner had recently retired, and they'd probably want to team him with a new partner. She also had a feeling Jessie Summer was going to be one closely watched young detective. What if they put her with *him*?

Her mind suddenly focused on a hot and dusty day over twelve years earlier. She had been a teenager then, on the verge of quitting school, tired of the whole thing. Her head had been pretty messed up in those days, she reflected, with good cause. She had skipped class and gone looking for her older brother, Jerome, who hung with some other boys on Sistrunk Boulevard in the middle of the northwest section of Fort Lauderdale, the "black" section. She had idolized her brother, and when she spotted him with a group of other boys, she began to edge up to him, hoping he wouldn't chase her away as he usually did. Jerome *was* scolding her for skipping school when the shooting broke out, a drive-by shooting. Jerome grunted, doubled over and fell onto the dirty sidewalk. She remembered now how she had knelt on that hot cement, cradling her brother as the red blood pumped out of his body. All of the others had run off and she was alone. Suddenly the police were there. The white police. They pulled her away from Jerome and sent him away in an ambulance. No one would listen to her as she screamed that she was his sister, and they would not let her get into the ambulance with him.

Mitchell remembered sitting on the sidewalk and listening and watching as the white police officers did their work around her, like she wasn't even there. One of the cops was that tall and gangly one with his hat jammed on the back of his head, his unruly straw-colored hair fighting to get out from under it. Melody remembered the words now, words spoken on that hot day.

"Hey, Les, what are you doin' over there . . . tryin' to make this into a real crime scene?"

"Nah," said the big cop, "just fillin' in the blanks on this crummy trash complaint . . . that's all."

Mitchell stretched now, still wrapped in her thoughts. Jerome had died and her life had changed. The good things about her home had already been poisoned before Jerome was killed, so now there was no reason for her to stay. She went out on her own, and her pain and anger forced her to choose between dropping out of the society she was angry at or hanging in there, playing the game, and making herself into something that could effectively fight back. She stayed in school, struggled through various jobs, and eventually became a police officer, and she never forgot where she came from. When she heard those old cheap words, "You can take the nigger out of the northwest, but you can never take the northwest out of the nigger," they had their own meaning for her, and if people thought she was "militant," that was fine.

"Hell," she said now, "I *like* who I am, and I like being a cop, excuse me, a *sergeant*, here." She had almost an hour before she would go downstairs to the briefing room for the promotion ceremony presided over by the chief. There she would trade her gold detective's badge for a gold sergeant's badge. Feeling better, she opened the file in front of her and began reading through it.

That same Monday morning Jessie Summer sat cross-legged on her living room floor, sipping from a mug of hot tea. The strong rhythmic music coming from the stereo was *Heart*, and in contrast to the beat of the music Jessie sat perfectly still, her body relaxed but motionless, while her blood and her mind felt and responded to the hypnotic energies of the rock and roll. Her eyes were open and she gazed beyond the screened back porch jungle by potted and hanging plants and ferns, out to the clear blue and cloudless sky to the south. Her breathing was deep and slow, coming down from the intense workout she had just put her body through.

She wore bright yellow sweat pants and an old gray T-shirt with the tattered remains of a college rowing team logo on the front. The mug warmed her hands, adding to the heat she had generated in her body, making the T-shirt damp with perspiration. She took another sip and continued her slow inner exploration of herself. She was exploring her body with her mind, touring, checking on trouble spots, backing up and re-examining old injuries, sounding, listening, testing. Her body, she knew, would give her what she wanted, what she needed. She was a warm, tight, healthy physical machine, and she could do the job.

Inside though, inside her mind and heart...worried her. Her knowledge of her own vulnerability brought with it the chilled edges of fear, and her *awareness* of the fear might make her more vulnerable. It was beginning to impact her, try as she might to protect herself, to turn a strong shoulder to the subtle probings of emotional pain. It was getting in . . . getting to her. She was jolted by the sudden picture in her mind of the children in the photos scattered on the jeweler's office floor, and she realized that she was already making a connection with those images and a long-repressed childhood memory of her own. She had kept it buried for so long, and now . . .

She shook herself, and as she did, said out loud, "Just shake it off, Jessie. Just shake it off like water off a duck's butt."

"Duck? Duck? Awk . . . *duck*?"

She looked to her left and burst out laughing. She finished the tea, stood up in one motion, and said, "No . . . duck's *butt*." Kicker and Freeway followed her into the bedroom.

Freeway was a mitred conure, an iridescent green parrot with a touch of red on its head, extremely pigeon-toed feet, and an unpredictable vocabulary. His partner, Kicker, was an old cat, a calico with a rust and white checkerboard face. Some years ago she had been in an accident, and from her hips down she was immobile. Her hind legs lay flat against the floor, her hips turned so she could use her front paws to pull herself around the house. She moved fairly well and could make herself comfortable most of the time.

Freeway had learned that he could stand easily on Kicker's hips and ride along as the cat pulled herself across the floor. He spoke for both of them in his own stuttering and raucous way, and he would spend hours grooming her. They were almost inseparable in their symbiotic relationship, and often Jessie would find them both fast asleep after some exerting adventure, the bird comfortably cradled within the front paws of the cat.

Jessie watched as Freeway and Kicker came into the bedroom, the cat pulling herself along easily, the bird cocking his head this way and that. Jessie peeled off her sweats and T-shirt, checked the clock, and stepped into the bathroom to take a fast shower. A short time later Jessie picked up her keys and looked around the house once more before going into the station. She had the white helmet with black visor in one hand. The crisp white uniform shirt with the shoulder patches made the tan on her smooth arms stand out, the shiny leather of the gunbelt and Sam Browne, black, in hard contrast to her tawny blonde hair. The black calf-high boots gleamed.

She thought about her decision to wear the uniform one last time, and knew it was the right one. She would be driving her Camaro in to work today anyway, which she had always done at least once a week so she could leave all clean uniforms in her locker. She wore biking clothes when she rode the Raleigh in, and then changed. She'd do the same now but would need to have the locker full of practical and professional-looking detective-style outfits. She grimaced. What *was* female detective fashion, anyway?

No matter. Today she would stand in the briefing room along with all the other cops and watch with pride as Melody Mitchell received her sergeant's badge. Her own name would be called out too, recognizing her assignment as detective, and because her motorcycle assignment was rare, she wanted to be *in uniform*, boots and all, when they called her name.

She sighed as she picked up the "loaner" automatic pistol they had given her, checked it, and slid it into the holster. Time to go. She put Freeway into his wrought-iron cage, bent and petted Mister Jones, her small dust-mop dog, scratched Kicker under the chin, and said quietly, "Bye, guys." She looked at her reflection in the full-length mirror once more. A pretty but sort of tough-looking motorcycle cop stared back. She blew a puff of air and supposed she looked pretty impressive in her motor regalia, but sometimes she felt like a little girl . . . all dressed up and pretending to be a cop.

Detective Les Stillwater was not pleased.

He ran one big hand through his straw-colored hair, hardly disturbing the unruly tangle. He was getting a new partner, sort of. Baby-sitter would be another way of saying it. His old partner had just retired, up and left the place as he had been threatening to do for years.

Without warning, his thoughts skidded from his professional life to his personal life, of which there was little to talk about, he reflected. Partners there too, he thought, a double-edged sword. He had been married and divorced once. His former wife had retained custody of the children, a boy then almost ten years old and a girl two years younger. That's how he saw his kids, as they were then. His former wife had taken them from the state, leaving only a photo album, some memories and the rare phone call. He had never met or even spoken to the man she had married after the move, could not picture what kind of father that man would be to *his* kids. But were they still his kids? His feelings of frustration and helplessness were aggravated by those of selfishness and guilt. Maybe he should have tried harder, maybe he should have . . .

A phone rang on another desk and it brought him back to where he was. He stood and stretched his six-four frame, hitched his pants up by wrapping his hands around his thick leather belt near the large silver and turquoise buckle, and sighed audibly.

He looked up and saw Melody Mitchell sitting at a desk reading that fresh homicide file. He had gone downstairs earlier to see the promotions ceremony and had told himself that he had no feelings either way about Mitchell making sergeant. Jessie Summer being announced as a new detective didn't bother him either. Then he saw the captain motion to Mitchell, then to him, and he followed them into the captain's office.

The captain was a small man with dark hair and very fair skin and an analytical mind. His name was Orsen Allen. He had been called "O-A" for a time, which was then changed in the mysterious ways of police nicknames to "Hi-ho," because of his diminutive stature, his intellectual work ethic, his uncomfortable attitude toward female police officers, and his brisk and energetic way of entering the lobby and marching up to his workplace in the Detective Division every day. It was said that anyone watching this would expect six more somewhat like him to follow, all whistling the same tune.

Captain "Hi-ho" Allen cleared his throat, waited for Stillwater to close the door behind him, and began the meeting. "Company policy," he said reverently, "is that we in Homicide work as two-man, um . . . two-detective teams, for all the right reasons. Les, you know Jessie Summer is coming up to the Division. She was selected because she has shown herself to be a good cop so far. Normally she would work with the general duty group until she got her feet wet, and we would bring an experienced detective over from one of the other squads to be your new partner. She *is* new, but she's a central part of this jewelry store case, so, Les, I want you to keep her with you while you work this case. I know there will be the usual resentment from the troops because she comes to Homicide, but that's the way I want to set it up for now."

Stillwater just nodded at the captain. Like all good cops, he had already heard of the plan. It's still a baby-sitting job, he thought. "Sergeant Mitchell," the captain continued, "I know you've got a couple of days until you're due to actually work with your patrol squad. I'd like you to use that time to work with Les on this investigation . . . and with Summer . . ."

Sergeant Melody Mitchell shrugged and said evenly, "No problem, Captain Allen. I'd be happy to help out." Why doesn't he tell me the *real* reason he wants me to "work with" big old cowboy Stillwater, she thought. Then she looked over at the big detective and nodded. He nodded back, and she was heartened to see he didn't look any happier about it than she was.

The captain decided to charge on, better with statistics and graphs and clues and trends than with people and personalities. "About this shooting yesterday," he said, "will there be any special problems because it was a female motor-cop that did the killing?"

"How do you mean that, Captain? The guy's dead, shot in a robbery by a cop."

Hi-ho played with a pencil in his hands, looked at Mitchell, and said, "Anytime a cop kills a citizen, we must look at any special textures involved, like when one of our white officers kills a black suspect. The case looks simple, but I don't want us to be caught flat-footed by some abstract thing because a woman is involved. The media went crazy with it yesterday, and there'll be more. The officer, um, Summer, is probably considered attractive in a strong sort of way. She's out there riding around on that motorcycle, although I can't imagine who approved *that*, and I just want to make sure this doesn't become a circus. I want fair, impartial and professional . . . right?"

This time both Mitchell and Stillwater remained silent, neither wanting to say what they felt about what they had just heard. The captain leaned forward, made a note on the pad in front of him, and went on quietly, "I know that Captain Ford was on the scene. This Jessie Summer isn't part of his famous 'pussy posse,' is she?"

Mitchell spoke now, her voice tight, "Look, Captain Allen. This case will be worked like any other homicide, thoroughly and professionally. As far as the media excitement about Jessie Summer goes, we'll have to ride it out. As far as Captain Ford, this department thrives on denigrating and lascivious rumors, most of them unfounded ... and if he does have any female fans here, I *doubt* if Summer is one of them."

Stillwater nodded and smiled, and the captain, perplexed, motioned with his hand for more. Mitchell went on, "I know Jessie Summer. She's a lady, and one of the rules she made early on was that she would not date within the department, ever. She told me once that female police officers are very socially vulnerable within such a close peer-group society, and that she felt it would be dangerous and unwise to play where she worked. As far as I know, she plays no politics, she keeps her head down and her nose clean, she has a solid record, and she would never belong to a 'posse,' Ford's or anyone else's."

Captain Allen had a strained grin on his face as he listened to Mitchell. He said nothing, but thought, Those dangers never bothered *you* though, did they, Melody?

"Tell you what, Captain Allen," said Stillwater quietly, "what Sergeant Mitchell here says is just about what I've heard about that gal. Never any funny business around here ..."

Mitchell, her face muscles tense, jumped back in, "Here's the important part, Captain. I was on the scene yesterday. I've taken Summer's statement and gone over the lab reports and looked through the file. I'd say right now this is a good shooting. Summer was absolutely justified, and she did a good job. You don't have to worry about how the department will look on this, and you can pass that on to the chief. I think there's more to this deal than a simple robbery. In the meantime, um ... Les and I will keep you briefed on our progress." She stood, and so did Stillwater.

Captain Allen watched them leave, aware that she had just terminated his meeting.

* * *

The Comm Center tracked Jessie down in the Traffic Office. A call had come in from one of her informants, a person she had helped some time ago who occasionally passed on unimportant information. He was a colorful old guy, forever involved in some scam at one of the local race tracks, a half-time artist working the fringes, tenuously "connected" to persons in the mob. Jessie called the number given, heard all the background noise, and guessed her informant was at his "office" in the Floridian Restaurant on Las Olas Boulevard. Could she come alone to a meeting with an important person at the small Italian place out on North Beach? It would be good for everybody. She asked who the important person was, and actually heard the voice gulp loudly before it said, "Dominic Tatari."

Jessie sat in her old Camaro convertible dressed in jeans, a pullover and a lightweight jacket. She ran her fingers through her thick blonde hair. She watched the front of the restaurant and mused. Funny, he had changed the name, she thought, with all of that supposed family pride involved. The name had been Tatarinello years ago, the Organized Crime guys had told her, and Dominic had changed it when he was just an up-and-coming soldier for one of the New Jersey families. She had met him briefly a year ago during a murder investigation, and now Dominic Tatari, well-known local crime boss, wanted to meet with her.

Her Camaro was a "classic," but it could be moody. The driver's side door was stuck, so Jessie climbed up and over, walked across the street, and went into the restaurant.

Jessie was shown to a corner table, and she sat now with her back against the wall, easily able to see the entire dining area of the place and part of the hallway leading to the kitchen. She sat with her left hip forward, her left arm on the table. Her right hand lay in her lap close to the semi-automatic pistol on her right hip, under the jacket.

Just habit.

Tatari came in through the front door, gave the waiter a look, and came to the table. Jessie stood, watched his hands, then shook the offered hand briefly. She looked at him as he sat in the seat to her left. His hair was still black but very thin, plastered back over his shiny skull. His face was full, puffy and pitted under the eyes. His arms were hairy and soft, and his simple white shirt strained across his bulging middle. He looked tired and edgy, and absently played with the obligatory diamond pinky ring on his left hand.

"Thank you for coming here," he said softly. "I told them how you would sit." Jessie nodded and he went on, "I wanted this meeting in a public place . . . open, okay? I know you are always working, always covering yourself." He paused, looking at her face, "You are much more attractive in real life than in the paper or on television. I saw your face, your name, and I remembered you."

Jessie nodded again, silent.

Tatari spoke rapidly to the waiter in Italian, and within seconds two cups of coffee sat before them. He sipped his, then said, "Last year when that tourist from Philly got himself killed by the pimp and left in the trunk of his car many policemen thought I was involved, yes? Big trouble for me, because of the digging . . . because he was supposedly a criminal from up north and came here to see some friends of mine. Then, because of your fine police work, because the pimp's hooker who had been with the guy *confided* in you and it was learned the *pimp* killed the guy, the crime was solved and the heat went away from me." He made a face, "Well, some of the heat . . . and for a while anyway."

She shrugged.

"Look, uh, Officer Summer. I asked for this meeting because I have respect for you and what you did then, and for what you did yesterday . . . and because I need help on a personal matter. It requires a special kind of professional trust and secrecy, and I'm afraid that within my own . . . structure . . . I can't find those things anymore, not on this level of personal importance." He paused, then lunged on, "I have a son. You know of him? Good. I have tried to give my son what he needed, and I have tried to hang on him a cloak of respect, self and otherwise. And yet he does things that make me wonder if he really is my boy, or if I've failed completely as his father." His eyes went out of focus. "We lost his mother years ago, and I often think she was lucky to only know him as a wonderful child, and not what he has grown to be." He stopped, and Jessie was aware that she was hearing words Tatari had probably not spoken before now.

They both sipped their coffee, and Jessie sat back and waited. Tatari leaned forward, his hands cutting the air. "My son has all the toys, yes? Cars, boats, travel, all the clothes, cash in his pockets . . . and with all of that, the girls . . . okay? Now he is forty years old, *forty*, and he acts like a spoiled brat, and does things that anger and shame me." The skin around his eyes tightened as he lowered his voice, "Now drugs. Now not only does he stick the shit up his nose . . . excuse my language . . . now he is the big businessman, the big importer. He's gonna make it big with the Latinos down in Miami, okay? He takes his father's money and *name*, without my approval, and goes into the drug business." He leaned back then and grimaced, "The Latinos, they take one look at him and know he's a baby. They don't know if I'm behind him or not, probably don't care, and they've got him figured six ways from Sunday before he even makes his first deal."

Jessie ran one finger around the rim of her coffee cup and said quietly, "I'm a cop, but I'm not a *narc*. Are you sure you've got the right cop here?"

"Listen a little more, okay?" said Tatari. "Hear the whole thing, then you'll see." He took a deep breath, then went on, "So, my son, the businessman, he gets behind in the game to the tune of a quarter of a mil, and the Latinos start getting antsy and then noisy and now pushy, making threats. I've heard it all before. The problem is, my son is very scared, and not capable of pulling the money together to get them off his back. I see that something is not right, but I wait. Finally he comes to me, to Daddy, to explain his problem." Tatari was very still, then shook himself and said, "This is not the only problem with this son of mine, I'm afraid, but at least *this* problem I can understand." He looked around the restaurant, the waiter reflexively moved toward them and was waved away, and he continued. "The Latinos are willing to forget the whole thing if my son will bring them the money today . . . cash in a bag to a hotel in Miami. I have the money, but I cannot let my son deliver it."

Jessie took another sip of coffee, guessing what was coming.

"Instead of a quarter mil," said Tatari, "I have a bag with an even three hundred thousand in it. I want you to take it down there for my stupid son, for me, and convince them that the extra fifty is enough to make them close the books. Okay?" Jessie sat up and pursed her lips, thinking, Pretty dramatic for a syndicate heavy, and it hardly sounds rehearsed at all, but what does he *really* want? She said evenly, "Will you offer me money too, or am I to do this because you're a good guy?"

Tatari shook his head irritably, "You know better than that, and so do I. I would not offer *you* money for anything. No . . . no, it will be a trade, of course."

She waited, very still.

Tatari leaned forward again. "You do this for me today, and within the week your police department can make a couple of significant arrests on a murder case that's been on the books for months." He rubbed his face with his hands. "Look, I'm talking about the three bikers shot so many times with the automatic weapons in that crummy bar out on Davie Boulevard. It is known now that one of the dead was an informant for the police, yes? And the police know damn well the bikers were doing the porn and the dope and the hookers with some more *ethnic* connections, yeah? And your guys just can't put anything together on it, can't find the right witness, the right person with enough troubles of his or her own who would flip for you in a heartbeat given the right doorways. Yeah? Yeah?"

"Yeah," said Jessie, not meaning to sound like him, "but now that you've said that, what's to prevent me from having you dragged in for holding info on a murder? How do you know I'm not wearing a wire right now? Why don't I just bust you, clear up the murder later, and let Dominic Junior get himself contributed to the Artificial Reef?"

Tatari actually smiled. "I must tell you that somehow it just doesn't work when you try to talk tough. But . . . I asked myself those questions before I set up this meet. I guessed you'd help my son on the possibility of me helping you down the line somewhere because I'd *owe* you, and you know how we are about that kind of thing. I trust you, Officer Summer, you see? Whether it means anything or not coming from me, I don't know, but I do know that a police informant was killed in that deal, and I know how *you* guys are about *that* kind of thing." He toyed with his cup for a moment, then without looking up, said quietly, "And I guessed you'd help me if I told you that the killing you did yesterday had to do with more than a simple robbery. Maybe your people have already guessed it, I don't know. I know it could be closed because it *looks* like a simple robbery, and that would be a shame... because there is something very ugly there that would interest any good cop, and it's possible I could learn more and pass it on to you if I wasn't so worried about my son." He sat back, crossed his arms over his belly, and waited.

Jessie felt very cold in the pit of her stomach, a dread knowing. She wiped her lips with her napkin and thought, No way, absolutely not, no frigging way. But she looked into Tatari's eyes and said, "You guessed right."

Jessie drove back to the station deep in thought—examining what she was about to do, looking it over as a cop, considering the legal and criminal aspects of it... then the potential yield—and knew she could do it without losing any sleep at all. She had to pursue any avenue that might lead to an answer. If Dominic Tatari wanted to play some kind of game, she knew she could play too. She also knew that most people she worked with wouldn't touch it with a ten-foot pole.

She was going to do it, and she had to do it alone.

Jessie found Mitchell on the phone when she walked into the Detective Division, and Mitchell smiled and waved her over. Jessie noticed Mitchell was not at the same desk she had worked at the day before and wondered why until big, gangly Les Stillwater, gruff and awkwardly polite as usual, walked over carrying a folder.

"Mornin' there, Jessie Summer. How ya doin' today? Get through the night all right and all? Settlin' down a bit after that deal yesterday? Did you know we're partners now, you and me? And Mitchell too, I mean, she's gonna work with us some on this jewelry store ambush and we've both got a feelin' it will turn into a can of worms before it's all over... what do you think?"

Jessie, not knowing which question demanded an answer, just

smiled and shrugged. She *was* jolted a bit at hearing she would be teamed with Stillwater, who had a reputation as a "dinosaur" cop, a holdover from the bad old days of police work.

But Jessie was comfortable around the big detective, aware of his reputation as a cop who got results, and she sensed that under the rough exterior was a gentle and caring man. Stillwater ran one hand through his disheveled hair, looked through the folder in his other hand, and said, "I've got to amble down to the lab for a few minutes, would ya tell Sergeant Mitchell I'll be back shortly? Thanks." He slouched off, his cowboy boots scuffing the floor, his slacks baggy in the back and threatening to slide off his hips at any moment.

"Hey, Jessie," Melody Mitchell hung up the phone and smiled, "I see you've met your new partner . . . and mine too, temporarily. It should be a learning experience for all of us." She paused, thoughtful, and said in a quieter voice, "You know . . . for everything that Stillwater is supposed to be, he's the first person around here that has addressed me by my new rank . . . and it sounded natural." She made a face, then went on, "Oh yeah . . . I got the full criminal history on the one you killed. Geraldo Gomez, Latino bad boy. Had a varied record going back to his teen years, everything from auto theft to armed robbery. Did some hard time, but not much, considering the number of arrests, and almost every one of his arrests involved a weapon."

"Any of his armed robberies in the past include jewelry stores or child pornography?" asked Jessie. "Not a one," said Mitchell with a strange grin, "and he rarely strayed from his home turf. I think he was just hired muscle, easy to find in Miami these days. Probably worked cheap, no real quality, but not asked to do tricky things either. I've got queries going with Dade County and Miami PD to see if he's hooked into any of the established groups, or where he would be brokered from if that was the case. Right now he's just a bad boy with a long history, a *dead* bad boy. That little automatic pistol he tried to shoot you with came from a residential burglary reported a couple of months ago in Hialeah." She stopped and looked closely at Jessie. "And what's on your mind, lady? Besides the killing, I mean. Want to talk about something?"

Jessie knew her agreement with Dominic Tatari was a deal with the devil, and she knew she could not drag Melody into it . . . or Stillwater either. "No, I just need some time. Uh . . . do you think it will be okay if I skate out of here for a couple of hours? I just need to get out for a while." Mitchell smiled and shook her head and said, "Get out of here, girl. Go home, go for a ride on that goofy bicycle of yours. Stillwater and I will be buried in paperwork most of the day, and the captain is upstairs with the rest of the staff right now. You're covered, now go."

Jessie and Dominic Tatari were together, side by side in their cars, for less than a minute. They met on the upper parking level at the far east end of the Galeria Mall, near the beach. Tatari told Jessie what the Latins had said, gave her the bag, and wished her luck. Before they parted, he asked one more thing. Would she come to his house off Bayview Drive after it was done? Come along to the right side of the house by the large hedge, all the way to the back, and tell him how it went down. Would she do that?

It was a place where a President met a Pope.

It was a place built by a man who wanted to bring a villa of sixteenth century design to Miami, by a man who could afford the artists, builders and gardeners to make it real. Over a thousand craftsmen labored from 1914 to 1916, and still more years were needed to finish the main buildings and garden. Material and art objects were brought in from all over the world to add to the grandeur. Its name came from a Basque word, and it was fronted by Biscayne Bay and largely surrounded by mangroves. Tourists and lovers of fine art and rare gardens came from all over the world to walk through the many rooms of the villa, through the courtyard, and around the paths of the gardens to see the carved seahorses and Venetian urns, the fauns and nymphs, Italian sculptured figures, pink Istrian marble and ornate cast-iron gates. It was a place of art and history and peace.

The Latins were not pleased at first.

They were not pleased to call the hotel room number they had been given, only to have a female voice tell them they would have to go to Vizcaya for their money. "Vizcaya? What kind of game do you play with us? We meet here, in this hotel, as instructed."

"No," said the female voice, "we meet at Vizcaya, open and friendly, where we can be relaxed and you can take this bag with your money plus another fifty for your trouble. ¿Sí?"

Pause. "Sí."

The female voice told them the color of the hat the person would be wearing, which would match the color of the bag. The Latins tried to be tough, demanding, threatening, but the voice stayed firm. "Are you sure you want to play hardball," asked the voice. "Isn't this a good time to make this deal and then pretend you never heard of young Dominic?" After another pause the Latins gave the name they said would be used to confirm who they were, the name they had given to the father of Dominic. Then they agreed to Vizcaya ... one hour.

Vizcaya, open to the public, was perfect. People were there— tour groups, photographers, local artists... one casually dressed young woman with big sunglasses and a light blue baseball cap with a marlin stitched on the front. Under her arm a light blue bag. The young woman sat with her back to a vine-covered wall of stone, at the far end of the Mythological Garden Walk, where eighteenth century statues stood in silent observation.

When she was approached by the two Latins in their guayabera shirts, one yellow, one white, both wearing sunglasses and scowls, she smiled. They pointed to the bag she held under her arm, but she just shook her head and spoke quietly for a moment, taking her time, making sure they understood that after today there would be no more contact, there would be no more deals, no hassles at all ... or there *would* be the kind of sustained and determined trouble for the Latins that made business impossible, made sleep impossible, ¿comprende?

The Latins, not afraid of the girl, but aware of the business implications imparted by her words, and guessing there were others covering her back, nodded their understanding. The girl nodded, her right hand now in the blue bag by her side. With her left she pointed to a delicately carved statue of a mythical goddess fifty feet away. One of the Latins walked there, bent, and picked up another light blue bag. He examined the contents carefully for over a minute, then straightened and grinned at his partner. He stood a moment and looked all around the gardens, made a small motion to his compadre, and they moved away toward the west reflecting pool.

Jessie found the house on a street off Bayview Drive, a big house with lots of landscaping and a low brick wall out front. She parked two houses down and walked back. It was early evening, and she was tired. She would meet Tatari, tell him how it went, and get out of there before she got kissed on both cheeks.

She went along the right side of the house by a large hedge, all the way back to the door that led to Tatari's private study as he had described it earlier. She looked beyond the screened-in pool area to the cement seawall and canal flanking the rear of the property. Must be nice, she thought as she knocked lightly and waited. She knocked again, harder, and was rewarded with silence. She walked to the edge of the screened-in patio and looked to her left, to the glass sliding doors leading to the dining room and study beyond. She had a sinking feeling even before she saw the distorted pale skin of a forearm and hand pressed against the glass of the sliding door at floor level. Darn it, she thought, I guess this whole thing *was* a little too simple.

She drew her weapon, tried the side door, found it locked, and went to the screen door. It was also locked but she pushed in the screen in one corner and unlatched it. She stopped and listened. She stepped through the partly open glass sliding door into the dining room, felt its emptiness, and took a quick look at the body of Dominic Tatari, senior. Dead with a vengeance, dead with a terrible scowl on his face, the left side of his head crushed in.

She stepped past the body and, moving in a crouch, searched the rest of the house for bodies, dead or alive. There was no one. The interior of the house was plush, richly furnished with all the audio and video toys and a full kitchen. The bedrooms were mannish and comfortable, and the house was neat to a fault. She found the door to the garage, opened it, and saw one car, a new Mercedes sedan. There was space for another. She moved to the front door and found it locked, the deadbolt thrown, and next to it an alarm panel, turned off. She turned back to the study. The wall panelling was dark wood, and around the living room were several intricately carved pieces, mahogany or teak. At the entranceway from the living room to the dining room and kitchen were a matched set of heavy wooden figures, dark, with an oiled gloss. She looked over her shoulder at the locked front door, and then at the partially open sliding door the body pressed against, where she had entered. Could have had a key and gone out the front, she thought, or simply stepped out here and gone the back way.

She tapped her foot on the tile floor of the dining room. No sign of ransacking, no real sign of a struggle, except that Tatari's shirt was torn and both his hands were balled into fists. In one was a piece of colored paper, crumpled between his fingers. She stood over his body and saw that he had hit and rolled, coming to a stop jammed against the glass door. The lab guys would probably choreograph it exactly, once they got a look at the spatter pattern of the blood and other stuff on the tiles and glass. He had been clobbered, no doubt about that. Jessie tucked her gun against one hip, rubbed her face hard with her hands, and said quietly, "Phooey."

She carefully used the kitchen phone to call out the troops, requesting detectives Mitchell and Stillwater, then retraced her steps in leaving the house, and stood in the early evening half-light at the edge of the drive near the low wall. Should she have called this in instead of just easing out of there and letting things unravel naturally?

She turned when she saw the car approaching. So soon? Then she saw it was a big Cadillac, no police unit, and the three men in it were staring at her as the car neared the drive. She saw the one on the right side turn and say something to the driver, who was big and dark, and the car stopped suddenly and was thrown into reverse.

Jessie was already running toward it, gun in hand, but the car accelerated back up the street violently, weaving slightly until it slid out onto Bayview Drive. Then, tires screaming, it roared north, still too far away for Jessie to see anything about the tag other than it was a Florida registration. She could see that the guy on the right side had sharp features and lots of hair, and for a tilting second she knew she had seen him before. She could see the one in the back, staring at her with his mouth open. He looked very much like photos she had seen of Dominic Tatari, the son. She gave a quick thought of running back to her car to give chase, realized she had a crime scene to protect, and stood there in the street, her eyes wide, breathing hard.

THREE

CAPTAIN ALLEN HAD ONE OF those sailor's coffee cups with the non-skid bottom. He sipped from it now as he silently read through a thin pile of papers in front of him. On the other side of his desk sat Jessie, flanked by Mitchell and Stillwater. Jessie knew she should have felt uncomfortable, but she was tired, and found all she could do was wonder why Hi-ho needed a non-skid bottom on his coffee cup, since it was well-known that he and the other admin warriors around there rarely left their desks, and their desk-tops rarely, if ever, moved. It was just past eight in the morning.

"I know it's in your report, Officer, uh, Detective Summer," said the captain, "but why don't you verbalize for me why it was *you* who came upon the body of Dominic Tatari. The chief says the OCU captain was piqued that his guys weren't called in if you had something going with this syndicate type, understand?"

Spare me, thought Mitchell, and looked over to see Stillwater roll his eyes.

Jessie laid it out for them, step by step, from her informant's message to the first meeting, then back to the house in the evening. She told the captain everything... almost. She only left out the part about the money, the Latins and Miami.

She told the captain Dominic Tatari had asked for the meeting through the CI because he wanted to give away an eyeball on the biker murders on Davie Boulevard, confirming there was an OC connection into the bikers' activities. He laid the ground rules during the first meeting, and set it up for Jessie to come back later. He had hinted there might be something else he'd have to say, something about the jewelry store deal she was involved in. She didn't tell the OC guys until she had something to talk about. "The guys over in OC *know* Tatari knows who I am because of that murder case that came out of their prostitution stings last year. That's the *only* reason I even knew who Dominic Tatari is... was," she ended.

"And he was doing this because he had become a Fraternal Order of Police booster...?" asked the captain.

"No sir... it's in the report. He told me he was doing two things. He was banking a favor on me which he might be able to call in down the road, and he was hurting somebody in a competitive group by putting the finger on them." It sounded lame even to Jessie, and she saw Stillwater looking at Mitchell intently.

The captain chewed on this for a moment, then asked, "Do you think this 'competition' got wind of your first meeting, and killed him before he could give them away?"

Stillwater spoke now for the first time, "I was on the scene, Captain, and I saw the report and the photos. Sure didn't look like a gang hit to me, not at all. Jessie found the place secured like someone had a key and locked up as they left, forgettin' or not noticin' that the glass door was open near the body. And that Caddy with the three guys showing up and then high-tailing it smells like unfinished business to me."

Jessie was very still, and the room was quiet for a moment.

The captain pushed a couple of paperclips around his desk-top with a pencil. "Okay," he said finally, "I hear you, Les. And for the record, after the OC guys *did* get there they had a field day going through the house for papers and phone numbers and stuff. Besides some money they impounded, and a phone book full of numbers that looks like the Who's Who of local and northeast syndicate members, it was pretty tame. No big secrets, no mysteries. Just a clean house and one dead crime boss."

"What about that piece of colored paper found in Tatari's fist? What did that turn out to be?" asked Stillwater.

Mitchell, surprised by the thoroughness with which Stillwater had looked things over, answered him, "It turned out to be part of a photograph. It showed one leg, the buttocks and part of the torso of a young child, probably male. The child was naked except for a pair of white socks with a small bear on the heel. The other side was a close-up of part of a face, pink skin, and written across it in ink were the words: 'More like this.' Lab told me this morning they think it is part of a pornography photo book. Their guess is the 'models' are kids.'' She was looking at Jessie now, who looked back wide-eyed.

"So," said Captain Allen brusquely, himself a family man, "not only was the dead Tatari a syndicate crime boss, he was also a pervert."

Jessie, Mitchell and Stillwater were silent.

Allen leafed through the papers and photos again, humming to himself. Then he looked up and said grimly, "Look, um, Detective Summer. This doesn't look good at all. First you do the shooting and now you're dealing with this bad guy and then find him dead ... while you're *supposed* to be learning the ropes here in your new assignment. You are *supposed* to work with ... Sergeant Mitchell and Detective Stillwater. They are on the jewelry store situation ... and now *this*. We need to clear up one homicide before you go out and find others, so why don't you kill time with Melody and Les until I get some answers or direction from upstairs. Right?"

After they left the captain's office, a secretary gave Jessie a phone message. The same informant needed to see her, soon. Jessie showed the note to Mitchell, who nodded and said, "We'll *all* go."

He sat near the phone brushing his full head of shiny black hair. His sharp features were relaxed, the oily lids covering the dark eyes closed now as he derived an almost sensual pleasure from the pull of the brush. He wished he was not working, wished he was back home where his little one would brush his hair for him, and he could just lie back and enjoy it. He opened his eyes and looked at the Piaget watch on his left wrist. But he *was* working ... and it was still too early to call California, but he could call San Juan or New York when he was ready.

The brush poised over his head for a moment as he heard someone walking outside the door to his room, soft voices. Then he resumed the rhythmic strokes as he determined there was no threat. Stupid hotel. He hated hotels. Too many records, no matter what sophisticated false identities one had available. The brush stopped again and he scowled, thinking of why he was in another hotel. Tatari, the younger Dominic, just couldn't maintain, couldn't be cool. He had been staying in a beachside condo owned by Tatari, without the elder's knowledge, and it had been fine for working purposes. But now, with the old man being found dead and the newspapers doing speculative stories and the cops running around with big grins on their faces, he didn't even want to be in the same *town* with Dominic. But he had to, for now.

He wondered for a moment if he should fly away from Fort Lauderdale. There was a negative surge taking place, and during his thirty-nine years he had been around the world enough times to know you pay attention to the signs when they tell you to take care. He remembered the bad feeling he first had about the young Cuban hired through the Miami broker. Big, tough, fast, experienced . . . the guy had come highly recommended. Turned out to be a two-bit thug really, no class, and no discipline. Good old quiet and reliable Humberto hadn't arrived yet, so the young Cuban had been hired to help out. The idea had been to make the little jeweler see the light, that's all. Just make him understand his position, and to convince the man it would be best if he accepted the next part of his contract with them, instead of backing out as he had threatened. The man had been a steady customer of the bait product and had indicated interest in the next phase. And he had the money. When he began signalling his reluctance, they decided to speak with him, just to keep things tight.

He put the back of the brush softly against his lips and kissed it. But no, he thought, the Cuban had to get too rough too fast, and there was nothing I could do about it . . . and then that exquisite woman policeman was there in the door, backlighted by the soft morning sun, and the Cuban learned quickly that he was not so tough and fast after all.

He felt an odd sensation in his groin, a warmth, and smiled. He was familiar with those stirrings, but usually they were only ignited by his little ones, or thoughts of them. How interesting, he thought, the image of the female cop with her gun is arousing me. A dominating female presence, touched with violence . . . is that it? He shrugged, then stretched, putting those thoughts away for now.

But there was no denying that things were not orderly. The jewelry store thing was a mess . . . although, with the jeweler out of the way we can now concentrate on more *definite* clients, he thought. But there was a real possibility the police would link what they found there with the death of Tatari. He stopped again, thinking of the female cop. Was it coincidence that put her at both places in such a short time? He didn't like coincidences. Was there more to her than local cop? Perhaps some preventative action against her would be required.

Wait, he thought then, go slow.

He glanced at the phone and thought of the ones in California with their safe places set up like little movie studios, with fancy bedrooms and playrooms and the lights and equipment. He knew there were places like it in Florida too . . . productive, professional set-ups with the developing and printing and mailing all going on from one group of buildings. The talent was there too . . . models . . . they never called them kids. Yes, they recruited the talent mostly from south of the border, but once in a while they came up with a nice blonde-haired, blue-eyed local, snatched and drugged and used and thrown back out onto the street . . . maybe on the steps of a church where they would probably be found. They weren't really inhumane, after all.

He sighed, "paper-cup talent," people in the business called them; use them once, throw them away. Fair-skinned, blonde and light brown-headed models were the ones considered most precious. Most of his samples came from South or Central America, or his native Philippines, so they were dark, with various textures and hues to their soft skin, and those big brown eyes and rich black hair. Easier to obtain, he thought, just as marketable, and in his opinion . . . just as pleasing. Of course, during the six or eight hours the models were in the complex many photos and films were taken, with several different adult models and props. Yes, they got full use out of the paper-cup before they threw it away.

Well, he thought, there certainly was money to be had from the portfolio and films with the young ones involved. He made a face.

The photos never *did* it for him, and he did not understand the great craving for them. He understood the money though. No, he wasn't interested in pictures or films of the very young and flawless talent being used for sex. He preferred the real thing, understood *that* market, and worked very hard—as quite a specialist, he believed— to supply those discerning enough, and rich enough, with what they really wanted.

Kids as lovers.

He grinned now as he thought of what one of his partners in Manila said the last time they were together discussing business, "Baby . . . if it's got hair on it, then they're too old." He began to brush his hair again, waiting.

Here in the States, he thought, the magazines and films are big business. The organized guys ran it, or tried to control most of it, though even some of *those* groups drew a line when it came to using the very young talent. That's what the trouble was between the younger Tatari and the old man . . . that and the dope and the natural fear and resentment spawned when a father and son struggle over control of their turf. Dominic was a fool and a loser even *before* he began packing his nose with cocaine. But, he reminded himself, we did need the name, didn't we? The name and some of his money to get those doors open, get the mailing lists, get things going with the magazines so we could make our unique little pitch, yes?

Yes.

"More like this," they said. Okay, I'll call California and make sure they do more like that, just for our valued customers. Then, after they've been pleasured by the images and their imaginations have been fueled, they will be cautiously approached. They will be felt out, to see if they had the desire and money to actually have a little one all their own . . . to do with what they wish. There was a market in other parts of the world, sure, and this was his first try at offering it here in the States, but he knew the money was here and waiting.

He stopped brushing, pulled more hairs from the bristles, threw the brush down, and said harshly, "Stupid old jeweler, stupid Cuban hot-head, stupid Tatari." Then he reached for the phone.

* * *

The informant's name was Charles. He was a small man, trim and neat, fastidious in dress and theatrical in mannerisms. His thick hair was professionally colored and styled, his nails were manicured, and his age was a carefully guarded secret. His charm, and almost desperate clinging to the "quality days, the *dignified* days when we carried ourselves with a *subdued* flair and certain style," gave away the fact that he was not part of this "new generation, all clamoring to burst out of the closet and wave themselves in front of everyone."

Jessie had first come to know Charles as a victim. He had flagged her down one night as she drove past in her squad car. Wringing his hands, he told her he had *foolishly* let this *delightful* young friend take a ride in his car. He had met the young friend in this quiet little bar, he explained, was *immediately* taken with him, and didn't think the young man would be gone long. This had been *hours* ago, he went on, and since then the young man had driven to his poor little apartment, *looted* it according to a neighbor, and was now driving around town spending his money and ignoring *his* efforts to get back his car.

Jessie had driven the distraught little man to the various bars he pointed out, and miraculously they found the car, with the "young friend" still in it. Even though encouraged by Jessie to do so, Charles had refused to press charges. Jessie recovered his property, got the car back, and sent the young man packing with a few words of warning. Charles was so taken with the way Jessie had handled the whole mess, he decided then and there he would help out his favorite police officer every time he had the chance. His help would come in the form of interesting information.

"So who killed him, Charles? Who knocked off old man Tatari?" asked Jessie now. Stillwater and Mitchell sat in the front seat of the detective unit, the big detective behind the wheel. Jessie sat in back beside Charles. They were parked behind Wolfie's Restaurant, across Sunrise Boulevard from the Galeria Mall where Charles worked at a fashionable haberdashery.

Charles' head was on a swivel, "Oh, Jessie . . . if I knew that I'd be *somebody* now, wouldn't I? *My*, I'd be the most popular man in this town."

"Yes, but I know you hear a lot of things, Charles... things that happen. Somehow you always seem to hear about them."

"Sure, you're right, Jessie." He stopped and fidgeted for a moment, looking at the two detectives in the front seat before going on, "But this is like one of your *squad* meetings, with everyone *staring* at me."

"Oh, Charles," chided Jessie, "you've met Melody before, and Les is my new partner now that I'm a detective. They've both heard me talk about what an interesting person you are, so they decided to come along. We're all on the same side, Charles."

"Well. I *am* interesting, and quite *rare*, really. And I guess it's all right." Charles paused, swallowed, and went on;"I know you need information, but this time there's nothing on the street at *all*." He looked all around again, then in a flash of cop mindset, surprised them with, "Well... doesn't *that* tell you something though? I mean, if it was an *inside* thing, you know, *business*... well then, maybe I'd have heard something. I can tell you right now that if I had heard anything *before* this horrible thing happened I would have gone straight to Dom with it *first*. After all, he *has* been good to me through the years, and always treated me with... with... oh, *my*."

Stillwater sat stiffly behind the wheel, staring straight ahead. Mitchell looked down at her hands in her lap, and Jessie gently patted Charles on the shoulder until he composed himself and went on. "Oh, dear. Anyway... but it's *quiet* out there, like everyone is just reading the papers and wondering what happened to poor Dominic Tatari. Maybe it was just some *off-the-wall* thing."

"So why call for this meeting then?" asked Jessie.

"Dom told me to meet with him that same day I set up *your* meeting at the restaurant with him... the day *after* you killed that *animal* who tried to shoot you at the jewelry store. Anyway, *after* your meeting he gave me instructions, something I was supposed to pass *on* to you." He squirmed around for a moment, playing with the lobe of one ear and looking all around the parking lot, then back at the three cops.

The cops waited.

Charles leaned forward then, and in a conspiratorial whisper, said, "There's a place called Dreamland—if you can imagine that—out west off State Road Eighty-four. It actually *used* to be a gas station, but now it's a beer bar with *exotic* dancers. It's shabby, really. A girl dances there . . . and occasionally hooks for the right guy. A girl called Starlight, real name Joan." His voice dropped even more. "*She* drove the shooters to that bar on Davie Boulevard where those *biker* types were murdered. Drove them, waited, and carried them *away*. She knows the shooters *and* the man who put it together. This guy owns 'Dreamland,' and if I understand what Dom was telling me, he's not really an associate of Dom's, but *somehow* connected. He might be some small-time competition, or know some of the same people, you know? According to Dom, besides the skin dancing and the prostitution, the guy is into *pornography*. I had the feeling talking with Dom that he didn't *like* the guy *or* his dirty pictures."

He stopped and gulped several deep breaths. Stillwater had glanced at Mitchell at the mention of porn, but they stayed quiet. The small man went on: "*So*. Starlight, or Joan, she can *finger* the whole gig, and Dom *said* she would. Said she's junked out on cocaine, the poor thing, and pissed at this guy because he was screwing her and *then* did some coke with Joan's thirteen-year-old daughter and screwed *her*. I guess the kid's messed up now, and Joan is not at all pleased. Dom said that Joan was just waiting for the right police person to come along, get her daughter off the street and into a place where they can clean her up, help *her*, Joan, get off the nose candy . . . *protect* her and the kid, and she'll give you the complete story, *full* of goodies like where they bought the automatic weapons, who her bosses' connections are . . . *all* that stuff."

He seemed surprised at the silence when he was finished, and he sat back in his seat, depleted.

Mitchell and Stillwater were chewing on what they had heard. Jessie waited, then said quietly, "Was there nothing else, Charles?" Charles looked hurt as he said, "Oh, Jessie, you know *I* wouldn't hold out on you. That's all Dom gave me, really. I don't know if he thought he was in *danger* or something . . . he didn't *act* like it." He wiped his face with a handkerchief. "This whole thing is so *weird*."

All three cops nodded.

"But don't *worry*, Jessie," said Charles as he opened the door and turned to get out of the car. "You are *so* right about me hearing things, I mean some of these tough guys tell me the *damndest* tidbits. Well, I'll call the *minute* I get something good." He held the door open as he leaned in, looked at each of them in turn, and then said to Jessie, "Maybe this doesn't mean anything, but Dom was one kind of bad guy, and his *son* is another. What *I've* heard about the younger Dominic isn't pretty at all . . . some really *kinky* stuff, *completely* out of bounds."

In the late afternoon of that day the Broward County Sheriff's Office took an incoming 911 call from a frantic mother of a nine-year-old boy. She had sent the boy to a nearby grocery store to pick up a couple of things on his bicycle. The trip should have taken ten minutes, but an hour had passed and there was no sign of him. A patrol deputy was dispatched to the North Lauderdale residential neighborhood to check out the validity of the call, and within a few minutes asked for more units to help in an area search. One of the Sheriff's Office helicopters was sent to the scene also, and within a short time helped direct a ground unit to a dirt path through a small wooded area near the grocery store. Laying alongside the path was the boy's bicycle, his backpack with one torn strap, which contained the items his mother had sent him for, and a melted ice cream bar. But the boy was gone. Also found in the dirt were tire tracks from a truck or van, and a witness told one of the searching deputies of an old beat-up van cruising the area in the afternoon. The deputies on the scene took it seriously, but the boy's mother was not consoled by their technical expertise and professional intensity. Her boy was gone.

While the deputies still toiled in North Lauderdale and the day turned to evening, a different kind of phone call was made.

"Uh, hey, Dominic . . . this is Scammer."

"Yeah?"

"I got a good one, I think . . . he's real clean . . ."

"So why the fuck you got to call me? You know what to do."

"Yeah, I know, but with all the shit goin' on about your old man and all, and I hadn't heard from you in a few days, and the last time we talked you told me to get a light-haired one, a blonde one maybe. This kid is beautiful, but I've had to dope him good . . ."

"*Goddamn*, Scammer! I don't need a fucking resume on the kid . . . if we can use him, *use* him. Get him over to Frog's and *do it*, then let me know when the proofs are ready. And don't talk to me on the fucking phone about this shit . . . why don't you just take out an ad in the goddamned paper?"

"You want me to take out an ad in the paper . . . ?"

"Forget it, Scammer . . . just *do* the kid, okay?"

When Jessie got home that afternoon, she spent an hour doing isometrics and stretching exercises. She took a lawn chair and a book and sat in the sun, trying to catch the final rays of the day. When the shadows got long, she went inside, showered, and called her mother. They spoke for quite a while, Jessie mostly listening to her mother's worries. Jessie tried to be patient and understanding and reassuring. They hung up laughing, friends.

She made a cup of tea and sat listening to the music of Keiko Matsui, wondering again if her mother would ever get over her guilt feelings about what had happened when Jessie was a child. Her mother chided her often about finding the right man and settling down, and Jessie suspected her mother's motives were somehow connected to proving that Jessie had come out of it all right.

She wondered about that.

She knew she could be comfortable around men on the job, liked being around them, in fact, and often suspected she could be better friends with one than with another woman. She could be comfortable around men in a light social atmosphere too, the emphasis on *light*. Even when she was attracted to a man, she found herself backing off and closing up when it came time to explore their physical selves.

She sipped her tea, musing. She had taken a look at things early on, and had decided not to even *try* to play where she worked. Not that she wasn't tempted sometimes. Most of the guys she worked with were nice people, and some of the single ones were definite hunks. One or two had even shown her a sensitive side that made her think they could help her through her . . . problem. Several had let her know they wanted to spend some time with her out of uniform. She had tried not to puncture any male egos, but she had said no. She would not date anyone she worked with, brass or otherwise. She wanted to be known, liked and respected as a cop, a cop the others could work with and count on, that's all. She knew how vulnerable a female's image could be once it was in any way compromised, and in the cop's world, *any* lack of one's own sexual identity would be compromising.

She went into her bedroom and looked at her reflection in the mirror. So, she thought, that leaves "civilians," non-police types. Just the job and what it did to a person were hard enough, people paid the price emotionally and physically. A cop's world became pretty small after a while. It was known that it took a cop to understand a cop, and the hard irony, she knew, was that, while it was hard for a cop to keep a relationship with someone, that same cop *needed* a relationship. So she had tried dating civilians.

She was healthy and smart and attractive and proud. She walked with her head up and her back straight, and she liked to look men in the eyes and have them look back. She expected any man she was with to *be* a man and act like a gentleman. She had been told that she could be "intimidating," yet still feminine and vulnerable too.

A week ago, always concerned that Jessie wasn't going out every night, Melody Mitchell had set up a meeting at a local lounge with a man described as sensitive, successful and selective. Her purse, which contained her off-duty weapon, slid off the bar as he introduced himself and landed on his foot. It only broke one of his toes, but she had not heard from him again. She frowned as she remembered another, a trial lawyer, who worked very fast. Long before Jessie felt they were comfortably into the *talking* stages, he was telling her how he felt it would be a real *power trip* to sleep with a cop. Goodbye.

She reflected that, thankfully ... or unfortunately, it usually didn't get that far. Men who weren't cops would find out what she did, and even if they were attracted to her, they would have trouble with it. The wimpy, sensitive man of the seventies had come back to being intelligently macho in the eighties, and his strong, compassionate and understanding jaw thrust him into the nineties. Physical fitness was in, quiche was still in doubt, and men liked to think of themselves as the male animal.

Jessie had decided to go to bed with the book she had tried to read that afternoon, and then the phone rang. She picked it up and said, "Hello?"

"Officer, um *Perdóneme*—Detective Jessie Summer?" asked a male voice.

"Maybe. Who is this?"

"Yes, I understand your caution, and I apologize for calling at this awkward hour." Pause. "My name is Miguel, um, Homicide Detective—Sergeant Miguel Tirado ... with Miami PD."

"Miami PD? What ... ?"

"Yes. My office received a query from your Sergeant Mitchell ... Melody. About the man you shot and killed at the jewelry store. I am the one who sent her what she told you, and I have exchanged more information with her since then ..."

"Like my home phone number?" asked Jessie, who knew she should have been annoyed.

"*Exactly*."

"If this is police business, Sergeant Tirado, don't you think we can handle it on *duty*, say with a phone call during my shift to the FLPD Detective Division offices?"

"Absolutely correct, Detective Summer, and in fact I *will* be calling Melody in the next day or so with more information from down here."

"Fine," said Jessie, "so why are we having this conversation *now*?"

Tirado laughed again, a gentle laugh that sounded rich and masculine to Jessie even over the phone line. "Ah, right ... right. Well, I heard about the shooting, I saw your photograph in the newspaper, then some film of you on the television news. Then, well ... Melody told me some little things about you. I knew we would be working . . . that there was the *possibility* we'd be working together on this homicide of yours because of some connections to *my* town . . . and I wanted to hear your voice."

"You wanted to hear my voice?"

"Yes. Correct. Absolutely."

"Goodnight, Detective-Sergeant Miguel Tirado."

"Goodnight, Detective Jessie Summer."

Great, thought Jessie as she hung up the phone, another groupie.

FOUR

Ramone Cindao sat in the back of a new rental Cadillac driven by Humberto Rawls. Humberto, his partner, remained quiet. Ramone glanced at the wide shoulders, broad back and full head of black hair on the man behind the wheel, and acknowledged once more the good luck that had brought them together so many years earlier. Humberto was solid, tough, professional and confident. He was Ramone's battering ram and raging bull when his own razor-like machinations were ineffective. He rarely questioned Ramone's decisions, took a reasonable share of the profits for his loyalty, and added to their capabilities as a team. "Loyal" was the main word in those thoughts, mused Ramone, even in this awkward venture. He knew Humberto didn't care for the United States, and didn't like being here, but he came with Ramone anyway. Ramone was glad Humberto was here, and sat back in his seat as the big man drove him toward his meeting with Dominic Tatari.

As the Cadillac moved through the heavy traffic in east Fort Lauderdale, headed for the beach, Ramone let his thoughts go to Isabel, his rare and precious one. Isabel was seven years old, a beautiful little girl with rich black hair, smooth flawless skin a shade darker than caramel, graceful limbs, pretty hands and a lovely face enhanced by eyes almost too big to be real. An orphan, she came from outside Lloilo, on the island of Panay, in the Philippines.

He had managed to move her to Manila. Her new home was one he owned and financed from the background. He had staffed it carefully, and did not scrimp on the operating budget. Isabel was told she was in a special place for special children, children who were beautiful. She was given plenty of good food, dressed in clean and almost-new clothes, and actually pampered. He knew she liked having her long hair brushed out in the evenings, and was comfortable when one of the old women who worked in the house rubbed her back as she watched television, which she considered to be a magic thing.

Ramone had begun to visit her once she was settled in. He brought her a small bracelet once and, another time, a gold locket. He was gentle with her, teasing her about growing into a lovely young woman, and it wasn't long before she was relaxed about his touch. He knew he did not frighten her. He restricted his touching of her to lightly stroking the skin of her arm, or absently running his fingers through her hair.

There were other children in the house, of course, most of them girls Isabel's age or younger. Ramone thought of it as his private little garden. He would visit sometimes, and gather the children all around him and tell them of faraway places like Germany, Japan and the United States. He told them that the government in Manila had so many troubles it had little time for them, the lonely ones. He told them in other parts of the world, wonderfully rich places, there were people who very much wanted a beautiful child of their own, but for some reason or another, couldn't have one. He had watched their faces as he told them how sad this was. But then he had added that some of these people knew of this house in Manila where there were children, who, through no fault of their own, were alone in the world, with no family and no future except to live on the "Ermita," Del Pilar Street, and in the brothels of Manila like the "little lost ones." He told them it was possible to make arrangements for these wealthy people in other countries to bring children from Manila to *their* house, as their child, and friend. He told them these people would give them gifts and clothes because they would be so happy to have them.

He remembered the modeling sessions he had set up for some of the children, especially Isabel. No skin stuff, but brushed and dressed and lighted just so. The photos of her were beautiful, and he had even presented her with one in a small silvery frame to keep, so she would believe him when he told her how beautiful she was.

Ramone was brought back to the present by the intruding clanging of bells, and looked up to see that they had been caught by an opening bridge. Humberto brought the Cadillac to a stop one car behind the gates, put the car in the parking gear, and got out to walk over to the sidewalk where he could watch the boats go by. Ramone stayed in the cool comfort of the car, still thinking of Isabel.

One evening he had taken her out onto the front porch of the house, held her hand, and told her of a very nice but sad older man who lived in America. The older man lived in a place called Florida, which was lovely and had weather much like Isabel was used to. Disney World was there, and other fun things. This man had seen pictures of Isabel and wanted her to come live with him so he could raise her like a daughter and buy her presents. Ramone had explained it would mean she would have to leave Manila to start her new life, but she would be with someone who knew she was special and beautiful, someone who *needed* her.

He smiled now as Humberto got back into the car, the gates went up, and they continued on their way to the meeting. He remembered Isabel asking him, "He has a swimming pool right at his house? And he would take me to see Mickey and his wonderful castle?"

Stillwater was having doubts. He and Melody Mitchell were sitting in his car behind the station. Jessie Summer would be busy for an hour with the Shooting Review Board. He played with the ignition key for a moment, then looked at Mitchell. Hogslop, he thought, look at us. How is this ever gonna work? Look at her sitting there, sharp as always, her brain working overtime. I know she's carryin' that secret grudge around in her heart. She comes from a part of the street I could never *really* know, and I know she saw me from the other side once. Besides, it took me eight years to get my gold badge, and she came slidin' right up with less than two years on the road and some time in Juvenile. Is she that good, or is she just that black? "Aaaahhh," he said as he ran one hand through his hair. And what kind of question is *that* to ask a new, temporary partner . . . huh?

Mitchell looked back, matching his stare. What is it, Stillwater, she thought. I see you looking at my threads, and I already know the questions in your head. Look at you, an honest-to-god polyester wonder. I heard you went out on the day you got your detective badge and bought one whole week's worth of doubleknit polyester pants, shiny short-sleeved shirts with wide collars, unbelievable ties and a couple of checked sport coats. A sartorial bumpkin, with your wide belts and cowboy boots. You're one of those guys that listens to the old Charley Pride tunes and says, "He sounds like *us*, but he looks like *them*." She had another thought and unconsciously took a deep breath. I've heard the talk too . . . about the divorce and the loss of your kids and how you've been living the job like it's your whole life since then. And finally there's that *thing* I remember about you, Stillwater. I've *seen* you out on my street.

She sighed then and thought, Dammit . . . why am I thinking this stuff with a couple of fresh homicides to clear up before I take on my new job down in Patrol? She rubbed her nose. Hell, this cowboy *did* pound the pavement over *there* for a long time before his tin turned to gold, he must have *something* beneath those unspeakable clothes.

"Coffee, partner?" asked Stillwater.

"Sure thing," replied Mitchell.

Dominic Tatari liked the way things were going. It was exhilarating to know his old man was finally out of the picture, permanently. He was ready to fly, ready to get *his* hands on the throttles, ready to *do it*. For too many years he had struggled for recognition and respect under the shadow of his father. He had enjoyed many years of being the "gangster's kid" with all the money and toys, but as he got older he felt more and more left out . . . *cheated*. Hell, the hard guys, the powerful guys, would ignore him when his old man was around. Even guys his own age, punks, would push right past him just to shake his old man's hand or have a few words with him. Sure, his old man had thrown him some scraps . . . a few small clubs, some of the vending machine action, and he had encouraged him to get involved in the powerboat racing thing for the "legit exposure and fast society ruboff," But it wasn't enough, and every time he tried to take more of what was rightfully his, the old man would squash it.

Okay, he thought ruefully, so he *had* screwed up a couple of times. The telephone boiler-room scam brought some heat with it, and some of his cocaine deals went sour. His face darkened as he thought of the dope deals. He had tried to explain to the old man that it took some time to get established, that there would be some losses. His old man had laughed at him. Just recently there had been that small deal with the Latins from Miami. So, he owed them some money, big deal. He could have handled it, but his old man had insisted on taking care of it *for* him, wouldn't even let him carry the money to the beaners. And the frigging chicks, holy shit, the old man would never shut up about it. So a couple of times they turned out to be a little young. Hell, I *like* them young. Yeah, there was some hassle over that last one, some bigwig's little twat daughter, but some of the old man's bucks and some pressure in the right office and the charges were never filed.

He rubbed the thick stubble on his chin now and reflected, The young ones, man . . . they're the *best*. Bitch gets a couple of years on her, tumbles in the sack with one or two guys, and all of a sudden she's an expert . . . gets *demanding* . . . challenging a guy. They see me driving that fucking fiberglass super-dildo with thirteen hundred horsepower, and they spread their legs and *expect* things from me, actually get *pissed* at me and make fun of me if it ain't up to their bullshit standards. Fuck it. The *young* chicks, man, when I pull that honcho out of my pants their eyes get wide and they do what I want and they're happy as hell I even *look* at them.

Now, with the old man gone, he could turn the focus of the organization's business to what *he* wanted to concentrate on . . . making money from sex. He liked being the one who ran the show that made money from people paying to watch or participate in sex, of any kind. He enjoyed being the boss who came around to the several topless clubs he owned through dummy corporations. The girls knew who he was and usually went out of their way to please him. He had some connections with the biker element, and he had a piece of their local hooker action. His money didn't go through the dramatic surges it would in the coke market, but it was always steady. People would line up and dump money into his pocket to watch his strippers take off their G-strings, or to spend a few minutes with a nineteen-year-old chick with a tight ass, leather pants and a tattoo that read: Live to ride, ride to live.

Yeah, he liked the way things were going. His new thing, he called it his *baby*, was just getting off the ground . . . but it looked good.

He saw the Cadillac park across the street from where he sat in the small Italian restaurant and pizza place on the north beach. He liked to come there now, to test the air. It had been his old man's second home, the place where he'd have his little meetings with his old cronies and soak up the scent of tomato sauce. When *he* walked in *now*, the manager practically busted his ass leading him to *the* table, and the waiters stood by nervously, watching for the smallest sign that he might need something. It was great, and about time. He watched as the driver of the Caddy, a big guy, got out and waited for his passenger, then crossed the street with him. When they came in, the big guy looked around, let him look . . . all he'd see was the standard decor, wall art of Venice, checkered tablecloths, candles melting down over wine bottles wrapped in straw. When the big guy was done looking, he leaned against the door, no expression on his face.

The other man was Ramone, of course. Ramone from the Philippines, Ramone with some money and lots of interest in the porn business. Ramone who would pay good money for quality photos and films of children, and Ramone who could even supply living, breathing, beautiful children a man could *own*. Dominic Tatari put on a welcoming smile, put out his hand to shake, and was rewarded with a limp and wet momentary clutching.

"So, Dominic, you said on the phone you have something for me?"

"Yeah, Ramone," said Dominic as he laid a large buff envelope on the table. "Today I've got some stills here, but the product can be ready to ship or distribute within a couple of days."

Ramone opened the envelope and nodded as he examined the

contents. "Yes . . . yes, he is a lovely little boy, very pretty. Nice quality to the photographs also."

Dominic smiled.

"But, Dominic, he looks very sleepy in these shots. Are the drugs too strong? Remember, fantasy is created for the viewer by the impression that the boy is engaging in these acts because he *likes* to, yes?"

"I understand perfectly, Ramone. These shots were taken late in the session, and you have that trained eye that picks up things the regular customer would probably miss. The boy is alert in the films and other stills, and it looks very good."

"Very well, Dominic," Ramone hesitated. "We have been doing quite well with our California suppliers, and we are dealing with you to see if we can work solely with the Florida houses. Of course, if the quality is consistent, the better price will make the difference."

Dominic nodded, knowing he was being squeezed, but expecting it.

Ramone closed his oily lids over his eyes for a moment, then opened them and went on, "But, Dominic, you also know that we are using these films and photos as bait toward our real product, yes? And you understand the money in the future will far surpass any in the pornography business . . ."

Dominic wet his lips and smiled. "I understand perfectly, Ramone, and I'm glad to be part of it." He paused and then said quietly, looking down at the placemat on the table, "I hope you will also consider me a potential customer. I would like a young one for my own. I know I have introduced you to others with money you might deal with, but I am asking that you not leave me out."

Ramone stood, a mild look of surprise on his face, and a slight smile. He shook out his hair, ran one long finger over his delicate lips and said softly, "You are more a man of the world than I first realized, Dominic Tatari. Yes, there is a lovely little girl waiting to travel here, and at this time I'm not sure who she'll go to. It depends on several things, not least of which is money. Her name is Isabel, and you will be enchanted by her."

After Ramone and his big partner had gone, Dominic sat over a cup of coffee, thinking. The timing of his old man's death couldn't be better. He had represented that strange group of old gangsters who had made fortunes during their lives while involved in every imaginable criminal activity and then got on their high horse and denounced the child porn business. Stupid bastards. Couldn't they understand that money is money, no matter where it comes from?

He left the restaurant and walked across the street to the lot where his Corvette was parked. He saw the beat-up van parked nearby as he unlocked his door, and then the driver of the van hurried toward him from the shadows of a garbage Dumpster.

"Scammer! What the hell are you doing here, man?" asked Tatari as the young tattooed guy stopped in front of him. The young guy said nothing, he just looked around the lot wildly, obviously agitated, and apparently coked up pretty good too. Dominic went on, "Easy, ol' buddy, take it easy. I showed our man the shots you brought me last night, you look great in them. Did you dump the kid somewhere where they'll find him?"

Scammer leaned in close to Tatari and washed him with his foul breath as he said grimly, "The fuckin' kid is *dead*, man. He wouldn't fuckin' cooperate at *all* at first, so we roughed him up a little, and when that didn't do it, we socked him with the drugs like you said." He licked his lips, his hand tight on Tatari's forearm, his eyes wild. "Kid overdosed, I guess. Cold as stone this morning . . . so I cut him up pretty bad, then took him out west and dumped him into a drainage ditch. *Jesus*." He leaned against the Corvette then, his arms crossed over his chest.

Tatari thought about it for a moment, forced down an immediate feeling of dread and fear, took a couple of deep breaths, and went over the whole thing in his mind. Then he put his hand on Scammer's shoulder and said quietly, "It's all right, Scammer. If they find the kid's body, they'll think it was the work of some child molester, and they'll work it in that direction. Did you clean out the van after you dumped the kid—and make sure that ugly little Frog photographer forgets *all about* it?" Scammer just shrugged, and Dominic went on, fighting down his anger, "Well, *do* it. Listen, it wasn't your fault, man, it was an accident. If the kid had done what you wanted, it wouldn't have happened. It's his own fault. We'll make some good money with these shots, and there'll be more in the future."

Damn, he thought, guess I'll have to get rid of this asshole now, and his partner too—Frog. Well, maybe I'll just do Scammer and use Frog some more. We'll see. He made a fist and hit Scammer lightly on the chin and said, "Don't worry about it, guy... you did good. Now get out of here."

Stillwater and Mitchell sat drinking pretty good coffee out of foam cups in the back lot of a donut shop in the south end of the city. Stillwater had turned so his left shoulder was against the doorpost and window, his long legs seeking comfort under the steering wheel. Mitchell sat on the passenger side, looking into a small notebook.

"The lab guys didn't come up with much on Tatari other than what we already knew. Cause of death was blunt trauma, the crushed skull, murder weapon could be anything of size and weight." Mitchell paused, then went on, "The wounds indicate that whoever did the pounding was in a *very* violent mood... indications of several impacts, each of which could have been fatal, or in the very least, render him unconscious."

Stillwater ran one hand through his hair. "Hit him, put him down, and then kept hitting him. Really pissed off, crazy, and going for it." Mitchell remembered the neat study, the lack of signs of struggle, and countered, "Scared maybe. Hit Tatari the first time. Then, frightened of what he'd done, frightened of what will happen when the old man gets up, or comes to... well, he decides in *fear* to finish him off."

"Great," sighed the big detective. "There goes our first degree. What are you, a defense attorney?"

"No, Les... just trying to picture it, that's all."

They were silent a moment, then Stillwater mused, "I wonder how ol' Jessie is doing in that Review Board. Think she'll come out of it okay?"

"Sure," Mitchell said, nodding, her mind far away. "It was a righteous shooting, she did it by the book, her ammo was legal and all that, she'll be fine." She sipped her coffee and, staring out through the windshield with unseeing eyes, said, "Hear about that missing kid the Sheriff's Office is working? They sent out a BOLO on him. Not a trace so far, and it's not a domestic thing either, with dad or mom snatching him from the other."

"Yeah," said Stillwater, feeling the dread that all police officers feel when discussing child-related crimes. "It's bad, no doubt. Why do you ask? Think it's related to this mess we're working?"

Mitchell sighed, "Hell, I don't know. We've got that torn part of a child porn photo in the dead Tatari's fist. We've got child porn at the jewelry store. We've got death, sex and children. Maybe I have kids on the brain for some reason."

They both sipped their coffee, looking out the windows, not comfortable with each other, partners only because they were in the same car. Mitchell checked her watch, saw it was still early, and said, "Les, I guess I'll leave it to you to go out to that 'Dreamland' bar and see if you can get next to Starlight-Joan. See if she's real, take a look at her. Then we can brace her somewhere and make our pitch."

"You don't want to come with me?" asked Stillwater, knowing the reason, but wanting to hear Mitchell say it.

"Well, yeah, Les, but that place is more like your—I mean, I'd stand out—and the two of us *together* . . . Sheesh, even those people out there would make us for cops." She moved one finger around the rim of the coffee cup, uncomfortable with being forced to say the obvious.

"More like what? My kind of place? 'Cause it's out there in the southwest, ridgerunner land? Hell, that's not even a redneck bar, that's a scumbag bar." The big detective gave a huff and waited.

"Sure," answered Mitchell, "but you know what I mean, Les. How many blacks do you think hang out there?"

"Don't know. Never been there."

"This salt-and-pepper partnership gonna be a problem for us, Les? We're not going to be able to work the biker-bar murders or the Tatari murder because we're a black and white team and we'll be spotted wherever we go? Is that it, or is there something *else* about this deal you don't like?"

"Well, yeah," said Stillwater quietly, "there is."

Mitchell sat up in her seat, rolled down the window on her side, dumped what was left of her coffee, crushed the cup in her fist, and looked at the big cowboy. She was tense, feeling her anger rising and not wanting it to, but knowing there had to be a time. "So what is it, Les? Got yourself a black partner? A partner who made detective in a couple of years, while it took *you* eight years? And the only reason your partner made it so fast is, she's a black female? And *now* she's a *sergeant*? Is that it, man? Think I'm here because I'm a minority, and our department has a reputation for kissing minority asses? Is that *it*?"

Stillwater actually smiled, a small smile. "Now that we're on the subject, why don't you tell me you're *not* the one with the chip on her shoulder. I know that was your brother shot dead on the sidewalk all those years ago. I don't remember it because you were there, I remember it because of the anger I felt when we learned who the shooter was and the homicide guys couldn't make a case because they couldn't get *one damn witness* to come forward and put the finger on him."

Mitchell was very still and found her heart pounding. She had never spoken to Stillwater or any other cop about that day and had never had a chance to let her feelings out. She just remembered the pain and anger. She pressed her lips tightly together and nodded.

Stillwater went on, "The guy that killed your brother walked around for almost ten years after that, still doing his dirty deeds, and you knew who he *was*, didn't you?"

Mitchell nodded again, swept by all the old feelings of guilt and revenge and impotency and the desire to *do* something.

"You know we finally nailed him on a solid first degree murder charge and conviction after a sloppy home invasion deal out near the county line, don't you? He was sentenced to death—" said Stillwater—"and you know who it was that finally put him away . . . right?"

"You did," Mitchell said quietly.

Stillwater rubbed his hands over his face, sighed, and looking straight ahead, said, "I'm a different person now than I was those years ago . . . and so are you."

Mitchell remained quiet. Stillwater, embarrassed and unhappy with himself for sounding long-winded and pompous, looked away.

After a long moment of silence Mitchell said hesitantly, "Well, maybe it's good we got this whole thing in the open now, hash it out and go on from there, be . . . partners."

"It ain't worked out yet."

"Yes, I know, Les, but we're talking complex subject matter . . ."

"That's not the problem."

"What?"

"You asked me if there was somethin' about this deal I didn't like, and then you tore off on your 'complex subject matter.' That's not the problem here . . . at least not *my* problem."

Mitchell waited, stung.

"We've been assigned as temporary partners, you and me," grunted Stillwater as he leaned toward Mitchell across the front seat. "We're working homicides, serious stuff, until you move on to your Patrol assigment. And there we are in the captain's office and Jessie is explaining to him why she happened to be at Tatari's house, okay? I'm listening and so are you, and it's all well and good for the captain to hear that bullshit story." He sat up behind the wheel. "But I'm your *partner*, or I'm supposed to be, and I know there's more to this whole gig than what Jessie told the captain. Everybody *knows* you and Jessie are good friends, and I've got a feeling you know the real story, and you didn't share it with *me*. I've got to know the whole dang story on any case we're working, and if you're worried about keeping a secret for that little filly, then have her sit in while you *both* explain it to me."

Mitchell looked at him, saw the intensity, saw the open honesty, the determination, and nodded. "You are right, Les. I felt it too. But whatever she's holding, she's holding it close, because she didn't tell me either."

Tiffany Eastin turned her head just enough to see beyond the pool deck and out to the dock that ran the length of their property on a small canal that made a dogleg off the Intracoastal Waterway. The house was located in a part of northeast Fort Lauderdale called Bay Colony, where even the meanest piece of property was in the million-dollar range. The Eastin house was made of raw brick, unfinished wood and lots of glass, with a huge wooden pool deck, sculpted tropical gardens and a dock over the seawall big enough for a large yacht.

Tiffany was in a chaise lounge, sunning. She wore only a miniscule G-string and a perfect tan. Her light blonde hair was pulled back into a ponytail, and the nail polish on her fingers and toes was a subtle pink. Her body was firm and trim and muscular, a lovely product of good genes and years of determined athletics, diet and pampering. Her legs were long and almost too slim, her stomach firm and flat, her breasts round and smooth with jutting nipples. Her arms were shapely, again with that hint of good muscle under the velvet golden skin. Her face was a pallet of contradictions, plain in one sense, with a jaw perhaps slightly too strong, a nose too small, pale blue eyes slightly too far apart, thin lips enveloping a too-wide mouth. Somehow the parts came together as remarkable and memorable. Her face, cruelly examined under the raw light of a hot sun, was interesting—but seen when it was ready to be seen, after the careful makeup was lovingly applied in the right light, accented by expensive clothes and jewelry and atmosphere, her face was powerfully beautiful. Tiffany Eastin's face was seen once in the pages of a society magazine, or glanced at from across the room at a Palm Beach, Fort Lauderdale or Miami gala, and not forgotten.

She turned her pale blue eyes now toward the dock and saw the red, white and blue thirty-two-foot Rapier speedboat nudge up to the dock, her brother Jack at the controls. She lay back on the lounger, rubbing tanning oil across her smooth arms slowly. She always took her sun topless, and she was not shy about nudity.

Jack Eastin deftly secured the boat to the dock, raised the outdrives, buttoned on the canvas cover, checked all the lines again, and joined his sister on the pool deck. He was tall, almost six-three, and slim. His face was sunburned, but not painfully so, the skin red but smooth, almost a gentle blush. He had a young boy's face, open, friendly, unlined, the kind of face you expected to see checking the sails on a racing sloop off Newport, or playfully perusing a piece of fine art in a Palm Beach gallery. His face would be the one that broke into a grin as he passed you in the S-turns at the Miami Gran Prix, his strong hands nonchalantly caressing the wheel of his Porsche Turbo. He'd smile at you and tip his glass of champagne at one of the local yacht or country clubs, or as he handed you a Perrier after the 10K Heart Run. His face was open and honest and fun and healthy. He would laugh at being described as wholesome, but for his own reasons. He looked like a handsome, rich playboy, which he was.

Jack collapsed now, Indian style, onto the deck beside his sister and said, "Too much sun, Tiff, you know what they say about too much sun."

She ignored him.

He went on, not caring, "I was hoping to bring someone *new* and *fun* home this weekend, at least this afternoon, but I got bummed out and said, 'Forget it.' The new boat runs great, and I think it's just loud enough to make everyone look up and watch when I bring it against the dock at any of the waterway places." He frowned. "That's where I've been, up and down the Intracoastal, stopping at *all* the places, hoping to meet someone *neat*. You wouldn't believe it, Tiff. They'd take one look at that Rapier logo on the stern and immediately start asking me about Dominic Tatari ... Senior *and* Junior."

Tiffany opened her eyes.

" 'Isn't that one of those boats that *Tatari* races?' I was asked about a dozen times," said Jack, biting his lip. "Just because old man Tatari was found dead and his son races one of our boats, that's all anybody wanted to talk about. I just got sick of it, the *speculation* in their eyes."

Tiffany reached out and brushed her brother's soft cheek with the backs of her strong fingers. Maybe it's true, she thought, what Father always said about Mother suckling you too long. Poor boy, your day has been ruined and now you're pouting.

Their mother had died when they were children. An accidental drowning had been the official word. This of course did not mention the fact that she had been roaring, sloppy drunk after a long and bitter party, that she was found naked in the pool, or that she had apparently decided on a swim after being timorously rejected by one of the young parking valets who had worked the party.

Jack and Tiffany had been enrolled in college, partying more than studying, when their father died. Mister Eastin and a very young blue-blooded Venezuelan girl died in a metallic tangle at the bottom of one of the mountain roads leading out of Caracas one foggy night, and within a relatively short time—legal manipulations and in-fighting taken into account—Jack and Tiffany became the sole heirs to their late father's fortune, which was very real, solid and carefully structured to last.

One of the local Eastin investments was the formation of Rapier Marine, builders of high-performance and racing "cigarette" boats. Promotional factors and Jack's very real interest led the firm into sponsorship of an offshore racing team. Since there were no local movie stars available, the team had been headed by the well-known and comparatively wealthy Tatari family, specifically young Dominic. The firm got good publicity, the boats were stunners, Tatari looked darkly handsome and exciting at the helm, and it worked for everyone involved.

Jack and Tiffany enjoyed being young and beautiful and rich; they wore it well, and were not shy about using their wealth to get what they wanted. Jack was like the kid in the candy store with a bag full of nickels. Tiffany, however, learned, to her surprise, that she liked the power and control, and she found herself partying less and working more. She made it clear to the family accountants, lawyers and corporate managers that she intended to be the new *boss*, a hands-on heir who would work at controlling and increasing the fortune left to her and her brother. She was still maturing, but had already perfected a cold and tough persona she wore and displayed when she chose to.

If anyone in the social register thought it odd that a beautiful sister and her handsome brother lived together in a stunning house in Bay Colony, they kept it to themselves. The Eastins were sought after. Guest lists brightened when their names were included. They were young and dynamic and lovely ... and wasn't being a bit eccentric fun, too?

Tiffany soothed her brother's face now and thought about him. Jack *was* like a big kid, she mused, and when he went out to "meet someone fun," he meant just that. He would bring home young girls *or* boys and they would ... *play*. He had every video game sold, and board games and darts and sailboards and the racing boat and bicycles and motorcycles and an incredible collection of toys. She sighed, knowing that more than once she had watched her brother with younger boys, chasing each other around the pool deck in their underwear, snapping towels at each other's rumps. Her face darkened as she delved deeper. He *was* at his mother's breast for too many years, in all the different ways. Spoiled certainly, but it went beyond that. She remembered that even as a child she had sensed some kind of sensual bond and dependency between her mother and Jack, and how he had withdrawn completely for several years after her death. Tiffany's father had credited *her* with the eventual recovery of Jack, but he didn't know—or acknowledge— the price.

She ran her fingers over his brow, bit her lip, and thought, And lately we've seen another part of sweet Jack, haven't we? She felt herself shudder in the hot sun, pushed the present into the background for the moment, and went back to musing. She had replaced the mother for Jack. She held him and comforted him, played with him and encouraged him, and finally became all things for him. She was his sister, his mother, his buddy, his partner and . . . everything. She smiled at him now and he smiled back. She thought, And, yes, between what *you* like, Jack, and what *I* like . . . we are *quite* the strange and amusing couple.

FIVE

JESSIE WAS ON HER WAY down the stairs from the third floor, where the Firearms Review Board had found her actions to be "justifiable" and "within departmental guidelines."

She sighed.

The Board had found in her favor, but it took the opportunity to reprimand her for not breaking in on the radio and demanding backups, and to chastise her for not using Patrol units to secure the scene until the SWAT team could arrive to handle the situation. She sighed again, remembering that the complaint about the SWAT team came from the captain who *headed* the team, and that her explanations had washed against the patronizing faces of her bosses with no effect.

Two down, one to go, she thought. Her trial by the media had been mercifully brief and surprisingly fair. She thought they spent too much time on the fact that she was a female officer, but, besides that, it was not too bad. The grand jury would hear her shooting in a few days, she would testify briefly, and that would be the end of it. Well, sort of, she thought.

She reached the landing between the two floors. As she turned, she came face to face with two other female police officers, both in uniform. Jessie knew them both but did not work or socialize with them. One had very long black hair, fair skin, small breasts and big eyes—made even bigger by what appeared to be theatre makeup. Her name was Cindy Banter, and she stood there now, one hand on her hip, beside the other cop, Lynn Cappadonna. Cappadonna was chunky, wore no makeup on a face that begged for it, and had hair bleached to the consistency of white straw cut in a wild, spiky shag and carefully manicured and painted fingernails. Her nails were painted bright red, *very* bright red . . . within the department the color was known as "fuck me red."

Banter was called "CB" because she never stopped talking and was reportedly easy to get a handle on, and Cappadonna was known as "Linseed," a play on her name augmented by the rumor she would use any lubricant necessary to get what she wanted. Cappadonna took the cigarette out of her mouth, blew some smoke into the air through pressed lips, and said to Jessie, "Hey, Summer . . . you survive your oh-so-dramatic shooting and go right to the Homicide squad? Are you a spitter or a swallower?"

"Yeah," said Banter with a fake smile, "it's amazing how there are all these qualified *and* senior cops waiting for a shot at a gold badge, and now here *you* are in plain clothes."

Cappadonna barked a short laugh as she elbowed her partner, "*Real* plain clothes."

Jessie just shook her head, trying to ignore them. She turned to walk between them, but Banter stood in the way and sneered, "What's the matter, Jessie? Can't talk with your mouth full, or is it just that you don't have time for us lowly patrol types now? Tell us the truth . . . is Bert Ford your rabbi?" Then she and Cappadonna laughed, gave each other the high five, and turned away.

Jessie fought to keep her face from turning red, took a deep breath, and walked down the steps.

By the time Jessie neared Stillwater's desk in the Division area, her mind was busy, wondering who owned that Dreamland bar, what the connection was to Tatari, where was young Dominic, who killed the old man, who was the man with the long, shiny black hair that she had seen—yes, *twice* now—and how did it all tie in with child porn and death. The thought of the porn triggered it again, the memory. Instead of color glossies, they became black and white prints, and she was in them. She realized that the prints were just the images she retained in her mind, images of that one afternoon when she stopped being a little girl . . . images of disbelief, disgust, helplessness and betrayal. A door slammed nearby and she came out of it. She shook herself and went on, remembering most the helplessness, and brushed by a caress of sadness.

Early the next morning a bent and twisted old man walked alongside a two-lane road off Orange Drive, in the small town of Davie, west of Fort Lauderdale. The old man carried a large bag in one hand and a stick with a nail in the end of it in the other. He searched for aluminum cans in the dirt and bushes near the side of the road, thrown there by people in passing cars. He sold them by the pound to a recycling plant. On his right as he walked north was a small, weed-choked drainage canal, the smooth contour of the still water broken here and there by the curve of an old tire or the bulk of a discarded washing machine. As the old man neared the edge of the canal to spear a beer can, he saw something in the water that looked . . . out of place. He leaned closer, peering, not sure of what he was seeing, then sure, but not believing his eyes. Horrified, he stepped back, dropped his bag and stick, and wiped his face with shaking hands.

He had discovered the badly cut-up body of a little boy.

The old man hurried awkwardly back to his ramshackle pickup truck, dazed. He drove into town like a zombie and actually parked his truck, got out, and walked right by a Davie police officer sitting in his squad car to get to a pay phone. He was trying to dial 911 when his eyes focused on the young patrolman three feet away. He dropped the phone, told the cop what he had found, and climbed back into his truck and roared out to the scene, the squad car right behind him.

After taking a quick look at what the old man had discovered, the young patrolman used his radio to urge the dispatcher to call out "everybody." He had the old man carefully back his truck out of the area, making sure he stayed on the pavement. He positioned his squad car to block the road a quarter-mile to the south and had another unit do the same to the north. The patrolman was aware of the BOLO on the small boy missing from North Lauderdale.

Because they were careful and thorough, the Davie police, assisted by the Broward Sheriff's Office lab people, not only recovered the body of the small boy, they also collected several articles of clothing, a beer can, two partial footprints near the edge of the canal, and a good impression of a tire print just off the pavement a few yards from the body. The faces of the men and women working the scene were grim, and when the body was pulled from the dead water, two of the officers, one a veteran with children of his own, became violently ill.

Within the local police community, news of the boy's body being recovered, and the condition it was in, spread quickly. Homicide detectives all across South Florida kept an ear to the ground for more information: evidence found, description of wounds, probable cause of death. They searched their files and memories for similarities to other cases, or peculiarities of suspects they had known in the past. Cops heard about the body, and the hope of finding the boy alive was almost therapeutically replaced by a cold, burning desire to find the animal who did it and . . . get him.

Detectives Stillwater and Mitchell were already having a bad day when news of the boy came through the Division. Hi-ho Allen had badgered them about the Tatari murder, wanting to know why more progress wasn't being made. He also repeated his admonition to them about Jessie. She was still skating on thin ice as far as he was concerned, and they were to babysit her, closely. They both said "yes sir," and trudged back to their desks.

Now Stillwater said to Mitchell, "Sarge, do you think this murder . . . uh, this boy they just found . . . could in any way be tied in with what we've got goin'?"

Mitchell pulled gently on an earring, examined her partner's face, the bags under his eyes, and said quietly, "He was grabbed in North Lauderdale, found in Davie. We know there are too many sickos out there to count . . . but we've got this damned child porn stuff surfacing here and there in our cases, and we've got a potential informant angry because a bad guy messed with her daughter. We've got kids being victimized all *over* this case." She paused, then went on, "Are you feeling all right this morning . . . partner?"

Stillwater, struggling with his own feelings about children, his or anyone else's, nodded mutely. Mitchell cleared her throat and said, "I guess it wouldn't hurt to get everything we can from Davie

PD and the Sheriff's office on it, just in case." Her eyes went far away for a moment, then came back cold and clear, "Kids *are* involved, woven *through* this thing."

Jessie came in then, took off her multi-colored flowered backpack, ran her fingers through her damp hair, and sighed. She looked at the faces of her partners looking at her and said, "You guys heard about the little boy, huh?" She saw their nods and went on, "Jesus . . . let's go *do* something, okay?"

Charles barely opened his apartment door to the insistent knocking when it was violently pushed against him by Dominic Tatari, who slammed it behind him as he watched Charles fall to the floor. He bent, picked Charles up by the front of his shirt, took two steps and dumped him onto the small couch covered with throw pillows. There were beads of sweat on his broad, tanned face, and his voice came like a hiss.

"Yeah, it's *me*, you little fruit—the one and *only* Dom Tatari now!"

Charles said nothing, but pulled his shirt together where it had torn.

"Tell you why I'm here, Charles," continued Tatari as he stood over the smaller man with his fists clenched. "I know you always supplied the old man with shit you heard on the street. You've always got your face in somebody's ass, and even there you hear stuff about what's goin' on. The old man is *dead* now, and I'm the new guy, get it? Now, you fucking tell *me* your little 'tidbits,' yeah?"

Charles watched him as he stalked around the small living room. He saw how agitated Tatari was, his unfocused eyes, and guessed the guy was doped up or scared . . . or both. Still he said nothing, and Tatari raged on, "None of the old man's old pals are doing *anything*, except the lawyer we've always had. He *tried* to get the old man's body released for a proper burial, but the cops said it's an 'on-going investigation,' the pricks. The lawyer stuck it back in their ass, though, by telling them *I* wouldn't talk to them about *nothin*! . . . and they've backed off."

Tatari turned his back on Charles then, and Charles thought about the little .25 automatic he kept in his nightstand drawer in the bedroom. But then Tatari turned again.

"Fucking guys my dad used to work with are circling like goddamn *vultures* now, trying to dive in and rip off pieces for themselves, like I'm *nothin'*. Shit, I knew already I'd never keep the out-of-state stuff, the trucking company, the vending machine outfit—their managers made deals to save themselves. Fuck them. But the local shit, man . . . those are *mine* to keep—the clubs, the carpark valets, the used car lot. For one thing, those managers are *young*, they understand *cocaine* money, how strong it is in this fucking tropical wonderland. They are hard and hungry and working for *me* now."

Still Charles was mute, carefully watching the bigger man's fists, like fleshy orbs spinning around the room, carrying pain with them if Tatari let fly. He watched Tatari's face and thought, Comes the inquisitor . . . becomes the confessor. Tatari picked up a phone notebook next to the telephone, flipped through it, then threw it on the floor.

"Things are happening *fast* now, and I've got to stay loose, stay *liquid*, man. The cocaine is one source, of course, but there are *other* ways, too. Oh, I see the look on your little fucking face, Charles. You don't *like* the movies and the mags? It *sells*, baby . . . it makes *cash*. Guys buy it by the pound, take it home, and beat their meat and come back for *more*." He paused for a moment, a smug look of bemusement on his face. "And it goes *farther* than just movies and shit, too . . . but that's not for you to know right now."

Charles sat up on the couch, ran his fingers through his hair, and shook his head. He tried, "Dominic—"

Tatari hit him open-handed against the side of the head, toppling him onto the cushions again. "Shut *up*, faggot! Listen . . . it isn't respectable? Is that it? You want fucking respectable? How about Rapier Marine, the oh-so-fucking-lovely and fashionably *perfect* Eastins, huh? They're part of my future too, Charles, isn't that nice? They are more than just fast boats . . . they've got *balls* . . . they'll be part of the way I'll make enough money on my own to climb out of the stink of spaghetti sauce and cheap red wine!" He took a deep breath and rubbed his face hard with both hands, collecting himself. In a quieter voice he went on, "*You* . . . you work for me now. Get me the word on the street . . . and don't even *think* about going to the cops, or you'll be *dead*."

He leaned down to Charles again, grabbed him by the shoulders, and lifted him bodily off the couch. He patted the small man gently on the cheek, then sent a terrible uppercut crashing into Charles' belly. As Charles doubled to the floor, Tatari hissed, "Don't fuck up, you little fruit." As he left, he slammed the door hard enough to break two glass jalousies.

Charles lay on the floor in the fetal position, taking ragged breaths. After a few minutes he forced himself into a kneeling position, then shakily stood. He picked up the broken glass by the front door and carried it to the trash can in the kitchen. He returned the phone book to its place. He stopped in front of the mirror to fluff his hair and check his face for bruises. He looked toward the door where Tatari had gone, and in his soft voice, said, "Little *fruit*, huh? Before this is all over, I'll be a pineapple up your *ass*, Dominic!" Then he walked slowly into the bathroom, carefully knelt until he embraced the toilet, and vomited.

Jessie's burning desire to *do* something was held in check for most of the morning by Stillwater and Mitchell's plodding and procedural paper chases. She excused herself. She knew she was wandering, waiting, wasting time. She felt uncomfortable, felt the need for *movement*. She went to her locker, got out her workout clothes, and prepared to change into them. She could grab an hour's workout, she thought, get the juices flowing. Then she had another thought, left the workout clothes on the bench, and walked to where the weight room was and took a look. It was busy, with five or six male officers pumping iron and shooting the breeze. She wasn't comfortable working out around the guys, so she decided to forget it.

A few minutes later she was back at Stillwater's desk. Les and Melody were nowhere to be seen, but a man sat at the desk. He saw her coming and stood as she approached. Jessie did not recognize him from any of the local PD's, but he looked like a cop, and this was confirmed when she saw the badge and a Visitor ID pinned to his belt. He smiled and pointed to two notes lying on the desk. She gave him a nod and picked up the first one. It was from Melody, and said she and Les were on their way to the Sheriff's Office to check out some info and she'd call later . . . she suggested Jessie use the time to "go over the files to see if we've missed something." Jessie cleared her mind of the irritation she felt at having been left behind as she looked at the cop standing there watching her with a smile.

He was just over six feet, and had a solid look without appearing chunky. His black hair was cut in a close shag, and his dark eyes waited under heavy brows that seemed constantly in motion. She held his gaze for a moment, felt the pull of those eyes, and thought they were the darkest, saddest eyes she had ever seen. His skin was smooth and the color of a good summer tan without the red highlights, maybe a little darker than amber. He had big, attractive hands with long fingers and scarred knuckles. Under his indelicate nose he wore the inevitable thick but well-trimmed mustache. It too was black, and didn't hide his full lips or white teeth, or that amused smile. He wore no jacket but had a pale green thin-striped tie with a perfect knot at his throat, and a long-sleeved white shirt that bore his initials on the right cuff. She guessed he would have them custom-made. His trousers were tan and pleated, with a thin belt, and his loafers shined. His jacket would be on a coathanger in his car, she thought, and it would be a pale tweed, light gauge. She took his strong right hand as he offered it.

"Detective Jessie Summer," he stated in a rich and pleasant voice she had heard before.

"Yes."

"Encantado. Sí . . . muy encantado. I am Detective-Sergeant Miguel Tirado, from Miami PD. We spoke on the phone."

"Yes . . . we did," she said as she gently took her hand from his, feeling the lingering warmth.

"I had to come to Broward County today, for a meeting with some Homicide officers at Hollywood PD. Since I was so close, I thought I'd stop by here, too."

"Because you have that information for Sergeant Mitchell?"

"No."

Jessie realized she was staring at him, examining his eyes. They still stood at the desk. He shrugged then, his big hands open, and said, "Actually, I must go now . . . I am due back in Miami in a short while. I am here because I wanted to meet you. I tried to think of some clever, case-related pretense, but I'm afraid I'm guilty of being distressingly clumsy at that sort of thing."

She smiled at his awkwardness and said, "I'll withhold adjudication."

He gave a small bow, and as he turned to leave, said, "Until the next time we meet, then, Jessie Summer."

"On some case-related thing, Miguel Tirado," replied Jessie, and saw him smile with those sad eyes. She watched as he walked out of the Division area, saw more than one female head turn, and was glad he did not work for Fort Lauderdale PD. Then she glanced down at the second note on the desk. It was a phone message from Charles: "Please call. Urgent."

The guard at the gatehouse protecting the entrance into Bay Colony hesitated, bothered by Jessie's car. The Camaro was over twenty years old, but it *was* a convertible, and the young woman driving it was attractive and knew who she wanted to visit. He waved her through, and she was glad she didn't have to flash her tin . . . the badge could get you in but shut you out at the same time. As always, Jessie enjoyed driving with the top down. The sun on her arms and the wind in her hair felt good as she made her way through the winding streets, past all the magnificent multi-million-dollar homes with carefully manicured lawns, brick driveways and docks out back, on the water. While she looked for the right address, she thought about what she was doing.

Allen would probably have a heart attack.

She had called Charles, then met him in the Galeria Mall. Charles looked pale, even though nattily dressed, as always. He told her about his visit from Tatari, what was said, and about the warning. He seemed convinced young Dominic was serious. Jessie found she was not surprised when he had suggested maybe Dominic had killed his father during some kind of quarrel, but she *was* surprised to hear the name "Eastin."

Dominic Tatari was definitely a suspect in his father's death, but she knew she couldn't confront him. It would be done by Melody and Les, probably through an "invitation," and the same lawyer that had tried to claim the body and kept Dominic from saying anything before would be present, and they'd get nothing out of it. For now she couldn't do anything about the biker killings either, not until that dancer had been contacted.

What about the connection between Tatari and the Eastins? Now there was something very interesting indeed, and since it was public knowledge that Tatari raced one of those Rapier boats, a company owned by the Eastins, wouldn't it be natural for the police to ask some routine questions?

Jessie found the house and pulled into the sweeping drive. It was a sprawling place, with lots of glass, brick and thick Florida shrubbery. She walked to the front door and pushed the button, and as she did, she took stock of her appearance, running her fingers through her hair and smoothing her dress. She wore her "schoolteacher's outfit," a pale yellow, belted dress with short sleeves, with flat shoes to match. The dress had a small collar and fit her tightly across her hips and breasts. She heard chimes from somewhere inside the house, and in a moment the door was opened by a stout older woman in a maid's uniform, with apron. She was dark-haired and olive-skinned, with a closed face. Latin, thought Jessie, as she smiled and asked for the Eastins.

Before the older woman could say anything, Jessie heard a female voice from inside the house, "Who *is* it, Lona? I'm not expecting anyone." And then Tiffany Eastin stood behind the maid, her head cocked to the side while her hands fooled with an earring. Jessie recognized her from photos in the society columns. Tiffany Eastin, dressed in a tennis outfit, looked over her maid's shoulder.

"Yes?"

Jessie flipped open her pink badge case and showed her tin as she said, "Sorry to bother you, Miss Eastin. I'm Detective Jessie Summer, Fort Lauderdale Police Department. I'd like to speak with you for a few moments, if I may." The maid saw the badge, a frown closed her face even more, and she backed away and disappeared.

Eastin looked Jessie over carefully, appreciatively, and then said, "My, aren't *you* the extremely female person to be a policeman.

Are you selling those Fraternal Police stickers or something? We always like to support you people."

"Actually, I'm investigating a murder, Miss Eastin. A syndicate crime figure murder . . . and your name popped up right in the middle of it," Jessie said quietly, her eyes flashing.

Eastin's hand went to her throat, and Jessie noticed the perfect nails and large diamond ring on the woman's right hand. "Oh," said Eastin. "Please come in, although I must tell you I'm due to meet friends in a short while."

Tiffany led Jessie into a large and airy living room that overlooked the pool and deck area. The house was lovely, pale gray and white, with large Bahamian watercolors and Haitian oils on the walls. As they sat, Jessie on a white leather couch, Tiffany on a matching chair, Jessie heard a man's voice coming from another room, but she couldn't make out what he was saying. Eastin asked if she wanted anything to drink, Jessie said "No, thanks," and they sat for a moment, examining each other.

There was a great energy and vibrancy about Tiffany Eastin, and to Jessie it seemed she actually looked too good, too healthy, too made-up. The tennis outfit was an expensive Evert piece, designed for a serious player. They sat at right angles to one another, their knees inches apart, and Jessie was startled by the woman's overt sexuality and uncomfortable under her appraising stare.

"I must tell you," said Eastin, "that, though I'm dismayed to learn I'm considered part of some murder investigation, I'm *enchanted* to find *you* being the police person who will question me." She paused and gave a small smile. "Frankly, I would expect one of those perfectly boring, shopworn detectives, plodding along in his frayed sport jacket, interrogating me as only a man can interrogate a woman." She licked her lips. "Tell me, um, Officer Summer, do you think I need a lawyer? I *do* engage corporate and financial lawyers often, and I *know* my family lawyer would have an absolute hissy if he knew I just sat down at *home* to talk with a cop . . . even if she *is* lovely."

Jessie hesitated, knowing already that this woman needed no advice on how to take care of herself, legally or otherwise. Then she said, "You would have to make . . . that determination. I'm here informally today, but if you are uncomfortable with that, I would have to go back to my bosses and then we'd have subpoenas, *then* the lawyers, and probably the *media* would hear of it, and—"

"*Uncomfortable?*" Eastin replied as she crossed her arms over her chest. "Not at all. Please proceed."

Jessie watched the other woman's face as she said, "I'm here because the victim, Dominic Tatari, was an associate in one of the businesses you own, Rapier Boats."

"Rapier *Marine*," corrected Eastin with a grimace that stretched her face. "Yes. We've already had some feedback about that, business-wise ... its structure as one of our holdings, and the speculation that his death might change the company's relationship to us. It was quite a *shock*, of course, and unpleasant to read that Mister Tatari had questionable connections."

Oh, please, thought Jessie, but she nodded and added, "We understand his son, Dominic Junior, drives one of your boats, races it, and it is tied in with promotion for your company."

"Yes, Officer Summer," said Eastin, "that is correct. We know Dominic only as a competitive man, good looking—well, many women seem to find him attractive, that being what they're *into*— and fun to be around. He has been a positive image for Rapier, and personally, I've always felt just a little sorry for him, trying to live up to what his dad wanted him to be." She paused, reached out and touched Jessie lightly on one knee with her long fingers, and went on, "We ... my brother Jack and myself ... we find him to be a pleasant person, nice company, and that's all. Rapier Marine is just one relatively *small* unit within our holdings."

"What to you know about his business dealings? How involved is he in his father's operations?" asked Jessie, moving her knee slightly.

"I'm sure you'd have to ask him, Officer Summer," said Tiffany coldly. "Why, we'd have no idea at all ... that would not concern us in the least." She cocked her head to the side and studied Jessie's eyes for a moment, a smile coming back to her lips. "Jessie .. I find it fascinating that a woman like you would be in your line of work, and I'd love to learn more about it ... more about you. Why don't you come to a party we're having tonight, here? It's just a little thing, really, maybe fifty people or so, and not one of those dreadful affairs where we all have to drag out our most expensive gowns and jewels to try to impress each other. My brother likes to get people together occasionally, very informally, for *fun*. Dominic Tatari . . . Junior, will be here tonight, you can meet him if you like, and more importantly, maybe you and I can get together and *really* find out what makes each of us . . . tick.''

Jessie was thinking it over, knowing she'd say yes, when a tall good-looking man, his cheeks flushed, bounded into the room. "*Tiff!* Guess what? I just got off the phone with Dominic. He *is* coming tonight . . . isn't that great? Maybe we can learn how much *he* knows about what happened . . . to . . . his . . . dad!"

Tiffany stood quickly, but Jack was too excited. "And guess what else, Tiff! He said he might bring that guy I was telling you about. Ramone from the Philippines! That's what *he* calls him, 'Ramone from the Philippines.'"

"Jessie Summer . . . my brother, Jack Eastin," said Tiffany with a weary look at Jack, and Jessie wondered if the woman had purposely not introduced her as a cop. Jack Eastin shook her hand strongly for a second, dropped it, then turned and hurried off, saying over his shoulder, "Oh, she's lovely, Tiff . . . congratulations. Tonight is gonna be so *neat!*"

Jessie had risen from her seat while being introduced to Jack. She saw Tiffany glance at a thin, flat gold watch on her left wrist and knew the interview was over. As she let Tiffany lead her to the front door, Jessie idly speculated how much more Eastin's watch cost than her own small gold oyster Seiko. Eastin said apologetically, "Little girls grow up to be women, and little boys grow up to be big *boys*, right?" She smiled as she closed the door, saying, "I'm serious about tonight, Jessie . . . please come."

Dominic Tatari finished his drink and stood, looking around the quiet bar. He had stopped off at the Dreamland Club in the early afternoon to talk with the manager about increasing the door charge, and to take a quick look at Joan, the dancer known a "Starlight," to see how she was holding up. He had been surprised and mildly irritated to find Scammer there too, sipping a beer and speaking quietly with Joan while she was still in her street clothes When he walked in, Joan had hurried over and kissed him on the cheek, then went back to the dressing room. Scammer had hesitated, then he had come over too, and now sat quietly at a back table.

Dominic felt edgy, licking his dry lips and cracking his knuckles, his face sweaty. He told himself it was the cocaine he had been doing, not fear. He looked down at Scammer and said easily, "Listen, Scammer, my man. I think we should hold off for now on any more photo sessions, know what I mean? Let's not worry about snatching any new talent for the time being. Hell, we've still got a great inventory of stuff, and it might be time to take a break." Scammer nodded into his beer. "What's bothering you, man?" asked Dominic, one hand on the younger man's bony shoulder. "You don't look good. Need some cash?"

Scammer looked up then, shrugged, and said through clenched teeth, "I don't like what's goin' on about that kid I had to *dump*? The papers have been makin' a big deal out of it."

Tatari nodded in an agreeable way. "Yeah ... it's a thing to worry about, but not too much really." Scammer looked confused. Dominic went on in a fatherly tone, "You and I both know it was an accident, and there's *nothing* to connect us with the body. You did a good job of cutting him up so the cops would think it was some perverted wacko, not businessmen like us ... and you cleaned out the van *real good*, right? Here. Here's a couple hundred bucks. Why don't you go out to one of those other bars you hang out at and have some fun? Maybe get some broad to clean your pipes for you ... do you good. I'd like to meet with you in the morning so we can make sure we're completely clean ... but I won't call you *too* early. All right, guy?"

Scammer stood then, too, stuffed the bills into his jeans, and grinned. "That's the way," said Tatari.

Before he left the bar, Tatari went back to the dressing room, patted a couple of dancers on the ass—they let him, he was the owner—and found Joan putting on her heavy eye makeup. "How's it goin', Joan?" he asked. "Need anything? Doing okay?"

"Yeah," said Joan cautiously as she stared into the mirror, "*I'm all right.*"

"So what is it then, worried about Babe?" asked Tatari.

Joan turned to look at him then. She wore only a G-string and high heels as she sat before her small makeup case. She didn't bother to cover her small, flat breasts as she said, "Shit, yeah, I'm worried about Babe. What do you think? She's doin' that fuckin' *crack* now, man. Before, it was just a little coke for fun. Shit . . . she's only thirteen, man." She stared at Tatari, her cheeks red with anger, afraid to say what she wanted to, It was *you*, Dominic, who gave her the coke the first time, you who wanted to fuck her so bad you got her stoned to do it. Came on to me like *I* was what you wanted, and all the time you were gunnin' for her, you prick.

Tatari reached out and patted her on the arm. "Hey, I told you before. I only gave her a little because she asked for it, said she had already used some that *you* had left laying around, said she was all grown up." Joan said nothing and he went on, looking around the room and lowering his voice, "Joan, *honey*. Hell, I've given you extra money. I gave you a big job that time you drove the car, and you got a bonus for it. What do I have to do?"

Joan took a long, slow breath and gathered herself. "You're right, Dom, you did help me, and I appreciate it. I just get all worked up and worried about her. She's all I've got." She began to cry then, big tears, and Tatari tore a tissue from a nearby box and handed it to her. She swallowed and went on, "I'll . . . I'm waiting to see if it will just pass, this crack shit. Maybe she'll let it be on her own." She wiped her eyes carefully and said meekly, "Sorry, Dom, I didn't mean to dump on you."

As Tatari nodded into her face sympathetically, Joan thought, *Right*, you big asshole. Thanks for nothin'. I've got Scammer sniffin' my shorts now, and once I give him what he wants, he and I are gonna find a way to take what *I* know and what *he* knows and either sell you down the river or sell our silence to you for big bucks. I'll get Babe into a clinic then, straightened out, and we'll get *out* of this hole. She smiled sweetly at Tatari and dabbed her eyes.

"Let me know if there's anything you need, honey," said Tatari as he patted her on the cheek and walked out of the room. Out in the main room again, with its fifty or so wooden chairs and two "stages," he saw Scammer was still there, leaning over the bar talking with the manager. He waved at them both curtly and left. Once outside, sitting in his Corvette, he rubbed his face with both hands and thought, Oh man... those two losers have got to *go*. I've got a good chance to get something going with Ramone, and these two idiots are coming apart at the seams. He thought about doing a line of fine cocaine he had in the car, and decided to wait until later, proud of his self-control. He drove slowly out of the lot thinking of the young girl, Babe, Joan's daughter. He remembered her nubile young body, untouched before him, the smooth skin and sweet taste, her responsive little nipples, and her anxious willingness. Shame, he thought. Well, maybe just *once* more.

Scammer had purposely waited to see if Tatari would leave. After he did, he waited until Joan came out of the dressing room wearing a frilly pink outfit that showed off all of her long legs, a little cheek of her ass and the dark nipples on her breasts as she leaned forward with her cigarette into his lighter's flame. "Guess they'll start comin' in pretty soon," she said, glancing around the room. "Hope I make some decent money tonight."

Scammer nodded, liking the way she looked, imagining her on her knees in front of him, looking back over her shoulder at him, wanting her. "Listen," he said, "I can't hang around here tonight, but if I did, I'd do *this*." He leaned forward, pulled on the pink and black garter she wore on her right thigh, and slid in a folded twenty-dollar bill.

Joan saw the grease under his nails, the rough fingers and the denomination of the bill. She smiled, leaned toward him, hugged him for a moment, kissed him wetly on the lips, and said, "Aw ... you're a sweetheart, Scammer, and a gentleman." She tilted her head to the side, examined him, and went on softly. "Maybe I *need* a gentleman in my life." Scammer nodded and grinned inanely. Joan stood, patting him on the leg. "Hey, honey ... it's that time. Gotta go shake it. It's just as well you're leavin'. I don't mind if other guys see me with no clothes on, but if I'm gonna get naked for you, it'll be for good *reason*." She winked, and Scammer left, practically strutting.

Right, thought Joan. Then she looked around the bar, saw that a couple of regulars had come in, and sighed. Got to make some money quick, she thought. Maybe this will be a good night to pick out some jerk and do some business. She didn't hook often, and it didn't seem like a big deal to her. Well, she thought, we'll see if anything good comes cruisin' into this pigsty tonight.

SIX

Jessie was putting the finishing touches on her light makeup. She was dressed in black, shiny heels, black pleated slacks and an emerald green pullover blouse with three-quarter sleeves and a loose turtleneck. She wore a black belt with a large gold buckle, a gold necklace and gold shell earrings. She had combed a little mousse into her hair, and as she applied her lipstick and looked at herself in the mirror, she thought, Not bad lady, not bad at all.

She could see the gang patiently watching, reflected in the mirror behind her. Kicker lay on the floor near her bed. Mister Jones sat on his haunches in the open bedroom door with his head cocked to the side in apparent canine curiosity, and Freeway eyed her from his perch on top of the closet door. As she watched, Freeway moved from the door onto the doorjamb directly behind her. The ledge provided very little room, even for his tiny, grasping claws, but he seemed confident as he eased his way to the middle of the jamb, his yellow eyes watching her and blinking slowly.

Jessie looked down at the black clutch purse lying on the sink counter. The bulge made by her small off-duty revolver was visible, but only she would know what it was. It would be okay . . . but was what she *planned* tonight okay? She thought about her earlier conversation with Melody Mitchell. Jessie had called Mitchell at home in the early evening. She had answered the phone sounding sleepy and a little grumpy. Jessie could hear soft jazz in the background, and the hint of sadness in Mitchell's voice as they talked.

She told Melody about her invitation to the Eastins', that Tatari would probably be there, and that she was going. There was a pause in the conversation, the soft jazz comforted them both, and Jessie had found herself thinking about Melody's loneliness.

Jessie knew Melody worked hard at her image of party animal—"So many men, so little time," and all that. Mitchell was attractive, female, full of energy and on the prowl, and she was never without male attention. But Jessie was aware that, though Melody spent apparently hot times with lots of men, she never *maintained* a relationship with a man. On the rare occasion that they let their hair down, Mitchell would shrug it off with the excuse that she was "still looking for the right one." Jessie wasn't convinced, but considered herself Mitchell's friend, and if Melody was uncomfortable talking about it, so be it. She thought they made an awkward pair of siblings... Mitchell going through dozens of men and having no man, and she spending *no* time with men and having no man.

But Melody had broken into her thoughts then when she addressed the work situation. "All right, Jessie," she had said on the phone, "Les and I both guessed you'd go stir crazy hanging around the Division area all day, and *I* should have guessed you'd go charging off, tilting at windmills. Go to the party. Now you can tell ol' Hi-ho Allen I gave you permission, if he gets his boxers in a bunch. But if you have any conversation with Tatari, stay away from *anything* linked to his father's death or you'll have to stroke him with Miranda, and he'll just laugh in your face. And watch that supposedly virginal ass of yours... I *still* think this case goes deeper than we realize. Les and I will be checking out 'Dreamland' later tonight, and we'll all compare notes in the morning. Have fun..."

Jessie sighed now, saw movement in the mirror, and lifted her eyes in time to see Freeway lose his grip, flutter his clipped wings rapidly, and then fall forward on the doorjamb, his small talons digging into the jamb hard enough to keep him from falling all the way off. Instead, he rotated, head down, until he hung upside down in the center of the doorway. As she watched, his head turned far enough for one yellow eye to meet hers, and in a small voice he said, "Uh-oh." Jessie shook her head and laughed, "Uh-oh indeed, you silly bird." She rescued him, grabbed her things, locked up, and left.

Jessie was let into the Eastin home by the maid, whose dour expression did not change as she nodded Jessie through the door. Good evening to you too, sourpuss, thought Jessie, and moved through the living room area. The room was full of people, and she looked out onto the pool deck. The lights, in the water of the pool and hidden in the delicate landscaping surrounding it, made the scene very pretty. There were many people on the deck, drinks in hand, in smiling conversations. Soft contemporary music wafted from unseen speakers. There were tables inside and out filled with bottles of champagne and various plates of canapes and dips and cold seafood and caviar and other goodies, with attendants standing by, ready to serve.

Jessie scanned the faces in the group. The first thing that struck her was that almost everybody was pretty and handsome. The women looked pampered and groomed. She was relieved to see that it *was* a casual affair, most of the women wearing slacks or simple skirts or dresses. There was no hiding the obvious care that these ladies took of themselves, with modern hairstyles and manicures. The quality of the jewelry stood out also, and Jessie guessed that if all the tennis bracelets worn at this party were stretched end-to-end, they would easily cover the distance from Saks to Neiman Marcus in the Galeria Mall.

The men had that look too. Most were in their late twenties to early thirties, but even the few older ones were fit and trim. Casuals again, straight out of *G.Q.* and the better men's shops, and the men wearing the clothes had that healthy vibrancy one pictures at the polo matches. This must be where the expression "beautiful people" comes from, thought Jessie as she stood next to a large bookshelf surveying the group.

She turned to find Tiffany Eastin standing beside her with a smile and two glasses of champagne. Eastin wore silky harem pants with slits up the sides and a simple cotton top tied just under her breasts, leaving most of that flat and tanned tummy exposed. Her shiny blonde hair was brushed out, there was a hint of pink on her lips, and she was barefoot. She looked at Jessie teasingly and said, "I'd offer to take your purse, but I'll bet you'd rather just hold onto it, huh?"

Jessie nodded, her smile tentative.

"Don't worry, silly, no one will know there's a gun in there," said Tiffany in a conspiratorial tone. "In fact, Jessie, I'm the only one here who knows what you *do*." Jessie took the offered champagne. They looked into each other's eyes as they sipped, Tiffany touching her glass to Jessie's, making a nice ring, and added, "I'm so glad you decided to come. I hope you have a good time even if you feel like you're working. Dominic is here already, so I'll let you handle *that* any way you like, but most of all, I'd just like you to have fun, okay?"

Jessie, liking the taste of the champagne, smiled and nodded. "Sure thing, Tiffany. I'm not here to talk business with him or anything. I just wanted to get a look at him when he didn't feel threatened." Eastin gave a short laugh, sipped from her glass, and crinkled her eyes as she said, "Don't *all* men feel threatened *all* the time ... always having to deal with the supposed potential of that little penis of theirs?" She enjoyed the wary expression on Jessie's face for a moment, then touched her lightly on the arm and turned away. "I'm going to mingle, why don't you, too? I'll check on you later."

Jessie moved through the talking and laughing people, smiling and saying hello and introducing herself when it seemed appropriate. Everyone seemed nice, most of the women were open and friendly, even when they couldn't hide their curiosity. The men met her with appreciation, and it didn't take long for her to recognize the gentle speculation about whom she was with, and what were the chances for someone else to get to know her better. She was not comfortable with the territorial female games and the predatory male games. She understood them, but found a perverse security in knowing she was just an observer. She filled a small plate with hors d'oeuvres, had her champagne glass topped off, and headed for the pool.

The evening was cool, the sky clear and showing many stars. Being near the water always made Jessie feel good, and she could hear the gentle lapping of small waves against the nearby seawall. She knew the canal behind the Eastin house connected with the Intracoastal Waterway a short distance to the east. She moved closer to the water and suddenly stiffened, her drink stopped on its way to her lips. She took a breath, let it out, and let the glass resume its path. She sipped and looked down at the dock near the sleek racing boat up on its hydraulic lift cradle, down to where Jack Eastin was in animated conversation with Dominic Tatari.

She moved as close as she dared, straining to pick up some of what they were saying. Jack was doing most of the talking, pressing for something, almost insistent in his open, boyish way.

"C'mon, Dominic. I know you're the one who really has his ear. I want you to put in a good word for me, tell him I'm for real, that I want to make a deal with him."

"Well, sure," replied Dominic with a grin, "I know that . . . but he's very cautious, and he's told me more than once that he wants to be sure the deal can work, that the person he deals with is sincere. That's his word, *sincere*."

They turned away from the boat now and began walking up the steps from the dock to the pool deck. Eastin pressed on, "My money is sincere, is it not? What does he mean?"

"Oh, he knows about your money, don't worry, and he's already spoken with your sister," said Tatari as they reached the deck.

"My sister?" gasped Jack. Then he saw Jessie and stopped. "Dominic Tatari, I'd like you to meet . . . um . . . Jessie, right?" He saw her nod, then turned back to look at Tatari. "Jessie is my sister's new *friend*, Dominic." It was obvious that the way he said it was supposed to mean something to Tatari, but Jessie couldn't tell if the other man knew what it was.

Tatari took her hand in his, gave it a firm shake, and looked at her with a questioning gaze. She met his eyes, not wavering, waiting. She could feel him struggling with recognition, and hoped the party blonde whose hand he was holding looked more like one of the many female fans he had around the powerboat circuit than a cop he had seen standing in front of his dead father's house. He released her hand, his face relaxed, and he said in a bored tone, "Nice to meet you."

Jack, apparently anxious, nodded his head at Tatari, smiled at

Jessie again, and said, "I hope you're having a good time, Jessie." Then he walked away, toward the center of the house. Tatari nodded at Jessie again, hesitated for a second, then followed Eastin, smiling at people by the pool, giving a small wave here, a handshake there. Then he was gone. Well, did he, or didn't he? thought Jessie.

Tiffany's lips were very close to Jessie's left ear as she whispered, "How's the investigation going? Learning anything new about who murdered the gangster? Did Dominic have anything exciting to say?" She had one hand on Jessie's shoulder as she leaned close, her eyes wide. Jessie wondered if the party and the champagne were already getting to Tiffany, and if not, why would the woman act like it was? She moved away slightly, turned her head, and shrugged. "Dominic seems to be busy with your brother, Jack."

Tiffany's brow furrowed as she looked toward the house, then she returned her look to Jessie and smiled. "I'm sorry I haven't been able to spend more time with you tonight. I'm being quite the hostess, you see." She licked her lips. "Most of the guests won't be staying late . . . I hope you do. Maybe we can go for a swim, or relax in the Jacuzzi for a while. God knows, I'll need it after a long night of being polite."

Jessie was saved from replying by a small group who came up to them, led by a distinguished older gentleman with a neatly trimmed mustache, who said, "Say, Tiff . . . good little get-together here. Everyone's having a wonderful time." He turned and shook hands with Jessie then and said, "I'm William. They call me 'Old William' in this group because there's another, younger, William running around here somewhere, probably making lewd suggestions to pretty women without the ability to back them up. Wouldn't be surprised to learn he had already shaken *your* tree to watch the fruit jiggle. And you are . . ."

"Jessie Summer," said Jessie. "Nice to meet you, Old William."

Tiffany said, "Isn't she lovely, Doctor Bill?" Then, to Jessie with a wink, "Doctor Bill does new faces and bottoms and *boobs*, and I can assure you he's *very* well known in *this* crowd."

"Never have had to do *you*, though, right, Tiff? Don't fix it if it ain't broke—that's what *I* say," replied Old William with a knowing look at his small entourage. Then he turned back to Jessie. "So what are you—a model? Movie star? And you're all *real*, aren't you?"

"I work for the city," said Jessie. Then she paused and added, "I'm in administration right now."

She could see the gleam in Tiffany's eyes as Old William asked politely, "Oh . . . how interesting, and *what* exactly do you administrate?"

Before Jessie could answer, a younger man in the group hit Old William lightly on the arm and said with a laugh, "Who *cares* what she administrates, you old fart? The way she looks, she can do any damn thing she wants." Old William looked at the younger man sternly, then looked back at Jessie, smiled, and said, "I quite agree. Now—let's get some more champagne before that bunch from Sea Ranch Lakes drinks it all up." He lead his adoring group back toward the inside of the house.

Tiffany waved at someone at the other side of the pool deck and said to Jessie, "Nicely handled. Think about my invitation, okay?" Then she hurried off. Jessie rubbed her forehead with her fingers, put her drink on a passing tray, and headed for the interior of the house to find a bathroom. She found one in the main hallway leading from the front door area and went in. When she came out a few minutes later, she stopped for a moment in the hallway. To her right was the living room and the party. To her left the house extended into other rooms. Bedrooms, she supposed, maybe a game room or library back there, too. She turned left, walking slowly. She passed two closed doors, and when she came to another left turn in the hallway, she was rewarded with the sound of Jack Eastin's voice.

"Sure you don't want to come out and join the party, Ramone? It seems funny, you coming through the side door and all. Tell your friend he doesn't have to stand outside in the dark. The people here are nice, and there's no one to worry about or anything." Jessie could hear a muffled reply, and then, faintly, Dominic Tatari's voice. "Sure, Ramone, Jack understands caution—don't you, Jack? We're just glad you could come and meet with him. Things sound good, don't they?" Again, the muffled voice. Must be sitting at the far end of the room, thought Jessie. Then she tried to picture the layout of the house in her mind. She knew the room they were in faced the back of the place, the far edge of the pool deck, then the dock.

Eastin's voice again. "Gee, I'm excited about this. I'm so glad it'll all work out, now that the problems are all taken care of."

"Taken care of, all right," said Tatari.

"Guess there's not too much more business to discuss for now then, right, Dominic? Ramone?" said Jack. "It's all settled now. What's that you've got there, Ramone? For me *and* my sister? Why her, too?" Jack's voice had a plaintive juvenile whine to it now, and Jessie's curiosity forced her to move. She turned and quickly walked out of the hallway. She passed quietly through the living room, out onto the pool deck, then stopped. She looked for Tiffany, didn't see her, then walked quickly to the south end of the deck. Then down two wooden steps, onto the dock, and toward the very back corner of the house.

She stood in the shadows, her feet in the soft dirt of a small garden, the plants and bushes reaching up to her hips. She was only ten feet away from the sliding glass doors that formed the east wall of the room where Jack Eastin, Dominic Tatari and another man huddled together examining something that Eastin held. The third man, who, Jessie knew, had to be "Ramone from the Philippines," had the shiny, long black hair, the sharp features and the oily eyelids she had seen before.

Jessie let out a sharp puff of air, unaware she had been holding her breath. She could not see what the men were examining, and her eyes widened and she felt a cold knot in her stomach when Ramone quickly turned his head, looking out through the thin white curtains and glass, out into the soft darkness. She knew he couldn't see her standing there, but when his eyes, questioning, searching, passed by where she was, she felt a chill. She stood in the periwinkles and hisbiscus, the aloe and jasmine, and felt the whisper of fear that comes from wondering if you're into something way over your head.

Suddenly Ramone stood, shook hands with the other two, and moved to a door at the south end of the room. A few more words were exchanged, the door was opened by Jack, and the dark-haired man left. Jessie stood still until she heard the sound of a car being started and saw that both Jack and Dominic had left the room. Then she turned and walked quickly back along the dock, stopping to knock the dirt off her heels. She looked up as she began to walk across the deck, and there was the dark maid, Lona, holding a tray and staring at her with no attempt to hide her suspicions or distaste. Jessie caught her breath, then smiled at the woman and walked past her. She went inside, through the living room again, and down the hallway. She passed Tatari near the front door. He was saying goodnight to a small group of people as she went by. She felt his eyes on her, tried not to turn, finally did, and saw him staring at her. She met his gaze, thought she saw a flicker of anger in his eyes, and smiled. He turned away and left. She moved on and got just beyond the bathroom door when she was met by Jack.

Eastin saw her and said absently, "Looking for the bathroom? It's right here." He began to pass her when she pointed at the object he held and asked, "What do you have there, Jack? Looks like some kind of pretty locket." He stopped reluctantly, nodded, and held it out in front of him. "Who *is* this lovely little girl in the picture, Jack?" asked Jessie quietly.

"Oh, just a friend of a friend." He began to move down the hallway, and Jessie smiled and asked, "Is the picture a surprise for your sister?" She saw Jack's face darken. He began to respond, bit his lip, and turned his back on her and walked off.

Jessie gave about ten seconds of thought to Tiffany's invitation to "stay for a swim." Sure, she'd like to learn more about Tatari—and now Ramone—from Tiffany, and the best way to do that was to keep her talking. But she was tired, and she had the feeling she may have already stretched all her luck for the night. She was also uncomfortable with getting too close to Tiffany, in an undefined way. She wanted to examine her jumbled feelings more deliberately. There was an attraction, she could feel it, but she had never felt that type of attraction from or toward another woman before, and it worried her. Her feelings about *men* were still a seemingly hopeless dark tangle, and she wondered if the things she felt with Eastin signified ... something. Mostly she was tired, and her head was pounding with what she had seen and heard. Ramone from the Philippines, Ramone from the jewelry store, Ramone from dead Tatari's house... and now Ramone with the Eastins.

Others were already saying goodnight when she found Tiffany by the pool, laughing and telling a story to a group of Old William's followers. Jessie waited until she was finished, let the laughter die down, then moved closer until Tiffany saw her. She still held her purse. "Don't tell me you're leaving already?" said Tiffany in obvious disappointment. "Aren't you enjoying yourself?" Jessie smiled and took Tiffany's hand, "I've had a wonderful time. You have nice friends, and seeing you was best of all." She saw Tiffany's face light up, and felt a little guilty. "But, hey, I'm a working girl and my day starts early and it's already been a long month this week, you know? I've got to go... but I'll take a rain check on a swim."

"Great," said Tiffany with a smile. "Come over. We'll get out there and snare some rays and talk all we want without being interrupted by anybody. How's that?"

"I'm looking forward to it, Tiffany. Thanks again." As Jessie reached the door and stepped outside, a hand on her shoulder startled her. She turned to look into Tiffany's face as the woman said, "I got so caught up in your leaving, I forgot to ask about your investigation. Did you make any progress? Did you find out who killed Dominic—I mean, the father?"

Jessie tilted her head. Behind Tiffany she could see Lona the maid watching her. "Not really, Tiffany. It was an interesting night for sure, but that's all."

Tiffany shrugged and smiled, but still looked relieved.

Jessie drove the old Camaro home slowly, still enjoying the night air with the top down. She thought about the night as she drove, trying to put some order into things. She decided it was too raw, she was too close to it. The night-time streets of Fort Lauderdale whispered past as she drove, and then her mind took her back to that day she had tried to forget, had tried to bury. She acknowledged with a jolt that this case was unearthing the memory of that day, and it frightened her.

She remembered Sanibel Island, the motel room, the man who was the "friend." She remembered his relentless forcefulness, his hands, his breath, his weight. She could feel his prying fingers, remembered how her panties had torn, how the elastic had stretched and dug into her skin as he pulled at them while she struggled. Back came the mocking thoughts, Did you really struggle? Did you try hard enough to stop him? Was it *your* fault? She remembered her mother's laughter choking to a halt when she and the boyfriend walked in suddenly and saw them on the floor. She remembered the angry words, the denials, the shame.

An ambulance roared past her on U.S. 1, going the other way, and the siren snapped her out of it for a moment. Then her mind charged on, reviewing the years that came after, the years of uncertainty, of confusion. She remembered her last year of high school then, when she let a boy . . . do it. She had felt all the normal peer pressures, had felt all the normal things happening to her body at that time, and *wanted* to do it just to know, like many girls that age. But there was more, she knew even then. She had wanted to know if she *could*, if it would be . . . whatever it was supposed to be. It had been a disaster, though mercifully brief. The boy had been hungry-hot, hurrying, pulling at her clothes. Then he was in her, pounding, and she felt the wet grass on her bottom and his hands squeezing her and a roar filled her ears and then he was standing over her, zipping his pants and leering, and she felt exposed and dirty. She did not talk to the boy after that, and finished school counting the days until she could get away from the stares.

She sighed now, and ran her fingers through her hair. Since that time she lived a sexual-social dichotomy, desiring a physical relationship with a man, desirable *to* men, craving for some acknowledgment of her own sexuality, and incapable of satisfying *any* of them.

"You all right, ma'am?"

Jessie turned her head to see a taxicab beside her car in the street, the driver leaning across the front seat, looking at her. He was a thin black man with a snap-brimmed hat and big ears. "I was behind you," he said. "You've sat through two cycles of this light . . . you okay?"

She smiled and made an excuse about having too many things

on her mind, thanked him for checking on her, waved and drove off. As she drove, she wondered idly if Old William could install a plastic zipper on her memory box. She thought of Melody and Les then, and wondered how *their* night was going, then put on an old Judy Collins tape and turned the volume up. She listened to the music and tried to figure out who she was, what she was doing, and whose "friend of a friend" the little girl in the locket picture really was. She felt sad, and trembled slightly with a flutter of fear.

While Jessie sipped champagne at the Eastins', Melody Mitchell sat in her unmarked car sipping lukewarm coffee. She had backed the car into a row of used clunkers in a lot across the street from the Dreamland Bar, had seen Stillwater arrive in his beat-up pickup truck a few minutes later, and settled down to wait.

When Les Stillwater had first entered the bar wearing faded jeans, a cowboy-style shirt and his boots, he saw that most of the men there were dressed in similar fashion . . . cowboy or construction. He hadn't been impressed by any of the dancers, and had taken only a few minutes to identify Starlight from the other men around the bar talking about her. She seemed to be the favorite.

He had watched Starlight for a few minutes and then began tipping her, first with ones, then, as he had more beers, an occasional five. She smiled at him more often, making eye contact as she danced on the stage in front of him. She stood with him for a few minutes during a break. They made small talk about nothing; she patted his arm and disappeared into the dressing room.

Stillwater motioned to the bartender for another beer and watched the action around him.

"Still having a good time, cowboy?" asked Starlight. She had freshened up in the dressing room and returned smiling to Stillwater's side. Les just grinned. Starlight stood close to him and ran one hand slowly up and down his left arm. She put her lips close to his ear and said quietly, "Listen, cowboy. I can tell you like what you see of me. How'd you like to taste it?" Stillwater's eyes went wide; he put his head back and licked his lips. Finally he said, "Well, yeah . . . but . . . ?"

She squeezed his arm, her lips brushing his ear as she whispered,

"I can leave and we can go to a place down the road. The problem is, I'm dancin' here so I can make the money. If I leave with you, I'll lose a night's tips."

Stillwater frowned as he considered this. Then he smiled and said, "Hell, that's no problem, darlin'... just tell me how much you'd make, and I'll cover it."

"One hundred dollars."

He whistled, but smiled.

"Wait outside, cowboy. I'll change and square things with the manager, then you can follow me to a little motel out on State Road Seven."

Stillwater had his boots off and his shirt unbuttoned, and Starlight was down to her bra and panties. She took off the bra, rubbed her breasts, smiled again, and said, "Cowboy, I've got to see the money now, okay?"

"Sure thing." He pulled out five twenties and put them onto the worn bedspread next to where she sat. He waited until she picked up the bills and counted them before he stood, reached over, and unlocked the door. Melody walked in quickly and closed the door. She had her badge case in her hand and flashed her tin at Starlight. The dancer looked over at Stillwater, who was now holding up his badge for her to see, and she slumped down onto the bed, covered her breasts and said, "Dammit."

Starlight cried as Mitchell read her the Miranda warnings. She cried as she got dressed, and she cried as Stillwater put his boots back on and pulled out a pair of handcuffs. She stopped crying when Mitchell said quietly, "We know about your daughter, and the trouble you've got." Starlight sat up on the edge of the bed then and listened. "We know your daughter's on crack, and that it's not your fault," continued Melody. Starlight nodded, her face changing from dejection to desperate hope.

"But we're *cops*," Melody said grimly, "not social workers. We can nail you tonight for this bit of hooking. Even better, we're moving closer to making arrests on a shooting at a biker bar that you might know about... everybody involved is going down hard, *including* the driver. When you go down hard, Joan, you think we've got time to worry about your daughter? No way... she's doin' the shit now, where do you think she's headed?''

Now Starlight cried again, holding her head in her hands. Mitchell's voice softened. "We know you drove the car; we know your boss made you do it. If you'll help us—that means give us info, statements, *and* be a witness in court—if you'll do that, we'll protect you and your daughter, and maybe you'll both have a chance to make another start." Starlight seemed to think for a moment, then looked up, her face streaked with makeup, and said quietly, "The man is a pig. He's been trying to get into the pornography business, only he takes pictures of kids, or teenagers and stuff. Two of those guys at the bar were somehow involved in the selling of it and they wanted more control. The third guy Dom suspected of being an informant, so he had them all killed."

She put her head down and did not see the look the two detectives exchanged. "Dom? Dominic Tatari?" asked Mitchell tightly.

"Yeah," continued Starlight, "he owns that joint I dance at... my frigging *boss*, okay? I can tell you who did it, how Dom got the guns, all of that, but I've got to know you can do right by me and my kid." She paused, then rubbed her face with her hands, turning her palms purple. "I think she's home now, I hope so anyway. We had a pretty bad fight before I went to work tonight. I almost didn't go, but I really *do* need the money." She looked at Stillwater, who met her gaze.

Mitchell said, "Okay. Why don't we wait until we can get you inside and take formal statements before we go any further? Do you want to get your daughter and come with us right now?"

Starlight hesitated, rubbing her nose with the back of one hand. Then she shook her head and said, "No. If it's okay with you, I'll keep on like nothin' has happened for right now. I want to make sure Babe, that's my daughter, is home and okay, and I want to get some other things squared away before I get with you. Will that be all right?"

Stillwater looked at Mitchell. They knew it would be better for the case if Starlight kept on with her life and work as if everything were normal, but they also knew they could lose Starlight as a witness if she got scared after thinking it over and bolted.

"Look," said the dancer now, "I'm not gonna run. I'm tired,

okay? It don't matter to me what you think of me... but I love my daughter and I want to make things better for her." She ran her fingers through her hair, waited while Stillwater lit a cigarette for her, and went on. "I know we'll do a statement and all, but let me tell you this much right now. A guy named Scammer did the shooting, along with two Cuban guys that Dom hired from some broker in Miami. One called himself Benny, the other, The Jet, and they were laughing about it. I don't know their real names. The broker's name is Salvatore, and they call him Salvatore Hat because his last name sounds like hat in Spanish. He also sold the guns to Dom."

Mitchell and Stillwater nodded, concentrating. Starlight stood, holding her bag. "I've got to get home and check on Babe." Stillwater handed her a business card for a construction firm with a number written in pencil on the back. "Call us every day until you're ready, and we'll pull you right out of this mess. We'll trust you if you'll trust us, and together we can get rid of Tatari and get some help for Babe," he said gruffly. She hesitated, then gave him a quick hug. As Mitchell reached for the door, Starlight muttered, "Listen, I hate that sonofabitch Dominic. He's a pig. He has these clubs, thinks he's a big man. He's messed my daughter up. He likes those pictures of *kids*, and he was bragging to me that they've got something 'special' coming up. I don't know what it is, but I know it has to do with kids and he's damned excited about it, the creep."

As Starlight walked out the door, she handed the five twenties to Stillwater, who folded them back into her palm. "Look, keep it," he said awkwardly. "I think you're pretty nice anyway." She smiled, surprised. Then she hurried across the lot to her car and drove away.

"Dominic Tatari, huh?" said Mitchell as she walked with Les back to his pickup truck. "Ain't *he* some shit."

Stillwater, a troubled look on his face, said, "Man... sumbitch is all *over* this case. I hope we're not playing him too loose."

"Too-loose *Latrek*... we ought to be bouncing that bastard off the walls. I hear you, Les, but you know, if we bring that scroatbag in before we have our total act together, that lawyer he's got will brush us off like lint," countered Mitchell, pounding one fist into an open palm. "We've just got to be cool... just like we've been preachin' to our antsy partner, Jessie. We don't need to go to the office now. I'll just make some notes on what she said, and we can formalize it in the A and M."

"Sounds good to me," said Stillwater. "I've had it for tonight."

"Good," grinned Mitchell. "I want you fresh tomorrow so *you* can explain to Hi-ho about the hundred bucks you just paid not to get laid—and hopefully not *screwed* either!"

They left, each driving home in different directions.

Starlight, or Joan, as she liked to think of herself when she was home, stood in the soft darkness in the dingy old rented house, looking down at the sleeping figure of her daughter. "God, she looks so innocent, sleeping like that," she thought. "I'm so glad she's home. Can those cops really protect us . . . can they help us? Or should I use Scammer to get money from Dom and make a run for it with Babe on my own? Oh God, please let me make the right decision for once in my life!"

She went into the bathroom to wash off the night.

SEVEN

Humberto knew Isabel had never before ridden in an airplane, but he could see she was not afraid. She had her face pressed against the window when she wasn't watching the stewardesses. He had made sure she had been properly dressed, in a new cotton dress and canvas shoes. Her black hair was carefully braided into one thick braid that hung far down her back, with small white combs on either side. She called him "Uncle Humberto," as did the other children at the house Ramone had set up. He knew she was comfortable with him, having been in his company in the past.

He had his head back against the seat rest, as if dozing, but he noticed she glanced to her left to look at him. He watched as she tentatively reached out with one finger and touched him on the wrist.

"Uncle Humberto?"

"Yes, Isabel?"

"I wish I had a picture of the nice man I will live with, to know what he looked like. But do you know Ramone told me the last time that maybe I would go to live with a beautiful woman instead?"

"Whatever Ramone thinks is best for you, Isabel."

"He said the beautiful woman might take me shopping and we would be friends. Anyway, he told me not to worry about the person I will live with. He said they would be nice, and I will be happy."

"That's good." He saw her look out the window again.

"Uncle Humberto," she said in her soft voice, chewing on her lip, "I can't believe I'm really going to America."

"But you are . . ."

"Yes. Look out there, Uncle Humberto, out the window . . . how beautiful the clouds are."

He grunted gently, then closed his eyes as she stared out the window. He did not look forward to the next couple of days, even though he was a veteran traveler who had trained himself to relax and catnap around the world. Still, there were many miles to cover, several Customs and Immigration points to get through, each time hoping the false documentation Ramone had purchased for the girl would hold up. His own papers were always in order, it was a rule he had lived by for years now. False, yes, but always close to accurate and always of the highest quality. Too many years smuggling guns, then narcotics, with Ramone were behind him; too many times the subtle kiss of fear had brushed him as he prepared to pass through some official gate on a covert and criminal mission. He heard the girl sip from her cold drink, paused, then went on with his thinking.

He was not sorry he had hooked up with Ramone. It had been good. He had made plenty of money, had lived his life of adventure with lots of gifts along the way, and had few regrets. He was part owner of three brothels in Manila, he took a nice percentage from a small narcotics ring operating out of Singapore, and he was even investing in a factory with Ramone, where the Koreans made almost perfect counterfeit purses and belts and luggage with the logos of expensive designer goods on them. With the money came the women, and he enjoyed their company with gusto, the frequency matched only by the variety. He had an oriental philosophy about carnal matters. He knew his tastes were fairly traditional, if gluttonous, and he knew about Ramone and his thing with children. It didn't bother him. His size and nature had won him jobs at the doors of some wild places all over the Far East when he was young. He had been a bouncer and manager at dingy whorehouses and fancy clubs, and he knew sexual preferences could never be guessed at or limited. It wasn't Ramone's desire to sleep with children or the selling of them for sex that bothered Humberto, it was just the sheer logistics of the thing.

Humberto liked the Far East, the Pacific Islands, his home in Manila. He was comfortable with the oriental-Polynesian melting pot, the complex nuances of doing business—any kind of business—there. Guns were simple, so was hot jewelry. Narcotics... well, you had to stay on your toes, and the knife often came from behind, but the money was there and it was all so simple. Memories of dirty little battles from his past brought another thought to Humberto, another rare moment of self-examination. He had killed many times during his career in crime, but before Ramone, it had always been in the heat of conflict, a turf war or debt collection. Ramone had early recognized his talents and... gratification... and had used him occasionally as a weapon. Humberto had embraced the reality that Ramone liked it, the killing, with the same oriental tolerance and passive acceptance of what can't be changed as he did Ramone's sexual preferences. He left that and went back to his thoughts of *business* with Ramone. Besides the guns and dope and jewels, prostitution was as old as dirt and easy to manage and profit by... even the special stuff, like children.

He opened his eyes and scanned the scene around him. He listened. Everything was normal aboard the plane. He felt no interest focused on him. He decided to sleep, knowing the hours ahead of him. But he was restless and thought some more. Keep it simple ... and keep it on your own turf. The money might be less, sure, but it would be so easy to sell this girl to one of the houses on *this* side of the earth. Why the hell did Ramone have such a fixation with doing business in the United States?

At that moment Ramone Cindao sat cross-legged on a towel wearing only a small bikini bathing suit. His rubbery brown skin shined with suntan oil, and his long black hair was heavy with water. He sat with his back straight, both arms lifted as he rhythmically pulled the brush through with his right hand, then smoothed it with his left. His face was tilted toward the sun, his eyes closed, a slight twist of sensual pleasure on his lips.

Humberto would never understand, he thought, could never really grasp the importance of bringing Isabel all the way around the world just to sell her. The money was very good, yes, but he had easily made as much in the past with the heroin and cocaine. And yes, the girl could be sold in the Pacific regions too, brokered out to one of the speciality houses perhaps, a percentage of the intake retained, and so forth. But it was intangible, and that's why Humberto would never see it.

Ramone knew Isabel as a sweet and almost achingly precious lover, a rare and priceless thing. He had never actually sampled this one's pleasure, but he had others, and he knew there was nothing equal to it . . . nothing. Having an exquisite child as a lover was unmatched. Others felt the same way, this had been learned. People would pay for what almost all societies had labeled off limits. The special photo albums, the videos of the children . . . the way they sold told him what he needed to know. They were the bait, and now it was time for the real thing. Yes, Humberto, he sighed, it is awkward and dangerous and the money is good but possibly not worth it in your eyes. But there is something . . . special about what I am doing, something erotically magical, no? I, Ramone, will sell to one of these rich Americans my little Isabel. She is priceless, but there will be a price. They will pay me a healthy down payment and then installments every three months or half year. For as long as they decide to keep her.

The brush stopped again, his eyes opened and he frowned, not seeing the Fort Lauderdale beach he sat on, not seeing the sailboats gliding past off the first reef, not seeing the occasional beachcomber walking by. Yes, he thought, for as long as they decide to keep her. That was the problem and the beauty of these children. They grew and, in his mind and probably the minds of his clients, they became less attractive as they grew. Their wondrous, childlike beauty became gross. Textures changed, bodies thickened, even the smell was different. And then what?

He nibbled his lip as the brush beat a silent tattoo against the meat of his thigh. And then I take them back, he thought. I give my client a guarantee that, when they are no longer pleased with their lover, they will quietly and without any fuss simply be . . .

gone. At that time, more to Humberto's understanding, they will be sold off or traded to one of the established houses in the Far East, or maybe even one of the places in South America where we have just begun to make contacts. These houses would still look on the product as very valuable, and there would be no delay in making the deal.

The brush began again and did not miss a stroke as he thought, She will not go willingly, so we will nail her with the drugs, quick and brutal. She will become addicted. She will cooperate or get no drugs. She will be in pain and alone. We will describe for her what her illegal status is in the powerful United States at that time, the jail that awaits her, and when we are finished, she will beg us for a fix and a chance to work for us anywhere in the world. Simple.

He heard a scream and opened his eyes. A few feet above his head hovered a seagull, wings outstretched, eyes and beak darting back and forth. The bird was focused on a large mullet washed up on the beach in the weeds at the top of the tide line. The gull circled around again, bent his wings slightly, and landed in the sand near the dead fish. Ramone watched in silence as the bird pecked at the carcass, stared at him, tried to drag the fish out of the weeds, then stopped and stared again. Finally, with an indignant screech, the bird flew, circled Ramone and the rotting fish once more, and flapped away.

Ramone resumed his thoughts. Isabel was a beautiful child, and in his mind he wished he could freeze her right there, just like that, because as she begins to grow she will become . . . less. Okay, he thought, what about those eager clients? What of Dominic Tatari and his empty boasts of sexual prowess? He has the money, yes, and he got me into the Eastins' circle, and he seems to have a growing interest. It is only a matter of time before he has real problems with the police, though, and his desire seems perverse to me. He stopped. Why is it perverse if Tatari feels it, but not when I do? He mentally shrugged. Because it is.

Then there are the Eastins. Jack, so much like a child himself, and Tiffany, so much harder and hungrier. Well, they were the upper crust, and with them the money is absolutely no problem. So. Who would pay the most? Who would be the safest and most reliable to deal with? Who won't back out when the time comes to actually take possession of the product? Who wants Isabel badly enough to play this my way?

He stood now, stretched his body in the hot sun, bent for his towel, and turned to walk back into the condo. The seagull came back, wheeling out of the blue sky, and lighted near the dead mullet.

Starlight passed the lit cigarette over to Scammer, smiled, and lay her head down on his naked chest. In her mind she was Starlight again because she was working, and Starlight was what Scammer called her. His chest was bony and hard, and she could hear his heart beating under the pale skin. She moved her right hand down his belly and began to gently fondle his testicles.

"Ummm, that was so nice, Scammer," she said softly.

"Yeah," he said, and she could tell it was through a grin. It had not, in fact, been nice for her.

Scammer had not needed much encouragement. Halfway through their first cold beer, a couple of smiles, and his hands were impatiently pulling at her blouse, his legs pushing her against the kitchen counter. Starlight had purposely not worn a bra, and Scammer's fingers were soon squeezing her soft breasts, his hot mouth on her nipples. She had held him, her head back, murmuring words that would propel him. She had turned him so his hips were against the counter, kissed him long and wet, and reached down and unsnapped and unzipped his jeans. She had smiled at his leer then, and knelt in front of him there in the kitchen. She worked at his fantasy while he sucked down his beer and held the back of her head with one hand.

She had managed to stop long enough to get them both into the bedroom, undressed, and into bed. She tried not to notice his breath, his dirty fingernails, his soiled underwear. His tattoos, to her, looked cheap and garish. He came against her body like a starving hyena upon an injured rabbit. His rough hands and fingers were impatient, his lips and tongue running over her skin wetly, but never stopping long enough to give her pleasure. He entered her with no concern for the timing, made himself comfortable, and began a pounding rhythm that made her put her arms up over her head, her hands on the plaster wall to steady herself and push against him.

He had hung above her like that, grinning, pounding, grasping, until, long before her breathing had changed, he finished. He finished with an arched back, a spasmodic clutching at her breasts, and a series of grunts that ended in a satisfied hum as he pulled out of her, and, using his hand, rubbed his sticky wetness all over her belly and his fingers, which he then shoved into her mouth. She had sucked them gently, with a smile, and had wondered then if he had been playing to an imaginary movie camera the whole time.

She looked up at him now, reached for the almost finished cigarette, took a long drag, and crushed it out in a small ashtray beside the bed. She sat up, ran her fingers through her hair, and laughed. "Wow," she said softly. He just grinned. She rubbed his chest with his fingers and ran her tongue over his lips. She looked at him and said, "You know what, Scammer? I think we fit together pretty good, like we were meant for each other." He nodded, his eyes watching hers. "I like being around you," she went on. "It's like I've got a friend, and more. I need that, you know. It's good to have a friend sometimes . . . a partner."

Scammer scratched and said, "Uh-huh."

"You remember, I told you a little of my problems with Babe?" she asked. "How I need more money and a way to break out of this fix I'm in?"

He nodded slowly, not completely sure what fix she meant.

She stopped rubbing him, her chin went out slightly, and she said defiantly, "Scammer, I've got to break away, and I think I can do it . . . if I have help." She tried to hold his gaze, "Will you help me, Scammer?"

"I don't know, Starlight, it depends on what—"

"Look. I'm talking about Dominic Tatari. He's got a hold on me, I'm dancing at his crummy club and he's screwed around with my daughter. I know you work for him too."

Scammer stiffened. He felt anger welling up in him, and he looked at her hard. He wasn't sure about all this now. He knew Starlight was supposedly Tatari's chick, but how much had Dominic told her? He grabbed her left elbow, gave it a squeeze, and said quietly, "Just what the fuck are you talkin' about here, huh? You got problems with Tatari, take it up with him." He squeezed harder. "What the hell, you call me over here, let me bang you, and it's all so you can pull somethin' over on Tatari? Forget it."

She shook her head and pulled her elbow out of his grasp. "Aw, Scammer," she said softly, "I invited you over here because I'm attracted to you. I wanted you to make love to me." She turned her head away and went on. "Yeah, I'm his occasional lover, but that asshole is more interested in my baby daughter than he is in me. I'm a healthy woman, Scammer, and I need a *man* to satisfy me. That's why you're here in this bed right now, I *needed* you to fuck me."

She could tell he liked that, but he still looked at her in doubt. She bunched one fist against her leg and began again, "I think the cops are watching him, the club . . . and maybe some of the other stuff he's got goin' on."

Scammer's eyes widened, but he remained silent. She continued, "He's gonna take a fall eventually, and I'm thinkin' he'll sell us out when he does."

"What do you mean, sell us out?" asked Scammer, his thoughts on the pieces of little boy in the canal. He grabbed her arm again. "What do you think you know about me and him?"

"I drove for you, remember? You and the two Cubans the night you went into the bar and killed those guys. You were coked out of your skull, but you do remember it was me, don't you?"

"Yeah."

"All right then. There's that, and I know you've been doin' some porno stuff with him."

Scammer sat up in the bed now, glaring at her. In a soft voice he asked, "And just what do you know about *that*, huh?"

She matched his stare. "Hey, all I know is, you're in the business with him. I figure he uses you to make the girls crazy like you did to me, then he gets it down on film and sells it to men who *wish* they could fuck like you do." She felt him relax and charged on. "Scammer, I don't know the details, and I don't want to know. I also *don't* want any dealings with the police. I don't trust them."

He grunted, and she went on, her voice thickening with intensity.

"But I trust you, Scammer... and *me*... and together I think we can mess over Dominic pretty damn good. We can get ourselves some heavy bread, and get the hell out of here before it all falls apart." She had his attention now. She took his hand, smiled, and said, "I'd understand if you wanted to go your own way after we did it. I'd like to have you stay with me, but I'd understand if you didn't."

They looked into each other's eyes. Both knew the lie, and both were relieved by it. He scratched his belly, chewed his lip, and asked, "So what have you got in mind?"

Babe had promised her mother she'd spend the afternoon at a friend's house, but she never made it.

She walked to the end of the block, made the corner, and spotted Dominic Tatari's Corvette coming the other way. She waved tentatively and instinctively looked over her shoulder toward her house. She saw Dominic smile and pull the car over near her. The right window slid down as he leaned across the seat, saying, "Hey, lady! This *is* timing... I was just looking for you."

Babe could feel the cool air coming from the interior of the car, could smell the rich, leathery scent of it. She thought of his hands on her, so knowing, so sure. She thought of the rush of the cocaine. Dominic made her feel like a woman. She frowned and looked over a shoulder again. Her mother loved her, yeah, but her mother treated her like she was still a little girl. She smiled at Dominic, who pushed open the car door. She climbed in, gave him a quick kiss, and they drove off.

The afternoon had turned into early evening, and in the small house on the west side of Fort Lauderdale, Starlight, the dancer, and Joan, the mother, began to worry. It had been dark for over an hour. Babe had not come home, and there was no answer on the phone at the friend's house. Starlight looked at Scammer slumped in a chair, wearing only his jeans, and thought. Maybe they went for a pizza or something... but I *told* her to be home before dark. Starlight was tired. She had discovered that talking with Scammer about her plan to extort Tatari tired *him*. He had helped himself to more beer as he listened, and as he began to feel the effects of the beers, he wanted to fool around some more, but the only result of the drinking on his sexual prowess was to make it somehow more violent and sloppier at the same time.

He burped now and scratched himself. She turned away, knowing he was very drunk and would probably fall asleep in the chair. She wanted him out of the house before Babe came home, but didn't know if she could get him into his van. In between the drinking and the playing with her body, he had listened to her plan and agreed to be part of it. They would tell Tatari they wanted a meeting. Dominic would come alone and they would tell him that unless he gave them cash . . . here they had argued, Scammer had rambled on about one hundred thousand, two hundred and fifty thousand, and Starlight had stayed with fifty thousand each, enough for her to get safely away and yet not too much for Dominic to get his hands on quickly . . . they would both immediately go to the police, tell all, and work deals for themselves for testifying against him.

She looked at Scammer. She was afraid of Tatari, and she knew that, even if he was concerned about her blabbing to the cops, he wouldn't be afraid of doing something to physically stop her . . . maybe threaten Babe. But with Scammer in on it, she thought, Dominic will have to go easy, because Scammer was tough, hungry and crazy. In addition to the safety given by the presence of Scammer, they would tell Dominic that they had already written out statements that were being held by a friend, to be given to the cops in case anything happened to them.

She looked out through the screen door of the old wooden house, out into the darkness. Well, she thought, that part is bullshit, almost. She hugged herself, worried about Babe, and thought about the scribbled note she had pushed into the mailbox early that day. She had addressed it to the policeman, Stillwater, at the station on Broward Boulevard. In the note she retold what she had said in the motel room, with just a little more, and a promise to keep in touch. She had sent it off more to reassure the cops than to threaten Tatari . . . kind of throw them off the scent of what she really had in mind. She turned and walked back to Scammer, began rubbing his face, and said, "Hey, lover . . . time to get up and get going."

* * *

Dominic Tatari drove slowly up Ravenswood Road from Griffin Road, Babe snuggling beside him. It had been a very pleasurable afternoon for him, and he had been surprised to learn how late it was when he began thinking about taking Babe home. He had driven her to a small but neat apartment he kept in Dania, just south of Fort Lauderdale. The place was leased in a false name and he used it occasionally for covert meetings and liaisons. It was in a quiet neighborhood, people minded their own business there. Babe had been happy and excited, and it wasn't long before he had a little cocaine in her nose, her clothes off, and her hands pulling him into bed.

Her young body excited him, and she was willing and adventurous as long as he made the right noises about her being a grown woman, capable of pleasing him as a man. Being with her brought him to sexual heights he rarely knew. He was greedy and impatient at times, but even this didn't put her off. She just didn't know any better. Once, as they rested, her face pressed softly against his lower belly, her arms under his buttocks, he found himself thinking about the black-haired, brown-eyed little girl that Ramone was bringing in. She was just a *child*... what would it be like with Ramone's baby? The thought of it had aroused him, and Babe did not protest when he pushed her face further down his belly until her wet mouth was on him.

Finally he had gathered her together, loaded her into the car, where she sleepily rode with him back toward her house. He planned to stop his car a few houses from Starlight's place, pat Babe on the ass, and kick her out. Then he could turn around and drive out of there without having to take any crap from Starlight again. He knew he'd have to deal with it eventually, but not tonight.

He was humming to himself as he made the turn off Ravenswood Road onto one of the side streets. He slowed the car and stopped humming when he saw Scammer's van parked in front of the house. He felt his stomach churn. Things were snowballing. Through clenched teeth he said, "Those stupid cunts."

Babe sat up then, her hair tousled. "What, honey?"

* * *

Tatari pushed open the door, shoved an impassive Babe past a wide-eyed Starlight, and stomped into the living room. He saw Scammer standing there, obviously drunk, and Starlight glaring at him. She went to her daughter, took her hands, and looked at her closely. Babe, rocking slightly on her feet, her eyes wide and unfocused, her hair a mess, her mouth loose and swollen, said quietly, "Hi, Mom." Then she gave a lopsided grin and turned away. Starlight whirled around, her face pinched, her fists on her hips, and snapped at Tatari, "You piece-of-shit *bastard*!"

"Hey. Fuck you, Starlight. What are you doing with this asshole?"

There was a strained moment of silence during which Babe moved behind Starlight and hugged her gently, and Scammer stood there swaying, a can of beer in one hand.

"I'll tell you what I'm doing, Dom. I'm cementing my partnership with Scammer." She was heartened to see Scammer straighten, an angry look firming on his face. "I've had it with you molesting my Babe, and I'm not gonna let you do it anymore."

"Molesting? How do you molest a cocaine whore?"

"Here it is, Dom," Starlight hissed. "I drove Scammer to the bar when he and the beaners made the hit. I know about the dope and the hooking, and I know about Babe. Scammer knows about the hit and the porno, and he knows you'll give him away when you're ready." She had seen Tatari's eyes widen at the mention of porno. She charged on. "Scammer and I are both going to the cops. We've got a letter of protection waiting to be delivered in case something happens to us. We're going to the cops and tell them every single thing we know about you and what you're into—"

"But you'll deal with me first, right?" Tatari seemed frozen.

"Aw, Mom," interrupted Babe in a plaintive voice, "what's all this hassle? He's my lover now, no kidding, and he'll give me money and I'll come back and pick you up and we'll ... it will ..." She drifted off, her eyes wandering across the ceiling.

Starlight watched her for a few seconds, then turned back to Tatari. "Yeah. We'll deal with you first, shitface ... for lots of money." She paused and looked at Scammer, who took a step forward and put the beer carefully down onto a coffee table. Then she went on. "You give both me and Scammer fifty grand each, cash, tonight, and we'll get out of town and out of your life. You know I mean it, Dom. All I want is to get Babe *away* from you. But I need the money to run."

Scammer nodded and buttoned his jeans.

Tatari licked his lips again and looked at them both. He rubbed one hand over his face, stole a glance at Scammer's empty hands, and went on, "I got paid earlier today for something I had going in Miami. I've got twenty-five grand in a briefcase in the back of my car. I'll give you the rest before noon tomorrow, but you've got to promise me you'll both get out of this area. You'd better be *gone*, got it? If you come back on me, I'll kill you both." He turned for the door.

Starlight took Babe's hand and reached up gently to pull a tangled lock of hair from her face. She tried to get her daughter's eyes to focus on her and said quietly, "Aw, honey."

Tatari came back less than a minute later carrying a briefcase. He set it down on a chair near the door, opened it so the top faced the room, and reached in. He seemed to be counting with his hands, which Scammer and Starlight couldn't see, and when he straightened up, his face was grim. He was holding a large automatic pistol with a bulbous silencer on the barrel.

Scammer saw the gun, his mind screamed for him to move, his body tried to respond, and then a flashing hot poker ripped into his guts, punching him down and back. He arched his neck to see Tatari and felt another slug punch into the center of his chest. He went down in a heap, his hands clutching at the bubbling mass of his belly, his lungs on fire.

Starlight turned instinctively to Babe, wrapped her arms around her, and tried to push her back toward the kitchen and the side door. Then she felt two incredibly powerful kicks to her back. She tried to hang onto Babe, but her arms folded down to her daughter's waist, and as she slid to the floor, she looked up at Babe and whispered, "Run . . . honey . . ."

But Babe didn't run. She watched her mother kneel in front of her, saw all the blood, and was confused. She frowned and tried to clear her head. She looked up at Dominic.

Tatari shot her three times, the last time right between the eyes.

* * *

Pierre LaPont, known since his teenage years as "Frog," was uncomfortable. A familiar part of his discomfort was caused by being out of his studio, away from his darkroom, without one single camera, not even a thirty-five. He felt naked without a camera and overexposed when away from his studio. Adding to his discomfort was the fact that he was driving Dominic Tatari around late at night. Tatari was definitely acting strange, and LaPont didn't like the feel of what was going on.

LaPont's studio and darkroom and home were all part of a rundown collection of warehouses and storefront businesses off Old Dixie Highway in central Fort Lauderdale. It wasn't a place for wedding photos or a record of this year's dance recital. LaPont was in the shabby underworld of his trade. Professional, but shabby. He was proud to say he was technically proficient, his equipment state-of-the-art and his abilities unquestioned. His clients were private detectives specializing in divorce cases, blackmailers, industrial espionage agents, false document procurers . . . and the pornography makers, his bread and butter.

His French ancestry and physical appearance gave him his name. He was squat, with short, thick legs and fat arms. He leaned into his pudgy belly and his large square head lolled on rounded shoulders. His skin was pale and sweaty and his wide-set, heavy-lidded eyes, small nose with flaring nostrils and gaping mouth with thick wet lips gave him the look of one who at any moment might send a writhing tongue snapping out to pick off a passing fly. He knew what he looked like, and he preferred to look at the world through a camera lens.

It had been almost midnight when his front door buzzer had gone off. He looked through the peephole, hesitated, and unlocked the door. It was roughly pushed aside, and then Dominic Tatari was standing over him, looking like a graverobber on the run. LaPont had met Tatari once, briefly, and had not ever spoken to him about business in any way, even though he knew that Scammer was backed by Tatari. Scammer would show up with the young teens or kids—boys or girls—tell LaPont what he wanted, and they would do it. He was proud of the quality of the portfolio he had put together for Tatari, had received most of the payment in cash, and was still making the requested number of copies. The first thing he thought of with Tatari standing there was the last shoot he had done with Scammer and that boy. It had turned into a real mess, with the kid overdosing and all. The photos turned out great, but LaPont remembered the fear that had welled up in him when Scammer came at him, his eyes wild, his voice tight. The kid had died, Scammer was trying to figure out what to do with the body, and LaPont had gone back to his camera, hoping to shoot the action. At the time he thought it would make some interesting shots: Scammer bent over the kid with knife in hand, rolling him over . . . but Scammer had gone crazy when LaPont began shooting, actually threatened him, made him stop. After seeing Scammer's reaction, LaPont had been happy to please him, and was glad when Scammer loaded the body into his van and left. Shortly after that, Scammer brought the cash from Tatari, and that was the end of it.

Until tonight, that is.

He followed Tatari's directions in his old nondescript station wagon. Tatari told him they were going to pick up Scammer's van. Scammer had gone out of town on some deal and was worried about his van sitting in front of some chick's house. Tatari wanted LaPont to drive the van away from the house, north into Pompano Beach, and leave it parked in a warehouse district where there were lots of junked cars. LaPont didn't understand the whys and whatfors, but he sat quietly now, just doing as he was told. Tatari instructed him to walk to the nearest all-night joint after he parked the van and take a cab home to his studio. After that, he was to forget it. This was a two-stick and one-carrot deal, Tatari had told him. The carrot was one thousand dollars cash, tonight, which Tatari had held under LaPont's flared nostrils. The first stick was that, if LaPont didn't do it, Tatari would make sure that in the morning every cop in town would be trooping through LaPont's studio. The second stick was that, if LaPont kept Tatari waiting one more minute, Tatari would kill him then and there.

LaPont drove.

Tatari had LaPont stop at the end of the quiet residential street of Ravenswood Road. He told LaPont to get out of the wagon and walk down the street until he came to the house where the van was parked. The keys were in it, and all he had to do was get in and drive away. Tatari would take the wagon back to the studio and be gone. LaPont could drop off the van and come home later. As LaPont stopped the wagon in the darkness, Tatari grabbed his arm, leaned over, and in a terrible voice said, "Listen to me, Frog. Do this for me tonight and there'll be more money and more business in the future. Screw this up, or back out, or say anything to *anybody*, and you won't *have* a future. Got it?"

LaPont got out and waddled down the street, leaving a sweaty mist trailing behind him in the darkness.

It took less than ten minutes for the Fire and Rescue Units to arrive on the scene of the woodframe house fire off Ravenswood Road, but there wasn't much they could do. Neighbors had seen the flames, smelled the smoke, and called 911 in the early morning hours after midnight. The nearest had tried to do what he could with a garden hose after pounding on the bedroom windows and front door before the heat drove him back. The house was completely consumed, and as the firefighters contained what was left, they learned that a young woman and her daughter lived in the house, but no one knew if they had been home. The woman's old car was out front.

The firefighters were especially interested to learn that the fire seemed to just leap into being. Several parts of the house were burning furiously within minutes, and there had been the smell of gasoline . . . and something else. When the first powerful flashlights pierced the black and smoky area that had been the living room, the firefighters' eyes confirmed what their noses had already hinted at. The Broward Sheriff's Office was notified.

The day was crystal clear, with forever blue skies, a slight breeze out of the southeast and temperatures in the mid-eighties. It was the kind of day that made you long to be outside if you were trapped in the air conditioning, or made you put your face to the hot sun in exalted glory and appreciation if you were out in it. It was a day for good tanning oil, a clean beach or sun deck around a pool, and a friend to share it with.

Jessie felt her nipples stiffen as her bikini top came off, and within her embarrassment, wondered if it was because of the cool breeze that swirled around them, the sudden change of temperature across the soft skin as the top was pulled away, or if it was the situation . . . and the company.

She had gone into the station early that morning, hoping to speak with Mitchell and Stillwater. All she found was another note for her on the big detective's desk: "We've got a problem with this guy Salvatore the Hat down in Little Havana. We've gone to Pompano PD ref a van they towed last night. Looks like Tatari Jr. owns the Dreamland Club through a dummy corp! Check with you later, Les." She had been approached by Hi-ho Allen as she finished reading the note, asking why she wasn't with the two detectives. She explained about the note and he nodded brusquely and admonished her not to do anything operational without them, or without briefing them *and* him first. He reminded her there was still plenty to do with the paperwork, supplements and phone calls. She listened patiently and told him she would get right on it. Then he reminded her that her schedule was not structured, and if she wanted to get out early, he was sure it would be made up "later." She told him she'd dive into the paperwork for a few hours, and then get out into the beautiful day and catch some rays.

Well, she thought now, here I am in just my bikini bottom with the warm sun washing against my breasts. Did I lie?

She had arrived at the Eastins' house less than an hour ago. Tiffany had answered the door, apparently very pleased that Jessie had actually accepted her invitation. Tiffany had been covered by a thin terry cloth robe, with her hair pinned up, full of energy and with a big smile. She assured Jessie they were alone. It was the maid's day off, and brother Jack had gone for one of his boat rides. She showed Jessie a bedroom where she could change into her suit. Jessie had prepared herself, walked through the cool interior of the quiet house, saw that Tiffany was already on one chaise longue near the edge of the pool, and joined her. Tiffany greeted her with a large frozen margarita and a grin.

Jessie looked up from her own breasts now and into Tiffany's eyes. She had never seen anyone so absolutely naked, and she felt a jumble of emotions because Tiffany's nakedness fascinated her. Eastin wore no bathing suit, no top, no bottom. She had small, delicate holes in the lobes of her ears, no jewelry anywhere, and soft pink polish on her nails. Her blatant nakedness, Jessie realized, came from the fact that she was clean-shaven, everywhere except her head. Eastin's firm and female body, with its nicely shaped breasts, smooth, round bottom, long legs, muscular arms and perfect tan, was pleasant to look at, yes, but she was so close and so naked that Jessie almost felt like averting her gaze. But she didn't.

Jessie wondered what it would be like to have no hair . . . down there, and guessed it would make you look like a little girl again. Jessie's hair was darker blonde than Tiffany's, but she still didn't have to worry about her bikini line or any of that. She let her eyes wander over Tiffany's body again and felt the woman's sexuality wash over her with the same intensity as the hot sun. Tiffany Eastin did *not* look like a little girl.

"Oh," said Tiffany in a hushed voice, "you have such beautiful breasts. I don't know why you were so reluctant to take that top off. Like I said, it's very private here, and it feels so good to let the sun caress you in places it usually doesn't." Her gaze lingered on Jessie's nipples, first one, then the other, and she smiled. "I can tell you like the way it feels."

Jessie licked her lips and nodded. She *did* like the way it felt, but she wasn't comfortable with the way Tiffany looked at her. She swung her legs to the side of the lounger, stood and stretched, stepped to the edge of the pool, and dived in. They had both been in and out a couple of times, the cooling water so refreshing after the sun. She felt the bubbles from her dive surround her and the tickly feeling of the water against her bare skin as she knifed across to the other side. She came to the surface, let the water pull her hair back, and climbed out. She stretched again, liking the way the water beaded up with the suntan oil on her skin. As she walked back to the lounger, Tiffany lifted her third margarita to her, smiled, and said, "Jessie, that is some classic body you've got there. People pay big money to the plastic guys to have boobs that look like that, and the butt, those legs . . . and yours are all God-given." She let her eyes examine Jessie from head to toe as she said it.

Jessie, wanting to lighten up slightly, said with a laugh, "Sure, it's all natural, but if I don't watch it, don't work out all the time, it will become more than full-bodied, if you know what I mean. I bicycle a lot, and hit the gym often, because I'm afraid to turn my back on it. I had a man tell me once my body was almost 'Rubenesque,' and I felt pretty good until I checked out some of Rubens's paintings with all of those nice pink and very round ladies."

"Do you like the way *my* body looks, Jessie?"

"Yes."

"Hmmm."

Jessie put her knees onto the lounger and then lay flat on her tummy. She noticed her lips felt dry again and her breathing was a little shallow.

Tiffany put down her drink, picked up the tanning oil, and knelt beside the lounger. "Here," she said firmly, "let's get some oil on that skin that's been hidden so you won't have the big peeling problem in a couple of days." Before Jessie could think of a response, she felt the hands, soft yet strong, on her back, kneading oil into her skin. It felt good. Jessie turned her head to the side so she could look back at Tiffany, their eyes locked, and then Jessie arched her back, resting on her elbows. She cleared her throat and said, "Tiffany, tell me how you could be involved in business with a man like Dominic Tatari and act so naive about the true source of most of his finances."

Tiffany's hands stopped. She blew out a puff of air, bit her lip, and said coldly, "*Boy* . . . you sure know how to change a mood, don't you?" She was motionless for a moment, then her hands began again slowly. Several more moments went by before she spoke. "I guess I can't forget for one minute that you are a cop, huh? And that you *are* working a murder case." She picked up her drink with one hand, sipped it, and put it down. Then she lightly ran her cold fingers down Jessie's spine. She went on. "Sure. When you're in business, you hear rumors, you check things out, you get info before you deal with someone. What I learned about Dominic didn't put me off. If he had syndicate connections, it wouldn't be a factor in our business ties. I would not have been pleased if his name was constantly kicked around in seedy deals or police problems or whatever, but it wasn't. He was always respectable, especially in the last couple of years, which is when our involvement began—business involvement, I mean. He was a nice old guy, really.''

Jessie's intuition told her there was some tension behind these words, but she just waited. Tiffany began rubbing the backs of Jessie's arms now, and then lightly down her sides, all the way down to the top of the bikini bottom. She sighed, "I kind of liked him . . . Dominic. He used to invite me to his place off Bayview Drive for coffee. Mostly just to talk, and sometimes to swim in his pool. He told me he enjoyed watching me prance around topless." She paused, cleared her throat. "I . . . I would just go topless around him, that's all. I mean, we were friends."

She rocked back on her heels and took another drink. Jessie turned and their eyes met again. Tiffany put the cold glass down and slowly ran her hands over her own breasts, letting her fingers rub around her hard little nipples as she stared at Jessie.

Jessie smiled a small smile.

Tiffany laughed, shook her head, and said, "Whew, lady . . . I think I've had too much sun and margarita. I'm running my mouth just when my lawyer would be strangling me to keep it shut."

Jessie laughed too, feeling the drinks more than she had realized, put her head back down . . . and waited. Tiffany said in a quieter voice, "Maybe it's because you're here, you're so close, and your skin feels so good beneath my fingers." She was silent for a moment, took a deep breath, and went on. "Just so you'll hear it all from me and not think later I was holding back, both Jack and I liked Dominic, and we both visited him from time to time, but we hardly knew him at all. I know Jack likes to hang around with the *younger* Dominic because he's the macho raceboat driver who knows how to party."

Jessie turned now, leaning on one elbow. Tiffany still knelt beside her, and without saying anything, poured more oil onto her hands and began rubbing it onto Jessie's shoulders. Jessie felt the heat and the strength, and she shuddered in the sunlight when the backs of Tiffany's hands brushed over her nipples, which immediately responded. She could see Tiffany's nipples were very stiff now, her nostrils were wide, her tongue constantly darting out to lick her lips. A palpable musk seemed to envelop them, and Jessie took a deep breath and hung right in there.

"When I was at the party the other night, Jack showed me a picture of a little girl," said Jessie in a husky voice. "Said some friend of his named Ramone had given it to him." Tiffany's hands stopped again and her eyes narrowed as she stared at Jessie. She pursed her lips and said in a harsher tone than she wanted, "Jack said that? About Ramone?" Jessie shrugged and nodded. "So who's Ramone, Tiffany? I thought he was some racing pal of Dominic's . . . Jack acted like he was somebody special." She purposely said no more about the girl in the photograph, not wanting to get too close—yet.

Tiffany stood now, her hands on her hips. She shook her hair out and stretched all the way up onto her toes. As she did, Jessie deliberately let her eyes wander all over Tiffany's magnificent body. She wanted Tiffany to see how she was watching her. Tiffany did see, and it helped her shift the tensions she was feeling, helped her gather her thoughts to focus again on that which was most immediately on her mind. She turned away, stepped to the edge of the pool, and dived in, a long flat dive that barely made a splash. When she came up at the far end, she was smiling. The clear blue water of the pool was patterned by rippling white light bands, and Tiffany's body shone in the water, supple and alive. She swam back toward Jessie, and when she got to the shallow end of the pool, she put her hands between her legs and said, "You're making me crazy, you *know* that, don't you?"

Jessie smiled, stood, and walked down the steps into the cool water. She gently splashed a handful onto Tiffany's breasts and lay back, her head against the tiled edge, and said easily, "I didn't mean to upset you, Tiffany. I'm just naturally curious, I guess." Tiffany shrugged. "No big thing. My brother does his thing with his friends, and I do mine . . . that's all. I don't know this Ramone person, but you're probably right, he must be part of Dominic's crowd. Jack and his friends, who can figure?"

Tiffany swam toward Jessie now, the bottom part of her face submerged. She stopped a foot away, and said matter-of-factly, "Jack and I both socialized to some extent with Dominic Senior. We've both been to his house. Jack pals around with Dominic Junior for fun and they apparently have a mutual buddy named Ramone. I'm sorry I over-reacted . . . it must be some form of sibling rivalry." She slid forward, wrapping her arms under Jessie's bottom, slipping a couple of fingers under the edge of the bikini. She very gently kissed Jessie's right nipple, then the left, looked into Jessie's eyes, and said in a husky voice, "Is that enough police talk for now? Can't you see I'm so crazy hot for you, I can't stand it? Do we have to keep talking about Jack and Dominic and all this other crap?"

Jessie had reflexively put her hands on Tiffany's shoulders to push her away, but she didn't push her away, and she didn't lift her hands. She could still feel Tiffany's hot, wet mouth on her breasts, and liked the feeling. She and Tiffany looked into each other's eyes for a long moment, all of their senses impacted by the warm sun and the cool water and the hot sexuality of their nearness. Jessie felt repelled by what was happening, but also felt trapped. There was so much heat, so much sex surrounding them, that she couldn't breathe, couldn't move. She realized then that one thing she *didn't* feel was fear.

Tiffany put her face against Jessie's right breast again and gently bit the nipple and then rubbed her tongue around it. Jessie caught her breath, and Tiffany squeezed her bottom with her fingers, pulling the bikini down as she did, letting her fingers slide against the wetness there. Jessie arched her back, and Tiffany lifted her mouth and whispered, "You *know* how good it can be for us. I know you feel it too, and I know you've never been with a woman before. You want good sex, *safe* sex? This is probably the *ultimate* safe sex . . . and it is *loving* sex, not invasive, not subjugating." Jessie had her head back, her eyes closed, her mouth open. The fingers of Tiffany's left hand disappeared between her own legs. Her lips were around Jessie's navel as she said, "Let yourself go with your feelings now. I can feel your heat. I can feel the gentle swelling, can feel how the lips are opening, pouting. I know the slick-wet is there." She ran a pink tongue over her lips, softly bit the skin of Jessie's lower belly, and looked up into Jessie's eyes, which looked back wide and blinking. "I want you, Jessie."

"*Tiffany!*"

Jessie pushed Tiffany away, but still held her shoulders. Tiffany, her face reddening, her eyes flashing, pulled back and stood in the shallow water. Her hands were balled into tight fists. She looked out toward the dock, then down at Jessie, her eyes angry and sad at the same time. Neither of them had heard the approach of the boat to the dock.

Jack came into view then, walking quickly, his athletic body sheathed in sweat. He was obviously agitated, and barely glanced at Jessie in the pool as he called out again loudly, "*Christ*, Tiff, wait till you hear what's going on! I just left Dominic. You wouldn't *believe* how he acted!"

Tiffany splashed up the steps of the pool, walked up to Jack, put her fists on her hips, and spat out angrily, "Shut *up*, Jack ... just *shut up*!"

Jack shut up and just stood there.

"God*dammit*, Jack," said Tiffany, her voice tight. "You told me you'd be gone all day. You *knew* I was going to have company, and now you come crashing in here in some kind of panic. *Dammit*!" She took one of the large towels off a lounger, wrapped herself in it, grabbed the other, and walked to the edge of the pool and handed it to Jessie. Jessie had turned to face Jack, pulled up her bikini bottom from around her ankles, and hugged close to the edge of the pool so her breasts were covered. Her chest heaved with the deep breaths she took.

Tiffany sputtered to a stop, and then stood staring at her brother, apparently at a loss for what to do next. Her breathing was deep, too. Jessie stood, embarrassed and curious and ... flushed. She was caught up short by the intrusion, as was Tiffany, but even through the sensual heat that washed her body, she felt the friendly cooling of relief. She climbed out of the pool and retrieved her bikini top from the lounger.

Jack, as if noticing Jessie for the first time, made a face, spread his big hands, and said shyly, "Uh, hey, Jessie. Sorry to come barging in here like this. I didn't mean to, uh ... interrupt."

Tiffany began to say something, still angry, but Jessie smiled and said, "That's all right, Jack ... Tiffany and I were just playing." Tiffany looked at Jessie curiously for a moment, then took a long deep breath, looked at her brother, and said, as if straining to be calm, "Jack, you know I love you, but *damn* your timing. You could fuck up a wet dream!"

Jack shrugged, then seemed to remember what brought him there in the first place. He said, "Sorry, Tiff... really... but I've got to tell you something *right now*. Things are happening faster than—"

His sister cut him off with a chopping motion of her hands and her voice. "*Stop*, Jack! Stop. Now... just shut up about it." She paused, made sure he was listening, then went on. "We, uh, we have a guest, and it's not fair for her to have to listen to our business stuff. Go into the house and get a cold drink or something, and I'll be inside in a few minutes."

Jack hesitated, said, "Sorry again," to Jessie and went inside.

Tiffany reached out and took one of Jessie's hands in hers. She forced herself to smile as she said, "Oh well, lady..."

Jessie shrugged and said quietly, "Hey. I enjoyed this afternoon, although I must admit it seemed to be heading in an unplanned direction. I like talking with you and... being with you. Who knows? Maybe we'll get another chance one of these days, and you can finish what you were telling me."

Tiffany studied Jessie's face closely, brightened a little, and said, "Promise? I hope so... really."

Tiffany walked Jessie to the bedroom, where she could change, and then hurried to the opposite side of the house. She opened the door to a small office that had windows facing east overlooking the north end of the boat dock and the canal, and facing south overlooking the pool. Lona, the maid, sat in a straight-backed chair holding a 35mm camera with a long lens. She sat before the windows overlooking the pool.

"Did you get some?" asked Tiffany.

"Of course, Señora Eastin."

Tiffany was back at the front door in time to meet Jessie there. She grinned and stuck out her tongue at Jessie. "I'm afraid a cold shower isn't gonna take care of this lingering problem I've got now... know what I mean? I'm glad I've got one of those vibrators that's waterproof and just won't quit until I *let* it."

Jessie knew *exactly* what Tiffany meant, and she blushed and turned away.

* * *

As she drove away from the Eastin house, wearing jeans and a T-shirt, Jessie was a jumble of emotions. She was sure now there was more to the Eastin-Tatari thing than Tiffany was saying, and the tie-in with Ramone definitely needed further digging. Why was she so defensive about Ramone and Jack, and why did she try so hard to make her socializing with the dead Tatari seem so trivial? Was she being honest about it, or did she figure the police would come up with it anyway, and it was better to minimize it by admitting it so freely?

Her personal feelings surprised her. She had been aroused by the nearness and texture of a *woman*, had even let the woman touch her, for God's sake. She had never had an experience like that, had never even been curious enough to *want* to. Her arousal had been intense, but so had the sun's heat, the drinks, her motivation. Would she have allowed Tiffany to proceed, would she have participated ... enjoyed it? She shook her head, and said out loud, "No."

She was aware of the effects of the close call—"*Sapphos* interruptus"?—on her body. She still felt the heat between her legs, her breathing had still not settled down, and she still felt flushed. She blew out a puff of air, ran her fingers through her hair, and pounded one fist on the steering wheel as she drove through the afternoon traffic on U.S. 1, headed back to the police station.

EIGHT

Melody Mitchell looked tired and angry, her normally smooth brow creased as she stared at the file lying on the desk in front of her with an intensity Jessie was reluctant to break. She looked around the Division area, didn't see Stillwater, and put her bag down on a chair beside the desk. Mitchell let out a long breath, looked at Jessie, and shook her head.

"Hey, Jessie," she said with a tight grin, "I don't know if we're making any progress or not. Seems like we get a break on something, then the roof falls in somewhere else." She looked Jessie over carefully, then went on. "Sorry about having to leave you another note while we ran off and left you... Les was anxious to move on info we had. Thanks for leaving me *your* note. I hope your meeting with little *Miss* Tiffany did us some good. You got some sun, anyway... and you look a little, well... unsettled. Everything okay?"

Melody had once told Jessie she could tell when a woman had been "getting it on" because afterwards some women had a "freshly fucked look." Jessie wondered if her friend was seeing that in her face now. She nodded and tried to smile nonchalantly. "It was... interesting," she said. "I learned there was more to the Eastin-Tatari relationship than just business. Both the brother and sister knew the old man on a social level, and spent time with him at his home."

Melody leaned back in her chair, still studying Jessie's face. "Uh-huh."

"Where's Les, Melody? And what's going on up in Pompano?"

"Les has gone over to the sheriff's office to take a look at something their Homicide guys are working now." Mitchell hesitated, then continued, "The county fire units called them out to a small woodframe house off Ravenswood Road early this morning... found three bodies in the house after a fire had consumed it. It was arson, and preliminary peeks indicate all three bodies were dead before the fire started. Looks like they were shot."

Jessie frowned, trying to think of who or why the victims would have anything to do with their case, why Mitchell and Stillwater would be interested. Then her eyes began to widen.

"Yep," Mitchell said quietly, "the neighbors told the fire guys a young woman and her daughter lived there. The woman was a dancer. They even knew where she worked. We think it was Starlight and Babe. Don't know who the third person is yet, but they think it's a male."

Jessie was beginning to understand Melody's mood, and knew why Stillwater would go to BSO himself to get the information on the victims. "Darn," she said.

Mitchell nodded, then slowly placed one hand palm down on the file on the desk, "We went up to Pompano because of this van they got. We were there, some Davie people, and BSO lab types. Late last night, early this morning, Pompano PD marked units moved in on a silent burglary alarm near some warehouses off Dixie Highway. The alarm turned out to be false, but they had moved in like gangbusters." She looked at Jessie and managed a small grin. "You know those hot-rod rookies on midnights, like any department. I swear, I'm *ready* to take over a patrol squad just so I can work with a bunch of reckless hard-chargers again. Anyway... the rookies are standing around the scene of their alarm-that-wasn't, and a newspaper delivery truck driver comes over and says, 'Hey, aren't you guys gonna check out that van over there?' The van is sitting in the middle of an intersection close to the alarm scene. The lights are on, engine running, but no driver. Newspaper guy tells them that when they came charging into the scene, they almost ran *over* the driver of the van, who jumped out when they came up, and ran off."

Mitchell paused here, looked at her notes, and went on. "Description is: white male, short and fat with a panicked look. Witness said he 'waddled' as he split the area. Patrol units checked around, but he was gone. Then they looked at the van." She looked at the file again. "In the back they found a couple of large trash bags. There was some blood in them, some on the floor, dried hard. The bags had duct tape around their necks as if they had been taped closed, then ripped open. There was also some tape on a roll, a length of bloody rope and some rags."

Jessie frowned again and waited.

Mitchell's eyes went out of focus as she said quietly, "Sometimes we have like a single mind, cops as a group... you know? We manage to *tune in*, like with this van. There was a van spotted near the scene where the little boy was grabbed. The tire print taken near the body was consistent with a truck or van. The plastic bags and blood samples are being tested, and the tag on the van is registered to one John Skinner. Pompano was checking around with other PD's to see if it was reported stolen, and Les picked up on the name. In our nickname and streetname file one dirtbag named John Skinner is called 'Scammer.'" Mitchell saw Jessie's eyes widen even more and nodded. "*And*, the same witness who called the fire units to the dancer's house reported a van was parked in the yard early in the evening but was gone when they first noticed the flames."

They were both silent as they digested it all. After a moment Mitchell pushed back her chair, stretched, and added, "We're betting the tire prints from the crime scenes match the van's, and the blood will be the boy's." She made a fist with her right hand and began punching it into her left palm. "Shit, if all this *does* tie in, we're working a case with bodies piling up, and witnesses, victims and informants going bye-bye faster than we can do the paperwork."

Jessie ran her fingers through her hair. She pointed to the coffee machine; Melody nodded, and she went over and poured two cups. Jessie put creamer in both, extra in Melody's, and carried them back. As she got to the desk, Captain Allen walked up carrying a file. He looked at her, then at Mitchell, cleared his throat, tried to stand straighter, and said, "Glad to see you came back after your break, Detective Summer, and I see, uh, you were successful at catching some tan. Okay, I've given Melody my approval for tonight. I'm not entirely comfortable with it, being out of jurisdiction, but Mitchell's reasoning is sound. She and Stillwater will be with you, of course, so you'll be covered. I don't have to say I expect you to conduct yourself in a professional manner, and show those Miami people we've got good hard-working cops up here too. Right? Good." He turned away, then stopped and said to the file he held, "Oh, and I don't think an overtime card from you will be necessary for tonight because of your present, um, loose schedule." Then he walked back into his office and closed the door.

"Say *what*?" said Jessie.

"'Catching some *tan*'?" said Melody. She laughed with Jessie then, and Jessie was glad to see her lighten up some. Mitchell sipped her coffee and said, "I told you about my friend on Miami PD. Did he call you? He did, didn't he? He called today too, asking about your schedule."

Jessie tried to look annoyed, Mitchell watched her for a moment, then went on, "Miguel Tirado... they call him 'Tired Mike.' His parents came from Cuba, and he got that nickname because he's always bitching about things down there, especially if it concerns Cuban-Americans. He *hates* bad Cubans and goes after them like a crazy man. Told me once that all America judges him and all other Cubans by the few bad ones that pop up. So who can argue?"

Now Jessie tried to feign indifference. Mitchell sipped her coffee, saw Jessie's look, and grimaced. "And, *no*, Miguel Tirado is *not* one of the several Miami studs I have allowed to sample my rather Olympian boudoir pleasures." Jessie just rolled her eyes and Mitchell continued, "Anyway... You know I've called him about this Salvatore Sombiero dude—'The Hat.' Tired Mike says he'll make the arrangements, then calls me back all mystified and more pissed off than ever. He contacted Sombiero, who runs his businesses from some café down there in Little Havana, and Sombiero tells him, sure, he'll talk with some Fort Lauderdale detectives... as long as one of them is that blonde-haired lady cop who shot and killed the Cuban jewelry store robber."

Jessie made a face, put her coffee on the desk, and shook her head. "Why, Melody? How the heck does *he* know who I am?"

Mitchell shrugged. "Beats me, lady. You waste this jewelry store guy, and the next thing you know every bad boy in town wants to meet with you, trade with you, and get financial advice. Let's face it, you *did* get a lot of coverage when you smoked that clown . . . it was a different kind of cops-and-robbers thing, and probably in some circles you're considered attractive, in a butch-looking way."

She didn't move fast enough to escape the punch Jessie threw, and she had to scoot back in her chair quickly to avoid the shower of coffee that erupted from her cup. Jessie stuck her tongue out at Mitchell and walked over to the coffee pot for a handful of napkins. She didn't want her friend to see her face until she had a moment. She was sure now that Melody could see right through her. She took a deep breath and went back and handed the napkins to Melody, who cleaned up the desk and threw some on the floor . . . grinning but wary. Finally she straightened up, looked at Jessie again, and went on, "So I talked it over with Tired Mike, who had already told me he wanted to meet you, too." She rolled her eyes. "And we decided you and Mike could sit with this Hat dude, and me and Les could cover your backs. Of course, I had to clear it with Hi-ho before we took you down to piccadilla-eater land in the guise of a real homicide detective."

"I see," said Jessie. "And do I have time to go home and shower and change before we head south?"

"Sure thing, Jessie. It's barely four now, and we'll be going down there about eight-thirty, nine. We're all gonna take a break for a couple of hours, then meet back here around eight, okay?" Jessie nodded, and they both looked up as Les Stillwater came into the Division area.

Stillwater's face told them the story, but they waited until he came to the desk, took off his worn sportcoat, kicked a chair around backwards, and sat down heavily. He ran one big hand through his hair, then down across his face, and said, "Ahhh."

They waited.

"Definitely Starlight and the kid," he said in a subdued voice. "And the third one's a guy. Full autopsies aren't done yet, but, with what we know, it could very well be that asshole, Scammer."

He rubbed his face again, this time with both hands, as if trying to wipe the images out of his eyes. He didn't look at Melody as he added, "Damn! I should have gathered her and her daughter in, I should have brought 'em in as soon as we knew what she had on this case."

The pain was still evident on Stillwater's face as he straightened up, shrugged, and said, "All three were shot. It's an early look, but the way they were found and the location of the wounds makes it look like an execution. Murder-suicide was kicked around, with the male doing the murders and then waxing himself, but it's not consistent with the number of holes in people. That, and the nice fire that crispied the whole bunch afterwards." He leaned forward, staring at Mitchell. "If it *is* Scammer along with Starlight and her daughter, and it *is* a hit covered by arson, then it has to be a certain macho raceboat driver and owner of Dreamland that done it."

Mitchell nodded; Jessie watched their faces. Stillwater added very softly, "That sonofabitch."

Jessie saw a small plain car sitting in her drive as she turned onto her street. She still had the top down on the Camaro and had let her mind wander on the drive from the station to home. Her thoughts had stayed on the operational parts of the case for a few minutes, then had focused on the scene at the pool with Tiffany. No matter how hard Jessie tried, she found her mind filled with images of Tiffany's nakedness, and her own, and of Tiffany's fingers. To her irritation she found she was becoming aroused again, just thinking about it. Then she turned the corner and saw the unfamiliar car.

Miguel Tirado had a guilty look on his face as he stood on Jessie's front steps, a large bouquet of flowers held awkwardly in front of his chest. Jessie parked her car, watched him for a moment, then got out and walked across the lawn to where he stood. She thought he looked better today than the first time she had seen him. He wore casual slacks, soft leather shoes and a peach-colored polo knit. He looked tanned and fit, and his sad eyes had a glint of mischief.

"Ah . . . they say timing is everything in life," he said with a smile, "and now you have caught me in the act."

"What act?" asked Jessie.

"Um . . . the act of driving up here like a schoolboy to covertly leave these flowers and a note for you on your doorstep."

"And why would you do that, Detective-Sergeant Miguel Tirado?"

"Well, I . . . um, I would do this as an act of courting you. I felt it would be fun to leave you flowers, and maybe call you up before you went back to work tonight . . . and ask you out . . . on a date." He shrugged and made a face. "It must be painfully obvious that I am out of practice at this sort of thing, and a beautiful woman like you must have many offers of dates, presented in much more . . . mature ways."

"You know we're coming to Miami tonight to meet with you, and you came up here now to drop these flowers off while I wasn't home?"

Tirado nodded, looked down at his shoes, then back up into Jessie's face. Jessie surprised herself by saying with a smile, "I think your timing is absolutely perfect . . . come on in and visit for a few minutes."

Tirado accepted Jessie's offer of a cup of tea, watched as she put the flowers in a large glass vase of water, and waited in the living room while she put a pot of water on the burner, then excused herself. She had already introduced him to the gang, who inspected him with varying degrees of interest before turning to her with their demands of attention. She made her hellos, and they all settled down. Now, in the shower while she quickly washed away the afternoon, she felt her heart pounding and was angry with herself. What the heck is *wrong* with you lately, she asked herself, you're acting really *weird*. She toweled off, put on a loose-fitting white cotton button-down and a pair of khaki walking shorts, and heard the teapot whistling loudly.

She found Tirado had located the teacups and teabags and was pouring. "I guess it's too late to say 'Mi casa es su casa' at this point," she said to him with a small laugh, and he shrugged.

"Ah," he asked, his brows high above his big eyes, "you have the Spanish?"

"Un poquito."

She stood beside him, and they were both quiet as they stared at the steeping tea. Then he turned slightly and said, "Your home is really neat, very comfortable. I love all the books, and that big painting on the wall there is oil on *batik*, isn't it? It's unusual, but it works. And that view through your tropical garden on your back porch . . . very nice."

She looked at his face and nodded. Then she looked down at his hands. He had nice hands, she thought, long-fingered and very strong and clean, and a couple of scars across the tops of his knuckles to hint at another dimension. She stood close to him and could smell him, a bit of some men's cologne, but mostly just . . . man. Without saying anything he wrapped his fingers around her hand, then softly ran them across the skin of her palm.

Jessie was hit with a wave of emotion, as if his fingers on her skin released the mixed feelings she had recently been carrying around in her heart. She pulled her hand away suddenly, frightened by the intensity. "Oh, I'm sorry," he said, pulling his hand back. She shook her head and entwined her fingers with his.

"I've had this really strange day," she said softly. "I'm kind of mixed up . . . like I don't know who I am, or what I'm supposed to feel . . . or *anything*." He moved against her and she felt his arms around her, strong and warm, and she felt his chin on the top of her head, heard him take a deep breath even as she did, and as she did, she felt her breasts swell against his chest.

She pulled back slightly, still in his arms, and looked into his eyes. Still she saw the sadness there, but also strength and patience. The late afternoon sun had turned the inside of the house golden. She was *in* her own house, and although she felt the heat and guessed he did too, she was aware that he seemed to be waiting for her. With a sensation like that of standing next to the tracks as a loaded freight train roars past, leaving you buffeted in its wake by noise and wind and bits of paper and leaves, all of her questions and fears and memories about herself as a woman rushed through her . . . and she made a decision.

Without saying a word she turned to walk out of the kitchen, pulling him behind her toward the bedroom. He followed and she felt him pause as they entered the room with her big bed against the east wall. Much of the room was in shadow now, soft light and quiet. She stood at the foot of the bed, facing him, and waited, and as if he knew how it had to be, he moved to her and began to undress her. Her breathing changed with the opening of each button, she gave a small sigh as he unsnapped her bra, then a longer one as he unzipped the shorts. She stood with her arms at her side, her hands held with the palms out, fingers open. Her chin was raised slightly, her lips parted, and when he straightened after bending to help her step out of the shorts, he kissed her. He let the kiss begin tentatively, his lips warm and dry. He let the kiss approach her as one approaches a small bird, slow and easy, with no sudden move. He let the kiss wander then, across the skin of her cheek, down to her neck, against an earlobe, then back to her waiting mouth. And as his lips reassured her, his hands began to leave warm silky paths across her skin. She stood naked before him, her eyes closed, and let herself be comforted and mesmerized by those hands.

He stepped back from her for a moment, and when he returned, his clothes were gone, his skin warm all over, and he embraced her with his whole body. She felt him against her, felt the heat, his arousal immediate... and she was suddenly scared. She fought it, tried to force her mind to silence and just let his nearness and her desire finally end the confused turmoil, but the memories would not be denied, and the old feelings came rushing on her like a cold wind through an open window. "No," she said in a strained voice, her hands on his shoulders and pushing him away. "Oh God, no. I can't... it's just too soon... I'm not..."

He pulled back from her and let his left hand fall from her breast, down her arm, until it found her right hand. He brought the fingers of his right hand up to her lips and said gently, "Shhh. It's okay. We'll stop." He pushed her lightly until she sat on the edge of the bed, then he knelt in front of her. He used his fingers to lift her chin and waited until her eyes came up to his. He looked into her eyes for a long moment, saw the anxiety, the fear, and waited. While he waited he softly pulled on her fingers and played with the skin of her ear. He saw her relax, then gave a crooked smile and said quietly, "I am completely out of line, and have acted again like a schoolboy... a hungry and impatient schoolboy. My self-control is no match for your face, your eyes, your beautiful body.

I wanted you as a newspaper photo, and when I finally saw you in person . . . I must confess I wanted you *right then*. Don't be afraid of me now, it's okay . . . I'll leave you.''

Through her mixed emotions she was aware of his words, was aware that he knelt before her, accepting and responding to her denial. He gave her choice and control . . . and as she realized it, her need for him burned fast and hot, and the heat enveloping her melted the fears and covered the old memories with soft smoke. She stood again and pulled him to her. She kissed him, a long and searching kiss, and with one hand she reached down and took him into her grasp. He was silent now, and they fell together onto the bed.

In the time that she and Miguel Tirado spent together, exploring and sharing each other's bodies, Jessie made a discovery and affirmation. She realized that the memories she held of her experiences from childhood, her teen years and more recently, were just fragments of a greater and potentially positive whole. Her childhood memory of the motel room was scary and painful, her high school night sordid and confusing. What she had felt with Tiffany Eastin was sexual excitement and arousal, yes, but she had always known that was not the path she would take, that the heat between them had only been on the surface. The heat she felt with Miguel coursed through the very core of her. She felt her body coupled with his in perfect fit, complete . . . like it was supposed to be.

He took her totally, searching her body for the tastes and textures, looking for and finding those places and movements that would bring her the most pleasure. She took from him without inhibition and looked into his face through half-closed eyes during those times when her body tightened until it vibrated, then released in a torrent that left her breathless. Later, he was patient and gentle in guiding her hands and mouth on him, allowing her tastes and textures and the pleasure of giving pleasure. Their bodies came together gracefully, and they joined in many ways, each one a quiet adventure and triumph. They laughed out loud more than once, like children at play. One of those times was when they faced each other, her legs over his, joined and kissing. He had fallen back then, his hands on her breasts as she straddled him, her knees on the crumpled bedcovers. She had enjoyed that, the control, the movement of her hips against him as she looked down into his eyes until finally they closed and he called her name again and again as he arched his hips and she hung on.

The room was dark when she awoke, her face against the skin of his flat belly. She lifted her head to find him looking down at her face, his eyes bright in the shadows. His fingers played with her hair, and she felt his other palm on her back, warm. His eyes searched hers, but he said nothing. She looked at his face and smiled. Then she looked at the red glow from the bedside alarm clock numbers. "Oh my god," she gasped, "it's after seven!"

She disentangled herself from him and got out of bed, and after a moment he followed her. She went to the dresser and turned on a lamp, and they were both impacted with years of accumulated social mores. She looked at him, suddenly awkward in her nakedness and his. She bent down and scooped up her clothes and said with a shy smile, " 'Scuse me a second," and dashed into the bathroom, closing the door behind her. He hesitated, a stranger in her house, in her bedroom, then quickly dressed and left the room.

When Jessie came out a few minutes later, she found Miguel in the living room. He kept his eyes on her face until she would look at him, then he smiled. She gave him a crooked smile in return, started to say something, then turned and went into the kitchen where she busied herself rinsing out the unused teacups. Finally she looked at him and said quietly, "Um, I feel kind of foolish. I don't know if I should say I don't *know* you and we've . . . or if I don't know *myself* . . . and we've . . . I hope you won't think I'm . . . I didn't plan . . ."

He held a finger against his own lips and shook his head. "I think only that you are very beautiful, and brave and wonderful. That's all." He sighed and made an open gesture with his hands. "I don't want you to feel uncomfortable. I guess I should go—I think you and I are supposed to meet for the first time in Miami in an hour or so." She nodded, relieved that she wouldn't have to try to explain herself to him now, and as she did, she noticed he was holding the shell, which he had taken from the bookcase he stood beside. Odd that he would hold the shell, she thought.

He saw her looking at his hands and said quietly, "I was looking around at the things you have here and found it on the shelf. It is a rare one, is it not? I'll bet a couple of these spines are almost three inches long."

"It's a *Cabrit's Murex*," she said so softly he almost couldn't hear her. "And I found it when I was ten years old, on a beach I have never been able to go back to, until today." He waited for more, but she was silent, biting her lip and staring at the shell. He gently placed it back on the shelf, came to her, and kissed her. Then he left.

Almost two hours later, Detective-Sergeant Miguel Tirado, looking like he stepped out of a quality rum ad in his eggshell linen suit, bowed slightly and said, "Encantado, Detective Jessie Summer, sí ...muy encantado." Jessie let Tired Mike take her hand in his, their eyes locked as he lightly kissed her fingers. He straightened and said, "Welcome to our beautiful city, señorita. It is made only lovelier by your being here. Miami is indeed a wonderful town, and I must admit I am probably the best person you could find to show you all of its treasures."

"Sheesh," said Sergeant Melody Mitchell.

"Damn," said Detective Les Stillwater.

"Anytime," said Jessie with a small smile and a tone in her voice that made Melody take another look at her face.

The three of them had driven down I-95 in light evening traffic, exited at the Eighth Street ramp, and took it east to the Miami Arena. They noticed in the area immediately surrounding the arena even the palm trees looked new, while just a block or so away the streets were dirty and neglected, with a forlorn look to them. Mitchell and Stillwater had commented to each other about the street people proliferating the area, many of them sleeping on the sidewalks or hanging around on corners. Stillwater, riding shotgun as Mitchell drove, had looked at the arena and surrounding streets and grunted, "This place looks like a fat girl in a new dress who got off at the wrong bus stop." Jessie had remained quiet, sitting in the back seat, staring out the window. Mitchell had tried to drag her into the conversation on the drive down but gave up after a few minutes. She thought Jessie looked flushed and unsteady, preoccupied or something. Even as they parked the car against the curb at the northwest corner of the arena, they saw Tirado waiting for them near the ticket windows, and he had walked down the steps to meet them as they got out.

"Listen, Miguel," said Melody now, "ease up on all that Ricardo Montalban stuff, let go of Jessie's hand, and try to concentrate on the *business* at hand, comprende?"

"Sure thing, jefe," said Tirado as he reluctantly released Jessie's hand and turned his sad eyes toward Mitchell and Stillwater. He shook hands with Les while being introduced, looked him over, and said, "So, Melody, I wondered if you would get a new partner. Is this him?"

Mitchell shook her head. "No, he's Jessie's, actually. I'm just helping out temporarily."

There was an impish grin under Tirado's mustache as he said, "*I* know. One of you is the fashion police, trying to arrest the other. No, you are homicide detective partners, teamed to work *both* sides of the barrio. Clever cops." He gave an eloquent shrug. "So who could tell?"

Stillwater leaned over Mitchell's shoulder and growled, "Sarge, tell Little Havana's answer to Henny Youngman here we don't want to work in *Meeamee* long enough to require a green card . . . and we'd like to get *on* with this hat dance."

Before Mitchell could respond, Tirado gave a short bow, held out his arm for Jessie, and said quietly, "Permit me." Jessie wrapped her arm in his, slightly relieved that so far Tired Mike had kept up the pretense of their first meeting. Her head was spinning, though, with the nearness of him, and she felt a sudden thrill at the substance of their secret. But her emotions were fragmented. She couldn't shake the feeling that she had completely lost control a few hours ago, had acted with him like . . . a crazy person. What could he think of her? What did *she* think of her? It could not have happened.

Tirado leaned close to her and said softly, "You, my precious one, will ride with me, and I will tell you why I am sometimes saddened by what I see here in this wondrous city, how disappointed I can be in my fellow Cuban-Americans, how complex and difficult it is to work in this Pan-American melange. These two—"he jerked a thumb at Stillwater and Mitchell—"will follow us in their car, no doubt talking all the while of famous African-American rap singers, and of things that interest gay caballeros."

Mitchell was watching the way Jessie leaned into Tirado's arm and thought for a moment she saw some kind of awkward tension . . . or something. Then she saw the look on her partner's face after Tirado's last remark and said with a grin, "He means *happy* cowboys, Les."

Jessie felt like Princess Leia of *Star Wars* fame under the reptilian scrutiny of Jabba the Hutt. Salvatore Sombiero was a grotesquely fat man whose olive skin seemed to ooze a wet sheen. Every part of his body appeared puffed and distorted, his fingers, lips, eyelids. His thin black hair was carefully parted in the center and combed down in even, shiny streaks on the side of his round skull, and his jowls almost completely covered the open collar of his beige guayabera shirt. Incongruously, his nose was long and pointed, geometrically clashing with his Buddha-like ears. His body filled a large leather recliner, against which rested a pair of shiny crutches, angled, with resting places for his forearms. His creased dark brown trousers had an awkward fold to them, and his feet were covered in suede half-boots with high heels.

Cuban heels, thought Jessie.

They had come a few blocks past Calle Ocho and parked behind a small grocery whose owner Tirado apparently knew. Their conversation during the ride had been stunted and uncomfortable, with Jessie pulling it back to case-related subjects each time Tirado tried to talk about the afternoon. Finally he had shrugged and become quiet. He had been all business since their arrival in this part of the city.

They headed for a typical open-front cantina/ bar/ coffee shop/ restaurant. There were open areas on either side of the bar, Tirado explained, with the kitchen in the rear. Sombiero held court on nights like this, sitting against the back wall of the far open area. He and his people knew Jessie's partners would precede them. They were to go in, look it over, and take a table against the wall. From there they could observe Sombiero's table. There would be no trouble, Tirado explained, but they would see plenty of desperadoes—those who worked for Salvatore the Hat. He employed a mixed bag of beauties, Tirado added, "Nicos," Salvadorans, Hondurans, Panamanians . . . even a few Cubans, he was sad to say.

"He calls himself a commodities broker," said Tirado as they walked down the busy sidewalk. "He deals in everything from guns for El Salvador to toilet paper for Fidel. He's got his gordo fingers in every illegitimate pie in town, and *everyone* uses him for connections, info, sources." He paused then, and Jessie had seen the pain in his eyes. "He'll talk to me or one or two other policemen. He'll deal with all of the criminal elements, and he just *loves* to remind us that he is closely tied in with our Federal government through a couple of intelligence agencies whose initials I can't remember. There is speculation that he has a thick file cabinet full of unpleasant facts about state and local officials and 'upper crust' citizens. That, combined with the Federal umbrella he sits under as a reward for helping out in some of *their* dirtier little games, makes him a hard man for us to bust."

They had entered the cantina from the sidewalk. Jessie had seen Mitchell and Stillwater sipping Cuban coffee and watching, and she and Tirado were seated at Sombiero's table. His recliner was in the back corner, so both Tired Mike and Jessie could have their backs against a wall. She had settled and found herself under that somehow carnally appraising gaze. "We will speak English," said Sombiero in a naturally lugubrious voice, "since this is Florida, in America, and here English is the *official* language."

"Como usted lo quiera, señor," said Jessie with just a hint of disinterest.

Sombiero's oily lids exposed more of his yellowish eyes as he chuckled with surprise. He looked at Tirado, who gave him an impassive shrug.

"Let me begin again, Detective Summer . . . Tirado," continued the big Cuban—in English, to Jessie's secret relief. "I will guess that neither of you is wearing a recording device. Everyone knows of Detective Tirado's famous photo-like memory, and I am told, and it has been proven, that you, señorita, are a woman of *honor*."

Jessie thought of her first meeting with Dominic Tatari, his use of that word, and felt a chill. She nodded.

"It is true," Sombiero went on, "that I am a powerful man and well connected, as you said when you set up this meeting. And it is true that, because of my position here in Miami, I know many people, I hear many things." He took a deep breath, then rubbed one fat finger down the narrow bridge of his nose, "Of course, I have heard of the two locos called Benny and The Jet. Yes, it is possible that someone might have thought I recommended the Cubano who found himself very dead at the hands of this delectable lady detective." He paused, a theatrical pause. "But beyond that, I'm not sure I can be of any assistance to you."

All he needs is a fez, thought Jessie.

"You are full of shit, Sombiero," was all Tirado said. Then he sat back with his arms folded and waited.

Sombiero looked stricken. "Must you be so blunt?" he said. "So impatient? So rude?" He turned his head, snapped his fingers, and immediately a waiter appeared with a tray. He placed a small cup of coffee in front of each of them, with a plate of pastalitos in the center. Sombiero waved him away, picked up one of the small meat-filled pastries, and delicately ate it. Then he carefully brought the cup to his lips and sipped.

Jessie, perplexed by Tirado's open hostility, didn't want this to end up a waste of time. She looked at the large gold crucifix hanging under Sombiero's thick neck and said, "Maybe Detective-Sergeant Tirado allows himself to be patient when dealing with certain forms of criminal activity . . . when *other* forms make him feel hurried." Sombiero eyed her and she went on. "Detective-Sergeant Tirado did tell me you are a powerful man, a man who in some circles is considered a man of honor. Maybe he is impatient with you now because he suspects, as I may, that you are directly involved in this case. There are *no* men of honor involved in the criminal activities we are investigating."

She had Sombiero's attention now. His eyes narrowed and he tried to lean forward toward her. She tapped a finger against her lips, and said, "Benny and The Jet were hired and outfitted through you to kill some people in a bar in Fort Lauderdale. The young man I killed in the jewelry store was also 'arranged' for someone through you. There are common denominators weaving a pattern for us, and *you* are woven into it.'' She leaned forward now too, her teeth clenched, her face inches from his. ''The common denominator turns out to be children, *señor* Sombiero, very young children who are abducted for the purpose of making pornographic materials. Is this how you get your power? Your money? Are their tiny and innocent bodies some of the goods you proudly broker?'' She stopped, took a deep breath, and then spit out, ''Or are you a *customer*, too?''

For a moment both Jessie and Tired Mike thought she had gone too far. Salvatore Sombiero's face became blood red, he clenched his teeth, his eyes bulged and the right one spider-webbed when a blood vessel burst. He placed one huge hand over his coffee cup and it began rattling faster and faster until it broke into small shards of ceramic. The coffee and the blood from Sombiero's cut palm turned the tablecloth muddy brown until, without taking his eyes off Jessie, he swept everything—pastalitos, cups, tablecloth—onto the floor with a loud clatter.

Immediately several waiters hurried over, as did two or three men who had been watching from the bar. Jessie saw Stillwater and Mitchell move to get up, but a covert wave from Tirado eased them back into their seats. The mess was quickly cleaned up, a clean hand-towel was crushed into Sombiero's wounded palm, and he waved his hard guys away. They sat for several minutes, listening to the rasping sound of Sombiero's labored breathing.

Finally he said in a terrible voice, ''So. You want to be a police officer, but you attack me as only a woman can. In different circumstances I would be most pleased to show you that I need only *two* braces ... my third leg needs *no* crutch! I am a businessman and a *man*. I don't deal in filth and I don't seek pleasure from it.'' He looked at the two red spots high on Jessie's cheeks. ''You are quite angry, sí? What makes you so intense about this case—what is your reason?'' They stared at each other in silence, then he sat back and seemed to make up his mind. He played with the towel in his fist, and went on in a businesslike but oddly dispirited tone. ''Juan Coasca and Benny Sánchez. A businessman in Fort Lauderdale, through intermediaries, employed them for a mission in that city. I heard later it was a hit. I supposedly sold this man the automatic weapons used." He looked at Tirado. "Prove it." He waited, then continued, "Later, a man employed the young *perro* killed in the jewelry store. The man did not tell me how he would use this dog, and I did not care. The man called himself to me 'Uncle Sam,' and we laughed. He was a Pacific Islander of some kind, unpleasant, with a hungry odor about him. Very confident and smooth. *He* is one who is in the business you speak of . . . and stupidly accuse me of participating in."

Tirado interrupted, "Did he also buy information from you? What did he want to know?"

Sombiero pouted as he inspected the small cut in his palm, sighed, and said, "Maybe. He was curious about certain syndicate figures in Broward County, names, business affairs, that sort of thing. I found it oddly coincidental." Then he smiled at Jessie. "And you, Detective Summer, you were close to one he asked about, and you have seen Benny and The Jet. Oh yes, they remembered you watching them as they scurried off with the money . . . they commented on your beauty and made bold plans, should they ever see you again."

Jessie's eyes widened. "At Vizcaya? But that money was for . . ."

"For a payment to get Senor Tatari's stupid son out of a drug business problem?" said Sombiero with a wicked leer. "Yes, but only a *part* of that bag of money was for those cocaine cowboys."

"The rest of it went to *you*? Tatari sent money to *you*? But what for?"

Tirado listened intently, searching Jessie's face as she spoke, trying to follow this unexpected turn in the conversation.

Sombiero ignored her questions, saying instead, "Oh, and you *delivered* it for him, didn't you?" He was enjoying her discomfort, and went on in a placating tone. "Of course, you could talk to Benny and The Jet—Coasca and Sánchez—but they had some sort of drug-induced falling out and Benny sprayed a bar with a machine gun. He killed poor Juan outright, but he also killed an inconvenient knot of bystanders. He will be arrested when—if—found, but I have heard he left the Estados Unidos for the south. Or maybe he's decomposing quietly a few miles from here in the Everglades. Anyway, Señor Tatari is dead too, and we don't *know* who did that one, do we?" He folded his pudgy hands together, let out a long breath, and smiled. "And now I must insist we terminate this meeting. I have other business to attend to, and you have bruised my Latin honor you have heard so much about. I did want to meet the beautiful blonde police lady who killed that rental dog, but now that I have, I'm afraid I'm disappointed . . . not in her beauty, but in her attitude." He let his eyes slowly examine her again. "Still . . ." he began to laugh, a rumbling volcano of flesh, and winked.

Jessie stood, as did Tirado. She thought "loathed" would describe her feelings nicely, but she said quietly, "That 'rental dog' you have such disregard for had the same look of disappointment in his eyes the last time *he* saw me."

They left.

The four of them gathered where the cars were parked behind the small grocery and stood together in the yellowish glow of a street light. "Well," asked Mitchell, "was it worth the trip?" Jessie, preoccupied again, didn't answer, so Tirado did.

"Uh, yes," he said with a nod. "I'm sure Jessie will fill you in. For the most part he just confirmed, without hurting himself, things we already suspected." He looked closely at Jessie then, and added, "Of course, as in any meeting of this type, with a slippery eel like Sombiero, some of the things he said only led to more questions." Still Jessie remained silent, so the other three shook hands, promised to exchange report supplements on the night's activities, and said goodnight.

Tirado took one of Jessie's hands, brought it to his lips, and said quietly, "It was my total pleasure to finally meet you, Detective Jessie Summer. I have greatly enjoyed my short time spent with you, and hope sincerely we can get together again . . . soon."

Jessie felt his warm lips on her skin, looked into his eyes, and for one scary moment thought he would embrace her in front of the others. But he just stepped back and gave a small bow, and she smiled tentatively and said, "Maybe on some case-related thing, Detective-Sergeant Miguel Tirado."

* * *

The ride back to the Fort Lauderdale police station was a quiet one. After ten minutes of Mitchell trying to get Jessie to tell them about the meeting, and another five just trying to get her to say *anything*, she gave up. She watched Jessie's troubled face reflected in the rearview mirror and wondered what was bothering her more . . . the talk with the fat Cuban or the unexplained but definite interaction with Miguel Tirado.

To Stillwater's surprise and delight, Mitchell turned the car radio to 99.9 Kiss FM, and they listened to country tunes all the way home.

NINE

Humberto explained to Isabel they were now in the Bahama Islands, all the way around the world from home. The islands were smaller than at home, he had told her, and drier and sandier. But she had seen all the colors in the waters, the blue skies, and said the air was soft and warm like at home. They had stayed one night on the main island, then had traveled by small seaplane, which she had loved, to a smaller island called Bimini. He had told her this would be their last stop before she went to her new home in America, and that Florida was very close now. She seemed to like the hotel they checked into—the Big Game Club—and, child that she was, she asked him what kind of games were played there.

"Now we will rest for a few days, Isabel," said Humberto in his quiet, gravelly voice. "You can swim in the pool and we can walk around and see the people, and shop, and you can rest after your long journey."

"Did we really come halfway around the *world*, Uncle Humberto?"

"The long way."

The long way is right, thought Humberto as he watched Isabel play in the shallow end of the large swimming pool. He rubbed his eyes with his fists. I must agree with Ramone, however . . . Hawaii to California is nice, but the Customs and Immigration people there are too tuned in about small brown children entering the country in either place. Honolulu gets the covert influx from the Far East, and California has all those desperate Mexicans, Central Americans and who knows what-all pouring in. No, it was better to take longer and go through gates where the pretty little girl and her patient uncle did not set off any mental alarms. He pulled at the new guayabera shirt already sticking to him in the heat and looked at his watch. In a while he would take Isabel to lunch at a small marina down the road. As the child ate her hushpuppies and fried fish, he would talk with the Bimini islander who would provide Ramone with the cocaine he was bringing in to Florida when they made the crossing.

Now he absently cracked his knuckles. I hope we're not getting too tricky for our own good, Ramone, he thought with a frown. I understand the need to entice the stupid Tatari with the coke, and that huge fat one in Miami also. And I understand that the heat of the coke will take the focus away from Isabel. Yes, I understand all of the complex reasoning and illusion, Ramone, but sometimes I think maybe you are a little *too* oriental in your scheming.

He motioned for Isabel to get out of the water.

Dominic Tatari cut himself shaving. He wiped the blood away impatiently, began again, and cut himself once more, high on his left cheekbone near the first one. He held the razor up in front of him and saw how his hands were shaking. He dropped the razor into the sink, put his palms against the mirror, and leaned forward, looking into the reflection of his own watery eyes. He didn't like the fear he saw there. He dipped his head and splashed cold water across his cheeks and mouth. He kept his face down and watched as small drops of blood fell into the sink. All right, he thought, I'm experiencing fear. Haven't I felt pregame jitters before? Haven't I played hardball in some pretty tough circles and come out on top even without my crummy old man's help? He looked up again and saw that the twin trails of blood had left a grotesque pattern on the side of his face and neck. A fat glob of coagulating blood had formed at the bottom of his chin, and it hung there now like an obscene pimple.

"Fuck it," he said, "and the hell with them, the stupid assholes." It's your own fault, a voice in his mind said. You picked them to work for you, and you *knew* they couldn't cut it and you knew they'd turn on you eventually, even the kid. "But I had to do it," he said to his face in the mirror. Yeah, said the voice, you had to do it, but it was messy and unplanned and there could be trouble from it—even your pussy attorney has called and demanded back fees in cash, like *he* knows your shit's weak, too. Hell, the local news has already reported the fire and bodies, and some official has been quoted as saying the fire was suspicious... even these plastic, movie-star cops they've got down here will eventually figure out what happened. They'll know she worked in one of your clubs, and they'll know he had been seen with you. And the kid?

"Screw the kid," he said to the mirror.

You already did, said the voice inside him, and Tatari let out a giggle. Now you'd better start thinking straight... it might be time for a cool change. It would still be hard for the cops to make you on anything.

His eyes focused, and then he was jolted with the image of the blonde female cop. Seeing her at that party had been nagging him until he had finally remembered where he had seen her before, and who she was, the *bitch*. Well, he thought, I told Ramone about her being there, and he didn't seem too shaken. Said he'd deal with her. Fine. My weakest link now is that sweaty Frog. But hell, I let him go for now because he's making up more portfolios. Beautiful shots of beautiful kids for Ramone, so he'll see I'm tuned in like he is to the real young stuff. The Frog will be okay for now, and then I'll *do* his ass and the fire official can give the news another quote.

He still leaned against the sink, breathing hard, his eyes closed. Shouldn't have done so much coke last night, he thought. This has not been a good couple of days. It was a mistake to lose it with that friggin' Jack Eastin, but that bastard makes my skin crawl. I shouldn't have been so short with him, but it gets old, him all the time asking me about Ramone, him and his sister, big friends of the old man, sharing time with him—and secrets. Even when he was alive, they looked down their noses at me, like I'm some kind of punk. And now I've got the feeling that Ramone is playing to them, the prick. The more I think about it... Crap, he gives *Jack* a picture of that pretty little girl while I'm standin' there like a *nobody*.

He opened his eyes. I *do* want her, he thought, and either Ramone puts me ahead of the Eastins on this one or I'll *take* her from him. A grin twisted across his lips like a lizard's dismembered tail. Shee*it*, he thought, am I whacked out, or *what*? Do I give a shit anymore? I was nothin' to my old man, and now the other groups are movin' in on my turf, and runnin' those bullshit clubs takes too much time, and the cops are out there lookin' for me—I'll sell the clubs and other crap for quick cash, and take the girl and go somewhere I can walk down the street with her on my arm for people to see and envy. She won't be like these sluts around here with their gaping maws and laughing smirks, not like some sleazy twat I had to pay for to love me.

He wiped his nose with the back of one hand and thought, And there's that *other* asshole buddy of my old man's too, Fag-o Charlie. My old man didn't think I was shit, but he hung around with that little pussy. Okay, I need to meet with him again. Got to check in and see if the little puke has heard anything out on the street about the old man *or* the fire, and I've got to get him started putting the word out on the load of cocaine. I'll need buyers fast. Yeah, I'll take the girl away from Ramone if he won't give her to me, but I'm takin' the nose-candy *anyway* . . . for my trouble.

He turned away from the sink, and as he did, the heavy globule of blood fell away from his chin, rotated slowly through the air, and finally spattered across the cover of a glossy porn magazine lying on the floor by the toilet.

"No calls," Hi-Ho Allen told his secretary. Then he closed his office door, sat at his desk, and looked at Stillwater, Mitchell and Summer sitting across from him. It was midmorning, the day after their foray into Miami. The captain wanted to be briefed, caught up on the case. Jessie sat quietly as Mitchell and Stillwater described the most important developments. Some items were just in, and helpful, they said. The first, Mitchell told him, was a note addressed to Stillwater from Starlight—the late Joan. It backed up things they already knew, but added the fact that Scammer worked directly for Tatari in the porn business—he was the one who came up with the kids to be used in the films. "One would hope he is still burning," said Captain Allen in a quiet voice. The others were silent until Mitchell continued. The note also mentioned a photographer named Frog, said Mitchell. Frog's real name was LaPoint or LaPont, he had a studio on Old Dixie Highway, and he developed some of the porn film. His description could fit that of the suspect who had abandoned Scammer's van in Pompano, added Stillwater. Hi-ho furrowed his brow at this.

Next, Melody said, the crime scene guys, quietly going about their business, had sent up a report showing that, while Tatari's house appeared to have been hastily wiped down, both Tataris and at least one more male and female, neither on local file, had been found and confirmed. The murder weapon had been identified, Mitchell read. It was a heavy teakwood figure, one of a matched pair that stood on small pedestals on either side of the entrance to Tatari, Sr.'s kitchen from the dining room. The figures were of the head and shoulders of a woman wearing a shawl or scarf with intricate designs and grooves cut into the wood to make the cloth effect. The one used to bludgeon Tatari had been cleaned and carefully put back in place, but close examination brought out small particles of skin and blood trapped in the grooves. These particles matched the dead man's.

Captain Allen tapped a pencil against his lips, waiting for more.

More parts of the puzzle, or even more puzzling, narrated Mitchell with an apologetic grin, were the results of the paper search on the jewelry store where this whole thing began. Jessie frowned as she heard again that the store had been jointly owned by the old man killed there and a small "investment group." The investment group turned out to be Dominic Tatari, Senior, and inquiries by detectives within the trade showed that the money behind wholesale purchases came from the jeweler's silent partner, and that the store was known to be a conduit for stolen goods going out of the country through Miami.

Lastly, said Mitchell, the Dreamland Club was owned by another bogus corporation . . . and the main name folded in among all the lawyer's secretaries' names was Dominic Tatari, *Junior*. This Tatari put together the biker hit—and probably killed Scammer, Starlight and Babe.

Captain Allen interrupted, "*Probably*, hmm? Listen, this is all good work evidence, leading us to our goal, but that's all it is so far. You people know how the Tatari lawyer butted in at the beginning, trying to get the old man's body released, and making sure the son clammed up." He stared at the three officers, then cleared his throat. "He'd love it if we jump too soon and file before we've really got our act together." Stillwater thought of the bodies piling up on the case while they got their act together, but stayed silent, along with Mitchell and Summer.

Mitchell stole a glance at Jessie. She and Stillwater had been surprised that morning when Jessie came in, very crisp and businesslike, and had told them the whole story of her original meeting with Tatari and the delivery at Vizcaya, everything. Stillwater had mentioned to Mitchell just before the meeting with the captain that maybe they should feel relieved—it had been obvious that Jessie was holding *something* in—and now they could get on with it. Mitchell had asked herself if Jessie wasn't *still* holding. So Mitchell had started by giving Captain Allen a slightly edited version of what had been learned from the meeting with Sombiero—Allen knew that large cash had gone from Tatari to Sombiero, he just didn't know who had been the courier. Now Hi-ho said, "So... after the jeweler is murdered, Tatari sends money to Sombiero, who had arranged for the young Cuban to be at the store with the other man who we think is this Ramone character. Was Tatari paying Sombiero for a hit on his own partner?"

Jessie, like the others, was silent. She thought the captain's guess was dead right, but still didn't know the whys, and she was angry about the fact that the more they learned, the more obvious it became that Tatari had used her, big time. Sure, he had given them Starlight, and she *did* clear up the biker bar murders, at least in the files, and this, in effect, gave away his *son*, but Jessie couldn't help but be angry with herself for being such a patsy. She had killed Tatari's hitman, then delivered the payoff herself. Only Mitchell noticed the small red spots high on her cheeks.

The captain was summing up. "So," he said through a steeple of fingers, "maybe Tatari went outside of his own circle to order a hit on the jeweler. It looks like this Scammer killed the little boy, and the younger Dominic is probably responsible for the three dead in the burned house. The prints found at the Tatari house *could* belong to one or both of the Eastins... at this point we know a lot, but I still don't think we have enough to get a warrant on anyone—*especially* the Eastins." He straightened his already straight tie. "I mean, some of our city and state administrators run in the same... social circle, if you read me." He blew out a puff of air. "And what the hell is this Ramone guy doing in the middle of this? Who is he? What's *his* game?" He looked at the faces of the three cops in front of him. Stillwater and Mitchell were relaxed, but Summer was curiously intent, almost agitated. He wondered again if it was a good idea, letting her work this case. He shrugged and concluded the meeting. "Your next step should be learning all you can about 'Frog.' Identify him, get next to him, and see if we can't legally get inside his sleazy mind and photo studio. G'bye."

Jessie rode the up escalator from the ground floor of the Main Library in downtown Fort Lauderdale. She could see Charles leaning on the rail near the restaurant, waiting for her. She had walked out of the captain's meeting just in time to get his message.

He smiled at her now and squeezed her hand for a moment, and she saw he looked his usual dapper self. His full head of gray hair was brushed out and styled, his body looked trim and fit, and he wore white jeans, pink soft-leather boat shoes, a white belt with gold buckle, and a long-sleeved pink button-down shirt, closed at the neck. "Let's just walk around while we talk, okay, Jessie?" he suggested. "I just love being around all these books." She grinned, and as he led her into the first open area, he said quietly, "No crooks, no cops. That's why I like this for a meeting place. Dominic thought I was out of my *mind* when I told him, but he came anyway."

He had told her on the telephone that Tatari had contacted him for a meet, very insistent and demanding. Charles made time for him right then, which had pleased Tatari. "He feels like a big man now, in *charge* of things," said Charles. "Hell, that guy is about as sharp as a marble. Big racing boat driver. How many brains does it take to hang on to one of those big bastards at full throttle?''

Jessie didn't want to venture a guess.

"I think he's doing *lots* of cocaine, that's what," continued the small man as he ran his fingers across the backs of a row of books. "He was all over the place as he talked to me. Asked me if I'd heard anything about a fire where three people were killed... *I* told him what I saw on the news. *Then* he wants me to quietly put out the word that some heavy coke is coming in. He thinks *I* can help line up buyers." Charles looked around nervously, saw no threat, and shook his head of hair. "Ignorant oaf has those young bouncers and lounge managers working for him, but he asks *me*. My god... so now I'm a *dope* dealer?"

Jessie just shook her head and gave a small laugh to show how off-base that was. They walked some more, and Jessie found herself reading titles and authors' names and wondering why she didn't come there more often. She turned to Charles as he spoke again.

"He thinks his old man somehow set *up* that murder at the jewelry store," said Charles breathlessly, "to break up some kind of porn ring that *he*, young Dominic, had going. I couldn't follow it all, but supposedly there was another guy there in cahoots with young Dominic who didn't *plan* on the old jeweler getting... killed. *That* guy is involved with the cocaine coming in, maybe soon, and some other thing that Dominic was all crazy-eyed about. Probably porno." He stopped between two rows of shelves. He spoke quietly, as one would in a library, and now put his hand lightly on Jessie's arm and said in a whisper, "Follow my thoughts here for a moment. There has been talk of Dominic's, um, *hang-ups* for some time. Word is, he likes real young girls, like *kids*, the creepy bag of fart." He grimaced. "Sorry. The reason I'm telling you is, he said 'the girl' a couple of times, like this other guy had some *girl* Dominic wants... maybe for this porn business, *I* don't know."

They were silent as they walked side by side back and forth between more rows of books, and Jessie found herself wondering if she came there late at night when everyone was gone, would she hear a soft and quiet murmuring from all those words and thoughts packed into volumes and volumes...?

"I feel *certain* he's got a big load of coke coming in with this other guy," said Charles as he picked a bit of lint off one sleeve, "and he's got this 'other business' which might have something to do with a young girl. The coke part is easy. It'll probably come in from the Bahamas, like half the frigging stuff *does* down here . . . it's probably his biggest deal yet—who knows? The funny thing about all of this is how I've been hearing in the bars that the whole damn Tatari thing is falling apart due to the vultures moving in, mismanagement and plain old *neglect*. Word is that Dominic will take a low bid on various holdings if the buyer can come up with quick cash . . . like he's *liquidating*, you know? All the years he *absolutely* pissed and moaned about not getting to take the reins of the Tatari empire, now he *gets* it and all he wants to do is take the money and *run*. What a peckerhead . . . sorry."

As they walked toward the exit together, Jessie thanked Charles and assured him it was good info he was getting. He again declined her offer of police protection, even though she told him she was worried about him, and pointed out that the three bodies in the burned house were probably Dominic's work.

"Oh nonsense, Jessie," he said with a big smile and wink. "God knows, I've been told I *talk* too much . . . but I doubt if I'll ever get *killed* because of it!" He waved and walked off, leaving Jessie alone in the stacks.

As Jessie drove away from the library, she tried to fit what she had heard with the pieces already in place. She remembered the child pornography strewn about the jeweler's office, the piece in the dead Tatari's fist. There was what Starlight had said about Scammer and Frog, and the character Sombiero knew as "Uncle Sam," who dealt in filth. Charles had done a good job, she thought as she pulled into the fenced lot behind the station on West Broward Boulevard, but he's wrong about one thing.

She got out of the car, slung her backpack over her shoulder, and thought, The little girl is the key.

"Ramone will be here in a few minutes, Jack. Stop sulking and come out of your room." Even as Tiffany stood in the bedroom hallway saying it, she fought to stay patient. "You've got to stop throwing tantrums every time I suggest we share something and both get enjoyment out of it." She heard the bed creaking, and the door was pulled open, and Jack stood before her, his face flushed. Behind him in the room she could see several stuffed animals, baseball cards, race cars and other toys strewn across the bed and floor. She looked up at him and waited.

Jack turned and moved past his sister into the hallway, and as he walked toward the living room area, he said without looking at her, "Oh, we've shared things in the past with no problems at all, Tiff . . . cars, boats, *things*. We even shared mommy and daddy while we had them, didn't we? And we certainly never fought about *them*." He walked into the kitchen, took a soft drink out of the refrigerator, and unscrewed the cap. He lifted it to his lips, then said, "This is different, Tiff, *so* different. I'm afraid you'll take advantage of me and *ruin* things." He took a long drink, his large Adam's apple bobbing. He licked his lips and went on. "Ramone is offering us a special gift, not like if we tried to go through some adoption agency or something to bring a playmate into our home. Even with all of our money, I'm not sure it would be approved. Besides, that's so *permanent*." He stared past her now, his eyes unfocused. "No. The poor little thing would grow and change, and we'd be stuck with it. With what Ramone has promised us, we can always have a lovely playmate, always the right age, always playful, always perfect." He lifted the soda to his lips.

Tiffany crossed the kitchen, got herself a bottle of mineral water, took a sip, and asked, "So, what's the problem, Jack? You know the games you want to play with her and the games *I* want to play aren't the same. And neither one will leave a mark on her all that much."

He looked at her and frowned. "I don't agree with that, Tiff. You like to play your games in bed . . . oh yes, you know I've seen you doing it." His face softened. "And you're so pretty and sweet when you do it, and then they want to be around you all the time, doing things with you. She'll be the same way. She's come so far, and she's so young, and you'll hold her and comfort her like you do me when I get scared, and then she won't want to play with *me*." Jack crossed his muscular arms, looked into Tiffany's eyes and pouted.

Tiffany began to relax, understanding now how to handle the situation. She rubbed her brother's smooth chest with one hand. "Do you think she'll *like* me more, Jack? Is that it? C'mon, you'll be playing with her all the time. She'll love being with you, and you'll be the best playmate she ever had. I'll take her to bed with me once in a while, sure, and I hope I can please her there. But I won't keep her there all the time, Jack, how could I? No . . . I think we can *both* make her happy . . . and keep her here with us until she isn't any fun, and then Ramone can have her back and bring us a *new* one." She reached up with both hands and cupped his face. She kissed him lightly on the lips. "You know I'll take care of you, Jack . . . I always have."

The doorbell rang.

Ramone Cindao had decided. The Eastins were the perfect couple for the deal. He smiled at Tiffany as she held the door for him to enter, and shook Jack's hand, noting the friendly grin and strong grip. The answer had solidified within the last couple of days. He had recognized that Dominic Tatari was like the worst kind of macho bull with an erection and an overblown male ego to protect. A young girl would stimulate Tatari, but he wouldn't know what to do with her when he wasn't tumbling her into bed. No, Tatari was useful, but he wasn't the buyer. That fat broker in Miami, The Hat, was a maybe, but the child would not be for *him*—he would simply sell her. No good.

He smiled as the Eastins made small talk and led him into the living room, and he sat on the couch. After a moment Tiffany brought him a cold lemonade. As he sipped it, he finished his thoughts. Tatari's current status was nagging him. There was talk on the street that the heat from the police was being turned up on Dominic, and now was not the time for *that*. He would like to finish the portfolio deal with Tatari anyway—*there* was some nice product that would turn a profit. Dominic was still good for local info too, like what he had told Ramone about that blonde lady cop being at the Eastins' party. This was definitely not good. The lady cop was magnificent, but she was showing up too many times. He wondered again if she was just a lady cop with the local police . . . or something *more*, and just playing a role. He had toyed with asking the Eastins what they knew of her but decided not to. He would caution them to be more circumspect about the deal now that things were coming together. Besides, he could always take action on the lady cop and make her ... *not* a problem.

"We're so glad you've finally decided to let us work with you on this," said Tiffany with a smile. "We could only guess you might have other potential buyers, and we just hoped you would pick us."

"That's right," said Jack with a grin. "We would be heartbroken if you thought someone else was *better* than us."

Cindao paused and lowered his eyes for effect. "Well, Tiffany ... Jack. To be open with you, I know financially you would have no problems." The Eastins shrugged. Ramone sipped from his lemonade and went on. "No, what troubled me, why I hesitated, was that you are brother and sister. In my, admittedly, meager experiences in this world, I have found it to be true that siblings will often fight over things or over affections."

Jack looked sideways at Tiffany, who kept smiling at Ramone, who said, "I really do want Isabel to be happy here for as long as you want her. I *don't* want conflict over her. She needs, above all, love."

Tiffany began to speak, but was cut off by Jack as he said enthusiastically, "But that's just *it*, Ramone! We *will* love her, and share her." He looked at his sister, grinned, and went on. "I'll tell you a secret, Ramone, so you'll see how we feel about each other." Tiffany's face took on a worried look, but Jack charged on. "We had made friends with Dominic's father, old man Tatari. Tiff used to go to his house all the time to swim and hang around. I would go too sometimes, but I didn't like the way that old man stared at Tiffany when she had no top on."

Ramone grinned at Tiffany, who just shrugged.

"The last time we were there, he was mean," said Jack, "accusing us of being in some kind of porn business with his son." Jack was so caught up in his tale, he missed the look that flashed between his sister and their guest. "Old man Tatari began waving some of his kiddie porn in Tiffany's face." Jack's face began to redden. "And yelling things, and Tiff told him to go to hell, didn't you, Tiff? But he started hitting her with the photographs, and he made me *angry*." He looked at his sister, then at Ramone. Then he bowed his head and said softly, "Tiffany and I are a team, and I had to make him shut up because he was wrong to yell at her." He gulped down the last of his soft drink and nodded several times as if mentally reviewing what he had just said.

Tiffany's face was flushed, but she was silent.

So, thought Ramone, the elder Tatari was found murdered, and even though young Dominic came to me in a panic asking for help in doing something with the body, and telling me he had found his father dead at the house, I thought he was just making it up. I thought *he* had done it. Ramone looked at Tiffany then and thought, And why are you letting your boyish brother tell me this now? A warning of his capabilities? A shared confidence to build mutual trust? And isn't it interesting that you will share a secret with me, but obviously you have not told Jack everything?

Tiffany broke the silence by clearing her throat and saying to Ramone as she matched his stare, "Jack may not be using the right example of how we feel about this, Ramone, but I think you understand what he's trying to convey." Ramone nodded gravely, and Tiffany, who sat on the floor next to her brother's seat, absently stroked his leg as she went on. "Other people have their games, we have ours. We will take care of Isabel, she will please us, and we will act in a quiet and responsible manner in this."

Ramone found he was becoming excited, knowing the dream was becoming reality. In some complex way he was sensing gratification from providing a rare and precious commodity to a unique and discriminating buyer. It was almost like selling a rare flower, he thought, delicate and beautiful, but ephemeral . . . fleeting in its colors and textures. What it was today, it could not be tomorrow, and therein lay its wonder.

"She's close now, Isabel?" asked Jack.

"Yes," Ramone answered carefully, "she has made the long journey and waits for me now with my trusted partner. She is in the Bahamas, and we will go get her soon."

"Why not let *me* take you over to get her in my boat, Ramone?" asked Jack, standing. "On a good day I can run over there really fast, and we'd have her back here in no time, and it would be *fun*."

Tiffany looked at him, and Ramone said easily, "You are very kind to offer, Jack, and I might take you up on it one day . . . but other arrangements have already been made. Besides, you understand that even at this point there is still the possibility of some . . . problem with the local authorities, and of course it would be better if you were not a part of that."

Jack looked disappointed, but nodded. Tiffany ran her fingers through her hair and stood. Ramone stood also and handed her a slip of paper with a series of numbers and the name of a bank in Singapore. Tiffany looked it over and said firmly, "Our deposit will be there for you to confirm in two days, and I agree with what you said about bringing her in. We'll let you handle that part, and we *will* be ready for her when she arrives."

Ramone took both of her hands and kissed them. Then he shook Jack's hand and walked to the door. "Maybe I'll bring her to you this weekend," he said with a smile, then left.

After the door closed, Jack turned and hugged his sister, lifting her off her feet and swinging her around the living room. She smiled down at him, her hands on his chest. He was very strong, and easily held her off the ground as he gushed, "Oh, Tiff, you were right as always! I don't know why I worry about things when I have you. You helped me at Tatari's and you helped me calm down before Ramone got here, and now, *look*—we're going to get her!" His eyes took on a sudden shine as he said, "Boy . . . I feel really excited now, *hyper*, even!"

Tiffany gave him a knowing look and said quietly, "You've been a good boy, Jack. Why don't you go into your room now, run a hot bath, and in a moment I'll come in and help you relax."

As her brother walked off with a grin, Tiffany shook her head and rolled her shoulders. *Whew*, she thought, that was close . . . though I doubt if Ramone gives a damn about what happened anyway. I wonder if this thing will really work. Ramone seems to have his act together, and Dominic will apparently play along. The police have been completely silent, there's nothing in the papers, and I haven't heard from Jessie Summer since that last time. She sighed, Damn, that was nice, and it could have been *real* nice. She thought about the beautiful color photographs Lona had taken that day. She had taken them to a small lab, a private place, in Palm

Beach for developing. Summer *was* delectable, but she was also a cop, Tiffany thought grimly. That little set of five-by-seven glossies should take the wind right *out* of any official moves, but Jessie was *hot*, and that's what Tiffany wanted to think about, not blackmail pictures. That, and the little girl waiting in the Bahamas, soon to be introduced to a whole new world of experience.

"I'm ready, Tiffany!" called Jack over the sound of running water, and Tiffany sighed contentedly as she walked to his bedroom.

Jessie got home around four that afternoon. She had gone back to the station after her library meeting with Charles to organize her part of the paperwork on the case to date. Les Stillwater had been called away to court on some trial from a year ago, and Melody Mitchell left in the early afternoon. She told Jessie she was having someone over for dinner and she wanted to go home and prepare things. Jessie asked if she meant *having* someone for dinner, and they parted in laughter, both glad that their relationship seemed to be getting back to its old self. Jessie worked for another hour, typing her supplements that would make a record of all the information, confirmed or unconfirmed, about the case. Then she left.

At home Jessie changed into old jeans and a work shirt and went out onto her screened-in back porch to tend to her "little jungle." She enjoyed nurturing the potted plants, ferns and small orchids. It had been a day of tentative rain showers, which by late afternoon had settled into a continuous heavy drizzle. Jessie spent an hour or so toiling with her small gardening tools and swept the last of the soil off the tile floor as the sky grew dark. She was putting things away when the phone rang, and she hurried in to answer it. As she spoke to her mother, she realized she still held the small spade she had been working with and carried it back to the porch and set it down just outside the sliding doors as she talked. Her mother was in a good mood, and the conversation was light and punctuated with quick bursts of laughter. Jessie considered telling her mother about Miguel Tirado and what had happened, but decided it wasn't the time. After they hung up, Jessie put on a pot of water for tea, stripped off her clothes, and hurried into the bathroom for a quick shower.

Jessie was out of the shower, had just pulled on an old pair of sweat pants, and heard the whistle of the teapot and the phone at the same time. She grabbed an old, large, comfortable T-shirt out of a drawer and shrugged into it as she hurried to the kitchen to turn off the heat, and answered the phone. It was Miguel Tirado.

"Jessie . . . I hope you don't mind my calling," he said briskly.

"Not at all, Sergeant Tirado."

Pause.

"Okay. Good. I . . . I have something to ask. I know of a small theatre, um, playhouse, in Fort Lauderdale, on Twenty-Sixth Street. There is a play there now, called *Papa*, by a local writer named John deGroat. It is about Hemingway, of course. I love all things Hemingway." She could hear him take a sip of something, then he went on. "I would like to take you there tonight, to see the play, and afterwards, dinner. Yes?"

"No," she said. Then, because the abruptness startled even her, she added, "It's been raining all day, and it's still raining and the wind is blowing and my feelings are so jumbled and intense that they're wrapped around me like an emotional Saint Elmo's fire." While she said it, she pulled the bottom of the T-shirt out so she could see the pattern on the front, and wondered about the coincidence. Printed on the shirt was a series of cats, all blue and facing the same way but one, which was red and facing against the tide. Above the cats was written "Hemingway House, Key West."

There was another pause, and then Tirado's voice. "If you won't go out with me, will you at least call me by my name, and not all this 'detective' and 'sergeant' stuff?"

"Okay . . . Miguel."

"Jessie, wasn't the other afternoon good, *more* than good? Was I imagining things, or did something very special happen then, did we not come together like two people who *should* have come together?"

Jessie wasn't ready for this conversation, but felt like she had no choice. "It was *more* than good, Miguel, more than I'd ever imagined it could be. It was special, and . . . well, very nice." She felt like a dolt.

"Okay, then."

She listened to his breathing for a moment. Then Jessie said quietly, "There are many things about me you don't know, Miguel, things in my past—and things more recent—that probably had something to do with . . . what happened."

He waited for her to go on, but when she didn't, said, "What kind of things? Whatever they are, I only want to know about them . . . about *you*."

"Things that have to do with *me*, with who I *am*, from my childhood . . . something from when I was a little girl, and that I've carried around . . . oh, *shit*. Listen, I am not some hot blonde who takes one look at you and drags you into her bedroom and rips your clothes off and . . . and—"

"And makes love . . . ?"

She still held the phone to her ear, but busied herself pouring the hot water into the cup, then adding the teabag. She stood, leaning against the kitchen counter, dipping the bag. Finally, in a small voice, she wiped a tear from her cheek and said, "Yes."

After another moment, Miguel asked, "And what do you know of *me*, Jessie?"

"That's what I mean . . . I—"

"I am a man who has lived all of his days to become the man you shared yourself with . . . and *you* are the woman who has lived all of her days to be there for me to share. I understand *completely* that what happened to us *is* special and rare, and of course there must be reasons, um . . . *causes* for such a thing to happen."

"You mean things like that don't happen to you all the time, Miguel?" Jessie said it to lighten the conversation, but Miguel took it very seriously indeed.

"*Never*," he said. "Never have I experienced such a thing, and all I could think of later that night was what could you possibly think of me, and I suspected you would never want to see me again because of the way I acted."

She squeezed the teabag, added a little milk, sipped it, and said, "It's still not easy, is it?"

Miguel was silent.

"Do you think it's too late to start from the beginning?"

"Maybe this *is* the beginning," he said, hope in his voice.

"Maybe we can go from here, learn about each other, find out if we . . . *like* each other . . ."

"Yes."

"So you'll go out with me then?"

"No, Miguel."

Silence.

She went on gently, hoping he could understand, "I have known for so long that it would be impossible for me to share what *we* shared with anyone that this whole thing has me totally off-balance. I . . . see myself in the mirror . . . my body . . . and I think of you and it's all *different* somehow. I don't know *what* I'm doing anymore, and if I'm going to begin something with you that might turn into something . . . important . . . I have to be . . . ready for it."

"So we'll go slow . . ."

"Yes. We'll go slow . . . and we'll wait until this case is done."

"This *case*?" asked Tirado. "The case is *the job* . . . I'm talking about *us*."

"I know, Miguel. But this case *is* us . . . or me, anyway—"

"Now I have to say I don't understand."

"And I'm not sure I can explain it to you, Miguel," replied Jessie as she hugged the phone to her ear with her shoulder and rubbed her forehead with her fingers. "I told you my feelings are jumbled. Somehow they are tied in with this case, I'm like . . . *drawn* to it. There's a little girl, and I'm . . . *drawn*." She stood in the kitchen, dark now because evening had come, and said quietly, "I'll have the time to work on *me*, maybe on *us*, . . . when all this is over."

She could hear him take a sip of something again, then heard him say calmly, "Okay. Tell me about something more recent. You said there was a thing from your childhood, and then a thing more recent."

So she told him about her afternoon in the sun with Tiffany Eastin. She told him about the nudity, about Eastin's coming on to her, about the touching. She told him of her mixed feelings of arousal afterward, and how confused she'd felt about herself.

When she finished, Tirado hesitated for a moment, then said, "I see, yes. If she and her brother are involved in this case, she may be hedging her bets with you. What I mean is, she may have deliberately made overtures to you as a way of . . . neutralizing your effectiveness as an investigator. Certainly you are aware of the problems a defense attorney could show with any testimony you tried to present to a court based on this meeting."

"Yes, but—"

"As far as your, um . . . *inner* feelings about what happened, she is a very experienced and sexually alluring predator. Perhaps she sensed in you a . . . vulnerability. It was an exciting day, hot sun, some drinks. I think you should stop beating yourself up about it." He paused. Then, "I mean, if you have *any* doubt about your femaleness, I can testify that you . . . uh . . ."

"Testify only to me, Miguel," she said, pleased.

"Of course. More about *her* . . . It is one thing to inherit riches, quite another to hang *on* to those riches. This Tiffany Eastin is a tough one, I'll bet. Who do you think is the toughest of the two—brother and sister? Who leads?"

"She does."

"Yeah, I'd watch her . . . watch myself when I was around her," he said.

They were both silent for a few minutes. When he began again, he sounded more businesslike. "How good is your Spanish, really?"

"Good enough to order off a menu, get travel directions, and fake out fat crime brokers in Little Havana."

"I enjoyed that, by the way, it was nicely done. So . . . when Sombiero said the Pacific Islander called himself 'Uncle Sam,' we did not laugh, no? But we thought, Could this be Ramone from the Philippines? How do you say 'uncle' in Spanish?"

"Tío."

"Correct. I thought about everything you have told me and everything Melody has sent to me, all the names . . . and I made a little list and carried it to a friend who works for the State Department. His family comes from Cuba, and he is a good man. Anyway. He is one of those computer worshippers, know what I mean? And he has access to files and current communications from several Federal agencies . . . from all over the world. I made it like a challenge, a game, and he loved it. This afternoon he sent me a very interesting bulletin." In a softer voice he said, "Jessie. The info originates in the Far East, and it concerns a Samuel Tío, a partner and a little girl." He heard Jessie catch her breath, then added, "I will make sure it is waiting for you at your front desk first thing in the morning, okay?"

"Yes," she said, her mind whirling. "Yes...thank you."

"Listen," he said with a small laugh, "you don't have to thank me. I'm doing it for my own good. The sooner you get *done* with this case, the sooner we can get...started, maybe." His voice changed. "Jessie, you are beautiful. I regret nothing. Take care." He hung up.

She held the phone to her ear for a moment, then slowly put it down. She stood in the kitchen for a while, going over the conversation in her mind. Then she changed into her riding outfit and rolled her bike to the front door. When she opened the door, she was hit in the face with cool rain and closed it quickly. She hesitated, took off her shoes, and poured a small tumbler of Gran Marnier. She drank it down, feeling the warmth, and looked out at the rain again. Then she put her shoes back on, pulled on her gloves and helmet, and pushed the bike out the door.

She rode the glistening wet streets through the dark Fort Lauderdale night for two hours. She rode hard, working her body while her mind traveled many paths. She was soaked to the skin when she glided back to the house. She took a long hot shower before going to bed.

Jessie sat at Les Stillwater's desk the next morning and read once more the papers from the buff envelope. She had ridden her bicycle into the station. The rain had finally stopped, but the streets were still wet. She had gone in through the front doors, picked up a large envelope with her name on it from the desk officer, and hurried back to the locker room to change. She had rolled loafers, pleated cotton slacks and a three-quarter sleeved blouse into her backpack, and she shook them out before changing into them. It would just have to do, she thought as she hurried to the Detective Division. Once there, she saw it was too early for any of her crowd to be around and settled down to read what Miguel's State Department contact had stumbled across.

The papers appeared to be copies of fax and Teletype transmissions and memos. Most had blacked-out spaces on them, so she understood they had been sanitized to the point where a reader could glean the info needed without knowing from whom or where they came.

She read:

Subject *Humberto Rawley* (see attached for crim bio/aka's/assoc) currently holding and moving under Philippine passport in name *Burt Rawls*. This agency obtained info in ongoing narc/weapons case Far East (see agency jurisdiction list). During hostile interview an arrested subject gave away Rawls/Rawley as buyer of false or stolen passports. Rawls/Rawley reportedly moving with female child, real name unk, Philippine passport name *Elizabeth Bell*. (Rawley flagged due to ongoing case equals narc/weapons/prostitution/false docs . . . see bio and assoc).

Subjects *Rawls/Bell* passport checks: Singapore-Delhi-Cairo-London-Jamaica-Nassau. Last known loc equals Nassau.

Subject *Ramone Cindao* (see attached for crim bio/aka's/assoc). Note: Subject flagged by several jurisdictions. Overlap probable. Clearance before arrest suggested. Manila agency reports home office close to moving on this subject ref narc/weapons/prostitution. Subject wanted ref child slavery/prostitution by several agencies. No cases made to date. Subject Cindao moving under Philippine passport name *Samuel Tío*. This is first record of that name use. Last passport check: Miami.

Subjects *Rawley/Cindao* known crim assoc many years. Several ongoing investigations target them, watch for overlapping. Weapons, radical group ties, crimes against children primary targets these subjects by several agencies.

Note: Level five this office warns any agent ref these subjects: They are experienced/dangerous. *Also*: Due to many agencies/jurisdictions with ongoing cases, proceed with caution ref arrest, equals subjects may by under umbrella by cousin agency as trade for info.

Jessie read it several times, unmindful of the bustle of dayshift secretaries and detectives arriving for work. Her eyes stared unseeing at the paper as she reviewed everything that had happened since the jewelry store. Now a little girl waited a few miles away . . . a little girl, real name unknown, who had been told something or scared somehow and brought halfway around the world to be *sold*. Humberto Rawley could have been the one driving the Cadillac that afternoon in front of Tatari's house, she thought, then he was sent back home to get the girl while Ramone lined up his buyers here. The cocaine deal generates funds, like the porn, but it's just false flame . . . like anti-radar chaff from a fighter jet. Cops and rip-off artists would focus on the dope, and Ramone would slide the girl in, trouble-free. Jessie looked at the papers again and said quietly, "Ramone Cindao. Humberto Rawley. Crimes against children. And female child . . . real name unknown." She pounded one fist against her leg as a tear dropped free from her eye.

Later that morning the rain was gone, the blue sky came with the sun, and the day became clear, breezy and warm. Tourists made their way to the beaches, further congesting Fort Lauderdale's already busy streets. Boaters were out too, sailboats and big yachts moving up and down the Intracoastal Waterway, causing the bridges at Commercial, Oakland Park and Sunrise Boulevards, along with Las Olas and Seventeenth Street, to open frequently. This served only to increase the lines of cars baking in the sun, air conditioners straining.

Jessie shared with Melody and Les the information on the intell sheet sent to her by Tirado. They understood her source was much like the "old boy" network. The info was real and could be acted on, but could not be backed up by documents or testimony. Melody agreed with Jessie's evaluation, but Stillwater cautioned them. He felt they should remember that cocaine was still *big* business, with heavy and fast money involved. They should focus on the drugs, and if they got the girl as part of it, all the better. They agreed they were technically unsure of what charges could be brought against anyone with the girl if she was unharmed at this point, but they had to find her anyway.

The info Mitchell and Stillwater shared with Jessie was more immediate. They had located the studio of one Pierre LaPont, underground photographer known in the local shutter circles as "Frog." Mitchell suggested they put the eyeball on the studio to get the feel of the place, then go knock on the door to see if Frog would talk with them. Then the phone rang, and when she hung up, Melody told the others she was wanted in a meeting with the patrol captain about her new assignment and schedule. "Finally," she said with a grin.

Les walked off to make a copy of Tirado's intell summary, and Jessie took the opportunity to ask Melody about the night before. Jessie saw that Melody's grin was in place, but her eyes had a hint of sadness as she laughed. "Oh, *Jessie*. That was some dinner, for *sure*. Lots of protein ... know what I mean? Un-*hunh* ... you should see the body on this hunk. *Too* tough. And my, he sure likes to play. You needn't worry, Jessie—I gave him a ride he'll not soon forget."

Then Stillwater came back, and Melody said to him, "So what you would like to do when you get over there, Les, is read Mister LaPont the *revised* Miranda warnings ... the ones that begin, 'You have the right to scream and bleed, and *everything* you say will be used against you if you survive this interrogation.'"

"That's the one, Sarge," said Stillwater with a grin.

Dominic Tatari beat them to the Frog's studio, and Pierre LaPont barely survived *that* interrogation.

Frog was again groggy as he opened the studio door in response to the heavy pounding, to find Tatari staring down at him. One look at Tatari's face convinced Frog to go easy, agree with everything, and pray the meeting wouldn't last long. Two things worked in Frog's favor. Tatari didn't know about Scammer's van being seized, and the portfolio Frog had produced with the last set of photos was of a very fine quality. Frog stood to the side wringing his hands as Tatari carefully examined the work under a bright light over the cutting table. When Tatari was done, he lovingly closed the book, turned away from the light, and said, "You do nice work, Frog. Did you make up fifty for me?"

"Sure thing," said Frog with relief. "There they are, all boxed and *everything*."

"No problem with the van the other night?" asked Tatari as he counted out the money. Frog just shook his head, but Dominic went on without waiting for an answer. "I parked your wagon in the alley behind this place like you usually do, and split. Everything worked out just fine."

Frog gulped. What had happened to Scammer was being graphically related out on the street, and the fact that Tatari so *offhandedly* killed Scammer, who Frog considered the meanest and craziest creep he had ever known, was terrifying. Frog had no doubt that Tatari had done it, and as he looked at the soft leather gloves on Dominic's hands, he wondered if he could get to the gun he kept hidden in the studio.

Dominic had similar thoughts as he put his wallet away and laid the display portfolio in the box with the others. I wonder if the little slimebag has a weapon here, he thought, and if I shouldn't go ahead and waste him right now. Could do him, take my time going through the crap here to see if anything ties me to Scammer or to Frog, and take off—hide his fat body, lock up, and come back tonight with my Zippo. This place would sure go up in a flash with all these chemicals and film.

He noticed Frog looking at him from the corner of his eye and thought, Yeah, that would clean things up, but what if that sonofabitch Ramone really *likes* this portfolio? We could make more money. He looked around again and smiled. Nah, he thought, too soon after the other three . . . get the cops all riled up. If Ramone and I can close the deal for this stuff and I can take possession of the girl from him—Tatari's face darkened—or even if the bastard turns me down and I have to rip him off, *then* I'll come back and snuff this asshole.

He told Frog, "Here's my car keys, put this box behind the seats." He waited inside while Frog did as he was told. When the fat little man returned, Dominic patted him on the shoulder firmly and left.

As Tatari's Corvette drove off, Frog scurried up the stairs inside the studio to the loft, then carefully out onto the rafters. Two cameras were mounted there, very sophisticated pieces of equipment he had installed months before. The cameras were quiet, and with their highspeed film and wide lenses could capture almost the entire studio area in sequenced still shots. There were several light and pressure switches in the place for Frog to covertly activate the cameras. Frog was, if nothing else, a survivor, and at the present time he was in a heightened state of fear and awareness. He wanted this deal to be over, and in the meantime he let his paranoia flourish unchecked.

Dominic Tatari traveled south on Old Dixie Highway only a block or so before turning off on a side street and heading west. He was thinking of the option of arranging a hit on Frog through Sombiero, since he had used him before with good results, and took little notice of the bicycle rider coming north on Dixie a couple of blocks away.

Jessie's thoughts were on the night before as she pedalled the bike through the residential side streets toward LaPont's studio. Les had had to take care of some things at the station, so Jessie took the opportunity to ride over on her bike, the perfect surveillance vehicle. She did not notice the Corvette as it turned off a main street ahead of her and disappeared from view. She pedalled slower as she came within a block of the address on Old Dixie, and adjusted the small flower-print backpack she always wore when she rode the bike. In it was her hand-held police radio and her service weapon, with extra full magazines. She was dressed in her biking outfit: black lycra bike shorts with a tight halter top, cross-training shoes with heavy socks, light leather gloves and a fiberglass helmet.

LaPont's studio was in the center of a small group of businesses occupying a row of warehouses. It was a bland wall of storefronts, each with a solid wooden door painted a different pastel color. The photo studio was the only one with no sign identifying it for potential customers. There were many cars parked in the area, and Jessie couldn't be sure if any of their owners were inside LaPont's place. She cruised past and continued north another block before circling back. She slowed, then stopped across the street a few yards from the door. She leaned her bike against a small palm tree at the edge of a low concrete wall and waited.

Ten minutes later Jessie saw Stillwater, driving one of the plain detective cars, come slowly past the warehouses. She made a small circular motion with one hand when he spotted her, indicating she would move to the rear of the building. She saw him nod, park the car, and slowly get out. He was almost to the door when she pedalled along the side of the warehouses and toward the back, looking for another entrance or alley that might lead to a rear door.

LaPont had climbed down from the loft, satisfied that his meeting with Tatari had been recorded, as had all of his meetings with Scammer, and he was beginning to breathe a little easier. He didn't hear a car pull up or a door slam, but suddenly he was aware that someone was at the front door. He never had walk-in customers, and his select clients always phoned first. He had a bad feeling as he pressed his eye against the peephole in the center of the door. The windows on either side of the door had been boarded up and painted over, so he knew whoever was there couldn't see him.

The person outside moved to one side of the door, but not before Frog got a quick look at him. Holy shit, he thought, look at the size of *this* guy. His breath came in short gasps as he watched one big arm with a fist stretch out, and when the knock came, it startled him. Tatari's venomous threats had spooked him. Oh god, he thought, it's either a hitman or a cop . . . who *else* looks like that? He decided he didn't want to know, grabbed his old .22 revolver from a nearby drawer, stuffed Tatari's cash into a pocket, and ran for the back door.

Stillwater pounded on the door. He wasn't sure, but it looked to him like the peephole had darkened for a second. He knocked again, sure that LaPont, or somebody, was inside. At that moment he heard the screeching of tires, a loud metallic crash and the painful revving of a car engine. He took off running, made the corner at the north end of the building, and headed for the back.

As Stillwater came loping up to a fence near the back of the place, Pierre LaPont, burning up the tires on his old station wagon, swerved crazily out onto the side street, skidded, and headed north on Dixie followed by a cloud of dust and blue smoke. As the wagon careened by him, Stillwater saw part of a chain-link gate in the street, and a small green metal Dumpster, dented in front, was rolling out of the alley. He saw Jessie's bicycle laying across the right side of the wagon's hood for a second until it fell onto the road, and for a flash he saw Jessie on *top* of the wagon, hanging onto the luggage rack as the car sped off. That was all he had time to see, then he turned and lumbered back to his unit, cursing. By the time he got to his car, Jessie and LaPont were already out of sight beyond a curve two blocks north.

Frog looked into the rearview mirror as he kept his foot on the gas pedal and tried to make his station wagon go faster. *Dammit*, he thought, what was that stupid girl doing back there on that bike? He knew he had hit her, but it sure as hell wasn't the time to be stopping. He stayed on Old Dixie, northbound, driving faster. As he approached the intersection known as Five Points, he was edging near total panic.

Jessie, clinging to the luggage rack on the roof of the speeding car, managed to turn her body so that she faced forward. She had found a gate one block behind the row of warehouses that led to an alleyway. She had ridden along the edge of the alley until she located the back of LaPont's business. Just as she had pulled up, the door opened, Frog hurried out and jumped into his car and started it up. She had pulled her bike against a small Dumpster and was swinging off it to yell at LaPont as the man made a quick backing turn and then jammed it into gear to come roaring right at her. She remembered jumping up and toward the Dumpster, then there was a crash, and she was lying on top of the car with her right knee aching like hell.

Now for one second she thought of trying to twist her backpack off so she could get to her gun, but the wildly rocking station wagon made that a deadly gamble. She thought she could edge over to the driver's window and yell at Frog to stop, but she doubted he would. She hung on, hoping he wasn't panicked enough to lose it completely and roll the stupid thing over. She looked back once, thought she saw Stillwater's car several blocks behind them, then looked forward again to see stopped traffic in front of them. Oh shit, she thought, what the hell am I *doing*?

A southbound train on the railroad tracks just east of Five Points had the whole area tied up. Frog looked into his mirror again, looked in front again, too late, slammed on the brakes, and rear-ended a bread delivery van at the end of the line of stopped cars. It was a step-van with no rear doors, filled with racks of bread and rolls. At that moment Frog was startled to see a figure hurtle across his windshield, bounce once loudly on the hood of his car, then somersault forward into the back of the bread truck with a crash. He was confused for a second, then thought, Oh *Christ*, that was the girl with the bike! He jammed the shifter into reverse.

Jessie, her fall broken by plastic racks of bread, shook herself like a boxer coming off a good punch. Suddenly she was very angry. She sat up, slid to the rear of the van, and jumped out as the station wagon was pulling back. She could hear the driver of the bread van off to the side, yelling obscenities at LaPont. She felt the pain in her knee but ignored it as she ran to the front of the wagon. She slung the backpack off and had one hand inside it reaching for her weapon as LaPont again put it into gear and accelerated along the left side of the stopped cars. Jessie, trying to run alongside, yelled, "Stop . . . *stop!*" at him, but he didn't even turn his head as he roared past her. The hood on the old car was crunched and steam was coming from underneath as the wagon roared through a funeral home entrance on the west side of Dixie, continued the wrong way for a few yards, and slammed over the concrete curbs at the corner in front of the old A&W hamburger place. Drivers waiting in traffic craned their necks to see what was going on.

Jessie knew Stillwater was coming up behind them somewhere, but guessed he would get hemmed in by the stalled traffic. She began running after the station wagon, one hand still inside the backpack. She saw that the car made it to the middle of the big intersection. It wobbled and bucked violently, its left front tire blown out after hitting the curb. The car headed at an angle toward the dry cleaner's on the opposite corner, but then Frog got it under some kind of control and headed north again. Jessie crossed the street still running, only a few yards behind the smoking car. She felt the sweat in her eyes, the burning pain in her knee, and the anger and fear in her guts. She wanted this guy, and sensed he couldn't go much farther in the lumbering wreck.

LaPont fought the wheel but the car pulled toward the left, and then it began stalling out, jerking him back and forth as he screamed and stomped the gas pedal. He was in a blind, raging panic now, not really aware of what he was doing, just hoping to escape. He narrowly missed a taxi at the end of the southbound lane of traffic, and then the wagon wallowed like a dying water buffalo as it came to a steaming, wheezing halt in the grocery store parking lot on the west side of Five Points.

Jessie, now running into the parking lot, saw Frog jump out of the car with surprising agility and take off across the lot on foot. She angled toward him less than one hundred yards back, limping slightly. She saw he had a gun in his hand, pulled hers out of the backpack, and let her eyes make a quick sweep of the lot. That's when she saw three *other* people with guns drawn, all pointed in the direction of the running fat man, and *her*.

Captain Bert Ford had finally agreed to take the two female patrol partners, Cindy "CB" Banter and Lynn "Linseed" Cappadonna, to lunch. He had come to realize that his macho swordsman reputation could have its downside. Apparently people actually believed in the workings of his "pussy posse." Banter and Cappadonna had been after him for months and he had finally relented, agreeing to take them to a small Chinese restaurant on Commercial Boulevard, where they gave cops a discount. Cappadonna and Banter were on their day off, so they were in civilian clothes, and they had been riding in Ford's car when Stillwater had broadcast the chase over the radio. They responded.

Captain Ford had already pulled off Dixie Highway into the grocery lot in an effort to get around the stalled traffic when Frog drove the wounded wagon in among the parked cars and people pushing shopping carts. Before Ford could unsnap his seat belt, both female officers shouted, "There he is!" and jumped out. They saw Frog waddling toward them, his eyes wild, and they both pulled their off-duty weapons, took firing stances, and began screaming.

"Freeze, motherfucker!"

"Police, asshole!"

But Frog didn't freeze, and Banter's big eyes bugged out and Cappadonna's spiked hair stood on end as they saw Frog point his small gun at them and fire it twice. Both of them tried to run backwards at the same time. They fired *their* weapons, bumped into each other, and twisted apart. Banter turned to her right and dove behind a parked car, but Cappadonna turned to her left, caromed off the front fender of Ford's car with her hip, and fell face down onto the pavement. During all this, Ford was crouched down behind the door of his car, watching wide-eyed.

Frog screamed, a high-pitched whine, as he ran wildly through the fleeing people in front of the grocery store. Even as Jessie got back to her feet after kneeling down when the bullets flew, she saw him crash through the front doors of the store and inside. She had seen at least one car window get blown out by the wild shots, but she was pretty sure LaPont had not been hit. She took a quick glance around and saw people lying on the pavement, some covering their heads or hugging each other. She could not tell if any had been shot, nor could she determine if Cappadonna had been hit. The bleach-blonde cop had stayed face down in front of Ford's car, and as Jessie ran to the front of the store, she could see blood coming from the front of her face.

Jessie could hear screaming even as she crouched, paused, then pushed her way into the grocery store. People were holding their hands to their mouths, pointing. Some were sprawled on the floor, some knelt by the registers. Jessie heard tires squealing behind her, looked, and saw Stillwater jump out of his car, gun drawn. She could see lights flashing in the distance. She turned to face into the store again, trying to see where Frog had gone. She followed the eyes and pointing fingers of the frightened people and began moving to her left, toward the produce area. Stillwater came behind her and moved off to the right, his face grim. The people in the store saw them moving, somehow instinctively knew what they were, and quieted. In a moment the only sound was heavy breathing and an occasional muffled sob.

* * *

Jessie moved forward, gulping quick breaths, her weapon in front of her, and when she found a frozen tableau of people standing and kneeling as silent as park statues, their eyes fixed, she knew she had come to the right aisle. Cautiously she inched her head around a stacked display of crackers and looked to her right. Halfway down the aisle, his back against a loaded shopping cart, his eyes as big as lottery balls, his face a mask of terror and fear, stood the Frog. The small black pistol was in his right hand, the hammer back. His left arm was held tightly across the throat of a little black girl, six or seven years old. The girl stood rigid, her eyes closed. Kneeling on the floor in front of them was an elderly black woman, her arms stretched out toward the girl.

Jessie felt herself become enveloped in a cold stillness. She took a long, slow breath and reached up and unsnapped the chin-strap on her bike helmet. She pulled it off with one hand and set it on the floor, then ran her fingers through her wet hair and across her forehead. She readjusted the grip on her weapon as a minute movement caught her eye at the far end of the aisle, and she saw Stillwater's right eye and part of his shoulder. She heard commotion behind her, sensed others rushing up, and used her left hand to wave them back, to caution them. She looked at Pierre LaPont, The Frog, and his hostage, and for the first time noticed the little girl wore a brace on her left leg, and a metal crutch lay on the floor near her. Jessie swallowed and, in the strained silence, even that sounded loud to her.

A police radio blared near the front of the store and Frog stiffened and screamed, "Don't even think about it! I'll kill her, I swear I'll kill her!" Several people gasped and Jessie heard the old black woman moan, "Oh Lord, oh Lord." LaPont moved his left arm, squeezing the girl harder, and yelled, "I didn't mean to shoot that lady cop out there, but I know I killed her, and now I'm *fucked*!" He took several deep rasping breaths, his eyes wildly surveying his surroundings. "I'm gonna walk outta here with this kid, and nobody better try to stop me!" The girl remained rigid, her eyes closed, and Jessie could see a tear running down her face as she began to sniffle.

Jessie looked behind her and saw many uniformed cops, then what she was looking for. Lynn Cappadonna leaned against Cindy Banter, with Captain Bert Ford beside them. They were near the check-out aisles, and Cappadonna held a bloody towel to her face. She must have busted her lip on the pavement, thought Jessie. She motioned to Ford, who crept toward her on his hands and knees. His face was pale and he was sweating freely. "How many were hit outside?" she asked in a hoarse whisper.

He shook his head, then whispered back, "None hit . . . all the shots went wild." Jessie turned back as he continued, "All the SWAT teams in the county have been called on this. Don't do anything stupid."

Jessie watched LaPont closely. She could see his hands shaking, the revolver in his right hand vibrating. The barrel of the gun was pressed against the skin of the girl's temple, just behind her right eye. The hammer on the gun was back, cocked, and Jessie saw with horror that LaPont's trigger finger lay inside the guard. All he has to do is hiccup, she thought, and that will be it.

Just then, LaPont tensed again and yelled, "I can hear 'em! I know they're moving in on me . . . I know they're gonna kill me!" He licked his lips, and the barrel of the gun slid off the girl's temple. He looked down at her, then carefully pressed the cold steel back against her head and yelled, "It'll be *your* fault if I shoot this kid! It'll be you cops who made me do it . . . I know you'll kill me, but I swear she'll be dead too!" He ended with a sob, and Jessie decided it was time to end it. She knew the SWAT teams had trained negotiators who were good at what they did, but she also knew how unstable this situation was, with that hammer back and Frog freaking out. She could not sit there any longer.

Jessie stood slowly, letting her weapon down by her right side. As she did, she ran the fingers of her left hand through her hair, blew out a puff of air, and said, "Mister LaPont, please . . . listen a moment." The inside of the store became very quiet. She moved to her left a bit, so that he could see her left shoulder and face. Frog tightened his grip on the girl and backed up. His hip hit the shopping cart, which moved slowly a few inches, one of the wheels squeaking on the tile floor. He licked his lips again, watching her. "I was on the bicycle behind your studio," said Jessie softly. "We were just there to talk with you, that's all. We need your help."

"You!" said LaPont. "When I saw that big one at my front door, I thought he was sent there to... and *you*... I thought I smashed you on your bicycle!" He paused and his eyes widened more. "Wait! I know you—you're that lady cop who killed the guy in the robbery. Sure, it was all over the news. You've got your gun now, don't you?"

Jessie ignored the question and went on in her quiet voice. "Mister LaPont, there's no reason to die here in this grocery store, and no reason to hurt that little girl. All we want to do is help you, so you can help us."

"What?" gasped LaPont. "*What?*"

Jessie took a chance and said, "Dominic is going to kill you, Mister LaPont. That's why we were there, to save your life." She saw the way he flinched at Dominic's name and she held her breath, her eye on the trigger of the gun. Finally he nodded slightly and she went on. "You have to put the gun down very carefully now. Even if we let you walk out of here with that little girl, where would you go? Do you want us to promise you a car and an airplane so you can make your getaway, while all the time our snipers put their sights on you? And *if* we let you get away from us, Dominic will kill you anyway." LaPont's eyes searched all around him. Jessie continued, "Look down at that frightened little girl you've got there. She's such a pretty thing, but she's already been dealt one bad hand, hasn't she?"

LaPont looked confused.

"Look at the brace on her leg, Mister LaPont, and those crutches," said Jessie in a whisper. "What kind of getaway can you make with her? Let her go now, put down the gun, and I'll make sure no one hurts you."

LaPont shook his head. "No! You're lying! I shot that cop outside and they'll kill me for it. They *will*!"

Jessie smiled, "No, Mister LaPont, you didn't shoot her. She got scared and fell down and hit her lip on the ground, that's all. She has a cut lip, that's where the blood came from. So far today *no one* has been hurt. No one." Jessie heard more commotion behind her and knew time was running out. She stepped out a little further, saw that Stillwater had crept closer behind LaPont while the small man's attention was focused on her, and saw Stillwater's weapon pointed at the back of the man's head. She let her faith in him take her to the next step.

"Look," she said in the same quiet voice, "here's my gun. I don't need it now because I know there will be no more shooting." She carefully placed the gun on top of the stacked cracker boxes. She took another step toward LaPont, her left hand reaching out. "Just turn the gun away from her head. It's time now, time for you to let her go. We'll take care of you now. We know you only take the pictures." She moved slowly toward him. "We know you wouldn't hurt a child, especially this one. Help us, and we'll make sure you are protected from the others."

She was very close to him now, her legs brushing against the kneeling woman, who still had her arms out in front of her, bent so that her thumbs rested against her lips. "Let her go now, Mister LaPont, before the SWAT team and the others get here and this turns into a *really* bad deal for you."

Slowly, slowly, the small black revolver moved down and away from the little girl. LaPont's left arm still hugged her throat, but as the gun moved away, Jessie could see he was trying to pull his pudgy finger from the trigger guard. "Careful," she said. "Just lay it on the shelf there ... that's right. Don't worry about the hammer now, that's right." LaPont kept his eyes on Jessie as he laid the gun down. Then he released his grip on the girl and began to fall back against the shopping cart. Jessie lunged forward, grabbed the girl in a bear hug, turned away, and rolled onto the floor beside the old woman. She kept her back to LaPont and tried to cover both the little girl and her grandmother as Stillwater made his charge.

The big detective's long arms and strong hands reached over the now-moving shopping cart, grabbed LaPont by the neck and shoulders, and lifted him bodily through the air. LaPont let out a piercing scream, hit the floor hard, and had the wind knocked out of him when Stillwater landed on top of his back. There was the thunder of heavy police shoes on the tile floor, loudly shouted belated commands, and more screams from the bystanders. LaPont was handcuffed, and Stillwater had to yell, "Take it easy—easy there!" at all the adrenaline-pumped cops running in to help.

As calm was restored, Jessie helped the old woman and the girl to their feet, still hugging them. The woman cried softly, and the girl comforted her.

Soon the brass came, and along with them, the media. The jurisdictional problems were worked out, and the charges. There were a few tense moments in a huddle of brass and detectives as Stillwater fought to keep LaPont's identity, or even his picture, from going to the media. The sensitive nature of a potentially violent investigation finally won the day for him. They were able to spirit LaPont, with a yellow emergency blanket over his head, to a waiting unit parked to the rear of the store. The media had plenty to shoot anyway, with Captain Ford and Officers Cappadonna and Banter giving vivid descriptions of their actions.

Jessie stayed with Stillwater, wanting to avoid any more publicity, feeling slightly sick to her stomach. Before they all cleared the scene, Ford hissed at her, "It worked, Jessie, but I told you the SWAT team was on the way. It might *still* be your ass when Allen and the Chief hear about the way you took this down." As he turned to walk away, he shook his head and said, "You must have a reason for jumping into these deals, but I'll be damned if I know what it is."

Then Cappadonna chimed in, her cracked and broken lips making her face even worse than usual, "You're a real swashbuckler, Jessie, you *glory hound*!"

Jessie rubbed her face with her hands as they walked away, and Stillwater, who had heard the exchange, said with a grin, "That's okay, Jessie. I want to hear the fairy tale they tell the Shooting Board about all the bullets they fired into that crowded lot out there ... and didn't hit anything but parked cars, lucky for them."

Jessie and Stillwater walked out the front door, through all the hubbub, and toward the detective unit parked sideways near the newspaper racks. They stopped and turned when they heard the little black girl, who was behind them, say shyly, "Ma'am?"

"Yes, honey?"

"I just wanted to say 'thank you' now for saving my life and for making sure my grandma's heart wasn't broken, 'cause she told me that's what would happen if anything ever happened to me."

She smiled, then looked down at her left leg and self-consciously moved the metal crutch behind her. "I heard what you said to that poor man about me bein' slow and him not bein' able to make a getaway because of me..." Jessie was kneeling now, brushing her fingers against the girl's face. She began to speak but the girl put her fingers against Jessie's lips and said, "You were right to say that to him, but I wanted you to know I can run pretty *fast*, and I can dance too, and I hope when I grow up I can be as pretty and as strong as you."

Jessie hugged her then, not trusting herself to speak. The grandmother smiled into Jessie's eyes, and Stillwater seemed to be studying something in the sky. Then another detective walked up and escorted them to another unit for a ride into the station.

Jessie and Stillwater drove back to LaPont's studio, checked that it was secure, and recovered Jessie's bicycle. The back wheel and part of the frame were badly bent, and Jessie stood frowning as Les juggled it into the trunk, tying the lid down with a piece of Crime Scene tape. She was quiet as Stillwater drove south on Old Dixie, across Thirteenth Street, to Seventh Avenue. When they got to Broward Boulevard, Jessie asked him to keep going south a couple of blocks, to the small park next to the New River and the Third Avenue Bridge.

Stillwater sat in the car as Jessie got out and walked over to a shady spot on the seawall, under a gumbo-limbo tree. She sat down and hugged her knees, rocking back and forth, and from where Stillwater sat, he couldn't tell if she was crying or not.

TEN

That same morning Salvatore "The Hat" Sombiero had another visit from the foreigner who called himself Uncle Sam. Their meeting was cordial. Sombiero was on his own turf, surrounded by loyal hard guys, and felt no threat. He was aware there was an irritable amount of local heat being generated by this foreigner, but business was business and he knew he could deal with it.

As it turned out, what the foreigner offered Sombiero was not exciting, or lucrative, for that matter. Cocaine. More cocaine was coming in, and the foreigner was offering The Hat a chance to buy in at pre-wholesale prices. How much cocaine, Sombiero had asked. One hundred kilos had been the reply, over two hundred pounds of fine quality nose candy. In an uncharacteristic sales pitch, Uncle Sam reminded The Hat that the toot could be cut and sold for the snorters, or cooked down into those dangerous and profitable little rocks for the crackheads. How boring, thought Sombiero.

They shared the small cups of bitter coffee and spoke of other business possibilities and connections. Sombiero was most interested in the time frame for the arrival of the coke. He asked too many questions, most of which his guest evaded, but got a few answers. To a possible buyer, the timing of the deal was important, so his guest assured him it was very soon, within a day or two. This did please Sombiero. Any answer to his questions pleased him, because a large part of his inventory to all potential buyers—good guys, bad guys, whatever—was information.

He and his guest wished each other well as they parted.

Ramone Cindao drove back from Miami confident that his plans were jelling nicely. Humberto had called him from one of the lounges on Bimini and explained in their simple code that he had made a deal for the coke, and he had also lined up two prospective vehicles for the other part. Humberto had worked with Ramone too long to express any misgivings he had about the complicity of the deal, but Ramone would have laughingly brushed them aside anyway. He felt things were fine, with the exception of the presence of that lady cop, and he advised Humberto to be prepared to leave Bimini for Fort Lauderdale on short notice.

As he took U.S. 1 north—slower than the I-95, but less terrifying—to Fort Lauderdale, Ramone reflected on his meeting with The Hat. He knew all about Sombiero's reputation as a dealer in information, and he was confident that before the day was out other ears would be warmly caressed by Sombiero's words of an incoming shipment of cocaine. A City of Dania police unit followed his rental car for several blocks through the small town south of Lauderdale. Ramone slowed, looking left and right, as if lost. He watched in his mirror as the police unit turned off and went back to his thoughts about Sombiero. "Stupid, fat pepper-belly," he said.

Jessie looked at her reflection in the mirror as she washed her face with cold water. She was in the ladies room down the hall from the Detective Division. She noticed that her hands shook slightly, she had a headache, and her stomach felt queasy. She mentally reviewed the monthly calendar, and sighed as she understood why she felt so rotten. That could explain why you've been so damn emotional lately, she thought. Then her mind flashed on an image of Miguel lying on his back below her, his chest muscles tight, his hands on her, and she said to herself, You're supposed to be *relieved* that this is happening now. She dried her hands on a paper towel, took two headache tablets from her purse, and headed for the water fountain. It was still bad timing, she thought. As she exited into the hallway, she spotted Stillwater motioning to her outside an interrogation room.

Pierre "The Frog" LaPont had gone weeping into his captor's arms. He was frightened, and it wasn't just the scene at the grocery store. The last couple of weeks had been working on him constantly. Being around Scammer was scary, then Tatari turned out to be worse. The threat of being killed was always there, and the pressure of knowing the police might be closing in gnawed at him daily. Now in the police station, he collapsed completely. All he wanted to do, he told Sergeant Mitchell, who had come back up to the Division as soon as she heard what had happened, was to get himself protected, and he would tell them anything they wanted to know.

There was concern in the detective's ranks that later, down the unpredictable judicial road, LaPont's confessions would be tainted by some appeal lawyer's claim that LaPont had been taken advantage of by overzealous cops. LaPont helped with this, explaining that he knew about lawyers and deals. Most important to him, he insisted, was that he be protected from the inmate population while in custody. The prison inmates wouldn't know the difference between him and a child molester, he explained, and he feared what they would do to him. He was pleased by the detective's assurances, and further pleased when he was told that the local news did not yet even know his identity.

"He's giving us a ton of stuff, Jessie," Stillwater said as he led her to a room adjoining the interrogation room. "He gave us Scammer on the little boy's murder, and as good as put Tatari right there, too." He paused, rubbed one big hand across his face, and went on. "He also told us about other children who weren't killed, just drugged, photo'd and dumped. Says the original negatives are still at his place, and we've got a team on the way there now—*with* a warrant. He told us he's got covert shots of Scammer in action, Tatari dealing with him, and other visitors." His eyes took on an angry light as he quietly opened the door to the room and let her in. "We wanted you to hear him on this one in particular."

Jessie stood to the side of the large two-way mirror set into the wall between the two rooms. Another detective was at the table beside her, monitoring the video and tape recorders. He nodded at her and gave a thumbs-up sign. Stillwater stepped out, knocked on the other door, and briefly asked Mitchell and LaPont if they needed another soft drink or anything. Receiving negative replies, he closed the door. It was a pre-arranged signal to Mitchell, who shifted in her chair beside LaPont and said in a gentle tone, "Listen, Pierre, I'd like you to tell me again about that photo session you did on Tatari's request. The one with the classy lady."

LaPont shrugged and said, "Sure, no problem. I told you it was different, because usually Scammer set everything up and brought the models and all." He stopped and raised his eyebrows. "You understand I was *afraid* of Scammer . . . he *made* me do this shit."

Mitchell waited.

"So," said LaPont, "Tatari calls and sets up this shoot. I had the impression he was just being the referral. Nice lady-friend of his, he says, she'll tell you what she wants. Do it, and no crap, okay? Right on time, there's the knock, but the lady is not alone— young teens with her, all girls. They're young but they're pros, chickens, you know? Very pretty stuff, no tattoos or any of that crap. The lady is a Madison Avenue chick, I'm talking *Palm Beach* here, a very fine and refined piece of uptown, er, pussy. Not like one of those expensive hookers either . . . didn't have the look."

He stopped momentarily to see if Mitchell would challenge his knowledge of class *or* hookers. Mitchell's face was tight, as if she fought to keep her feelings in check, but she said nothing. LaPont continued, "The lady has chilled champagne with her, a fat roll of cash, which she lays on me and the kids, and they all drink bubbly while I arrange what she wants. I have one part of the studio that's like a huge bed with silk sheets and throw pillows. In no time this lady and the kids are buckass naked, and, man, that lady was *really* naked, if you know what I mean. And they . . . had it. The lady was in charge, and she did what she wanted with the girls, and then had them do it to her. She choreographed the whole thing, even telling me if she wanted a particular posed shot or close-up. I just did as I was told, burned up a lot of film, and finally got tired watching them, really. That was a *busy* pile of splits—" he looked up at Mitchell—"Sorry. And they did it *all* . . . I mean, they did all they could without one of *these*." He patted his crotch.

Jessie, in the next room, held her breath. She looked at Melody through the glass, and saw the black woman's fists bunched on the small table, saw the tension in her stare. Her *own* face was flushed, and she realized her headache was worse than before. The Frog repulsed her, but his story fascinated her, and she already knew who the classy lady was.

LaPont finished with, "So, like I told you, Tatari set it up, but he wasn't there. The lady waited as the girls left, then took all of the negatives. She told me if I held any back, Tatari would have me killed, and if *he* didn't, she would cut my balls off herself, and I believed her. She left, and I swear I never saw her again . . . I figure it was some private kinky deal, like for her scrapbook or something." Suddenly he grinned. "Of course, I *did* have some negs she couldn't know about from those high covert cameras I mentioned. You guys will find them in my floor safe. The lady was in her late twenties, groomed and healthy. No jewelry, but that, uh, *pampered* look. Blonde hair, long legs, nice boobs with spiky nipples, good tummy, tight tush and a tongue that could pull the last olive out of a tall, narrow jar, I swear." He sat back, folded his stubby arms across his belly, looked up at the officers and giggled. Mitchell forced a friendly expression. "Mmm," she said. "And the man that set it up for you, Tatari's son—"

The Frog cut in, "No, uh, Sergeant Mitchell. It wasn't the kid. It was the old man. Dominic *Senior* was who contacted me for the lady."

"I've got something to tell you, Jessie," said Melody, her voice quivering. "I've got to tell somebody *right now* or I swear I'm gonna have to walk out of this fucking zoo and never look back."

They stood face to face in the ladies' room. Mitchell had slammed out of the interrogation room, grabbed Jessie's arm, and practically dragged her down the hall and into the only sanctuary she could find. Jessie saw how Melody hugged herself tightly, saw how the black woman's teeth gnawed at her full lips, saw how the tears had formed and rested precariously on the corners of her big brown eyes, and she said gently, "Tell me, Melody."

"People around here think I'm wrapped a little too tight because of what happened when my brother was gunned down on the sidewalk years ago, me bein' there and seein' it. They think I'm too quick with my fists because I beat that slimy child molester back when I was with the Sex Crimes Unit, and unprofessional because I had to ask to get transferred *out* of there. They think I'm a frigging sex goddess-maniac because I'm all the time dropping my panties for the next stud in line." She stopped for a moment, looked into Jessie's eyes, then turned her face away. She gazed at her feet, unmindful of the tears that now freely fell, and went on quietly. "Never knew my daddy, but my mother always had a man. One of her men raped me when I was eight years old... raped me repeatedly for about six months. Told me I had to do it for him, and then told me it would hurt my mother real bad if she ever found out, so I never told." It was very quiet in the room for a moment. Then Melody said haltingly, "He finally moved away, and that was the end of it... but, of course, it *wasn't*."

She looked at Jessie then, smiled a small smile, and reached out and took one of Jessie's hands in hers. "Took myself to a shrink," she said evenly. "Not that police department head doctor we're supposed to be able to trust... a private one, a woman. She told me all kinds of things about how I go from man to man seeking gratification and approval through the physical giving of myself. How I find it nearly impossible to hold *one* relationship together because my self-picture is so screwed up. *Shit*, if that ain't the damned *truth*. Men are hot for me, I get their balls all tightened up, rip their clothes off and fuck their *brains* out, Jessie, and the next day I can't even *look* at 'em—or myself—and I don't want to be around 'em after that."

She stopped again, and they stood there holding hands and looking at one another. Jessie began to speak, but Melody shook her head. "No... I don't know, Jessie, I just had to say something, to *tell someone* about it. Maybe it's this goddamned case, and that slimy Frog in there stroking his crotch and telling his freaky little porno stories. I swear to God, I'm just angry all the time, and this place, and the work we do and the things we *see* ..."

"You can talk to me, Melody," said Jessie softly. "I'm in this for my own reasons." As Jessie turned for the door, Melody said in a concerned voice, "Well, you know *my* reason, anyway ..."

"Yes, Melody," answered Jessie, without looking back at her friend. "And hear this. Maybe as many as one out of three. I heard on a morning news show the other day that as many as *one* out of *three* women in this country today may have been abused or molested as a child. I'll see you outside." Then she walked out and softly closed the door.

Captain Hi-ho Allen met with Jessie and Melody and Les an hour later. He listened to Melody's strongly worded request that Frog's capture be kept out of the news until they could wrap up his statements, catalog the seized evidence from the studio, and meet with the State Attorney to nail down a bullet-proof warrant for Dominic Tatari. Stillwater backed her up, telling the captain that Tatari would haul ass the minute he heard about Frog. He reminded the captain about Tatari's apparent liquidation of his holdings. Tatari was spooked, and if they wanted a shot at him, the bad guy from the grocery store had to stay invisible to the media.

Allen heard the request for a two-day minimum, then told them *they* had to realize how important this arrest was to the community and the Chief's office. This pervert Frog had photos of other kids besides the North Lauderdale boy. This could clear up missing person reports from all over, and if they ID'd any of the kids in the pictures, and these kids had been found dazed and drugged, their parents could be notified and professional help given, if they weren't already under therapy. Two days was too much to hope for, he told them, and then got to the real issue: Here was a chance for the positive police image to be shown. The people should hear on the news about the fine job their cops were doing. He didn't have to tell them the Chief's photo would figure prominently in all this ... right beside Frog's.

"You just do your jobs and let *us* worry about what to release to the media," he told them as he walked away from Stillwater's desk. Jessie watched him go, realizing he had totally ignored her.

Captain Bert Ford didn't think much of Captain Allen, but he understood Hi-ho's thinking perfectly. He knew what the Chief wanted, and he wasn't about to let a couple of detectives hold back on something that could help the entire department—and himself. He wasn't all that fond of Banter and Cappadonna, but understood that they knew how to tango when it came to mutual stroking. As for Jessie Summer, he had given her several chances and she had turned him down in that quiet, cold way of hers. She hadn't really done or said anything, she had just ignored him, and that pissed him off. She must be butch to reject *me*, he thought. More important was her always staging those hot-dog macho actions that made *her* look good and everyone else look bad. He could have saved that girl, he told himself, if Summer had given him a chance to move closer, but he had been trying to coordinate the SWAT teams. She had disobeyed a direct order from the ranking man on the scene. Actually, he thought, I could have wasted that little puke in the parking lot if those two patrol split-tails hadn't started jumping around and popping caps like a couple of twits. And of course, there was Summer running across the parking lot in her stupid bicycle suit, right in the line of fire.

He parked his staff car next to a pay phone and fished out a quarter. On the seat beside him was a file containing photos of LaPont being booked, the charge sheet and photos of himself, Cappadonna and Banter, and the Chief. He would give it to his source at the news and the source would break it wide open. He knew it would be meaningless for *any* info to be held back once Frog's identity was made public, so he was just priming the pump. After it broke, his source would do the payback in the form of Captain Bert Ford being portrayed in a quietly heroic way. For a brief moment he thought of Summer, Mitchell, Stillwater and all the other working hacks on the job. He dropped a quarter into the phone, dialed the number and thought, Damn hard-headed street cops just don't have their career priorities in the right order.

* * *

Les Stillwater drove Jessie and her beat-up bicycle home later that afternoon. Stillwater was quiet, preoccupied, and Jessie felt tired, hurt and sick. Her head pounded, her stomach wobbled, and her knee ached. All she wanted to do was get home, get out of her clothes, and lie down for a while with her eyes closed. On another day, feeling more alert, she might have sensed that they were being followed, or seen the rental car lagging behind them, might have seen it pull off when they turned into the driveway at her house.

But she didn't, and Stillwater missed it too.

Dominic Tatari truly enjoyed the feeling of the powerful racing boat he piloted eastward across the magnificent purple-blue Gulf Stream. He had left Rapier Marine over an hour ago, and knew the mirage-like first images of Bimini Island should be showing up on the horizon any minute now. He was alone in the boat, which was a production version of his thirty-eight-foot racer. The one he competed in was all decked out in warpaint, and had superfine blue-printed engines pushing perfectly balanced stainless steel props. He pushed his hips further back into the bolster seat, flexed his legs, and thought, This one right out of the factory isn't bad, either. Quieter, of course, with twin V-8's churning the props. The standard exhaust system wasn't loud, and it definitely got better fuel mileage than the tricked-out model. The hull was the same deep-V, hard-chined, heavy sliver of fiberglass that cut through the ocean, or crashed over it like a blue marlin on the prowl.

He had alerted the manager of the Rapier Marine sales office and dry storage facility, located just off the Dania end of Port Everglades, near the Florida Power and Light hot water cooling canal, that he would be needing a boat. He heard a slight hesitation and disapproval in the manager's voice, but a boat *was* available for him, and no one asked his destination. His good racing name and photo were all over the sales brochures, and his dead father's money, along with that of the Eastins, kept the accountants happy. It was Thursday afternoon now. The boat had been fueled and ready when he arrived for it. He had told the manager he'd have the boat back by late Sunday night. The security guard at the front gate would be notified and told to leave Mr. Tatari alone unless asked.

Now Tatari felt a subtle change in the movement of the waves and saw the first ghostly shadows breaking up the straight horizon. Bimini. Always a good place to visit, he thought, lots of fish, fun and chicks. And money to be made. He would tie up on the north island and check into the Big Game Club. Ramone would be there, and Humberto and the girl. If everything seemed right to Ramone, they would load the coke and the kid and come home.

He wiped the salt spray out of his eyes and thought about the situation. He knew that if his old man was around, he'd be screaming at him for taking too many chances. Why drive this mission yourself in a company boat when you could hire any number of willing idiots to do the job? Yeah. Well, things are too hot, too screwed-up now for doing things in a cautious way. Ramone and those mamby-pamby friggin' Eastins might not know it, but the heat was *on*. I'll show that rich bitch and her faggy brother who's got the balls, and greasy Ramone too. I'm takin' the cocaine *and* that little girl, and I'll be gone before they figure out what happened or where I am . . . and the cops will go sniffin' up their own asses, too.

He pulled back on the throttles slightly and let his mind go over things. My old man was a lying sonofabitch. Even when he was lying dead with his head smashed in, and I went to get Ramone to help me with the mess, I could hear him chewing me out. I still don't know who did it, but when that Filipino bastard told me about his gig with the jeweler, it worried me—maybe he and my old man got into it, and *he* cracked my dad's skull, the shithead. Well, in that case, this'll be payback time. A son should show his father some respect.

The color of the water changed from deep blue to emerald green, and he knew he had crossed the shelf and was over the reefs. The island could clearly be seen now, and he angled toward the channel separating North and South Bimini. His face took on a scowl as he brooded over what had happened earlier that day.

He had parked down the street from Charles' apartment and watched until the little man came home. He gave him a few minutes, then went up. He hadn't gone there to *shoot* the little prick, he thought. He didn't care about Charles, but he knew the heat was on and he sure as hell didn't need to aggravate things—that friggin' puke, Frog, he thought. That whiny, slimy bastard panicked and ran, let the cops take him, and then spilled his guts. Tatari had already been wired when he walked in on Charles, and when the snitch told him about Frog, Tatari shot him. Fuck. *I should have wasted Frog when I had the chance . . . I knew it.*

He was in the channel now, the sun getting lower in the sky behind him. Angling more to the left he watched the current sweeping the beach off his shoulder and let the boat idle easily into the bay. Almost no bridges left to burn now, he thought. *I'm my own man and on the run, even if the others don't know it yet. I'll act like a playboy tourist here for a couple of days, smile at Ramone, and hammer anyone who gets in the way when I make my move.*

He received a hero's welcome from the locals on the docks at Brown's Marina, and forced himself to relax as he headed into the weekend.

Six o'clock Friday morning the alarm kicked in. Jessie shut it off and lay back on the pillow. Her sleep had been interrupted by disquieting dreams, but she couldn't remember what they were. She saw her small dog, quiet cat and busy-body bird watching her from the doorway, and closed her eyes. She felt reluctant to get up and start the day, and she understood the cramps she felt in her stomach were being aggravated by the gnawing fear over the progress of the case.

That little girl was out there.

She pulled the bedcovers aside and slowly got up. She hugged a pillow to her face and caught the scent of Miguel. She lingered with it a moment, then slowly put the pillow down on the bed. She said her morning hellos to the gang and thought about the night before. The print media had the story of the hostage situation at the grocery store, with some photos of the location and a few of the police officers involved. Her picture had not been run, but the story contained her name and stated that she had confronted the gunman. The television news had blown the lid off it, though. Pierre LaPont was identified, there were scenes of his studio, and although Tatari wasn't named, the story told of a suspect associated with

LaPont, a man who owned topless bars, now wanted for murder. Within the hour both Mitchell and Stillwater had called. Stillwater was loudly angry and frustrated, Mitchell more subdued, pensive, dispirited. They felt control of the investigation was being taken out of their hands at a critical time, and they hated the thought that public image was more important to their bosses than actual police work. They promised to meet first thing in the A.M. at Stillwater's desk, to "proceed with vigor."

Miguel Tirado had called too. He had heard about everything, of course, and told Jessie he was both proud and worried about her. He had tried to kid with her a little too.

"Cars are made to be ridden on the inside, Jessie."

"It was the dirtbag express," she had replied, "and I only had a ticket for the cheap seats."

He had volunteered to drive to her house right then, to help her through the night. She had hesitated, at odds with her feelings. She knew how good his arms felt around her, knew how strong he was, knew he could make her . . .

"Not tonight, Miguel," she said. "I'm a mess, and I need to heal and rest and . . . be alone."

"There are times to be alone and times to share, Jessie."

"Yes, Miguel." They were silent for a time, and Jessie relaxed in the big man's even breath. "You'll be the first one I call."

In the shower Jessie thought about the last call of the night, the one from her mother. It had come after she was already in bed. Her mother had heard about the action from a friend in Fort Lauderdale, and she was upset and frightened again, full of misgivings about "that crazy job." That whole world was no place for her daughter, she had said, no place for a good girl, a talented girl who had better things to do. I tell people I have a daughter who went through college and now goes around talking to her shoulder, she had said, referring to the radio transceiver clipped to the uniform shirt. She thought being a detective meant getting away from all that shooting stuff. How long could Jessie go on living like a lady bachelor without even *looking* for a husband to settle down with? Her mother felt she should come down there for a couple of weeks, to stay with Jessie. Jessie had listened and tried to half-heartedly explain why she lived her life as she did, but she had said it all before, and she was tired now. Her mother heard the fatigue in her voice and finally said goodnight after getting Jessie to promise once more that she would be careful.

Now Jessie fed her gang, had a light breakfast, and took a couple of aspirins. Her knee was stiff, each step caused a noticeable pain, and she guessed she had probably torn something pretty good this time. She was ready to leave when the phone rang.

"Officer Summer?"

"Yes . . . ?"

"This is the Comm Center . . . got a message for you that just came in"

"Okay."

"Broward General Emergency says they've got some guy named Charles, says he's your informant. Somebody shot him twice, doesn't look good, and he's got to talk with you."

"Ten minutes—thanks."

The reception nurse recognized her and waved her through the inner doors of the ER. She was directed to one of the closest workrooms. It was small and crowded; several nurses and doctors leaned over a body on the table in the center of the room. The body was naked, with a small towel covering the groin area. The skin was very pale except where the blood had stained it. It was very bright red blood, Jessie noticed, as she walked closer and leaned forward.

"You Summer?" a man behind a mask asked brusquely.

Jessie nodded, looking at the face on the gurney, which stared up at the big overhead light. Charles had two tubes in his mouth, one in his nose and a loose bandage on his head. The doctor went on in a businesslike manner, and Jessie could tell he didn't like being interrupted in his work. "Took two bullets. One lower abdomen, one left side of the head over the ear. Lower shot glanced off the pelvis and went erratic. We don't know the damage there yet. This one to the head cut through the scalp, cracked the skull but didn't penetrate, and exited the back. Bad blood loss, as apparently he lay where he fell for hours, coming in and out of it. Finally managed to push a chair through the glass slats on his front door and someone heard it and found him. He was brought in here only an hour ago. When he's conscious, he asks for you.'' He looked at her then, his eyes almost black over the green mask. "He might make it, but he can't burn too much strength or time talking to you, understand?"

Jessie nodded again, pushed past a nurse, and leaned forward until her face was very close to Charles'. "Charles?" she whispered. "Are you in there? It's Jessie..."

The eyes that had been staring at the overhead light blinked and widened. They turned, and Jessie thought she saw recognition in them. "It's Jessie," she said again. "What happened?"

"Ta... Ta..." Charles tried to lick his lips with a bloody tongue. His mouth moved around the tubes. "Dom. Wild. Crazy mad. Dom comes with coke this weeeggg..." The small man spit up some bubbles of pink blood. The nurse wiped it away, and the doctor put his hand on Jessie's shoulder as if to push her out of the room. One of Charles' bony hands reached out and gripped Jessie's wrist, hard. He took two deep breaths and continued his labors. "Dom maybe Sunday."

"Where, Charles? Where will Dom come in?" asked Jessie, her whisper harsh.

"East house... old Dom house... marina... maybe..."

"The girl, Charles, what about the..."

Charles' eyes fluttered and he gulped violently twice. This time the doctor did gently push Jessie and said, "Enough, we've got to have him now." Jessie pulled her wrist from the tight grasp, turned to walk out of the room, and heard the struggling voice gasp again, "Careful, Jessieee... they... know... you..."

Mitchell and Stillwater were waiting for her when she got to the station. Jessie, who was still shaken, said, "Mom... Dad... I didn't think you'd be awake." Without a word Les pulled a chair and Melody put a fresh cup of coffee in her hands. They were silent for a moment as she sipped the hot liquid and got herself back together. She looked up at the two of them, nodded, and they went back to work.

Mitchell told Jessie they themselves hadn't been called to the shooting scene because none of the uniformed guys dispatched there knew Charles was their informant. They had the rough details. It went down in Charles' small efficiency apartment on the beach. He apparently knew the shooter because he let him in. Neighbors heard a loud discussion, but no shots. Hours later someone heard glass breaking. It turned out to be Charles' front door, and he was found. No good witnesses yet, only a sketchy make on the shooter. "But we know, don't we?" said Mitchell grimly.

Jessie told them what she had heard from Charles. It wasn't much, but each word was like a fiery signpost, showing them without question that the case they had been working on for so long was beginning to close in.

"So now we can add this hit to the info we've got out there on Tatari. All the local agencies have the BOLO already. No one at any of his businesses admits having seen him. His car was found parked in front of an apartment down in Dania, and at least two banks where he has accounts told us he recently visited his safe deposit boxes," said Mitchell. "That sucker's gone underground, running just like we knew he would, but he *still* takes the time to blow up Charles! What is *wrong* with these people, anyway?"

Stillwater said, "Power games and twisted minds—add money, spice liberally with coke, and it equals unpredictable and violent assholes doing things that make no sense."

Jessie ran her fingers through her hair. "Charles said 'Sunday' but we can't be sure, and he said either the Eastins', old man Tatari's house . . . is that still locked up as a crime scene?"

"Our lab guys are done there. It's locked, but it still has a dock," answered Melody.

". . . *Or* that Rapier boat place at the south end of Port Everglades," continued Jessie. They were silent, thinking of the possibilities. Finally Jessie said quietly, "What are we going to do?"

Before anyone could answer, they were interrupted by Captain Allen. "Mitchell, Stillwater, I'll need to speak with you both in a few minutes. Officer Summer, would you come into my office, please?"

Jessie looked at Mitchell, who just shrugged in irritation. She followed the captain.

After the door was closed and she was seated, Allen sat. He examined a file on his desk, then said, "Sorry to hear about that informant of yours. Guess it goes with the lifestyle." He cleared his throat. "The Shooting Review Board has found that you did not act improperly in the jewelry store shooting. Late yesterday afternoon the Grand Jury found no cause to indict you in reference to the same incident." He looked up at her. "This department feels you are completely cleared, and the matter is finished." He pulled her .9mm Smith & Wesson semi-automatic pistol from a drawer, cleared it, and pushed it across the desk to her. "This goes back to you now, and you will return that loaner to the armorer." He pouted and went on. "There are already questions about what happened yesterday with that hostage situation. Again you acted on your own, possibly taking action that could have resulted in catastrophe. Have you forgotten everything you learned since the academy about teamwork out here? Just because this type of John Wayne stuff works occasionally doesn't mean it's the professional way to do it. Understand?"

Jessie looked at him, and after a moment, nodded.

"Well," he continued, closing the file, "I'll leave any more on that to your immediate supervisor. You are off this temporary assignment with Homicide as of now. Report to the General Duty Detective Sergeant as soon as you leave here." He busied himself with a small pile of memos. She hesitated a moment, got up and left.

"Bullshit," said Mitchell when Jessie told her. "Are they jerking you around, or what?"

Stillwater pulled his sagging pants up, sipped his coffee, and said into the cup, "Brass assholes."

At that moment Captain Allen stuck his head out of his office and motioned to them. As they stood, Mitchell said, "Don't worry, Jessie. You can still work this thing with us, even if you're in General Duty. You're still a detective." Les stepped in to pat her on the shoulder awkwardly.

Jessie went across the Division area to see her new sergeant.

The General Duty Detective Sergeant was a man Jessie had worked with for a few months in Patrol when she was a rookie. His name was Hamilton, and she remembered him as fair, professional and likable. He had a pale round face and a quiet demeanor.

As she approached his desk, he stood and said, "Ah...Jessie, I wish I wasn't the one who got told to do this..."

She stood in front of his desk, waiting.

The sergeant handed her a transfer slip. "I got this first thing today. I had nothin' to say about it, and I'll tell you right up front I was actually pleased for a few seconds to learn you would be working for me. Then I saw what was going down, and...well, it sucks, it really does."

Jessie took the transfer slip that stated in neatly typed letters that she was no longer a detective. She had been assigned back to the Patrol Division. She looked at Hamilton and said with a wry grin, "Rats...I didn't even get kissed."

Jessie returned to Captain Allen's office. As she neared it, she saw Mitchell and Stillwater coming out, wearing angry expressions, and Captain Bert Ford going in. She wondered what Ford was doing with Allen—it was well known they detested each other. She walked into the office behind Ford. She laid the transfer slip on Allen's desk with a trembling hand and asked, "Did you have something to do with this, Captain Allen? And if so, will you explain it to me?"

Allen bristled. "You are way out of line to charge in here with such a disrespectful tone. I'm not required to explain anything to you, but just so you'll understand this time...the staff discussed the matter, and it was agreed that a transfer would be in the best interest of the department. *Sometimes*, Officer Summer, we have to consider the *common* good."

Ford cut in with a grin, "What's the matter, Summer? You made your point, now let somebody else have a chance to be cool."

"It has nothing to do with being cool, for chrissakes," snapped Allen. "Officer Summer, I told you earlier that your recent actions are being scrutinized. You are becoming too high-profile, too unpredictable. Another tour in Patrol might give you a chance to become reacquainted with how professional police work is done."

"But this isn't right," said Jessie through clenched teeth. "I'm as qualified as anybody for the job, all I need is a chance to prove it." She felt her cheeks flush, and she fought to keep the tears out of her eyes.

"There it is," said Ford, still grinning. "As soon as something like this happens, you girls start whining about job discrimination, or *sex* discrimination."

"What—?"

"Oh, come on," Ford continued, "you're blaming this transfer on the fact you're a woman, and not on your poor job performance."

Jessie jumped in, knowing it was an argument that would only make things worse for her, but she couldn't help herself. She felt the anger rushing up and she couldn't control it. "Are you telling me there's no discrimination? No selective assignments, no harassment of women cops who challenge bullshit—with all due respect, sir—like this?"

Ford jabbed a big finger in Jessie's chest and hissed, "Gimme a break, lady... we got skinny schedules all over the department because female cops are pregnant. One of 'em isn't even off her probation... she's sitting there on the front desk instead of out on the fucking pavement where she could be properly evaluated!"

"Who *impregnated* her, you—"

Allen stood, separating Jessie and Ford, who were chest to chest in front of Allen's desk. "That's enough!" Jessie and Ford glared at each other, taking deep breaths. To her horror, Jessie felt one huge tear form at the corner of her left eye, then roll wetly down her face.

Captain Allen composed himself and said, "There is no place for this discussion here, Officer Summer. Captain Ford, I must ask you not to use that kind of language in my office, and I would *caution* you about using it to a fellow employee."

Ford was too hot to care. He said, "Yeah."

Allen continued, "Jessie, I suggest you go to Patrol and find out who your supervisor will be. Meet with that supervisor and get your schedule. I recommend you take some time off. You seem distraught and emotional, and it could affect your job performance. Please leave now, and take any complaints through the proper channels."

Jessie felt a tear forming in her other eye, and bit her lip. She stared at the two captains a moment, then threw her gold detective's badge onto Allen's desk. "You can have this back," she said quietly. "My patrol officer's tin has always made me proud anyway."

Then she turned and walked out.

Les and Melody caught up with her in the hallway. "Hold it, little gal," said the big detective. Jessie turned, hugged them both, and began to cry softly. "This isn't fair, the timing, I mean. Normally I wouldn't . . ." Stillwater, misunderstanding what she referred to, patted her clumsily on the back.

She told them what had happened. "Off the case, huh?" said Mitchell. "Well, guess what? He told *us* to back off, too. Said there are other cases stacking up and we'd already spent too much time on this one. He said the staff was pleased with Frog's arrest, since that cleared up the little boy's murder, and who really cared about another dead crime boss? After the dead Tatari, he said Scammer, Starlight and Babe weren't a big deal either, and he was confident some cop would find Dominic after we put the BOLO's out on him. The case is pretty much a wrap, according to the staff; nail Tatari for murder, and maybe pick off a shipment of coke at the same time. No sweat, nothing out of the ordinary. Les can work it if there's time between other cases." She stopped and pinched her nose. "He also told us we'd done a 'fine job' . . . and told *me* I begin my new Patrol assignment today, right now." Melody shot a look at Jessie. "I am *out* of here."

Stillwater just snorted.

Jessie looked at them, saw the pain in their eyes, and walked away.

Jessie had a soft drink, then went to the ladies' room and washed her face. Downstairs she found Melody Mitchell in the Patrol Sergeant's office. It had been a half hour since the scene in Allen's office, but she still felt angry. Mitchell took one look at her and said, "Sit down here and talk with ol' hot-to-trot Melody Mitchell for a minute, girl. You look terrible."

"You don't have to talk about yourself like that to me anymore,

Melody," said Jessie with a weak smile. "And in addition to all the other crap . . . it's my period time."

Mitchell made a face and said, "Bein' around this place is like havin' the rag on all the *time*." She held up a schedule. "I just got out of my little meeting with the Patrol Captain. Got my squad assignment and the schedule. I lobbied for your bod. You work for *me* now . . . ain't that some shit?"

"First good news I've had all day," said Jessie quietly.

"There's more," continued Mitchell. "Our squad's got enough people to cover the schedule. You've got plenty of vacation time on the books, and I made out the forms for you. One week enough?"

The thought of some time to herself was nice, but Jessie shook her head. "Melody . . . we were just ordered to walk away from—"

"Look," Mitchell cut in, "this is *me*, Melody. We know it's not fair, but you're not a detective now and that case is out of our hands. You need to back off a little for your own good . . . regroup."

"We can just walk away, Melody? Knowing what all this might mean?" Jessie asked her friend quietly. Mitchell lowered her eyes to the desk as Jessie ended with, "Because the *staff* thinks the case is wrapped? Pardon my language, but screw 'em."

Melody was left wondering what to say as Jessie turned and walked out of the office.

Ramone Cindao sat on the beach with the young American couple. They were on the west side of Bimini, just north of the town area. The sun hung low over the expanse of ocean in front of them, heading for what promised to be a spectacular sunset. The couple's forty-five-foot sloop lay on the hook in the calm waters of the bay on the other side of the island. Ramone had spotted them earlier in the day, had seen the way they dressed in their homespun-style clothes, the book she carried, his knapsack, and decided to make his pitch. Humberto and Isabel sat on the beach too, about one hundred feet away.

"But everything we've read and heard about Aquino's government tells us she really is concerned about human rights and working toward a real democracy," the woman said. Her long rust-colored hair was in a thick braid, and Ramone could see she didn't shave under her arms.

Her husband had a full and shaggy beard, the same color as her hair. He had one gold earring and smoked a battered pipe. He gestured with the pipe as he spoke. "Sure honey, but you must always keep in mind that our government and big business was there cheek-by-jowl with Marcos, and they're still there. It's like Sam here says, things probably haven't changed that much for the *people* of the Philippines."

Ramone had approached them with a request for a ride across the Gulf Stream to the U.S., if that's where they were headed. It was, they had replied, but not until Sunday morning, and they were cautious about whom they let on their sloop, what with the crazy smugglers and pirates scattered all through the Caribbean, they laughed. Ramone had told them he understood, but there was a little girl who needed help. That got their attention, and he told them about the little girl who was a political refugee from Manila, whose father and mother had been killed by the death squads, and whose tattered family had fled in panic, somehow leaving her behind over a year ago. The family members had eventually made it to the U.S. and made contact with him. He hinted that he worked with a non-political group that tried to help bona fide political refugees. The girl had genuine Philippine identity papers, but there was fear that if she applied to leave the country she would be picked up by officials there. Ramone told the sailboaters he just wanted to get the girl to the U.S. without the American government rejecting her and returning her to the Philippine government—not Aquino, but those in the military structure. He fueled the situation by telling them the Bahamian government was aware of the girl, and would do whatever Washington wanted.

The young couple talked it over for only a few minutes before agreeing, apologizing for their seemingly flippant attitude before. They were glad for the chance to help their little sister cross the Stream. The husband took charge and made it clear, however, that under no circumstances could he allow any hard drugs aboard his boat. Ramone noted the "hard" distinction, and guessed there were probably a couple of pounds of good grass stashed against the inner hull . . . and smiled. They shook hands.

The girl alone would make the crossing on the sloop. That way, Sam could fly over and be waiting at the Bahia Mar gas docks in Fort Lauderdale. The couple had planned to stay in Lauderdale anyway, throwing the hook at the free anchorage at Las Olas Bight. They explained to Sam that they never flew a yellow quarantine flag, and the way U.S. Customs was set up, a boater coming in from foreign waters was supposed to call them on the telephone to report whether or not he was carrying any illegal contraband. Most of the time they forgot to call, he said.

Ramone told the couple the little girl would answer to Elizabeth, but, because of her traumatic childhood to this point, she was very shy and would turn away from most questions. He stressed the point that he was leaving the girl's fate in their hands, and hoped they understood the great chance for a normal life they were giving the girl, if all went well. The couple, secretly thrilled, nodded gravely and said they understood. They would make the trip a pleasant one for the girl and would not pry into areas of conversation that might make her uncomfortable. "We promise," the wife said, hardly able to contain herself.

The sun was almost gone when they were finished, and the sand flies were already making the beach untenable. They all stood, and the couple walked to where Isabel and Humberto waited. Without a word they both solemnly shook Humberto's hand and hugged Isabel. Then they walked to where their skiff was tied off.

Ramone watched them go, pleased with himself. The sailboaters were so low-key they'd be almost invisible, and realistic to boot. If things *did* somehow go terribly wrong, neither he nor Humberto would be anywhere near the girl.

Ramone, Humberto and Isabel joined each other at the hotel to have dinner together. Ramone walked with his arm across Isabel's shoulder; she hugged his hips, almost clinging to him constantly since his arrival on the island. She had missed him, she had said, and he knew she was feeling more frightened now that they were so close to her new life. He assured her again that her new home was beautiful and told her he'd be waiting on the dock when she arrived.

He had met that day with the Bahamian who would supply the cocaine. The man was almost too anxious, he thought. Apparently there was plenty of the drug to be had in the islands, and the price was nearly as cheap as it would have been at the source. Ramone had made sure Tatari stayed at the hotel while he and Humberto and the girl wandered the island and made their plans. The coke would be loaded that night, the two duffel bags simply tucked under the V-berths in the pointed bow of Tatari's boat. Dominic had told him all the normal boating paraphernalia would be piled on top of the bags, and that would be it. One of the bags had several one-ounce Baggies of the powdery drug near the top, for testing and samples. The cabin doors on the boat would be locked with a cheap padlock and the key would be thrown away, explained Tatari. Even if the cops somehow found the stuff, they had to prove that the boat operator had knowledge and access. Ramone had been happy to note that Dominic spent the afternoon playing with two secretaries from New Jersey, who were checked into the hotel, and it looked as if the games would continue into the night. Dominic seemed relaxed. Ramone had not yet told him what part the sailboat would play.

Now Ramone and Humberto waited outside while Isabel used the bathroom and freshened up before dinner. Quietly, without looking at him, Ramone said to Humberto, "Leave tomorrow. Do it... make it messy, so they will think it is just another rape-murder, then get out of there and fly to California, where I'll meet you. I'm afraid it is necessary, so I'll leave it to you. Understand?"

Humberto nodded. He was not displeased.

ELEVEN

Jessie left the station before lunchtime. She drove her old Camaro slowly through traffic, her thoughts jumbled. She went to the grocery store, enveloped in a comfortable loneliness as she pushed the cart up and down the aisles, taking things from the shelves in a haphazard way. Back at her house, she put the groceries away, made sure her menagerie had what they needed, and changed into her old sweats and a T-shirt. She turned the stereo to an oldies station, made some tea, and went out onto the screened-in back porch to do some gardening.

The sun was going down when the phone rang.

"Hello?" said Jessie, wiping her hands on a paper towel.

"Jessie? Miguel."

"Miguel . . ."

"Melody told me what happened, your reassignment and everything."

"Yeah, it stinks . . . I'm not sure what I'm going to do about it—the case, I mean. Can't do anything about getting jerked around."

"You could let this romantically-charged cop you know down in Miami feed you dinner and get you drunk on good rum and take you dancing . . . and other forms of nocturnal aerobics. Might make you feel better."

"Probably would."

Pause.

"Did Melody tell you about Charles, our informant?" asked Jessie quietly.

"Yes, she did. I know that hurts too."

"Yeah."

"Listen, Jessie," said Tirado. "About the case . . . El gordo, the fat hat, he asked me to meet him. Told me he wanted to speak with you again but knew there probably wasn't time, so he asked me to relay the info." He sounded full of energy and businesslike now. "He told me he'd been visited again by the foreigner who calls himself Uncle Sam. There was an offer of coke, a pretty heavy load. Sombiero says he listened but didn't commit. He said, by the way Sam was describing the deal, it would come in some time this weekend. That's all he would give me."

"That backs up what Charles told me," said Jessie.

"He had a personal message also," continued Tirado. "He said to tell you he is a bad man, yes. He traffics in many things, but he is not one who deals in any illegal way with children. He said to tell you 'Only a very *bad* bad man would hurt children,' and he is not one of those. I had the impression it was important to him for you to know that." Tirado paused. "One more thing, Jessie. He said Uncle Sam asked him what was known of you, something like 'what you really were.' Sombiero told me he got the feeling you should be extra careful on this case—"

"The case I'm *off* now?"

"Yes." Tirado paused again, then went on, his rich voice softer. "If I thought you were really 'off' the case now, Jessie, I'd remind you that you promised we'd possibly spend some time together once it was done. My offer of dinner and long walks and a chance to really *talk* to each other still stands . . . will forever stand." He stopped, and she could hear him breathing gently into the phone. "But in my heart I know you're not done with it yet, are you?"

"No, Miguel."

"So, I'll wait. And tell you only not to forget me when it comes time to look for reinforcements. Let me help you on this if I can. I will also confess to you that, although I have *beaucoup* confidence in you, I will worry about you until this thing is *over* . . . okay?"

"Okay, Miguel. I . . ." She began to say to Miguel that she

missed him, hesitated, then hummed a sweet goodbye to him.

After they hung up, Jessie called the hospital, first getting the runaround until Jessie was connected to a senior ER nurse who knew her and put her on hold while she checked with ICU. The nurse came back on with the information that Charles was still alive—there was serious internal damage, but the doctors felt good about the surgery, and the odds were he just might make it.

Jessie thanked her and hung up. She said a small, silent prayer for Charles—and for the "female child, real name unknown." She prepared a light dinner of stir-fried veggies, browsed over her bookshelves, found an old clothbound copy of a work by Anne Morrow Lindbergh, and became engrossed. She was surprised to learn how late it was when her eyes grew tired and she turned off the light, falling quickly into a fitful sleep.

Saturday morning came clear and hot, and Jessie was up early. Still sleepy, she walked to the kitchen badgered by the gang, especially Mr. Jones, who yapped and jumped at her feet. She put on a pot of water for tea and then opened the sliding glass doors to let the small dog make his first trip out into the yard. When he came trotting back, pleased with himself, she tried to work her body through some stretching exercises. Her left leg was stiff and sore and the stretching was painful, but after a few minutes it began to loosen up. She wrapped it in an Ace bandage, dressed in jeans and a pullover, and prepared to go out. She had no game plan, but she was too antsy to hang around the house.

Before she left, she got on the phone again. Charles was in the same state—alive and holding. She called the Marine Unit, and the FLPD Harbor Patrol officers said they would keep an eye peeled for Tatari and his boat, although they reminded her it *was* the weekend, and they were spread pretty thin. Then a call to her mother, who advised that she was still worried about her, but loved her very much. She grabbed the car keys, and the phone rang as she reached the door. She got it on the fourth ring.

"Hey, girl," said Melody. "It's me . . . your boss."

"*Buenos días, mi jèfe.*"

"Cut that out, you," laughed Melody. "You know us black folks can't even speak correct English, let alone one of those exotic heathen languages."

"*Se acuerdo, señor*," said Jessie, pleased to hear Melody's laugh again.

"Okay, okay. Listen, I got a fax for ya, hot off the rollers."

"Hit me . . . Sarge."

"Here it is: 'Subject Tio cleared Miami Customs Thursday PM. Local carrier, round trip single passage nearby island. Ticket to close Sunday PM. Take care'—that's in the message—'take care.' That Tired Mike must be one romantic stud-beaner, huh? Sends you a fax, all businesslike, then puts in 'take care.' Hm . . . be still, my heart."

"Melody . . ."

"Uh . . . do you want me to pass this on to Hi-ho or somebody, so it can be included in the file or somethin'?"

"Nope, just get a copy to Les."

"You got it. You have your take-home radio, right?"

"Yes, Melody," said Jessie, glad to have Mitchell as a friend. "I'll let you know if I need help."

"Good luck then, Jessie," sighed Melody. "And remember—don't get your panties in a wad if things start to break loose. You're on vacation even if you don't want to be, but if you happen to *bump into* somethin' out there, you revert automatically to on-duty status, right?"

Jessie smiled. "Copy that, Sarge." She hung up, and the phone rang with her hand still on it.

"I've got problems out here," said Stillwater. His gruff voice sounded agitated, and Jessie could hear traffic noises in the background and guessed he was calling from a pay phone. "I'm tryin' to work this thing even though we're *not* working it . . . but I'm skittish about rolling past that guard at Bay Colony, where the Eastins live. I could flash my tin, but I can't be sure if the guard isn't bein' greased on the side to alert people who live there."

"Why do you want to get in there, Les? It would be hard to take any kind of covert position without the whole neighborhood knowing it in minutes," said Jessie.

"That's what I figured, too, but I tried to get some help from

Harbor Patrol and they're short-handed and can only look in once in a while, if at all—the Eastins' dock, I mean." There was a pause. "Yeah, and I did some real detective work and found out Tatari *did* take one of those Rapier boats from that marina where they sell them. He was alone. I'm tryin' to flow from one spot to the other, but, as usual, the traffic is a bear, and I feel like I'm shovelin' shit against the tide."

"I'm coming out too," said Jessie, "so I'll cruise by all those places. Maybe I can get a look at the Eastins' dock from another isle or something."

"Okay. I think if they come in today or tomorrow, it'll be late in the afternoon when the boat traffic is really heavy. It's the same thing daytime smugglers have always done, and I guess it'll still work." Then he added, "Crap."

Before they hung up, Les told her to keep her radio on the detective channel. He'd call, using her off-duty number, if he learned anything. She agreed. Then she got out of the house before the damned thing rang again.

Saturday dragged by for them all.

The sun shone brightly, the beaches were packed, traffic east and west was slow, bridges opened and closed, jets took off and landed. Jessie managed to get into Bay Colony and onto an isle where she could observe part of the Eastins' dock. Jack's Rapier boat was secure on its lines, and there was no sign of life. She left and came back a couple of times, and drove by the other spots, too. Once, coming off the street where old man Tatari's house was, she pulled onto Bayview Drive just as Stillwater made his turn in. They looked at each other awkwardly, then she waved and told him to meet her at the Egg n' You restaurant, where they shared coffee and morosely read the papers.

Later Jessie drove south, into the port, and looked over the Rapier Marine facility from the outside. A narrow canal came off the Intracoastal Waterway south of the port and dead-ended at the drystorage docks. She saw that the Florida Power and Light hot water cooling canal emptied into that canal too, and remembered watching the gentle manatees, or "sea cows," feeding there last winter.

She met Stillwater again as it was getting dark. Mitchell joined them, having come off her shift and checked with Les over the radio.

They sat in the parking lot on the east side of Burt and Jack's restaurant located out near the cruise and naval ship berths at the south edge of the Port Everglades turning basin. They could see the Coast Guard station right across from them, and as the lights began to come on, they observed how the boat traffic had slowed.

"I'm tired," said Mitchell. "And I think I'm tired because we didn't do a damn thing today but fart around and worry about this situation."

Jessie felt the same way, and probably so did Stillwater, she guessed, but the big detective surprised them by saying quietly, "This case has been good for me."

Mitchell looked at him quizzically and asked, "How's that, Les?"

He had his arms folded across his chest as he leaned back against his car. He scuffed the ground with one foot. "It's the kids, I guess, and us workin' this case, and makin' headway, and keepin' after it even though they're tryin' to make a neat package out of it and put our asses on somethin' else." He rubbed one big hand across his face roughly, "Pride in myself... or something. And I been thinkin' about my own kids, gone since the divorce." He hesitated and they waited. Then he pushed on. "Dammit, I don't know. It's like I figured they had a new dad, and I was out of the picture. Now I feel like I want to clean up my act, re-establish contact, and *be* something in their lives that's... positive." He stared at his feet, embarrassed.

They were quiet for a moment, then Mitchell said, "I've got to admit, Les, your eyes have seemed more in focus than usual, and once or twice it looked like you'd combed your hair. But you've still got those *clothes*, man." Stillwater just nodded and smiled in agreement. Mitchell picked up a small piece of asphalt and threw it into the water. Then she said, "All this case has done for me is to make me more pissed off than I already was."

Jessie saw the pain in the black girl's eyes and the loneliness, but her thoughts about Mitchell's revelation were interrupted when

Melody added, "I don't think it's goin' down tonight. They would have been in by now. I say we pull the plug, and you guys can start again in the morning while I ride around supervising my patrol troops."

Stillwater nodded, then said, "What about getting Tirado to watch the Miami airport, and one of us watch the Fort Lauderdale terminal. That way, if Ramone *does* come back in, like your message said, we can tail him to where he goes."

Jessie shook her head. "Nope. Might spook him. He's hinky, he'd spot a tail in a second. Then he'd just take a dive and come up a week later somewhere else."

"What about notifying our government and the Bahamians that we've got info on a child smuggling case. I'll bet that would light a fire under somebody's ass."

Jessie bit her lip, still shaking her head. "No. No way."

Mitchell added with a huff, "Hell, it's the weekend. There *are* no governments on the weekend."

"What if every child in the world gets a tiny miniature ELT, emergency locator transmitter, surgically implanted into their bodies, say, the heel, or the buttocks," said Stillwater as the other two stared at him in wonder. "It would be set on 121.5, the Mayday channel, and could only be activated by a police agency as soon as the parent called in. I'll bet they could make 'em real small. They'd lay dormant until activated, then transmit for a good range for a couple of hours or more. We'd always be able to locate the child—maybe even if it was too late—if they were abducted or somethin'." He looked away sheepishly.

Jessie smiled and Mitchell rubbed her lip, hesitated, then said, "That's the scientific approach, Les. How about the spiritual-emotional-psychic approach? When a child is abducted or missing, all of the caring people in the world stop what they're doing, clear their minds, and begin thinking of that child... picturing them, saying their name over and over. It would be like a collective-consciousness desire that would bring a focused amount of positive energy onto that child. Maybe the child would begin to glow, or maybe one of the tuned-in minds would 'see' where the child was..." She stared into the darkening sky, enjoying what her mind's eye showed her. "All of our good energies combined would make the child glow and be safe, and that same energy would nail any person who was there to harm the child..."

The three of them sat under the few early stars, thinking about a better world and wishing they could help bring it around. Jessie hugged her two partners as she said goodnight.

On this night she didn't even try to fight it. The phone was quiet, apparently exhausted after its earlier labors, and there was no message from Miguel. Jessie put on her bike outfit and re-wrapped her knee. She had another "loaner," this time, a bike. Steve, the owner of the bike shop near Cordova Road, shook his head when he had seen hers, and gave her a similar one to use until her own was repaired. She cruised nice and easy, winding through the darkened streets, in and out of the dappled shadows. She thought of the little girl as she rode, and found herself humming a tune from an animated film she had seen a couple of years before. That girl was out there, somewhere. It was late when she returned home, and she remembered the last time she had ridden that late to soothe her feelings, and she sighed.

As the earth continued its inexorable roll to the east, the vast ocean changed from the wet blackness to slate to the metallic green that was the Atlantic. The southeastern-most Bahama Islands were brushed first by the edge of light rounding the great curve. Inagua and Mayaguana lit up, washed by uneven shafts of yellow-white— not much, but enough for a native fisherman standing in the shallows to see the ripples made by the backs of the baitfish, enough for him to swing his arms back and then heave the opening net with a barely audible grunt. The net fell with a hissing splash even as the light raced over Crooked and Long Islands, Rum Cay and San Salvador, where a group of desperate Haitians, cold and hungry and on the run to America, hoped their salvation would come. Still the light came, stronger now, more bright yellow and gold chasing the silver that edged the cumulus ridges. It caused the proud rooster to begin its raucous call outside of Georgetown, the Exumas, and over near Cutlass Bay, Cat Island, two independent marijuana smugglers looked at the dawn with a mixture of dread and excitement. Their old fishing boat, stuffed to the gunwales with burlap bags of grass, lay broken down. It would be a toss-up... would the engine part they needed from the States get there first, or the Coast Guard? Not concerned with the plight of those it warmed, the morning sun came to Eluthera, and New Providence Island, where slumbered a groggy Nassau, still smelling of rum and not too quick to respond. Andros, the Berrys, Abaco, and finally across the flats to Bimini, the morning brought with it a new day, a new chance, change, life and death. The morning brought Sunday to Bimini, charged on westward, and crashed against the Gold Coast of Florida.

Isabel watched the morning sun come across the broad expanse of water to the east. The hotel room was on the second floor, and the balcony faced the bay. Isabel knew it was Sunday and had awakened from a nervous sleep as the night was just turning to gray. She had crept silently out onto the porch still wrapped in a blanket, which covered the oversized Mickey Mouse T-shirt she used for a nightdress. She rubbed the sleep out of her eyes and watched the first pelicans and seagulls go wheeling across the sky over the bay. The swimming pool below her looked like a huge bowl of blue ice, rippled by an early breeze.

She turned in the webbed chair she sat in, her knees hugged to her chest, to look over her shoulder to the west, where *Florida* was. All she saw was her own reflection in the sliding glass doors to the room, the reflection of a little girl with sleep-tossed long brown hair, a pouty mouth and big brown eyes that looked back in question. A seagull cried and she turned her head back to the east as the fiery orange-red sun boiled up from the far horizon, burst through a line of low-flying puffy clouds, and kept coming to fullness, bringing with it the sureness of day.

After a quiet breakfast Ramone took Isabel to Brown's Marina, where they waited for the couple from the sloop to row in on their skiff. Isabel seemed quieter than usual to Ramone, and when he had tried to cheer her with stories of all the future riches in the

United States, so near now, it didn't help. The girl seemed distant, and Ramone was used to her being immediately entertained by him. He became impatient and snapped at her once after she gave him another noncommittal shrug. Ramone forced himself to stay calm, knowing, if Humberto was there, he would be cautioning him about the effects of stress at the near-end of a complicated deal. He shook off his irritation and had a big smile ready when the American couple tied off to the dock and climbed up for more hugs and handshakes.

Isabel was loaded into the small skiff with her bag. Ramone stood on the dock as the husband used the oars expertly to cross the bay to the sloop. Soon the three of them were aboard the sailboat, waving back at him. The American couple knew their boat well, and in a very short time they were under way, headed for the mouth of the channel. Depending on the seas and wind, the trip could take eight to twelve hours. The way the weather had been the last couple of days had the American couple guessing eight or less, and they had explained this to Ramone the night before. Ramone had again stressed he was leaving Isabel's fate in their hands, and the Americans assured him they understood.

Ramone watched them go now, Isabel sitting on the cabin roof near the mast. He was heartened to see the little girl stand and wave at him as the boat made the channel and turned out of sight.

"What's going on, Ramone? Don't think I can get the girl in? Changing things, trying to pull something over on me?" It was a sleepy-eyed Dominic Tatari, wearing shorts, a tank top and sneakers. He stood on the dock behind Ramone, who had been so absorbed in his thoughts he hadn't heard him approach. Tatari stood there now, his muscular arms folded across his chest. Ramone made a small waving gesture and shook his head. He was relaxed as he said, "No, Dominic, nothing like that. Come, let's get some coffee, and I'll explain." Dominic hesitated, then nodded, and they walked off the docks together. He respected Ramone as a player, but also knew the Philippine Islander couldn't read minds. Besides, the cocaine was now on *his* boat.

Over coffee Ramone spoke of the girl. The Eastins had the time, money and desire for such playthings, he said, but Dominic Tatari was a man on the move, a busy man who took his women when and where he found them, a man who made good money running a highly desired product across the Gulf Stream. Ramone had decided the girl would just clutter up the cocaine part of the operation. It would be unfair to ask Dominic to carry both when the heat could be generated from either one. The low-profile option with the sailboat became available, so he put Isabel aboard and sent her westward. That left Dominic with his go-fast boat, the cocaine, no hassles and the sure knowledge that there would be more little girls in the future for him to choose. Humberto was already back in Fort Lauderdale, Ramone told Dominic, available in case any surprises at all came up. Ramone would fly back today, so none of the three parties would have contact. It was like not bunching up, so that one grenade couldn't get everyone. As they headed back to their rooms, Ramone said, "We have come a long way, Dominic, and we are close to completing this deal. I am very happy for all of us."

Dominic, containing his growing anger, said, "Yeah," and choked up a laugh. "I like the way it's all coming together, too. Don't worry about my part of the run. I'll get the stuff in safely and I'll store it until we get a good buyer." He stretched and ran his fingers through his hair, not noticing how they shook. "Like we planned, I won't be leaving here until later this afternoon, so I'll arrive in Port Everglades with all the afternoon traffic. Since I've got time to kill, I'll be with those two sluts I partied with last night."

Ramone hid his distaste with a grin. "Some guys never get enough—right, my friend?"

Tatari strutted away. "See you in Lauderdale," he said over his shoulder.

Sunday morning came to Fort Lauderdale then, pink-orange-red probing against the silver as it came over the ocean and turned the beach yellow. Early joggers and speed-walkers were out, as were several people moving slowly across the sand in a high-tech version of the "Sanibel stoop," bent over and listening intently to earphones wired to metal detectors sweeping back and forth over the beach. One rusty freighter and one gleaming tanker lay offshore, both low on the water line. They waited for space in busy Port Everglades, and pulled on their anchors perpendicular to the shoreline. Traffic on A1A was light but would increase rapidly on a day that promised to be such a beauty.

Jessie awoke with butterflies in her stomach. She sat in bed a moment, her head in her hands, and speculated on what the day might bring. She got out of bed lost in her thoughts, went to the kitchen, put a pot of water on for tea, and returned to her bedroom. As she finished brushing her teeth, she noticed her small dog jumping around her legs. "Sorry, Mister Jones," she said sleepily. "You wanna go out, don't you?" The dog followed her out of the bedroom, past the kitchen, and across the living room to the rear sliding doors leading to the back porch. The dog whined impatiently as she unlocked the glass door and slid it open. Mister Jones jumped onto the porch on his way to the screen door and the yard beyond. Just as the dog leapt, Jessie sensed movement outside to her right—and Humberto came off the ground in a charge. He kicked the dog with his right foot, sending it crashing into the wall, where it hit and fell to the tile floor. At the same time, he lunged for Jessie with his left arm, grabbing the front of her night shirt and forcing her back and down.

Jessie, shocked and completely unprepared for the attack, fell backwards stunned, and Humberto was on her, kneeling over her, tearing at the nightshirt, ripping the cloth and pushing it up over her hips and waist. His left hand went to her hair as his right roughly tore away at her panties. Jessie didn't scream, but as she gasped, "What? What . . . ?" she realized what was happening to her. In that millisecond of comprehension she acted as she always told other women to act if they were attacked. She went berserk. She pulled her head to the left to get out of his grasp, and at the same time she swung both arms, her fingers taloned, at the big man's face. Her nails found one ear and his jaw as she kicked her legs, her shin and knee finding his groin. She heard him grunt, and his grip loosened and she forced herself backwards on the carpet with her elbows. Before she could wriggle out from under him, he was on her again, too strong, too confident—almost calm.

His left hand cuffed her against the right side of the head as his right fist pounded into her left arm. The burst of pain in her eyes and ear was like a white light, and she felt something let go in the swollen muscles of her shoulder. He lunged forward to put more weight on her and she instinctively slid back and raised up. He hissed and his hands flew to his face as her forehead smashed into his nose, but again her respite was too short. He was a veteran brawler, and he knew the outcome of this battle was inevitable. As she squirmed across the carpet on her rump, he came on, toying with her . . . smiling.

She tried to kick him, but he swatted her legs away and straddled her again. His huge dark form swam in her eyes as she felt a numbing helplessness envelop her. Barely able to lift her left arm now, she swung her right at him and he shrugged it off, his big right hand squeezing her breasts as the fingers of his left tore the remains of her panties away and dug roughly between her legs. She struggled up onto her elbows again as a roaring sound filled her head and tears filled her eyes. His hand forced her thighs open, reaching, probing, and she sobbed in frustration, shame and anger. Suddenly she was ten years old again, helpless, and he was so big and strong and rough, and she was unable to . . . she bumped against something with her right shoulder. She had backed all the way across the living room, and was up against the bookcase.

The man on top of her looked down for a second to shift one knee between her legs and she felt the hard edge of the bookcase dig into her skin. She flung her right arm up over her head, reaching, knocking things down, searching—she was *not* ten years old, and this was *now*—and her hand found what she sought and closed on it. Then, as he looked up to see what she was doing, she came down with her arm and hand with all the strength she had in her.

The longest spines on the Cabrit's Murex shell hit the left side of Humberto's face and punched right into his left eye. There was an explosion of blood and sticky fluid, and the big man reared his head back and let out a hissing scream. Both his hands cupped his face, the fingers like spastic spiders dancing across his skin, touching the sharp, burning thing that had entered his flesh. Jessie felt his weight go off her as he sat up on his knees, still hissing, one hand on the Murex, but apparently hesitant to pull on it.

And now Jessie heard another scream, a high-pitched wail of terror and pain, and she didn't know where it came from, and it frightened her to think it might be her. The scream continued, but now, using her elbows for leverage, she kicked him in the groin with both feet. Pain swept the part of his face she could see, and he grunted and fell backward as she frantically tried to scramble away from him. Her left shoulder failed her and he managed to get his right hand into her hair again as they both fought to stand. She came up with his pull and began hitting him in the rib cage with her right fist. He pulled her as he staggered back, his face on fire, enraged.

Finally, they went down, his shoulders across the sliding door track, his head over the tiled back porch floor. She lay across his chest, held there by his right arm. As she struggled to get free, he hit her again, in the temple this time, and his knuckles left a red welt. She gagged, flung out her right hand, and felt it plunge into her gardening tools.

Humberto was in maddening pain, trying to finish this while he could. He released his grip on her head with his right hand and moved it toward her throat, and she brought the small garden spade hard into the left side of his neck, under his ear. She heard him gasp and felt the blade dig into the flesh as she jerked it back and rammed it at him again, this time catching the side of his throat near his collarbone. He was twisting violently now, trying to throw her off him and squirm out of the path of that terrible, cutting blade. She heard him spit out a high-pitched grunt as she used all of her force to punch the spade into his neck once more, this time pushing it so hard she felt it cut through the muscle until it scrunched against bone. Hot, wet blood spurted against her fist and wrist and arm as he gagged and struggled under her. She began to cry as she hung on, twisting the spade in her fist, pushing it into him ... and still she heard that continuous wail all around her.

The fingers of his right hand were on her throat now, digging, but as she forced her shoulders off his chest, she felt them loosen, then fall away, and she looked into his face as the thick red blood bubbled out of his mouth, and his one angry eye began to fade and take on a curious and frightened look. The shell remained splayed over his left eye, and it looked to her like a small, alien animal on his face.

She stayed like that for several minutes, straddling his chest, her left arm hanging by her side, her right hand gripping the spade dug deep into his neck. She felt the shuddering breaths convulse in his chest... then he was still. She sobbed as she sat over him, her cries almost animal-like as she fought to keep her fear from devouring her. She forced herself to take several deep breaths, but began crying louder, close to breaking down completely. Then, under the keening scream that still filled her ears, she heard a small whimper.

She looked to her left and saw Mister Jones, conscious but in obvious pain, struggling to stand on all fours. His breath came in shallow gulps and his rear legs kept failing him. His tongue hung out and his big eyes looked at her blankly.

"Oh, my God," said Jessie weakly. She pried her fingers from the wooden handle of the spade and slowly moved off the big man's body. She knelt over the dog, lifted him gently with her right hand, and stood shakily. She stepped over Humberto's grotesquely splayed form, into the living room, where she lay the dog on a chair. She straightened, looked around, and found the source of the wailing: the teapot on the burner, sending rockets of steam up to the ceiling. She hurried into the kitchen and turned it off.

As the wail subsided into a gentle whistle and then stopped, she cocked her head and listened. Nothing seemed out of the ordinary ...just a quiet Sunday morning. She had a large yard with lots of heavy foliage, so it would be hard for any of her neighbors to see into her back porch. The struggle had apparently gone undetected.

Jessie, still in mild shock, her shoulder throbbing and the side of her head numb, slowly began to function again. She poured a cup of hot water over a teabag. From the hollow sound around her, she guessed that her right eardrum was broken, and her shoulder was torn badly. Suddenly she thought of the little girl and Ramone Cindao, and her mouth went dry. She looked down at Humberto's body, for surely that's who it was, imagined Ramone ordering him here to kill her. This isn't over, she thought—it's just *beginning*. She moved into the porch, placed her feet on either side of the dead man's head, grabbed his jacket, and pulled. She almost passed out, then fought back the bile in her throat. She gulped several deep breaths and tried again, this time moving the heavy body a few feet. Again she pulled, and again, until she had him stretched out lengthwise against the plants and ferns along the edge of the porch. She bent over him and reached out toward the shell. She wanted to recover it, to take it from him, to put it back on the bookcase shelf where it belonged. But she could not touch it.

Sobbing, she used an old towel kept with the tools to wipe the blood off her feet before stepping back into the living room. She closed and locked the glass sliding doors, and carried Mister Jones slowly into the bathroom and laid him down on the floor of the shower. She let herself cry softly as she carefully and painfully washed every inch of her body.

Ramone Cindao, traveling as Samuel Tio, took the morning Chalk's seaplane back to Fort Lauderdale. He arranged for a rental car and drove it to Bahia Mar, on the beach, and planned to have a leisurely lunch, read the local papers, and wait. He felt confident and excited about the prospects of the day, and knew Humberto could never understand the kind of thrill he felt as his plan came together. A vague feeling of unease swept through his mind like a chill breeze, but he shrugged it off in the hot sun, not wanting to diminish the intensity of this glorious day with foolish doubts.

TWELVE

As Jessie pulled her car behind the War Memorial Auditorium in Holiday Park, she saw Les Stillwater and Melody Mitchell standing beside their cars in the shade of a huge ficus tree that dominated the back of the building. Mitchell was in uniform, her car one of the marked units that had "Supervisor" on the front fender. They waited for Jessie as planned.

Jessie had managed to get herself dressed, forced down a couple of aspirins, and bundled Mr. Jones into a towel. She called the veterinarian's after-hours emergency number, then drove to the office on South Federal Highway, where they had cared for her gang in the past. The doctor arrived a few minutes later, and after checking the small dog, he concluded that a couple of ribs were probably broken. He told Jessie he would take custody of Mr. Jones, who would have to stay there for a couple of days. He had also been concerned about Jessie's condition as he looked *her* over. She told him the dog had been kicked by a neighbor, and that she had recently been in a car accident. He suggested she go home and take it easy. She left and drove to the park in a daze.

Now, as she slowly got out of her Camaro, both Les and Melody came up to her, and Les said, "*Dang*, Jessie! What the hell happened? You look like you've been mauled!"

"You're hurt," said Melody as she put her fingers gently against the side of Jessie's bruised face. "Seriously hurt. Looks like a minor concussion the way your eyes are dilated . . . you're holding your arm funny, and your throat is scraped. You can tell us what happened on the way to the emergency room." She tried to take Jessie's arm to lead her to the patrol unit.

"No," said Jessie as she pulled her arm away from Melody's grasp.

"Yes, Jessie. You're in no shape—"

"No." Jessie looked at them, tears in her eyes. "Listen to me, Melody, Les. Something terrible happened at my house this morning, and yes, I'm hurt. What happened has to do with the case, *our* case, and if I tell you what it is, you'll be duty-bound to take procedural steps . . . to . . . to do the right things." She paused, took a deep breath, and went on. "All I'll tell you is, I was attacked in an apparent attempt to keep me from working this case. Both of you have been hurt in the past, and you both still did what you had to do. Give *me* that chance now. Trust me, I can *do* this—I've *got* to do this."

"But—"

"But, nothing. It's going down today, we know it. The dope is coming in, the girl is coming in, Tatari will be there, the whole deal . . . and when it goes down, I want to be there." She leaned against her car and fought the urge to throw up. She looked into their faces, their eyes, "If I throw in the towel now and tell the brass what happened, you know how they'll react. They'll get caught up in my situation and fall apart on the rest of the case. They still think it ends with porno, coke and Tatari—but we know about the girl."

The other two were silent a moment, struggling with their feelings, weighing her words against how she looked to them and their feelings for her. Melody looked at Les, the big detective shrugged, and Melody turned to Jessie. "We're with you."

Stillwater hesitated. Then he nodded and said harshly, "Okay, let me ask you this: should we be looking over our shoulders for the badass who attacked you, or is he out of the picture?"

Jessie looked into his eyes. "Out. Big-time."

Stillwater's eyebrows went up, he made a face. "So be it. I talked with the narc sergeant. They've got a crack sweep going this weekend and can't help. Marine Patrol will keep an eye out again for Tatari, but they'll be busy too. I'll take the eyeball on that Rapier

Marine facility in the port. Melody is limited because she's on duty and will have to pay attention to her squad and zones, but she can listen in for us, and maybe sweep by old man Tatari's place once or twice, like on routine patrol. It's still locked up but there's supposed to be no one there—and it *does* have that dock." He ran one large hand through his unruly hair, looked at Jessie, bit his lip, and said, "Since you've been able to get into Bay Colony, you should take the Eastins'. It's agreed they might just sit there and have nothing to do with what goes down today anyway, so you'll also have to move around some—and I *mean* this, Jessie—if you start to feel worse than you look now, you get us on that friggin' radio and head for the nearest emergency room. You won't do *anybody* any good if you fall out because you're too damned stubborn to get your head examined."

The sailboat took a steady wind from her port side and easy following seas as she made her way west across the Gulf Stream. Isabel was delighted with the sailboat, the wonderful expanse of blue water, everything. Any misgivings had been swept away by the fresh wind, the creaking of the hull and stays as the boat moved through the water, and the feeling of freedom she had. So far, the only time she was uncomfortable was when she had to use the small toilet down below, near the aft cabin. The American woman kept giving her cookies and soft drinks, which was nice, but soon the need came, and when she went into the closet-sized bathroom and closed the door, the motion of the waves made her feel squeamish in moments.

When she finished, she rushed topside again and felt better immediately. Topside was where all the sights could be seen anyway. Big, pointy frigate birds circled over them, and clusters of flying fish jumped alongside the hull and went skipping across the waves. Once the American captain had yelled and pointed, and there, only a few yards from their path, lay a great big sea turtle, its back scarred and crusty, its head like a large coconut sticking out of the water. The turtle had disappeared as they passed by, its wide flippers splashing as it swam down underwater.

Isabel now sat as far out on the end of the bowsprit as she could go. She straddled the board with her feet hanging on either side. Every once in a while, when the stern of the boat was lifted by a large following sea, her toes would briefly splash across the top of the water and Isabel would laugh with glee. She hung onto the stanchions and leaned back, her long hair flying behind her in the wind.

She heard the captain shout again and looked down in front of the boat to see a group of dolphins playing on the surface. She laughed and pointed as the big mammals came closer, close enough for her to hear the air as it was puffed out of their blowholes. Isabel thought they were beautiful with their rubber-wet skin, triangle back fins and wide tails. The ones under the bow were just inches from her feet, and when they turned on their sides, she could see their eyes, and knew they were looking right at her. They seemed to smile at her as they played in the waves, jumping by two's and three's and running under the bow. Before long they began to disappear, until there was only one left, running just under the surface by her right foot. As she looked down at it, the dolphin broke the surface, smiled, and hit the hull with its tail, making a splash that wet her legs. Then it was gone, and Isabel put her face into the wind and looked westward.

Dominic Tatari took the Rapier speedboat out of Bimini later that afternoon. He took it easy going out of the channel, making a low-key departure in a clean boat. He wasn't worried about being bothered by the Bahamian authorities out on the water. He was well known on the island, and behaved himself there, and he guessed Ramone had probably slipped some cash to the local cops and customs people anyway, just as any careful smuggler would do. Once away from the beach and over the reefs, he pointed the long bow west, pushed the throttles forward, and settled back against the bolster seat. It would be an easy crossing with the medium following seas, and the sun felt good on his chest and arms. His mind became filled with thoughts of the little girl. He wasn't waiting for the next one, he was taking *this* one, and Ramone and the Eastins could have a good cry together after he and the girl were gone.

If he passed any sea turtles or dolphins along the way, he did not see them—and if he had, he would not have understood the big tears in the loggerhead turtle's eyes, and would have felt the smiles on the dolphins mocked him.

It became a timeless Sunday for those who waited.

Jessie existed in a cocoon of pain. She had a metallic taste in her mouth, and her head felt as if there were a plastic bubble around it. Sounds were muted and distant, and she felt dizzy and off-balance. Her leg was still stiff and sore, but she had been working her arm and could move it much better than before, although the pain was still there. She had vomited several times, and kept drinking ginger ale for her stomach. Without warning she would be seized by a vivid picture of Humberto, his hands on her, his breath, his weight, his fingers. His shuddering last breaths. His blood.

She had been across the canal from the Eastin home a couple of times and had seen absolutely nothing. There was no activity around the pool deck, the boat sat against the dock, and no cars came or went. When she checked in with Les, she got a similar report, and Melody was staying busy with patrol channel activity.

Jessie sat under a tree now, near the entrance to the Bay Colony gate. She sipped ginger ale and thought, What if we're wrong? Charles and Sombiero said it *might* go down today. Maybe they came in last night. Maybe they are all in some posh hotel in West Palm Beach drinking champagne and celebrating their good planning. Maybe the girl is here, and the life they've planned for her has already begun. Even in the heat of the day, Jessie shuddered. Damn it, she thought, everything points to today, we've got the likely places of arrival covered, and we just have to wait. And have faith. (Faith in what, she asked herself—in a world where bad things don't happen to good people?) She sipped the cool liquid and wondered about the world she lived in, about right and wrong, good and evil, life—and death.

Tiffany Eastin looked at her brother in frustration and disgust. You are such a little baby, she thought. She said evenly, "Jack, please. I am not trying to *run* things. I'm just trying to keep this simple and low-key. There's no reason for you to be upset . . . this is only the *first* day we'll have her. There will be many more days before we give her back to Ramone."

Jack, standing near the sliding glass doors leading to the pool deck, shrugged and replied with his back to his sister, "I think the first day is important. We want to show her we want to have fun, and I'll bet she would simply *love* a boat ride from that house to here."

"That house has been locked up since . . . since the police began their investigation, Jack," Tiffany said, fighting to keep her patience. "Ramone will have a new rental car, we'll have our sedate Mercedes, and no one in the neighborhood will give it a second thought. But if you go powering in there with your macho racing toy and tie up to the dock where there hasn't been a boat in who knows how long, every old fart on the canal will be wondering what you are doing."

Jack turned on her and pointed a finger across the room. "Who sees us arrive isn't the real issue, is it, Tiff? What you really want is to control what happens to us. Just like you always have. When Mom and Dad were alive, you always tried to boss me around, but they protected me. Since we've *grown up* and they're gone, you think you can be my mom and my big sister at the same time."

"And whatever else you want . . . right?" said Tiffany, her hands on her hips. She wore faded jeans, a halter top and sneakers.

"And whatever else I want, because *you like it*!" snapped Jack, as he pulled open the sliding door. He slid his feet into old boat shoes, jingled the keys in the front pocket of his shorts, and pulled at the webbed fabric of the tank top he wore.

"Oh, Tiff," he went on, "just this once, I think I'm right, and you're being too cautious and stodgy at the same time. I'm taking the boat for a ride, and then I'll meet you at Tatari's house like Ramone planned." He grinned at his sister. "*You* bring the car . . . and we'll let *Isabel* decide who she wants to ride home with." He closed the door and walked off across the pool deck toward the boat with long strides.

Tiffany watched him go, blew a puff of air at the shock of hair hanging over her forehead, and, in a kindergarten-school voice, said, "Can you say . . . *asshole*?"

* * *

Tiffany was wrong about her brother's boat causing a commotion in the neighborhood. It didn't have racing exhausts, so it was quiet. It looked respectable and so did the operator. If anyone did notice Jack ease in and tie up at Tatari's dock, they paid no more attention to it than a passing glance.

It was late afternoon when Jack climbed out of the boat, walked across the back yard, and came to the screened porch around the pool. The screen was still torn where Jessie Summer had let herself in weeks ago, but Jack didn't give that a thought as he let himself in. He saw that the sliding glass doors leading from the kitchen-dining area to the pool deck were locked and secured with pins. He figured the police must have done that when they left. There were no signs of a police search, no crime scene tape or warning posters. He used the key he had made from the one Tiffany had and let himself in a back bedroom door. Once inside, he realized with horror that Tatari must have had the place alarmed, so he hurried to the living room. Beside the front door was an alarm panel, but it showed an inactive light, and Jack let out a long sigh. Dumb cops probably didn't know the code, he thought.

He wandered through the house, looking in all the rooms. The house seemed quiet, poised, as if waiting. It was cool, the air-conditioning working the whole time. The only signs of a police search inside were closet doors and bureau doors being open and the black, soot-like fingerprint dust that powdered the doorjambs and some pieces of furniture. He walked through the living room to the kitchen and noticed one of the carved wooden figures was missing from beside the entranceway. The *right* one, he thought. He opened the refrigerator and saw it was still cold and well stocked. He grabbed a beer and looked around with a grin. It felt funny to be standing in the house where it happened, where he had done it to old man Tatari . . . but strangely exciting too. He remembered how angry he had been then, and the feeling of power he felt when it was over. Tatari had always treated him like a child, he remembered with a scowl, but he had looked at him differently at the very end. Yes. He shouldn't have said that stuff about Tiff, and those ugly photos he was waving in her face... what a creep. Served him right.

He thought of something else and returned to the living room. Along the west wall of the open room was one of those heavy old-fashioned wooden bars with the lift-open tops and bottles in circular racks. One side had an ice bucket and bar tools, and the other had the glasses and shakers and things. He thought about the last time he was there, how Tatari had reached in and pushed right... here, then pulled down, and the front panel in the center of the bar opened to reveal several shelves built under the liquor storage cabinet. The cops, in their general search, probably with orders not to destroy property and not having information on secret hideaways, would never have found this, he thought. He had seen the bedroom where they *had* found one floor safe and a wall safe, but they missed this. He knelt down, sipped from the beer, and looked on the shelves.

There was a lot of cash, in bundles. Looked like around one hundred thousand, he thought. The money looked somehow sinister sitting there, but it didn't interest him. Along with the money lay several large manila envelopes. It was from one of these that Tatari had pulled the ugly pictures he waved in Tiffany's face. He saw that his hand shook slightly as he knelt there on the carpet, opened one of the envelopes, and poured the photos out across his knees. More of the same, he thought grimly. Young, pretty people doing things to each other. Some were like expensive magazines, and he remembered tearing one out of Tatari's fist just before it was over. He emptied another of the envelopes and began spreading the pictures out with his fingers, drinking his beer at the same time.

Then he stopped.

Slowly he put the beer down and leaned forward. All of the pictures from this envelope were of girls, doing it. Suddenly he realized they were much younger than girls in the other shots. Some looked like they were not even teens. He picked up one photo, holding it like it might bite him, and examined it with a mixture of dread and anger. It had captured Tiffany with that look on her face as she gazed down at one of the young girls. Tiffany in this one, that one, he rifled through them. The pictures were very graphic, and in the ones where he could see her face, he recognized that look of rapture and power and control he knew so well, and it impacted him with a cold intensity he had never felt before.

He let the photos drop from his fingers and stared at them, unseeing. That filthy old man Tatari was right, he thought, Tiffany *did* do it on camera, and she must have been selling them somehow, or why else would she do it? He felt the cold beer on his wrist and looked down to see his hand gripping the bottle so hard his fingers were white. Ramone, he thought, she must have been hooked up with Ramone somehow and didn't even *tell* me. And she let herself get photographed doing it with these pretty kids, enjoying it the whole time, so she could sell the pictures to people like Tatari who would look at them and...

"*Tiffany!*" he shouted to the empty house as he threw the beer bottle across the room. Tatari knew, and Ramone knew, and they didn't tell *me*, he thought, tears forming in his eyes. They kept it to themselves, and all the time I'll bet they planned to use this little girl, this Isabel, for more pictures. He sat down in the middle of the room, legs crossed Indian fashion, and cried. He made a fist and pounded it onto the carpet, saying to the house, "I *know* Tiff likes to play with girls, and I know she'll do it with Isabel, but it's supposed to be our secret, a *private* thing, not to share with wicked old farts like some cheap skin magazine!" He thought of Ramone and Tatari and his sister conspiring against him, keeping secrets from him, and his anger turned to a jealous rage while he waited for them to arrive.

The sailboat docked at the Bahia Mar gas dock. Ramone was there to meet it, and he solemnly shook hands with the American couple onboard. Then they hugged Isabel again, the woman seeming reluctant to let her go, and wished them "good luck, and Godspeed." Ramone thanked them with a smile, and he and Isabel stood waving as the sloop cast off and headed for the anchorage near the Las Olas Bridge. Moments later Ramone held the door for Isabel as they climbed into the rental car. After he pulled out of the lot and onto A1A, he put his arm around the girl's shoulders, marveled at her simple beauty even in the plain shorts and loose cotton shirt she wore, and said, "It won't be long now, my precious."

* * *

It was only minutes later that Stillwater's voice came over the radio, steady but tense. "I see him, bigger than life. He's alone, I think. He just came off the ICW, and he's headed for the marina. I don't see anybody else on board, unless they're down in that forward cabin."

Dominic Tatari was turning off the Intracoastal Waterway into the access canal leading to Rapier Marine.

Jessie hadn't heard Melody on the radio for some time now, so she answered Les, "I just left the Tatari house a few minutes ago, Les, it was quiet, but I could only see it from the front. No cars. I'll head your way as backup. Maybe we can secure Dominic real fast, and by then the rest will show at the house."

Stillwater came back with, "That sounds right. He's almost to the dock now, and I'm gonna head for the front entrance to the facility. If I can detain him, we'll play the paper game until the dispatcher can dig up a Customs guy to do a search of the boat."

"I'm on the way, Les," answered Jessie, "but the traffic is *bad*. You be careful—he *is* a murder suspect. Just keep an eye on him until I get there."

"Roger-dodger, over and out, wilco," replied the big detective.

Tatari threw a line over a cleat and pulled the boat snug against the dock. He shut the engines off and looked around the marina. It was closed on Sundays, and there was no movement at all. The dry storage was for long-term contracts, and Rapier sales had an office in Bahia Mar. This facility was where they prepped the new boats and worked on mechanical problems. Seeing nothing out of the ordinary, he turned and used a screwdriver to break the small padlock on the louvered wooden cabin doors. He crawled inside, pulled up the cushions on the V-bunks, dragged out all the marine gear, and, finally, the duffels themselves. From the top of one he pulled several one-ounce Baggies of the cocaine and stuffed them into his pockets. Could use a little blast, he thought, and backed out of the cabin. As he stood, he felt eyes on him, turned, and saw nothing. He bit his lip, staring into the sky, and began to think of Ramone, the Eastins and the girl. This is bullshit, he thought, I'm here, not a fucking cop on the water or anywhere else to see me or stop me, and they've got the girl at the other end of town. Why the hell did I come *here* anyway? If I'm gonna make a move and get out of here quick, I've got to *do it*. He reached forward, made sure the clutches were in neutral, and fired up the starboard engine.

"*Whoa*, cowboy—shut it *down*! Police!" yelled Stillwater as he ran, pointing his .38 caliber Chief's Special at Tatari. The revolver had a two-inch barrel, small frame and a five-shot cylinder. It was an easy gun to hide in plain clothes, and popular with the older detectives. Stillwater had been hugging the corner of the hangar-like storage building, watching and waiting, and he had seen Tatari enter the cabin and come out. When Dominic started the engine again, Stillwater decided it was time to move. He was over twenty-five yards away, in the open now with the offices and huge sliding doors to the storage building behind him, and the docks and Tatari in front of him. His adrenaline was rushing through him as he charged.

Dominic heard the yell and saw the big man running toward him and knew immediately what he was. He crouched behind the bolster seat as he pulled his .9mm Browning high-power pistol from his waistband. He fired one quick shot, fear in his bloodshot eyes.

Stillwater saw Tatari fire at him, flinched, and came on. He wanted to get close enough to be sure of his shots before he fired. The girl, he thought, is in the cabin *right next* to Tatari. He hesitated just a split-second too long. Tatari steadied his aim and fired twice more. One slug hit Stillwater in the right lower leg on the outside, the other high in the right chest area. The .9mm slugs felt like hot high-speed drills boring into the big detective's muscle and flesh, and he felt himself going down even as he squeezed off two shots at his adversary. The hot, rough tarmac hit him hard as his body fell to the right and down. Just before his forehead crashed into the pavement, Stillwater had the grim satisfaction of seeing both his bullets find their mark. Tatari had straightened as he fired and was slammed back as the slugs seared into his stomach and chest on the left side. His eyes grew wide and his arms stiffened as he staggered against the portside. Blood covered the front of his shirt as he took several wobbly steps across the deck, his calves hit the transom at the stern of the boat, he sat, then slowly toppled over into the water, his eyes staring up into the sun.

Stillwater's world turned gray and spun crazily. He tried to sit up, wondered where his radio was, and looked in amazement at all the thick red blood everywhere. As he passed out, his last thoughts were, I hope somebody tells my kids I had the bullet holes in the *front*.

Jessie was out of her car arguing with the guard at the Rapier Marine gate when the shots were fired. The guard had lowered the thin metal boom across the entrance after Stillwater had driven through waving a badge. The man was confused and told Jessie there was no way he was letting anyone else through until he learned what was going on. She had her badge out, and he was shaking his head in disbelief when the gunfight began. Without saying another word, Jessie jumped back into her car, floored it, pushed the boom aside, and roared across the parking lot. Then she was out, running slowly, gritting her teeth against the pain. She rounded the corner and saw Stillwater down and bloody on the tarmac. He was struggling to sit up.

"Oh no, Les! What happened?" she yelled as she pushed him down to examine his wounds. She heard the gate guard come panting up behind her, heard him exclaim, "Madre de Dios!" and leaned over Stillwater.

"I shot the bastard dead. Didn't see the little girl..." said Les as he licked his lips. "... He shot at me and I killed him. Bastard fell right out of the back of the boat into the water, probably went right to the friggin' bottom." He tried to lift his head to look past Jessie. "I didn't see the girl, Jessie..."

Jessie keyed her radio and spoke those dreaded words, "Emergency, *officer down* ... officer shot." She gave the location and the dispatcher acknowledged immediately. Then she bent over Les, knowing the troops would respond from all over the area now, and the medical units. She brushed the hair away from Stillwater's forehead and put a wad of tissue against the wound on his chest. The big man's breathing sounded strong and not too raspy, and there was no blood in his mouth. Maybe he's not too bad, she thought. She heard Melody calling her number on the channel, and said into the radio, "Melody, Les killed Tatari, but there's no sign of the girl. We have to look for the others."

"I'm comin' from *your* house, Jessie," answered Sergeant Mitchell. "I was in that area on a backup call, so I swung by—I'll be at your location in a couple of minutes. Stay put."

Jessie knelt on the tarmac, cradling the wounded detective and staring at the boat where Tatari had died, and the water just beyond where he had gone to his grave. "You did good, Les," she said gently, but Stillwater had slipped into unconsciousness.

Mitchell pushed her car hard through the slowly yielding traffic, trying to stay calm. Her mind was filled with the fresh images of the scene she had just left. She *had* been on a call in the residential area where Jessie lived, and she had swung by to have a look, admitting to herself that she was curious, and realizing that she would open a can of worms once she found what Jessie had told them was there.

She had not used the house key Jessie had given her some time back to check on the place while Jessie was out of town, but rather had instinctively gone around back. The screen door to the back porch was unlocked, and she stepped in. That was when she realized she was standing in a puddle of blood. She had lifted one of her feet to be sure, swallowed hard, and let her eyes follow the thick stream from the step bordering the screen door to Jessie's back porch. The stream flowed along the edge of the screen wall to the body of a big man in a dark suit lying on his side among the potted plants. She moved closer and examined the wide, staring eye, and had to lean even closer to see what thing was impaling the other. She looked at the open mouth and cruel cuts and gouges on the side of the neck. She noticed how the skin of the face was ashen, and how thick the blood was everywhere. She saw the bloody footprints on the crumpled towel next to the glass sliding doors and gagged.

She had taken in the scene and had made her decision. She could be Jessie's friend *and* a cop supervisor at the same time. She contacted the dispatcher on her channel and called out the troops to the crime scene at Officer Summer's residence. As soon as the first patrol unit arrived, she had left there to go find Jessie. Then she heard Jessie's frantic call about Les Stillwater and headed that way. As she drove into the port, she pounded one fist on the steering wheel and said, "Oh, Jessie, *Jessie* . . ."

It took only a few minutes for the scene behind the Rapier Marine storage facility to fill with police activity. A sheriff's deputy arrived first, the port being their jurisdiction, and a medical unit was right behind him. As soon as they leaned over Stillwater, Jessie went to the boat, painfully climbed aboard, and searched for any trace of the girl. She found only the drugs. She leaned over the stern of the boat and looked into the water, but could not see Tatari's body. She climbed out of the boat and was walking slowly across the lot toward her car when Mitchell caught up with her.

"Jessie, hold up! Are you okay, lady?"

"I'm hurting, Melody, but still on my feet," Jessie said quickly. "Tatari's body is in the water, and we've got a call out for divers to do a recovery." She looked at the expression on the black girl's face and went on, "I guess you found Humberto's body—but the girl—"

"My God, Jessie, this while thing is totally out of control. Jessie, listen, I know you've got your reasons for hanging *on* to this fucking thing, but you've got to *let it go*—I mean, it is way past time to call out the goddamn *troops*. I will personally get in Hi-ho's paddy little face and make *sure* he understands this isn't over—okay?"

The medical team was yelling for some help to lift Stillwater onto a stretcher, and Mitchell turned to assist. When she turned back, Jessie was gone.

Benjamin Hardy was in his early eighties, retired and widowed for many years, and transplanted to Florida from Michigan at the insistence of his oldest son. He now made his home in Tamarac, west of Fort Lauderdale, and spent much of his time driving his old Chrysler all around the area, taking in the sights. He had heard of the FP&L hot water cooling canal in Port Everglades. Many kinds of fish could be seen there, he had been told, and even a manatee once in a while. On this Sunday he decided to cruise into the port, find the canal, and check out the fish.

He parked on Eller Drive, a few yards from where a small bridge crossed a canal. He wasn't sure if he was at the right place or not, but it would feel good to get out and stretch his legs anyhow. He opened his door, swung his legs out, and looked into the face of death.

Dominic Tatari stood there, leaning into the driver's side, an insane leer on his twisted face. He was soaking wet, his shirt front was covered with blood, and he held a big automatic pistol against Benjamin Hardy's face. Benjamin's eyes grew wide as he tried to pull his face away from that gaping barrel. Tatari cursed, grabbed the old man by the collar, and dragged him out of the front seat. As he brought the struggling man to his feet, Tatari struck him across the face with the gun, and as Benjamin Hardy's body sagged, Tatari threw him into the ditch alongside the road. Then he slid behind the wheel, started the car, and drove away. The whole thing had taken place less than one hundred yards from the Rapier Marine dock, but the police working there could not have seen it through the tall pines that edged the road, and could have only moved to that spot quickly the same way Dominic did, by swimming along the edge of the canal that branched off the Rapier Marine entrance canal.

Tatari drove slowly at first, trying to make his mind settle down and think. He had almost shot that old man in the face, but at the last second remembered the cops nearby. He fumbled in his pockets and found the other magazine for his Browning pistol. Holding the car steady with his knees, he snapped out the used magazine and pushed the new one in. He had no idea how many times he had fired and wanted to be sure the gun was ready. He laid it on the seat beside him. He let out a strangled sob and looked down at the blood oozing out of his shirt. His tortured mind told him he was hurt, but not dying . . . yet. He could keep going, keep on until he finished the thing. It was so clear to him now . . . they had set him up, loaded him with cocaine and snitched to the cops while they got the girl. Sure.

He felt cold and began to shiver. It was the wet clothes, he thought . . . and loss of blood. He looked around the front seat, then craned his neck over the back. He saw a folded jacket, grabbed it, and brought it up. He pulled over and struggled into it. The garment was a raincoat, an old, worn trenchcoat Hardy kept in the car to cover the dash when he parked. Tatari began driving again, feeling the warmth coming back a bit. He put the gun in one pocket, pulled a couple of the zip-lock Baggies of cocaine from his pants and stuffed them into another. He drove out of Port Everglades and joined the heavy traffic northbound on U.S. 1.

He couldn't know that Jessie Summer left the port only a few minutes behind him, and wouldn't have cared anyway.

Tiffany Eastin parked her Mercedes in the Tatari house driveway, got out, and went to the front door. She opened it with her key and went in. Tucked into her waistband was a five-by-seven manila envelope containing all the negatives and prints of her and Jessie by the pool. She knew Ramone would appreciate them, and she still hadn't decided whether to give them to him as a gift or not. Ramone had called her from Bahia Mar Marina, and she knew he would arrive any moment with the girl. She walked into the living room to find Jack kneeling in the middle of a pile of scattered money and photographs. She saw the open front of the bar and knew immediately what had happened. "Jack," she said tentatively, "I can explain what you've found there. Let me help you understand."

"You don't have to explain," shouted Jack as he held up several of the photos.

Tiffany chewed her lip, sensing how agitated he was, and worried about what he would do when Ramone got there. "Jack," she said in a placating tone as she gathered the photos and envelopes and stuffed them into the bar, "let's put these pictures away for now and talk about them later, okay, baby? Isabel will be here soon, and we don't want *her* to see them now, do we?"

"Isabel *should* see these! She *should* see that you posed for money! You let Ramone sell these pictures to filthy men like Dominic who look at them and . . . and . . ." Jack was breathing hard and there was a sheen of sweat on his forehead.

Tiffany looked at him and felt the panic begin to rise. Now was *not* the time to solidify this deal with Ramone, no matter how much she wanted that little girl. *Damn Jack*, she thought, I could never make him understand what those photos are all about. Then she remembered old man Tatari's reaction and shook her head. She had sold him a story while she sunbathed topless here at his house one hot, sunny day, a story about how she wanted to do some "naughty" posing, nothing lewd or out of line she had told him, just for fun. He had responded by telling her that many prominent local photographers offered "boudoir" sessions, lots of soft lighting and filters, filmy underthings, sexy stuff . . . but still legitimate. She had given him a teasing smile and told him she wanted some of the shots to be at least topless, and she was afraid of being too well-known locally . . . that the photographer would talk about her, or show the shots. She had asked him about, maybe, a photographer who was more "underground." Tatari Senior had hesitated, then told her he knew about a guy who was a real slime-ball, but who had a reputation for doing what was asked of him and keeping it to himself. He had even offered to arrange the session for her. It had happened as she hoped it would, without old Dominic knowing what *really* went on in that completely ugly little photographer's den . . . or she *thought* it had. Her brow wrinkled now as she remembered how shocked she was, and how stupid she felt when, *of course*, old Dominic had received copies of the shoot from that Frog character. Tatari had gone ballistic over them, waving them in her face and calling her names . . . all in front of Jack. At least she had managed to hurriedly put them all away after Jack attacked Tatari, and *he* had never realized she was the star of the porn the old man was so upset about. Until now.

She looked at her brother's face again and felt an intense anger building over her fear.

The hell with it, she thought, I'll just have Ramone take care of Jack once and for all—I'll be *done* with the sniveling idiot, and Isabel will be all mine. But all she said was, "Jack, honey. Never mind that just now."

At that moment they heard a car pull into the drive. A door slammed and a few seconds later the front door opened. Tiffany and Jack were frozen in place, waiting.

Ramone walked in, pushing a shy and adorable Isabel in front of him. He had a big smile on his face as he said, "So—Tiffany, Jack . . . she is here at last. Say hello to Isabel." There was a silence, during which Ramone continued, "Uh, Isabel has been traveling all day. Perhaps she could freshen up, a cold drink . . . or . . . something?" He was aware of an unpleasant tension in the room, one which he was all too familiar with.

Tiffany managed to remember her basic social graces, smiled, and said shakily, "Of course. Welcome, Isabel. Let's have a big hug." She moved toward the girl, who stood close to Ramone, her back to his legs. Before Tiffany could take another step, Jack uncoiled, stood, and lunged forward. He shouldered past Tiffany and picked up a suddenly frightened Isabel in his strong arms. He pulled her away from Ramone, who had reached out for her in reflex, and backed away, holding the girl to his chest. "No, *I'll* hug her, and I'll be her *best* friend, too, I don't care what you do."

Isabel looked at Ramone across the room and began to cry. Tiffany, seeing this, became even more angry at Jack. The girl was more beautiful than Tiffany imagined she would be, and to see her here, in the flesh, so lovely and innocent and *real*, made Tiffany determined to have her, no matter what the price. She tried to keep her voice under control as she said, "Jack. Go easy. Be gentle." She turned to Ramone, who looked worried, and made a "wait" sign with her hands. Then she followed her brother, who was talking to the girl as he carried her into the kitchen. A displeased Ramone followed them in.

"Let me get you that cold drink. I'm your best friend," Jack said to Isabel. He still held her to his chest, high, so he had to look up into her face, and he laughed. Isabel remained silent, small tears on her cheeks. As Jack got to the refrigerator, Tiffany reached out and grabbed him by one arm, pulling him. "Hold on a second, Jack. She likes me, too."

"No!" shouted Jack, and pulled away.

Ramone, having seen enough foolishness, pulled at Jack's other arm now. He was a smaller man than Jack, but had some martial arts background in *Arnis* and was sure he'd been in a few more back alley fights than had the well-heeled playboy. As Jack turned, Isabel slipped from his grasp, and when her feet hit the carpet, she began backing away from the three. She tripped over the remaining heavy wooden carving at the edge of the dining room entranceway and fell backward. Jack, seeing this, became enraged.

"See what you've done now!" he yelled. He pointed a finger at Ramone and said through clenched teeth, "Sure, you'd take *Tiff's* side! You're the one making all the dirty money with pictures of my sister, you bitch. It's your fault she's doing it—you and that greasy Tatari!"

Ramone tried to think of an answer that would calm Jack, but at that moment Isabel, crying, stumbled to her feet and rushed toward him, arms outstretched. Ramone pushed Jack's arm out of his way and bent to catch the little girl.

Seeing this, and fearing Ramone would leave with Isabel, and feeling his anger, pain and indignation rise beyond controllable levels, as it had done once before in this house, Jack turned. He picked up the heavy wooden carving and slammed it down on the side of Ramone's head while Tiffany screamed, "*No!*"

Ramone was just realizing that Isabel was not running to him, but *past* him, when the blow struck. The sudden impact left him stunned, his vision blurred, and a strange metallic taste filled his mouth. He tried to straighten up, tried to make his arms lash out at the bigger man, but before he could, the wooden figure came down again, crushing his forehead. The impact was so intense the left side of his skull exploded, and a sudden rush of hot blood gushed from the wound.

Jack, seeing the carnage he had wrought, and feeling the power he wielded over the other man, brought the heavy figure down again as Ramone reeled, his mouth open now, his legs folding. Tiffany was screaming at Jack and pulling impotently on his arms to make him stop, just like the last time it had happened. Neither she nor her brother saw Isabel run from the room, her back to the scene.

As Jack straightened and took several deep breaths, Ramone crumpled to the carpet, his skull crushed. His bloody face and ruined eye made a grotesque stain on the floor, and he vomited. His last thoughts were a cracked kaleidoscope of images, macabre and frightening. I'm so small and helpless, he thought, and this is so unfair. His tongue slid out between his teeth, and he died.

"Nice going, asshole," said a terrible voice, and both Tiffany and Jack looked up from the horror on the floor to see Dominic

Tatari standing in the middle of the living room. Tatari wore a rumpled knee-length raincoat and held a gun straight out in front of him. As he squeezed the trigger, Tiffany whispered, "Oh, Jack," and she heard her brother grunt as the gun fired twice. Jack was slammed back against the wall by the force of the bullets kicking him in the stomach, and he looked down in amazement at his own bluish-white intestines bubbling out the front of his pants. He slid to a seated position, his feet a few inches from Ramone's grimacing, dead face. He looked up then and said, "Tiffany?"

Tiffany knelt to him, shocked, and she heard Tatari begin to laugh. She turned and looked up at the gun as the burst of flame exploded from the barrel. She threw up one hand as if to ward off the .9mm insect coming at her. The high-speed bullet hit the palm of her hand, began breaking up, passed through flesh and bone, and impacted her squarely in the face, just under the nose. The bullet crushed teeth and bone and snapped her head back. It destroyed the upper palate, but the splinters stopped before entering the skull. The force of the blow hurled her backwards, and her head hit the wall, knocking her unconscious.

Dominic Tatari swayed on his feet, surveying the scene before him. He laughed again and snaked his tongue around cracked and dry lips. He looked closer at the bodies. They all looked dead, and that pleased him. At that moment he heard a soft sob to his left, from one of the bedrooms, and he remembered the girl.

Jessie drove through traffic on U.S. 1., yelling at people, blowing her horn, and weaving from one lane to another wildly. She was just a few minutes out of the port when Melody came over the radio with the news. An old man had been found near the access canal. He was alive but badly beaten, and his car had been stolen by a bloodied man who had to be Tatari. The car was a well-kept, older-model Chrysler, white over gold. Melody added that Stillwater was on the way to the hospital, and she was coming behind Jessie but would be a few minutes. "You know where he's going, Jessie, so watch your ass."

Jessie bulled her way through the turning traffic at Seventeenth Street, ignored the blaring horns, and floored it, heading north. She weaved back and forth, flying now, cleared Davie Boulevard in seconds and hung grimly onto the wheel as she pushed the old Camaro harder toward the New River Tunnel. She crested a slight rise in the road and slammed on the brakes, turning the wheel hard left to avoid rear-ending a line of stalled cars. Something had happened near the northbound tunnel entrance, and everything was stopped. She stood in the seat, looked out over the top of the windshield at the mess, and shouted, "Go back to New York, you idiots!"

She bounced down into the seat, floored it again, and skidded over into the oncoming southbound lanes. She blew through the light at the tunnel entrance, cars scattering in front of her, and leaned on the horn as she flashed her headlights on and off. She could hear other horns blaring even before she rocketed into the darkness of the oncoming tunnel exit.

Isabel had not seen anything of what had happened after she ran through Ramone's arms. She hurried into what turned out to be a large bedroom and cowered near a huge bed. She was terribly frightened and felt sick in the sudden realization that this dark house was full of evil and pain . . . she could *feel* it. These people Ramone knew were like crazy people, like there was something wrong with them, and they were wrapped in evil too. She would stay there, in that room, until Ramone and the others stopped arguing, and then she would make Ramone take her *home*.

When she heard the loud, punching gunshots, then the grown-up laughter, she began to cry. She heard cloth rustling, and the laugh again, and knew someone was coming toward the room. She had to get out, get away. She saw a door across the room and ran to it. As she put her small hands on the doorknob, she heard an animal-like voice say slowly, "Now where do you think you're going, little girl? Running away from your new lover? Come over here to *me*, sweetie."

She turned and looked over her shoulder at Dominic Tatari in the bedroom doorway. To her the horrible bloody man in the coat, his eyes wide open, looked like a nightmare monster. She saw the grin on his face and the gun in his hand, and she turned back to the door. She twisted the doorknob hard, but it wouldn't turn. She heard the laugh behind her and began to cry again. Finally she felt the knob turn and she pushed on the door, but it stayed stuck shut. She sobbed as she heard the monster behind her grunt and walk toward her. She saw a lever over the doorknob, shook it back and forth, pushed the door again, and felt it open just as the horrible man reached out for her. She felt his fingers tangle in her long hair as she cried out and ran through the doorway. Her head was pulled back for a second and then she broke free and fell forward onto the cold concrete of the pool deck. She sat up quickly and looked at the screen that surrounded her. What kind of room is this, she thought, and where is the door out of it?

Tatari felt his fingers slide through the girl's hair, lost his footing, fell backward, and slumped against the bed. Through the open door to the pool deck, he saw the girl get back to her feet and run off to the left. He moaned as he stood and lurched out the door after her.

Jessie skidded to a stop on the lawn across the street from the Tatari house. She saw two cars in the driveway, a rental and the Eastin Mercedes. At the next house sat the white-over-gold Chrysler.

She drew her pistol and ran painfully across the street in a crouch. She hopped the low wall bordering the yard and moved slowly between the two cars. She was moving toward the front door when she heard the shots, two, then one more. She felt a wave of cold fear and anger wash over her and moved up beside the door. There was no more sound for a few seconds, and then, as she slowly pulled open the front door to peer inside, she thought she heard a little girl crying. She put the gun up in front of her and swung into the living room.

As her eyes adjusted from the harsh late afternoon sunlight to the gloom of the house, Jessie saw the three crumpled bodies near the dining room. Ramone was face down in a puddle of blood, his long black hair spider-webbed around his head and shoulders, dead. Jack sat with his back to the wall, his knees up, his sightless eyes staring down at his insides. He was dead too. Tiffany Eastin lay beside her brother, blood all over her face. As Jessie moved forward, she heard Tiffany gag and spit up. Then she heard the scream.

Jessie turned away from the bodies and moved quickly to her left, into the bedroom. She saw the open door, checked the room quickly, her gun still up, and moved through. Her left shoulder and arm were still aching and weak, and her head pounded. She felt dizzy as she cautiously looked out into the pool area. No one was there but she could see the east screen door standing open. She heard the small scream again, very near, and took off toward it. As she rushed through the open screen door, the pain in her left knee caused her to grunt, and she thought she would fall, but she bit her lip and charged on as sweat dropped from her brow and stung her eyes.

She let her eyes sweep the back yards, listening again for a sound, and then heard another sob to her left. She crouched and moved toward a couple of large central air-conditioning units that served the house, and she saw them.

The little girl was on her knees in the dirt of a carefully manicured hibiscus hedge. She had one thin arm over her eyes and one thrown back as if to push someone away. Standing a few feet from the girl was Dominic Tatari. He weaved on his spread legs, and the open raincoat flapped around his knees. His face was an obscene mask, with flecks of spittle dripping from his lips. In one hand he held the weapon, in the other a bag of cocaine. He held the cocaine out toward the child, and in a raspy, gurgling voice, made grotesque by his efforts to raise the pitch, said, "Come here, little girl. . . . and I'll give you candy . . . Oh yes, I will."

Jessie, seeing the apparition before her, hearing the words, knowing the pain and suffering and loss this creature had caused, said in a tight voice, "Back away from her, *scum*." Then she pushed off with her right leg, determined to charge the animal and force him away from the girl. Jessie was totally consumed now, focused on what she knew she had to do.

Tatari, a surprised look running across his face, turned in a crouch toward the voice. His eyes widened at the sight of Jessie moving on him, and he grinned as he brought his gun up. "*You* back away, bitch—this one's mine!" He squeezed the trigger.

Jessie saw the bursts of fire and began shooting too. She watched as her slugs punched high into Tatari's chest, felt one of his bullets hit her in the left shoulder, and knew the next would take her in the face. She squeezed off another shot even as she understood she would die.

The force of Jessie's bullets threw Tatari back against the hedge, and he felt the burning pain, but saw that he had hit the lady cop. He brought the barrel of the gun around shakily so the next shot would hit her in the mouth. He choked on his barking laugh as he jerked the trigger again and sat down into the hedge. He coughed up a huge blob of blood, felt an unbelievable burning pain working up through his crotch and belly and chest, put his head back, and let the fiery blackness take him.

Jessie's left knee finally went out.

She was running hard, and her weight and strength caused her body to immediately collapse forward as the knee went, and even as the pain in her leg seared her, she felt the wasp-like bullet, the last Tatari had fired at her face, snap past her right ear. A few strands of dark blonde hair fluttered onto her shoulder and stuck to the blood on the wounded muscle as she fell to the grass. She rolled to her right as she hit and came up in a sitting position, her gun out in front of her, inches from Tatari's contorted face. She studied him sitting there for a few seconds, saw the blood, saw his tongue, the gun still in one hand and the cocaine in the other, and began to pull her trigger finger tight once more. She would blow his horrible face off, and that would be the end of it.

Even as she squeezed, but before the hammer fell, she heard a sob again and it made her look to her left. There was the little brown-haired girl coming to her on hands and knees, crying. Jessie felt her gun hand relax, felt the gun fall into her lap, and reached out for the girl, hugging her tightly. The girl's small arms wrapped around Jessie and squeezed hard as she crawled into Jessie's lap, crying loudly now. Jessie's left arm hung by her side, numb, and she used her right hand to gently stroke the girl's long hair as she comforted her. She felt the small heart beating against her breasts, closed her eyes, and listened to the girl's frightened sobs.

They knelt there in the sun, faces together, hugging each other tightly. After a moment Jessie pulled back slightly, smiled into the little girl's eyes, and said gently, "It's okay ... we're both okay now, little one."

EPILOGUE

One week later Jessie sat in her bed with her back to the pillow propped against the headboard. The bullet wound to her shoulder had cut through some muscle, but not enough to reduce her strength or performance once it healed. There would be a dimple scar there, the doctor had told her, but the arm would still work. The knee was a mess. Orthoscopic surgery had been done, the swelling was going down, but it was still tender and stiff. She had been treated for concussion, and while a complete test hadn't been done on her eardrum yet, she felt that her hearing was improving every day. At least she didn't feel sick anymore every time she stood up.

Her mother had arrived Sunday evening, while Jessie was still in the emergency room. Since then she had joyfully moved into the house, answering the phone, folding the towels the wrong way, and spending lots of time in the kitchen. In spite of her feelings about the job, Jessie's mother threw herself into the task of handling the media and police brass. Each morning she would brush her hair into some semblance of order, pull on another multi-colored, billowing housedress, and prepare to handle whatever distractions came toward Jessie during the day.

Tired Mike Tirado had been there that Sunday night too. He had been back almost every day or evening since, shaken, but proud of her. Each time he arrived, he carried flowers, and spent a lot of time with Jessie's mother in the kitchen. She thought of the words she and Miguel had exchanged the night before when he bent to kiss her goodnight.

"Is the case over, Jessie?" he had asked with a teasing smile.

"Yes, Miguel."

"Then it would be safe and ... proper ... for me to ask you for a date when you are on your feet again?"

"Yes, Miguel ... but ..."

"But?"

"But I would not want you to think we would ... you know ... on the first ... like last time ..."

Miguel Tirado laughed. "*That* will only happen again when *you* say it is time. Yes, Jessie?"

"Yes, Miguel."

Jessie had also spoken with Charles on the telephone. He was still in the hospital, but out of Intensive Care. He thought he'd be discharged soon, and would probably stay in Miami with his two widowed sisters for a while. Jessie, surprised that Charles had something as mundane as sisters, made him promise to come by and have a drink with her as soon as he was able. He became embarrassed when she told him what a good job he'd done, and said he needed a Certificate of Appreciation from the Chief's office like *another* hole in the head.

Les Stillwater was already out and about, limping slightly, one arm in a sling. He was supposed to be on "light duty," but he and Mitchell were wrapping up the case. The media had gone into an orgasmic frenzy over the story, keying on Jessie's role, and simply fascinated with Tiffany Eastin's involvement. Melody told Jessie the list of high-powered attorneys hoping to represent Eastin was impressive. Stillwater added that the lawyers might want to wait until the plastic surgeons tried to do something with Tiffany's face before they brought her in front of a jury.

Melody also told Jessie with a grin that so far the brass didn't know if she should be commended, reprimanded, or both. Word was, they had settled on attributing some of her decisions after Humberto's attack to the concussion she had suffered.

On a personal note, when they were alone in the bedroom, Melody told Jessie she had begun a "moratorium on going out with guys." She wanted to spend some time just being herself, to get to know herself as a person and a woman. Then maybe she could start this "boy meets girl" thing all over again. They hugged for a long time before Melody finally let go.

Captain Orsen "Hi-ho" Allen had been in contact too. Surprisingly, he had been the one wrangling with the feds and the Philippine government on Isabel's behalf. He called to promise Jessie a package of immigration forms to arrive soon. Hi-ho Allen did *not* tell Jessie of the brief but intense personal struggle he had suffered after being called to the scene at Tatari's house. He had arrived there after leaving the grim scene at *Jessie's* house, and was still jolted by what he had seen there. He had pulled the manila envelope from Tiffany's waistband as the wounded woman was placed onto a stretcher. He had taken a quick look, and hung onto them. Back at the station, he had carefully inspected each of the photos of Tiffany and Jessie in the sun. He had noticed that all of the negatives were there. Then he carried the whole package downstairs and out the back door. He had gone to a Dumpster near the jail entrance and had carefully, methodically, and completely burned every photographic image. If asked, he would have argued it was for the good of the department, but he was secretly pleased with himself nonetheless.

Jessie laid her head back now and closed her eyes. The image of the Murex shell filled her mind. She could see it as she first saw it, on the clean white beach, covered with sparkling sand. She opened her eyes then, and remembered Melody telling her the shell was at the Medical Examiner's office, and they wanted to know if she wanted it returned. She had told Melody to keep it for now. One day she would give it back to the sea.

She saw the little girl standing in front of the mirror in the bedroom, saw how she studied herself and her new dress as she brushed her long hair. Jessie remembered how lost and frightened the girl had been at the hospital until Jessie's mother had arrived. From that point on, there was no question of where she would stay until the immigration problems were worked out.

Jessie thought about that as she watched the little girl try on a new pair of shiny shoes, and she thought of how the girl had shyly asked if she could have her long hair cut . . . like Jessie's. Could it work? Would living here be right for her, and what she really wanted? Jessie rubbed her eyes with her fists, wincing from the pain in her arm. She wouldn't worry about it for now. The child was safe with her—and, after all, this wasn't such a bad place to grow up.

The little girl turned and looked at Jessie with a big smile. Her skin glowed and her brown eyes sparkled. She came to the bed, sat beside Jessie, put her arms around her, and hugged her tight.

Jessie returned the hug and thought, "Female child, real name unknown," you have a name. She lifted her face, smiled at the girl, and said softly, "Isabel."